JO BEVERLEY
FORBIDDEN

ZEBRA BOOKS
KENSINGTON PUBLISHING CORP.

Chapter 1

Three people sat at breakfast in the chill and dusty dining room of Grove House in Sussex. The burly Allbright brothers noisily washed down rare beef with porter. Their sister, Serena Riverton, huddled in a heavy shawl nibbling toast and drinking tea whilst reading a book of poetry.

Will Allbright stared blankly into space as he chewed and slurped, but his older brother, Tom, muttered as he went through the day's post.

"Duns, duns, duns . . ." He tossed three letters toward the smokey fire. "Ah, this is more like it." He tore open a letter and read it greedily. "At last! Hey, Serry, Samuel Seale wants to marry you."

His sister looked up, revealing a remarkably beautiful face. "What?" Then she went pale and rose, pushing back from the table. "Oh no, Tom. I won't. I *won't* marry again!"

"No?" the man asked, filling his mouth with food again. "What're you going to do, then, Sister? Ply the streets?"

Serena Riverton shook her head desperately,

shocked almost to witlessness by this turn of events. "I can live on the money Matthew left me."

Her younger brother Will, who was rather simple, turned to look at her. "That's already gone, Serry." He seemed surprised she didn't know, almost regretful. Serena knew better. In all their selfish lives, her two brothers had never regretted a wrong unless it got them into trouble.

In looks they were both John Bull—big, solid, ruddy-faced men in simple country clothes. They had none of John Bull's solid worth, however.

As she stood there numbly, Will shoved a final hunk of bread into his mouth and rose from the table to warm himself in front of the hearth. Having effectively blocked the sparse heat of the fire, he pulled out a guinea and began to toss it.

Serena dazedly watched that glittering coin and tried to find a footing in all of this. "Gone?" she echoed. "How can my money be gone? My husband is only three months dead. Where can it have gone?"

But even as she spoke, she knew. Gone where all the money in this dilapidated house went. To the tables, on a roll of the dice, on the speed of a horse, on the speed—for heaven's sake—of a cockroach!

She tore her eyes from Will's coin to glare at Tom. "That's blatant thievery!"

He forked up another lump of red beef. "Going to put the Runners onto me, Serry? 'Twouldn't do you a maggot of good. There's no getting blood from stones."

Stones, thought Serena wildly. That's what they were. As heartless as stones, and as stupid.

"You couldn't have lived on it, anyway," said Will.

6

Flick, spin, catch. Flick, spin, catch . . . "Three thousand? Loose change, that's what three thousand is."

Tom grunted his agreement. "Who'd have thought Riverton'd go through his fortune like that? We expected you to be a rich widow, Serry, or we'd have never been so keen to get you home again. Three thousand'd hardly keep you in gowns." His small eyes roamed over her very expensive russet cloth dress.

It was expertly cut—as Serena knew only too well—to display her figure, but she hadn't expected to be looked at like that by one of her brothers.

Serena clutched her heavy wool shawl around her for protection. "It would keep me in gowns very well," she said through her teeth. "I'm sure it's beyond your comprehension, Brothers, but it is possible to live a decent life on the mere *interest* of three thousand pounds."

"It'd be a damned dull one," said Will in amiable incomprehension. "You wouldn't want that, Serry."

Serena stalked forward and snatched his spinning guinea out of the air. "Yes I *would*, Will." She turned on Tom. "I want my money back. If you don't repay me, I will take you to court."

He burst out laughing, spitting food all over the table. "You need money to take someone to court, Serry, and even if you won, it'd be years before the matter'd be settled. You won't get far in the meantime on Will's guinea."

"It's a start." Serena tightened her grip on the coin, but Will grabbed her wrist.

"That's my lucky piece!" She resisted, but he roughly twisted her arm until she cried out and surrendered the coin.

Serena backed away again, tears in her eyes, holding her stinging wrist. She was forcibly reminded of her brothers' bullying cruelties. She'd been fifteen when she left her home, but she remembered. Why had she thought matters would be different now that she was a grown woman?

Tom saw her fear, and his eyes glinted with satisfaction. "Perhaps Seale'll pursue your rights for you, Serry."

She met his eyes. "There is no possibility of forcing me into another marriage, Tom, but especially not into a marriage with Samuel Seale."

"Don't fancy him, eh?" Tom seemed genuinely surprised. "Not a bad-looking man for his age, and rich as Croesus. All those mines, you know. Thought you'd prefer an older man like your first husband. You always seemed content."

"Content?" Serena repeated faintly, her mind dizzy from such a vast misunderstanding.

"Right-o, then," said Tom. "We'll wait for other bids."

"You will?" Serena was astonished to have won; then she took in his words. "Bids? What *bids?*"

Tom tapped the letter that lay open on the table beside his plate. "Seale offered ten thousand. Pretty fair, really. Father got thirty the first time round, but we won't get that now you're not a virgin."

"Thirty thousand pounds?" Serena heard her voice climb toward hysteria. "Father *sold* me to Matthew Riverton for thirty thousand pounds?"

"Guineas," corrected Will conscientiously, once more flicking his coin. "Towed us out of River Tick nicely at the time. Didn't you know? Course, you were only fifteen. Twitty little thing."

Serena put a hand to her head and choked back a cry. Twitty little thing. She'd realized years ago that she had been a stupid child to go so blissfully into a marriage, thinking only of new gowns and excitement and the feather in her cap of being the first of her group to wed.

But to have been *sold* . . .

Thirty thousand pounds. No, *guineas*. No wonder Matthew had been enraged when she refused to dance to his tune. When she tried to refuse . . .

"Face facts, Serry," said Tom. "Snap up Seale. We're up to our ears in debt again, and you're not such a prize now. You've still got your looks, I'll grant you that, but your maidenhead's gone. And most men want a wife with a dowry and the ability to give him children. You've neither."

"I had three thousand pounds," she said bitterly, but it was the other that struck like a blow.

Barren. She was barren. As if it were yesterday, she remembered the doctor making that pronouncement like a hanging judge. And she remembered Matthew's rage. "Barren! What plaguey use is a barren wife? Especially one that takes no pleasure in bed-work!"

His treatment of her had changed from that point on. For the first few years of the marriage, he had merely been rough and careless of her feelings. After the doctor's verdict, however, he had started to demand more, to demand services that went far beyond her marital duties.

If Serena could bear children, she might remarry for

that joy, but since she could not, she would never again enter such a state of legalized bondage.

But if she was penniless, what was she to do?

What *could* she do?

At the very least, she had to leave this room before she gave her brothers the satisfaction of seeing her in tears.

Serena turned blindly toward the door, managing the words, "The answer is still no, Tom, so you can cancel the slave auction."

For all of his size, Tom was quick on his feet. He reached the door ahead of her and thumped it closed in her face with a beefy hand. "You weren't *asked*, Serry. You were *told*." His eyes, closed in with rolls of fat, fixed on her malevolently.

Serena wanted to hit him, to tear at his piggy eyes, but she was small and her brothers were big and brutal. "You can't do it!" she protested. "I'm not fifteen anymore, Tom. I'm twenty-three and able to make my own choices."

"Don't be stupid."

"It is you who is being stupid! It's no longer possible to take a bride to the altar bound, and I'll go no other way."

"Don't be stupid," Tom repeated flatly. "If you give me any trouble, I'll sell you to a brothel. I'd get at least a monkey for you."

Serena swayed, knowing he spoke the plain truth.

He opened the door with a parody of courtesy. "I'll tell you when the bidding's done."

Serena walked numbly through and the heavy oak slammed shut behind. She heard her brothers laugh.

She fled to her room. Twitty, twitty, twitty. It rang

10

in her head. She'd thought eight years of marriage—years of slavery, years of horror—had at least taught her something, made her wiser. But here she was, a twit again.

She'd been so relieved, though, so incredibly elated when Tom had brought the news of her husband's death, that she'd not stopped to think. She had simply packed her belongings and returned immediately with Tom to her family home. She hadn't given a thought to legal matters. It hadn't even distressed her when she'd learned that Matthew had gone through nearly all his vast fortune.

What did money matter?

She was *free*.

Matthew would never again descend on Stokeley Manor and demand she play the whore for him. He'd never again punish her for refusing some intolerable indignity.

She was free.

Now she paced her chilly room, wringing her hands, trying to decide what to do. She would not lose that freedom.

Samuel Seale. She closed her eyes in horror. Another like her husband. A big, coarse man, gone fifty and deep in depravity. And she suspected Seale had the pox. At least Matthew had not had the pox.

She stopped her pacing, gripping a bedpost to halt the pointless movement. She must do something.

What?

Flee.

Yes, she must go. Go somewhere.

Where?

Her mind scrabbled for a refuge and found none.

There were few relatives, and none she'd trust to protect her from her brothers. During her marriage, her husband had kept her a virtual prisoner at Stokeley in Lincolnshire, forbidden all contact with friends or the local gentry. Though truth to tell, few of those worthy people would have been willing to acknowledge anyone from Stokeley Manor. No, there was no help to be found there.

She went back in her mind, seeking a friend. Back to innocence. Back to her school days.

Miss Mallory.

Serena had attended Miss Mallory's School in Cheltenham. She had been taken straight from there to her wedding. That small school had been her last place of security and innocent pleasures. She remembered Miss Emma Mallory as a firm but kindly autocrat, and a staunch believer in women's rights. Surely Miss Mallory would help her.

If Serena could reach her.

It was a long way from Sussex to Gloucestershire.

Money. She needed money.

A search of her room turned up two pound notes, a guinea, and a few smaller coins. Not enough. Where else could she find money?

Even when in debt, her careless brothers left coins about. She'd find them.

Clothes.

She had begun to pack a valise when she realized that it would be impossible to leave the house carrying anything without raising suspicions. She began to replace the garments in the clothespress. It was terrible to be fleeing with only the clothes on her back, but all in all, she would be pleased to abandon her wardrobe.

Every stitch she owned had been chosen by Matthew in London and sent to Stokeley as the whim seized him. All the garments were of the finest quality, but all were cut to show, to revel in, her figure.

Serena looked in the cheval mirror and let her shawl drop. How could russet cloth, finely trimmed, look so . . . so *bold?* But it did. The bodice exaggerated her full bosom, the skirt was cut rather narrowly, and the soft cloth shaped to her hips. Worst, though, was the perfume.

All her clothes had been drenched in it before she received them, and her maid/jailer had repeated the applications. Serena didn't know its composition, but it had nothing to do with flowers. She knew it was a whore's perfume, and that it had amused Matthew to make his fastidious bride stink of it.

Since Matthew's death, Serena had managed to wash the smell out of her linen and muslins, but she could not wash it from her heavier clothes without ruining them. Until her brothers released her funds, she could buy no others. . . .

Sickly, she realized there were no more funds.

She seriously thought of dressing in one of her sweet-smelling muslins for her flight, but at this time of year it would be insanity. She did fold some underwear and stuff it into her reticule. Surely carrying a reticule would not sound the alarm.

Her jewels! Matthew had given her many items of jewelry, though even then he had managed to make them part of his degrading games. She shuddered at the memory of those ornaments, but they could be sold and they were hers.

She clenched her fists in frustration when she realized that she didn't know where her jewels were. She hadn't wanted to know, but now they represented survival.

In Tom's room?

She was suddenly consumed with urgency, fearful that her brothers would come to drag her to her wedding or at least realize that she would flee. She grabbed her luxurious cape—camlet cloth lined with sable—grateful that it was very warm.

Another memory: It had amused Matthew to take her walking in the garden, naked under the cape, the silky fur tickling her skin, her face red as he stood talking to an oblivious servant.

One of his more innocent diversions . . .

She shook herself free of these thoughts.

Her heaviest gloves. Her sturdiest half boots. Her few coins in her pocket. She only had one bonnet, for Matthew had seen no point or amusement in bonnets, and it was very high with a large brim. She intended to use the hood of her cloak for concealment, and the hood would not cover the bonnet.

She went without.

The rings she wore on her left hand caught her eye, and Serena smiled grimly. There was a large emerald and a gold band, so much a part of her that she'd forgotten them. Surely she could survive for some time on the value of those.

She glanced around her room, checking to be certain she had taken everything that could be of use. When she had returned here with Tom as a widow, she had seen this dingy chamber—her girlhood chamber—as a haven. It had appeared to be a return to the innocence of her too-brief youth. She saw now that she had deluded herself. It was time to be done with delusion.

Heart pounding, she peeped into the cold and gloomy corridor. No one was in sight. She slipped down it to Tom's room and eased in, leaving the door ajar. He was not a quiet man. She'd hear him coming.

She searched ruthlessly finding a few more guineas, and not hesitating to pocket a gold fob she found in the dust behind his washstand. She saw no sign of her jewels, though. Where could they be? She didn't think her brother had a safe. Her eyes swept the room again desperately, but she could see no possible hiding place and dared not linger.

Next she invaded Will's room and filched a few more coins. She had nearly ten guineas now.

She swallowed a sound of despair. Ten guineas was a significant amount, but not enough to place between herself and starvation.

Death before dishonor.

Was marriage truly a fate worse than death, for it could be death she faced in this mad flight.

Serena realized she had been standing here too long, running over it all in her mind and hoping to see some alternative. There was none. She forced herself to move on, to go downstairs, to leave her home forever.

On her way to the side door, she stopped in the library. Her brothers were in the habit of spending the evenings here when rusticating—not reading, of course, but gambling. She smiled in grim triumph when she found a guinea and a crown on the floor.

The treasure showed that the lazy servants hadn't cleaned in here today, but that was no longer her concern. It was time to go. She turned toward the door, but then heard heavy footsteps.

Guilty panic choked her. She ran back and grabbed a book off the nearest shelf.

Tom walked in. "Into the books again?" he sneered. "Don't know why Matthew allowed it. You'll lose your looks hunching over books all day."

Serena closed the book on her finger, heart pounding. *He'll guess. He'll know what I'm planning.* "Matthew didn't care what I did during his absences, and I would welcome losing my looks."

"Don't be so pissing stupid, Serry. If you weren't a raving beauty I'd throw you out to scrub floors. You'd soon find marriage a better deal than that. I reckon old Riverton spoiled you."

He came over and twitched the book out of her hands. "What now? Byron? Keats?" Then he let it fall open and burst out laughing. "Oh, Serry, you are a one! Got a taste for it, did you? Can't see why you're so stiff-rumped about marriage, then."

Serena realized with horror that the book she'd mindlessly plucked from the shelf was one of her brothers' foul erotic tomes. She knew because Tom was waving an illustration in front of her. "Like that, do you?" he asked, eyeing the contorted picture.

Serena couldn't say no and not raise suspicion, but she couldn't force herself to say yes, either.

Her brother looked at her red face and shook his head. "And you can still blush, too. You're a strange one, Serry, and no mistake. But I can see why the men go crazy over you. Miss Prim and Proper with a whore's body and a whore's eyes. And a whore's mind, I see. That's your role in life, you know. Whore. With

16

your figure, and the way you move, and the look you always have of just emerging from a spicy bed . . ."

His eyes were defiling her again.

"Perhaps we should widen the bidding," he said thoughtfully. "There's not many want you for a wife, but a mistress, now, that's another matter. As a mistress you could go to the highest in the land—a lord, a duke even. Being barren's a feather in the cap of a Cyprian."

Serena just stood there, letting his words wash over her. She was leaving. None of this would happen to her.

He put the book back in her hand and patted it with a parody of fondness. "Off you go, sister, and study your trade."

Clutching the book, Serena hurried out of the library, her brother's coarse laughter echoing behind her. Once out of doors, she forced herself to walk calmly through the chilly November garden as if she had no purpose.

Her mind was not calm, though. Now more than ever she had to escape. She fretted over her chances and how to improve on them.

She had time. Neither she nor her brothers regularly ate at midday, and the servants wouldn't go looking for work. There was an excellent possibility that she wouldn't be missed until evening. She should be well away by then.

She had no doubt, however, that her brothers would come after her. She was, after all, worth at least five hundred pounds to them from a brothel. In fact, she was worth at least ten thousand because she'd marry even Seale to escape that fate.

Thirty thousand. Her father had *sold* her for thirty thousand. . . .

That thought, that thought of the old betrayal, almost took away her wits, but she concentrated fiercely on the immediate.

Escape.

She wandered into the orchard, then quickened her pace. Realizing she still carried it, she hurled the horrid book into a stand of nettles and clambered over a stile into open fields. It was three miles to the nearest stage post. She could only hope that if she reached there, a passing coach would pick her up. They went by every few hours, she believed, but Serena rather thought one needed a ticket.

She was only too aware of her abysmal ignorance of the world. She had been taken from school at fifteen and immured at Stokeley Manor. From that day on, she had never managed anything for herself, until these past three months when she had tried to bring order to her brothers' house.

She had to wonder whether she was equipped to survive alone.

But she had no choice.

Another stile brought her onto the country road. Serena made sure her hood was up over her head, in case anyone passed who might recognized her, and marched resolutely on.

Chapter 2

"Fancy a ride over to Canholme, Middlethorpe?"

Francis, Lord Middlethorpe, looked up from his deviled kidneys and replied to Lord Uffham, his host's son. "Why not? It promises to be a fine day." He turned to the young lady at the table. "Would you accompany us, Lady Anne?"

She was fair and slight and, though not shy, very quiet. She gave him a fleeting smile. "I would enjoy that, my lord."

She was his intended bride.

Nothing was settled yet. He hadn't spoken formally to her father, the Duke of Arran, who sat at the table immersed in his copy of the *Monthly Magazine*. Everyone knew the road they were on, however. Before he left Lea Park, he would propose and be accepted.

It was an excellent match. Anna belonged to one of the highest families in the land, and her portion was suitably grand. Both his family and hers were well acquainted and enthusiastic about the union. She was sweet-natured, clever without being bookish, and pretty in a pale, quiet way. He didn't at all mind the limp.

Francis was aware of a twinge of irritation at the very smooth propriety of it all, but he dismissed that as foolishness. Just because his friends became entangled in adventures and passions didn't mean he should do so. He had always known that wasn't his road in life.

He had come into his property and title at the age of twelve. Since then, he had been the sole reliance of his mother and three sisters. Certainly, his mother had ruled his life while he was a child and still ran Thorpe Priory with smooth efficiency, but her welfare depended upon him. His sisters, thank heavens, were suitably married now, and thus off his hands.

He had always known that it was his duty to guard his health, use his wealth wisely, improve his property, and marry suitably to provide heirs. He had probably delayed marriage rather longer than was wise. If he were to die without an heir, the estate would pass to a distant cousin with a large family of his own. In that event, his mother would lose all connection with the home she had built and cherished with his father.

It would have been pleasant, however, he thought wistfully, to have had one or two adventures in his life. His friend Nicholas Delaney had traveled the world and been in grave danger twice before he settled down. . . .

He realized he was being addressed and turned with a smile to Anne.

"Would you object, my lord, if we went a little out of our way? I have promised some books to the school in Kings Lea and would like to deliver them myself."

"Of course not. Improving tomes? Bibles?" He was teasing but she answered him seriously.

"They are already well supplied with those. How could you think otherwise? No, these are rhyme stories for the younger ones, and a few books of geography and such. All volumes that our schoolroom here will not need for many years, especially as Uffham refuses his duty." She directed her solemn reproach at her oldest brother.

"Good grief, Annie, I'm not yet twenty-five! Give a fellow a chance to kick up his heels before you shackle him for life."

They all laughed, but Francis reflected that he was only just turned twenty-five, yet no one seemed to consider him too young for shackles. . . .

"Marriage is not a shackle," Lady Anne countered with gentle firmness and a slight, betraying flicker of her eyes toward Francis. So perhaps she did catch the point.

Lucky Uffham. Uffham's future was clear, too—marriage and a dukedom—but at least he had no need to hurry. He even had two healthy younger brothers to buffer his conscience.

Quiet servants brought fresh coffee and removed used and cold dishes as the family lingered, making plans for the day. The duke's secretary came quietly in with the personal letters contained in the post bag, and they were distributed. Francis was surprised to find one for himself, for he had given his mother complete authority to handle estate matters in his absence and to open personal correspondence.

This letter had not been sent on from Thorpe Priory, however, but addressed to him here. He felt a prick of uneasiness as he snapped the seal and unfolded the sheet.

My lord,

I suspect you are being kept in the dark, and deception profits no one. For the good of all, I advise you to ask your mother about me. If she will not answer you, I will. I am fixed here at the Crown and Anchor in Weymouth for the next week

Charles Ferncliff

Francis was so startled he muttered, "What the devil? . . ." then hastily apologized.

"Is it bad news, my lord?" Lady Anne asked.

"I hardly know." Francis could not discuss this strange epistle here. In fact, the only thing to do was to show it to his mother to see if she had any explanation to offer. "I fear I must go to the Priory to look into a family matter. If you will forgive such a disobliging guest, I hope to return by this evening."

"Of course," said the duke. "No question about it, my boy. Your family's needs must rank first with you. Hope there's nothing seriously amiss."

"I don't think so, Duke," said Francis as he rose to his feet. Who on earth was Charles Ferncliff, and what possible connection could he have with his mother?

He ordered his curricle and sent for his greatcoat, gloves, and hat, but took nothing else. He expected to return in short order. By tacit agreement, Anne walked with him to the door.

"I'm sorry about this, Lady Anne." He offered a social lie. "It is just a matter that my mother cannot handle alone."

"A weighty one, then," Anne said with a smile. "Lady Middlethorpe is wonderfully competent."

"Indeed she is." It was excellent that Anne and his

mother had mutual liking and respect. They were even similar in nature and taste. Both had innate good manners, quiet decorum, impeccable neatness, and they never put a social step amiss. He suspected that once Anne was in charge of her own establishment, she would rival Lady Middlethorpe in competence, too.

Francis had an urge to speak to Anne now, to have it settled, but he came to his senses. He could hardly make his offer impetuously in the hall under the eyes of the Groom of the Chambers and two footmen. But he recognized that it was time to act. This evening he would speak to the duke. He would gain Arran's consent, arrange the settlements, and then commit himself to Anne for life.

He took her hand and kissed it warmly. "I will return as soon as possible. You know that."

She didn't mistake him and lowered her head, a delicate blush touching her cheeks. Then they heard the horses on the gravel beyond the door. Francis was assisted into his outer clothing and left.

Two hours later, Francis caught sight of the great wrought iron gates of his home, Thorpe Priory, and his groom blew a blast on the horn. The gatekeeper ran to swing the gates open and the man's family scurried behind to bow or curtsy.

Francis acknowledged them all with a salute of his whip but didn't check speed. Instead, he concentrated on steering his team into the long, straight drive to his home. The passing hours had increased his anxiety. Something most peculiar was going on.

He drew up the steaming team before his door, flung

the ribbons to his groom, leaped down, and strode into his home, shedding outer garments into the hands of waiting minions.

"My mother?"

"In her boudoir, milord."

He ran quickly upstairs, rapped, and entered.

Lady Middlethorpe, a handsome woman who had given her son his dark hair and fine bones, appeared caught in mid-pace before the fireplace. "Francis! What on earth are you doing here?"

He was startled by how agitated she appeared, for she was normally a lady of great composure. She was even fiddling with her fringed shawl—a habit she deplored. He crossed the room and gave her the letter. "I received this today."

Lady Middlethorpe glanced at it and paled. She appeared to read it for far longer than the terse words warranted, then she sat on a chaise and focused her sweetest social smile upon him. "You have just arrived? You must be parched, dear boy. Shall I send for tea?"

Francis could hardly believe it. "No. Cut line, Mother. What is that letter about?"

"Do not use cant in my presence, Francis!"

"I'll start into outright profanity if you don't tell me what is going on!"

He wasn't in the habit of speaking so forcefully to his mother, but instead of reproof she flashed him a distinctly nervous look, then concentrated on the fire in the grate. Her fingers returned to her tangled fringe. "I don't know why you have rushed away from Lea Park. It must appear peculiar to the Arrans."

"Mother," asked Francis, his patience severely

tested, "who is Charles Ferncliff, and what is that letter about?"

She sighed. "He is a young man who was tutor to the Shipley boys."

As an explanation it was totally inadequate. "But what is the letter about? What are you supposed to tell me?"

He thought she would not answer, but then she looked at him and said, "Probably that he is blackmailing me."

"Blackmailing! On what grounds, for heaven's sake?"

Her color now high, Lady Middlethorpe said, "He is threatening to . . . to expose my improper behavior."

"Imp . . ." Francis choked back a laugh. "Who the devil would he think you had been improper with?"

"Francis! Such language! And though *you* clearly think so, at forty-seven I am not yet in my dotage."

He stared at her, realizing that in her way she was still a handsome woman. She was slender and fine-boned, and her large blue eyes were still bright, her hair still dark. "Of course not, Mother. You know I have urged you to consider another marriage. But no one would ever suspect *you* of improper behavior."

"Thank you," she said stiffly, and perhaps ungratefully. "As for marriage, I would not be so disrespectful of your father's memory."

Francis could not believe that his gentle, loving father would have wanted his widow to take this view, but this was hardly the time to discuss the matter. "As you will," he said. "As for this tutor, Mother, the man must be mad. Why has he picked on you for such foolishness?"

Lady Middlethorpe shrugged, but her color was still

high. "As to that, my dear, I fear it is because I spoke to the Shipleys about him. Though he is very clever, he seemed rather rough-and-tumble, and inclined to encourage the boys to high spirits. I thought him not quite the best influence on young minds and advised the Shipleys of it. My opinion doubtless contributed to their decision not to retain him to teach the younger boys once Gresham left for school."

Typical, thought Francis. His mother meddling, thinking she knew the best for everyone. The poor tutor sounded as if he might have been fun, very unlike the dull and worthy Mr. Morstock who had prepared him for Harrow.

But then, he reminded himself, in this case his mother had been proved correct in thinking the man unsuitable. He was clearly a blackguard and quite possibly mad.

"And he's been pestering you. I wish you had told me sooner, but I'll take care of it now. What is he demanding?"

She gave a little laugh. "Oh, Francis, it is such a silly business. I cannot believe the man is serious."

"Serious or not, I will not tolerate such mischief. What is he demanding?"

Her artificial smile faded. "I insist you ignore the matter, Francis"

"I'm sorry, Mother, I cannot do that. What is Ferncliff's price not to spread these lies?"

She stared at him quite angrily. Francis met her look with one that said that he insisted for once in handling the matter in his own way.

At last her eyes shifted. "Ten thousand pounds," she whispered.

"Ten thousand pounds! The man is ripe for Bedlam."

"You won't pay it, will you?" she asked anxiously.

"Assuredly I won't. Putting my hands on such a sum in cash would be no easy matter and I have no intention of buckling under to a demented blackmailer. After all, his threats are toothless. He can't do much damage with a bundle of lies."

"All the more reason to ignore him."

"Not at all. He must be shown that he cannot disturb you in this way."

Her eyes widened. "What will you do?"

"I'm going to take up his rash invitation. I'm going to Weymouth to teach this tutor a lesson."

His mother surged to her feet. "No, Francis! I forbid it!"

Francis was beginning to fear that this matter was turning his mother's wits. "I assure you, Mother, it will be the most effective way to put an end to this. I want you to put the whole matter out of your mind."

She clutched at his sleeve. "But you could be hurt, dearest!"

He looked at her in incredulity. "By a *tutor?*"

"He . . . he is quite a well-built young man. Larger than you. Athletic. A stern letter from you would be just as effective. And far safer."

Francis felt a familiar exasperation. He'd been a slight, sensitive lad and his mother was in the habit of coddling him. He would have thought she'd discarded the idea by now. True, he was still of slight build, and he knew his good looks and dark eyes gave him a damnably poetic appearance, but he was well able to take care of himself and others.

He patted her hand. "His size will not matter,

Mother. I don't actually intend to sink to a brawl unless he insists, but he'll get the message more effectively face-to-face."

"Oh, dear." She released his sleeve and paced the room, wringing her hands as if she truly expected him to be going to his death.

"Mother," he said firmly, "you are not to fret yourself in this way. You will make yourself ill. I confess, I do feel inclined to beat this Ferncliff to a pulp just for distressing you so, but it will not come to that."

She turned suddenly, almost eagerly. "But what of Lady Anne?"

"What of her?"

"She will be most hurt that you have abandoned her. You must return to Lea Park with all speed."

Francis regarded her with genuine concern. "Nonsense, my dear. Anne will still be there in a day or two, and this business must be handled now. I leave immediately for Weymouth. You are not to concern yourself over this matter any further. This Ferncliff will never distress you again." He kissed her flushed cheek, then left before she could speak any of the further protests that clearly hovered on her lips.

When her son left, Lady Middlethorpe paced the room, wringing her hands. Dear Lord, dear Lord, what was she to do now? Why hadn't she realized that Charles could find out where Francis was and write to him there? Charles was not a stupid man.

If Charles and Francis met, it would be disastrous. She opened a drawer and took out the letter she had received that day, the last of a series of letters from Charles.

. . . I will tell your son all and show him the letters you have written to me. I am convinced that when he knows how it is with us he will not oppose the match. But I would rather you admit your feelings honestly to him, my love. I know you can be no happier than I with the current state of affairs. The memories of that one afternoon of ecstasy will never leave me. I am in hell.

As was she. The memories of that afternoon would not leave her, either, and unlike Charles, she had to live in this house, sit on the chaise where they had . . .

She buried her face in her hands, assailed by guilt and desire. How could she have behaved in such a way? How could she have so betrayed her position and her husband's memory by letting a younger and impecunious man make love to her in the home she and her husband had created?

How could she want so much to repeat the shameful act?

She had been so overwhelmed with guilt that she had engineered Charles's dismissal, hoping to thus dismiss him from her life. But he had continued to woo her.

Then she had argued that Francis would oppose the match. It might be true. She had no idea how her son would react to her union with a man like Charles.

Charles had not been deterred. He had been sure that he could persuade Francis of the suitability of the union. And that was probably true, too.

Now, cast into panic by Francis's sudden arrival, she had added a blantant lie to her deceptions. Charles had never blackmailed her, never demanded money. All he had ever demanded was that she be honest with her son and honest with herself.

She could not do it.

But now Francis was heading for a confrontation with her lover, and disaster could be the result. The lesser disaster was that Charles would tell Francis the truth, and her son would despise her. The greater was that the two men would fight, and one would die.

Francis had never been a rough, bloodthirsty boy or man, but ever since he had come under the influence of Nicholas Delaney and his Company of Rogues, Lady Middlethorpe had not been sure what he was capable of. All this talk of brawling worried her, but it was the thought of pistols that terrified her. Men issued challenges over the most trivial matters.

Lady Middlethorpe dropped into the chair in front of her delicate Buhl escritoire and dashed off two notes. Almost as soon as her son had driven off, a new team in the shafts, two grooms rode out from the Priory with these letters.

One was headed to Redoaks in Devon, home of Francis's closest friend. Much as she resented the influence Nicholas Delaney had over her son, he was just the sort of man to be able to prevent Charles and Francis from dueling to the death.

The other groom was headed to the Crown and Anchor at Weymouth with a note addressed to Mr. Charles Ferncliff. Far better for all if Charles could simply make himself scarce so no meeting would ever occur.

And, please God, that would be the end of it, and she would never hear from him again.

But at the thought, she wept.

Chapter 3

That evening the failing light found Serena and Francis in the same part of Dorset, though as yet unaware of the fact.

Serena was close to despair.

She had been lucky at first. She hadn't had to chance the stage picking her up, for she had been taken up by a wool-factor in a gig. The man was a stranger to the area, just passing through. There was reason to hope that after he dropped her at the Dog and Fiddle in Nairbury, he'd never be heard from again. To her brothers it would be as if she'd disappeared into thin air. She hadn't missed the wool-factor's speculative looks and hints about improved acquaintanceship, but the man had taken her lack of response in good part, and had driven off alone.

The Dog and Fiddle was a staging post and Serena had no difficulty in purchasing a ticket. She chose to go to Winchester simply because that coach would be the next one to leave. Surely she could lose any pursuit in that busy city.

The three-hour coach ride, however, gave her too much time to think.

The insanity of her actions began to dawn on her, but no alternative presented itself. Better surely to be out in the world with guineas in her pocket than to be sold to a brothel.

She knew her older brother would do it. Will might protest, but he was too weak a man to stand against Tom, and it was the brutal truth that her brothers had no use for her except to sell her for money.

Her faith in Miss Mallory was ebbing, however. She remembered the lady as firm and kindly, but that was eight years ago. She didn't even know whether the woman still lived. Even if she did, what could Miss Mallory be expected to do when Serena Riverton turned up on her doorstep begging for refuge?

Offer her a teaching position?

Serena almost laughed aloud at that.

Though she had developed a taste for reading during her marriage—for most of the time, thank God, she had been left alone in the country—she was not of an academic bent, and the selection of books at Stokeley Manor had been meager.

And she was Randy Riverton's widow.

Sir Matthew Riverton had been a rich Cit given a baronetcy for his generosity to the Regent—that is, he had given Prince George some fine and expensive works of art that he had lusted over. But Matthew hadn't moved in the first circles for all of that. In his cups he had been inclined to rant over the unfairness of life: The Prince hadn't made him a crony, and his wife couldn't give him an heir.

Even if he didn't have the entrée to Carlton House,

however, Matthew Riverton had been notorious. He had been infamous among men for his extravagant lewd entertainments. Serena could imagine the reaction of the fathers of Miss Mallory's pupils if they discovered their daughters were being taught by Randy Riverton's widow.

Taught what? they might well ask.

And with reason. During her marriage Serena had not been allowed to handle money and so had not learned household management. She had never possessed great interest or skill in needlework or music. Having left school at fifteen, her more formal education was lacking.

The only real training she had received had been from Matthew, and that had *not* been in skills suitable for well-bred young ladies. . . .

Serena became aware of something rubbing her foot. She looked down and realized it was a boot—a boot belonging to the mustachioed captain lounging opposite. He smiled and winked.

She turned hastily away, heat rushing to her cheeks. His boot tapped against hers, then slid up toward her ankle.

She turned back to glare at him.

He raised his brows in mock innocence and moved his foot, but the lascivious invitation didn't leave his eyes.

Serena pulled up her hood and huddled in its protection. Oh, but she hated her appearance that attracted this kind of attention.

Serena knew that without some man's protection this was the kind of pestering she must expect for the rest of her life, or at least until age rid her of her damnable appeal. She despaired of finding any respectable sanctuary.

Even if she could think to find a post as a governess or companion without references, her appearance would slam all doors in her face.

Serena looked out at the bleak winterish countryside and knew Tom had been right. It was her destiny to be a whore. It seemed God had designed her appearance for that role, and her husband had trained her for it. Trained her in what he revoltingly called bed-work . . .

She flicked a glance at the captain and he winked again, grinning. The invitation was unmistakable.

Then be damned to them all, she thought bitterly. If the choice was between marriage and prostitution, she'd *be* a whore but not in a brothel. She'd be a high-flying Cyprian. In fact, if she was going to be a whore, she'd be the best damn whore in England.

A boot tapped her foot again. Serena glared at the captain so fiercely that his eyes shifted and *he* colored up. And so he should. He couldn't afford her.

She'd be the most expensive damn whore in England, too!

If Seale would offer ten thousand pounds, what could she ask for herself? As Tom had said, her barrenness was no impediment as a mistress.

How were such things arranged?

At that point her resolution faltered, for she was unable to imagine how to go about entering a life of sin. Then she thought of Harriet Wilson.

The famous Cyprian had come to one of the house parties that Matthew had thrown at Stokeley Manor during hunting season. Orgy, more like. Serena shuddered at the memory, but she remembered Harriet as being quite kind to a seventeen-year-old who refused to have anything to do with low women.

Kind and pitying.

Serena could see why Harriet would pity the child bride she had been, obvious slave to her husband, forced even into improper behavior before strangers. Harriet had permitted no such indignities.

Harriet had even stirred herself to give some advice. "I'd leave him, dear," she'd said one day, catching Serena alone.

"I cannot. He is my husband."

Harriet had not protested but merely said, "If you do, dear, come to me and I'll help you. I'm sure I could find you a protector who'd snap his fingers at Riverton. You've a rare quality, you know."

"I *loathe* it."

Harriet smiled. She had none of Serena's beauty, but she, too, had something that drew men like a lodestone. " If you're lucky, dear, one day you'll see it as the power it is. It's like a cocked gun, aimed straight at the heart of this man's world. Learn to shoot straight."

So, thought Serena, she had a weapon against men . . . if she could only discover how to use it. It was clearly time to learn to shoot straight, and Harriet would be an excellent teacher. When she arrived in Winchester, she would not continue toward Cheltenham but would buy a ticket to London.

When she arrived in the cathedral city, however, the timetable in the bustling inn yard told her that she had missed the day's London coach. Serena looked anxiously over the crowd and knew she could not stay in Winchester. It was such an obvious center to check that it was only a matter of time before one of her brothers arrived here.

She must go on to a smaller town.

She bought a ticket on the next stage to leave, one to Basingstoke. The big horses were just being eased between the shafts, and so she spent a few coins on a pie from a passing pieman, keeping a wary eye out for any sign of pursuit. It was late afternoon now, and dark was slowly gathering. Her brothers would be on the hunt.

The guard called for the passengers to go aboard, but as Serena brushed the pastry crumbs off her gloves, she froze.

Will was riding into the yard, scanning it.

She ducked behind the coach, heart racing with panic.

The guard called again for the Basingstoke passengers. Serena wanted to leap into the stage and let it carry her away, but she knew Will might see her. And anyway, the booking clerk would remember her—everyone remembered her—and tell Will what coach she was on. It would then be a moving trap.

She choked back a sob of panic. What should she do now? She was aware of the temptation to give up. This was all too hard. She couldn't keep going.

But she must. She really would rather die than marry.

The main thing was to escape Will. She used the concealment of the coach to slip down the yard toward the arched opening into the street. A glance back showed her Will buying a hot pie from the same vendor who had served her. Would he ask about her? He looked as if he thought himself on a fool's errand.

Thank God it was lazy, stupid Will who'd almost caught her and not Tom. She still had a chance.

Once out of the yard, she headed out of town at a brisk walk, expecting to hear pursuit at any moment. There was no alarm and so she relaxed a little. Perhaps she could walk to the next village.

Then she realized she was too obvious on the wide highway. She could clearly imagine Will coming up behind her, chasing her down as if she were a frantic fox. So when she came to a smaller road signed to Hursley, Serena turned into it, speeding her pace almost to a run. When the road forked, she went right at random.

She was gasping by now and she slowed, trying to regain control.

This was madness! This was the road to nowhere, and she doubted that the coins she had left in her pocket would carry her to London. But back in Winchester Will awaited, and she'd rather *die* than fall into her brothers' hands. They'd never let her escape again.

She had made herself walk on. There would be a village ahead, and surely some way of continuing to London even if she had to take a cart or walk.

Now, an hour later, she was trudging along wearily, pondering the question again: Is marriage truly a fate worse than death? Because it was quite likely death she had chosen.

Slow death by starvation. Quick death at the hands of foot pads. Horrible death at the hands of a rapist. Death from exposure . . .

Dark was coming, bringing with it an icy chill. The

village of Hursley was ahead somewhere but might not appear in time.

Serena had always known that her exotic appearance disguised a prosaic spirit. That prosaic spirit had enabled her to survive her marriage, whereas a more sensitive woman might have been destroyed. Now her sensible head told her that a second marriage, even if like her first, was probably preferable to dying from exposure and certainly preferable to dying from rape.

Serena realized she had stopped to ponder this, and once again she forced her cold and tired legs into motion. She'd surely freeze if she stood still, and she wasn't yet ready to resign herself to an icy death by the roadside.

She felt the small purse in her pocket. Four guineas left, along with a few smaller coins. Some bulwark against the world, but little enough upon which to build a new life.

She swallowed threatened tears and pushed back panic. All would be well when she found a way to London.

She knew many women would be horrified that she was even considering becoming a Cyprian, but to Serena it was a case of needs must when the devil drives. To be a high-paid whore was infinitely preferable to marriage in her eyes. A mistress, after all, could leave her protector. She received money that she could keep as her own. She made the man no vows, and he had no power before the law.

A chill wind was picking up, swirling under her warm cape and gown. Her feet were icy. She anxiously scanned ahead but saw no sign of humanity, good or bad. There could be some shelter quite close, though, she told herself. The hedges here were high, and even though it was November, they obscured her view of the surrounding countryside.

She quickened her step, her mind returning to worry at her problem. She still had the option of returning home and marrying Seale. There was some hope that he would debauch himself into the grave even faster than her first husband, and next time she'd make sure to hold on to any assets that came to her. . . .

The fact that she was thinking of it told her she shrank from her practical choice.

A whore. Could she really be a whore?

What else had she been to Matthew, wedding ring or not?

At least this way she'd be in charge of her destiny.

A noise penetrated her tangled thoughts. Horses and wheels. Fearing pursuit, Serena whirled around.

A carriage!

No, a curricle.

A man.

No one she knew, she realized with sweeping relief.

All the same, her heart raced as she thought of being caught here alone by any man, but there was nowhere to hide. She turned forward, hastening her step, though she knew she had no chance of outpacing the four-horse rig.

It drew closer. The large, steaming chestnuts pounded past but slowed . . . slowed until the curricle was alongside and matching her speed.

"May I take you up somewhere, ma'am?"

An educated voice, but he could be up to no good accosting a woman on the road. Serena just prayed he would drive on.

The curricle kept a steady pace. "Ma'am?"

Oh, why would he not leave her alone? Serena turned slightly, staying huddled in the deep hood of her cloak. "I need nothing, thank you." She marched on.

The man didn't drive past. "Ma'am, it's at least two miles to the nearest hamlet that I'm aware of, it's cold, night's falling, and I suspect a storm is coming."

As if to prove his point, a few drops of icy water blew on a sharp gust of wind.

"I cannot leave you here," he said simply.

Serena saw it was hopeless that he go away, and she stopped to turn and look at him. No tame wool-factor, this. A blood, she thought with despair, reeking of fashionable arrogance from his tilted beaver to his glossy boots. His lean, handsome face was touched by wry amusement. At her.

"I have no wish to alarm you, ma'am, but the weather threatens to worsen, and it hardly seems safe or proper for you to be alone out here. And consider my predicament," he added with a slight smile. "I've been very well trained in the gentlemanly arts and am cursed with a kind heart. I cannot possibly abandon you. If you insist on walking, I will have to keep pace with you all the way."

Serena was seduced by his good humor and kindness, such rare ingredients in her life that she did not know how to resist them. A knife-sharp gust of icy wind decided her. She was in desperate need of shelter.

Cautiously, she approached the curricle and raised her foot to the step. He stretched out a hand and helped her into the seat beside him.

The very feel of his hand around hers, gloved as they both were, sent a jolt through her. Lean and powerful.

40

She was not accustomed to lean, strong young men. Her father, her brothers, and her husband were all strong men but heavy, with hands like bunches of rough sausages.

Once, young and innocent, she had glimpsed such men as this and had giggled with her friends about them, wondering which one might be for her. Since her marriage, they had been no part of her existence. He frightened her.

He did nothing alarming, however, but just urged the team up to a cracking pace again. "Where are you headed, ma'am? I'll take you to your door."

"Hursley," she said, looking firmly ahead and clutching the rail.

Now that she was raised above the hedge, Serena could appreciate the man's concern. Bare fields stretched on one side and bleak hills on the other. There were no nearby houses. Heavy, threatening clouds were rolling in from the east and in the distance skeleton trees tossed in strong winds.

"I have to pass through Hursley," he said, "so there is no problem in taking you there. My name is Middlethorpe, by the way. Lord Middlethorpe."

She flicked a wary glance at him. She had met few lords, and none she liked. Matthew had been a mere baronet, and his friends all lower still. Wealthy, to be sure, but not of high rank. The few members of the nobility who had hung around Matthew had been the desperate dregs. Another of Matthew's complaints had been that the cream of the aristocracy would not succumb to the lure of his lavish generosity.

The lords Serena had met previously had been out-and-out libertines, and she was sure that honorable

41

peers of the realm did not pick up chance travelers out of pure charity. She looked at the road racing beneath the wheels and wondered if she could throw herself from the carriage and live. . . .

"May I not have your name, ma'am?" he asked.

"Serena Allbright." Then she realized she had given her maiden name.

Why?

Doubtless because she wanted to wipe away all traces of her marriage. And because she shuddered at the thought that this man of fashion might recognize the name Riverton, might know her to be Matthew Riverton's well-trained wife. How could she know how far her husband's drunken boasting had traveled?

At least Lord Middlethorpe intruded no further, concentrating instead on steering his team with casual skill along the winding, rutted lane. Serena found her attention caught by his competent gloved hands, so subtly strong on the ribbons. Eventually, her gaze traveled up his caped greatcoat to his face.

He did not look debauched. His classical profile was quite beautiful, in fact. Since her own looks were flawed by a short nose and peculiarly tilted eyes, she had great admiration for pure lines.

Why, what an idiot she was!

Serena almost laughed out loud. She had been nervous of her rescuer's intentions, when just a short time before she had been planning a life of sin! Here, surely, was a candidate for protector. When—like the wool-factor and the half-pay captain—he tried to seduce her, all she had to do was succumb to his wiles and set her price.

Brought so close to it, however, her mind balked.

This man might be handsome, but he was still a man. He would expect what Matthew had expected, do what Matthew had done. . . .

But, asked her practical side, what choice do you have?

And this time, if it becomes truly intolerable, you can leave.

All the same . . .

Lord Middlethorpe must have detected her shudder. "Cold, ma'am?" he asked. "Shouldn't be long now. But the dashed wind's worsening."

He urged his horses to more speed. In moments, though, a rut caught a wheel and almost tipped them into the ditch. He threw himself over her to correct the balance as he hauled back hard on the ribbons. "Sorry about that," he gasped when he had control again. "Are you all right?"

"Yes, thank you." Serena straightened, all too aware of the power of his body so briefly against hers.

Then concern over that power was swamped by concern over the power of the elements. The wind was now tugging at her cloak like monstrous hands, and even buffeting the carriage.

" 'Struth," muttered Lord Middlethorpe. "I feared we were in for a storm, but nothing like this. I see a farm off to our right, ma'am. Do you know if it would offer shelter?" He was shouting now in order to be heard over the wind.

An alarming crack announced the separation of a rotten branch from a nearby tree. It whipped past the horses and he had his work cut out to steady them again.

Serena couldn't hear his muttered words and rather supposed that was for the best.

"Well?" he shouted. "I'm not sure we can make Hursley."

"I don't know," she shouted back. "I am a stranger to these parts."

He gave her an astonished look, but then steered the curricle into the rough lane leading to the farmhouse. A welcome light flickered through tossing trees.

Serena had no time to worry about what he thought of her. The winds were surely of almost hurricane proportions. She saw a nearby haystack shredded to blow in the wind, and a particularly sharp gust almost tipped the curricle over.

"We'd best get out and walk!" he yelled, and struggled down to go to the frightened horses' heads.

Serena saw he could not help her, and she clambered down as best she could. Her heavy cloak was being flapped like a cotton sheet and was as much hazard as protection.

She managed to make it to the other leader's head and reached up to grasp the strap, as much to anchor herself as to steady the beast. It worked to do both and they fought the wind toward the farmyard.

When they staggered into the yard the force of the wind eased a little, blocked by the sheds and barns. But now flying debris was much more dangerous. Serena let go of the horse and pulled her hood close as protection against the swirling dust and straw. She saw a bucket bowl along and collide with Lord Middlethorpe's shin; saw him jump from the pain.

Serena clutched on to a stone horse trough, wondering how she was going to make it to the house.

A plank ripped free of a sagging manger and whirled just past her head to shatter against a stone wall.

Francis saw her narrow escape and her predicament. Lord, she was quite a tiny thing. He had managed to tow the frantic horses into the shelter of an open barn, so he abandoned them and grabbed her. He shielded her with his body as they fought their way to the farmhouse door.

He knocked but no one would hear him in this racket, so he opened the door and pulled them both in, shutting it thankfully on the violence outside.

They were in a stark tiled corridor, lit only by one small window. Muddy boots and pattens lined it, suggesting a good number of inhabitants. Heavy cloaks and coats hung on hooks on the wall.

In comparison to the outside, the corridor was almost silent, and they were at last free of the raging wind. They both took a moment to catch their breath. With a deep sigh of relief, Serena Allbright pushed back her heavy hood and shook her head.

Francis was transfixed. Even tousled and pale, he had never seen such a woman in his life.

No, he thought, that was ridiculous. He'd seen any number of beauties of all shapes and sizes.

But not like this one.

His dazzled mind absorbed blood-red hair escaping from a knot and pale, flawless features . . .

No, not flawless. Her lips were too full, her short nose had a decided tilt, and her eyes . . .

Her eyes could not exactly be called flawed. Deep, dark, and huge, they sat tilted, under sensual, heavy lids. Despite the fact that he knew differently, those eyes said she was emerging, sated, from a well-used bed.

The effect was being heightened, he realized, by a most extraordinary perfume. It surrounded her, not heavily, but unignorably. It had nothing to do with the flower scents his mother and sisters wore, but was composed of spicy, musky odors that spoke of sex.

He realized with a jolt that the last time he had smelled such a perfume was on Thérèse Bellaire, the owner of a high-class house of pleasure and the most dangerous woman he had ever known.

A whore. Serena Allbright had to be a whore.

An available whore? his optimistic body asked.

With a conscious effort, Francis remembered to breathe. With an even greater effort, he summoned caution. He reminded himself that Thérèse Bellaire had been a viper who had almost destroyed his best friend, Nicholas. To find a woman such as this wandering the countryside could mean nothing but trouble.

She was looking at him quizzically. "They probably haven't heard us because of the storm, my lord. Don't you think we should tell the people here that they have unexpected guests?"

"I am wondering *what* to tell them, Miss Allbright."

"That we need shelter from the storm? In Christian charity they can hardly refuse us."

"I was wondering rather what to say about you. I am about my business. On my way, in fact, to Weymouth. What of you?"

She started in surprise, and he suspected that for a moment she had forgotten her circumstances, whatever they might be. "I have suffered a coach accident?" she offered tentatively.

46

"Then we must by all means arrange assistance for your coachman and servants."

Her lips twitched in acceptance that she had lied. "I have no good explanation to offer then, I'm afraid, my lord."

"Miss Allbright, I need to arrange for my horses, so we cannot remain here exchanging pleasantries. What do you want me to say about you?"

She raised her chin. "The truth, if you please."

He shrugged. "As you will." It was going to present a devilishly odd appearance, though.

Francis walked toward the door at the end of the corridor, but it opened before he reached it, spilling light, heat, and the welcome aroma of food. "Who be out there?" asked a gruff voice, and Francis saw the mouth of a shotgun pointing straight at him.

"No malefactors, sir," he said quickly. "We are just seeking refuge from the storm. You did not hear my knock."

Perhaps it was his well-bred accent that lowered the barriers, for the speaker came fully into view, proving to be a tall, gaunt man with a long, black beard. Behind him Francis could see a kitchen full of people.

"Never let it be said," the man intoned, "that Jeremy Post turned away good Christian folk in their hour of need. So who be ye?" Despite the words, the tone was grudging, the eyes hard and suspicious.

In the face of this biblical presence, Francis made a snap decision. "My name is Haile, and this is my wife. We will pay well for a night's shelter."

A moment later he was doubting his wisdom, as he heard a stifled protest from his companion; yet he knew he was right. It was all too likely that this patriarch would throw Serena Allbright back out into the storm if she didn't have a cloak of respectability.

A plain mystery woman might just have been tolerated, but this erotic siren? Never.

And if he was going to pretend to have a bride, it was definitely better not to give his title.

The man's sunken eyes took them in, lingering on Serena in intense disapproval, but then he lowered his weapon and stood aside. "Come you in, then."

The kitchen was filled with people and the smell of cooking. It was also full of the smell of stale, sweaty bodies, but Francis was past being particular. In fact, he thought, anything that masked Serena's disturbing perfume would be for the best. He took in a vague impression of about ten people of all ages as he steered his companion toward the fire. Above the hearth was a sampler declaring, *The eyes of the Lord are in every place, beholding the evil and the good.*

"Shem, Ham," growled Mr. Post. "Go see to Mr. Haile's horses."

Two brawny young men sitting on an oak settle near the fire rose surlily to their feet and clumped out.

"There, sir," said Mr. Post. "Sit yourself and your wife down."

Francis turned to assist his companion out of her cloak, noting its quality with some surprise. It was made of heavy camlet lined with sable and must have cost some man a pretty penny. Its removal, however, revealed a russet gown that would surely give Mr. Post palpitations, so low was it in the magnificent bosom. Francis had to drag his eyes away.

Serena Allbright did not seem aware of the effect of

her appearance and was intent on stripping off her leather gloves.

Francis's attention was caught again. She was wearing a handsome wedding band and a large emerald.

She was *married?* Some man owned this magnificent creature and let her wander around loose?

"Sarah," snapped Mr. Post to the huddle of women near a table. "Give Mrs. Haile your shawl. She'll be chilled."

A thin girl scurried forward to give up her black knitted shawl. Francis could swear that he saw Serena's lips twitch as she arranged it. She smiled sweetly at their host. "Thank you, Mr. Post. How kind you are."

Jeremy Post glared at her, jaws clenched on his long clay pipe. Francis knew he was wishing this whore of Babylon had never entered his domain. Francis was feeling a bit that way himself.

They took their seats and Francis said, "I thank you, too, for your hospitality, Mr. Post. It is fierce out there." The wind was howling, windows were rattling, and occasional crashes told of further damage.

"God's hand upon the sinners in the land," the man muttered. "Where be ye from, then?"

"I have property near Andover." This was entirely true. Thorpe Priory was situated there.

"Handsome property, I have no doubt," sneered their host. " *'Labor not to be rich: cease from thine own wisdom.'* "

Francis raised his brows. "Sounds like an instruction to idleness, sir. *'Strong men retain riches'?*" he offered as a counter proposal.

Mr. Post glared in confusion, but Francis heard a smothered sound. He didn't look, but he suspected that his "wife" was trying not to laugh. She was going to set him off; if they weren't both careful, they'd be out on their ears.

But he couldn't abide religious extremists of this type.

" 'A naughty person, a wicked man, walketh with a forward mouth,' " avowed the patriarch. "We don't hold with ungodliness in this house, Mr. Haile."

"I don't hold with ungodliness anywhere," said Francis amiably, though it was an effort to be pleasant.

He was seriously considering his options. The briefest thought assured him that they had little choice but to maintain their deception and stay the night in this most unpleasant household.

He looked around.

There was a degree of prosperity about the place—in the quality of the plain furniture and pots, and the hams and other supplies hanging from the beams. There was also an air of austerity. The clothes were drab, and the only decorations in the room—if such they could be called—were the biblical quotations.

Over to one side he saw a daunting message burnt into wood. *"Thou shalt beat him with the rod, and shalt deliver his soul from hell."* Beneath, on a ledge, was a rod, ready.

How many were subject to this tyrant?

There were four women busy preparing the meal, presumably Mrs. Post and three daughters. A young lad turned a spit by the fire and an ancient woman snoozed in a rocker. There were also the two young men who were out tending the horses. Shem and Ham. What were the odds the spit-turner was Japheth?

Despite his distaste for the environment, the thought of Jeremy Post as Noah, and the farmhouse as a bleak

50

Ark in the midst of the storm, twitched Francis's sense of humor, but he brought it to order. Clearly, laughter was not considered "godly."

"Don't hold with strangers, I don't." Post's harsh voice dragged Francis out of his musings.

"Pity," he said, stretching his boots out toward the fire.

Post frowned in his thwarted way. "Don't hold with gentry-types, either. *Better is little with the fear of the Lord, than great treasure and trouble therewith.*' You touch one of my girls and I'll not be answerable."

Francis shuddered at the thought of touching one of the Post girls. "I have my wife with me, Mr. Post."

"Aye," the man grunted with a blistering look at Serena.

A banging door announced the return of Shem and Ham, and in moments they were in. The two young men stopped dead at the sight of Serena, even in her shawl, and their mouths fell open.

"Stop gawking," snarled Mr. Post, and they both colored and looked elsewhere. "Remember. *The lips of a strange woman drop as a honeycomb, but her end is bitter as wormwood.*' "

"Mr. Post," said Francis quite pleasantly, "if your sons offend my wife, I will not be answerable for the consequences."

The man's hand clenched. "If it were godly to do so, Mr. Haile, I'd throw you and your wife back into the storm."

Francis let that wash over him, but godly household or not, he was concerned about the sleeping arrangements here. He was uneasy about any situation that would put Serena Allbright at the mercy of the young

51

Post men, who bore strong resemblance to bullocks scenting their first heifer.

He had to wonder whether he, despite his gloss of sophistication, was exhibiting the same panting awareness. He was aware of her to a distracting degree. Even the assorted smells of the Posts' kitchen could not entirely drown out her perfume, and as she was sitting close beside him, he was deeply aware of her body touching his.

He risked a glance at her. Her skin was amazing. It was like a pearl—flawlessly pale and yet glowing with an inner light. Her eyes rested on the plain wall opposite, and he could appreciate the extraordinary length and thickness of her lashes. Her nose had a decided tilt, but he could not make himself see it as a fault. It simply made her seem vulnerable and childlike.

Unlike a child, however, she sat in composed silence with never a twitch.

Was it weariness or discipline? He would not expect a loose woman to have such control. Was she wife or whore? Which did he want her to be?

Francis reminded himself that he was about to offer marriage to a virtuous young lady and dragged his eyes away.

It seemed that everyone had decided silence was golden, and it sat heavily in the room except for the sounds of the women's work, and a repetitive whistling snore from the old woman. Francis passed the time by trying to devise acceptable explanations for Serena's plight, but he found himself too weary to put much effort into it.

Then the supper was spread on the table. Plain food but good, thank the heavens: thick barley soup, slices of ham with cabbage, and fresh bread with gooseberry jam. After a lengthy grace, heavily larded with references to the virtues of a simple, godly life as opposed to one of idle luxury, they all set to. Francis ate with relish and noted that Serena did, too. Of course, he had no way of knowing how long it had been since she'd last eaten.

He knew nothing about her at all.

She was undoubtedly a problem, for what innocent reason could there be for a lady to wander around unescorted in November? It cast into doubt any idea that she was respectably married. The best he could imagine was that she was a widow turned mistress and callously abandoned by her protector. Even if her virtue was dubious, however, it wasn't in his nature to turn away from any woman in distress.

What on earth was he to do with her, though?

Since his trip to Weymouth could be sensitive, he had done without his groom. He could not possibly take a strange adventuress along. But he equally could not leave her here. Perhaps when he had a chance to speak to her alone, there would prove to be something simple he could do to straighten out her circumstances.

How could he arrange to speak to her alone in this cramped household?

As the meal ended, he realized that speaking to her alone was going to be no problem at all. They were to have a private room.

Chapter 4

The Posts kept country hours and on these short days the women went to bed as soon as the supper dishes were cleaned. The men would follow after the last farm-work of the day.

Before going out to see to his stock, Jeremy Post held a final, lengthy Bible-reading, including the pointed instruction: *"Keep thee from the evil of the flattery of the tongue of a strange woman. Lust not after her beauty in thine heart; Neither let her take thee with her eyelids."*

This was clearly directed at Shem and Japheth, but Francis thought he should perhaps take the words to heart himself. He also noted wryly that Mr. Post was not blind to the power of Serena's extraordinary eyes.

As soon as the big bible was closed, Serena and Francis were escorted—rather in the manner of dangerous prisoners being rendered safe—to the best bedroom, Mr. and Mrs. Post's own room.

When Francis attempted to demur, it was made clear that the house was full, and that this arrangement had been accomplished by Mrs. Post moving in with her daughters and Mr. Post with his sons. Francis knew a suggestion that he and his wife could do the same split would never be agreed to.

And considering the number of lascivious looks still being cast toward Serena by the sons of the house—including stripling Japheth—Frances wasn't sure he would be easy leaving her unguarded, even with the daughters.

When the door was closed on the small room, however, he shook his head. "I'm sorry. This is becoming rather awkward."

She perched on the edge of the big bed. "Aren't the Posts peculiar? Never fear, my lord, I won't fall into the vapors. I'd far rather be in here with you than out there with them. I'm not a sensitive virgin, after all."

The words were prosaic, but with her astonishing sultry beauty they dizzied him with a wealth of erotic promise.

He wondered what her reaction would be if he said, "But I am." It was true. Too fastidious to enjoy loose women and too kind to use pure ones, he was a peculiarity amongst his friends, though in fact they all thought he was just very discreet.

It was, however, yet another excellent reason for marriage. Thought of Lady Anne put him sharply on his guard. "I'll sleep on the floor," he said.

She scanned the room. "Where?"

He had to admit that short of sleeping under the bed it was a chancy proposition. The room was small and the Posts had filled every available space with chests of drawers, small tables, chairs, and other odd items. There was a narrow strip of bare floor on one side of the bed but it did not look inviting, and he could already feel the chill drafts that whistled across the bare planks.

"My dear Lord Middlethorpe," said Serena pleasantly, "this is, if you'll note it, quite a large bed. I suspect we can both sleep in it without being aware of the other. If," she added with a sliding look that stole his breath, "that is what you want."

Damnation! The woman was trying to seduce him! And he knew in his heart—and less noble portions of his anatomy—that he wanted to be seduced. He was no better than the Post lads.

He had no idea what to say and feared he was coloring up.

At his silence, her color certainly flared. "Surely, my lord, if anyone should be uneasy about this situation, it is me, not you."

Her heightened color made her ravishing. . . .

Francis took a deep breath and struggled for control. It wasn't as if he hadn't felt desire before and conquered it. He certainly wasn't going to leap into folly for a chance-met light-skirt.

Lust not after her beauty in thine heart, he reminded himself. *Neither let her take thee with her eyelids.*

He lounged in a hard chair beside the bed. "I assure you, you have nothing to fear from me, madam. Now, tell me why you were on the road in such weather."

All amusement fled and her lids shielded her eyes. "I dare not."

Dare not. An interesting choice of words. Francis considered the enigma. Her deep red hair was escaping its pins and curling into an intoxicating mass of fiery bronze in the light of the one candle. The curving line of her body from nape to hip was sensual beauty incorporated. Even under the ugly shawl, her breasts swelled with promise, pleading for the touch of his hands. Her perfume was weighing heavy on the chill air.

She was shadows and mysteries that his body yearned for, but he made himself keep hold of sanity.

Her rings glinted in the light, helping him to control himself. "What of your husband?" he asked.

"He is dead."

"Family, then?"

"I have none to help me."

"You must have a household, servants . . ."

"No."

Faced with such patent evasion, Francis's patience began to thin. It had been a hell of a day. Now it appeared he had a lying adventuress on his hands, and a growing desire he was determined not to assuage. "Where, then, were you going, ma'am, alone and on foot?"

She looked up reproachfully. "My name really is Serena and I invite you to use it."

"That would hardly be appropriate."

"Why not? We are about to share a bed."

"Madam," he said flatly, "I find you bold and damned fishy."

Color flared in her cheeks again. "Bold? It was no plan of mine to create this lie, my lord!"

"If I hadn't, you'd be out on your ear. As perhaps you deserve."

"I deserve no such thing."

"No true lady could be so cool at this situation."

Her magnificent eyes flashed. "Would you rather I have the vapors, sir? I will if you want. I have cause enough."

"What cause?" asked Francis quickly.

The lids came down again and she controlled herself. "I cannot tell you."

"Then devil take you." He rose to his feet. "Get into the bed." After a moment's thought, he decided he'd be damned if he'd sacrifice comfort to this woman's modesty. He took off his boots and cravat, then stripped down to his shirt and buckskin breeches.

Out of the corner of his eye he saw her scramble into the bed fully dressed and wondered if he'd misjudged her after all. At this moment she looked very uneasy, as any decent woman should. He blew out the one light and slid under the covers himself, keeping to the very edge of the bed.

It should have been easier to stay in control in the dark without the distracting sight of her, but instead there was a new intimacy. He'd never been in bed with a woman in his life. He thought he could hear her breathing and sense the distant warmth of her body. When she shifted slightly the bed carried the movement to him, along with a whisper of that devastating perfume.

He stirred restlessly. "Are you really a widow?"

"Yes."

"Then that perfume is hardly proper. It is more suited to a whore."

"Are you saying you do not like it?" There was a distinct edge to the question.

"That has nothing to say to the matter." 'Struth, he sounded like an outraged parson. "Go to sleep, Mrs. Allbright. I must be on my way early in the morning."

"On your way?"

"I am on important business." Then he registered

the panic in her query. "Don't worry, ma'am. I will take you on to Hursley."

And what, he wondered, was at Hursley? A lover?

He heard the bangs as the Post men returned to the house, and the sounds of them climbing the stairs and settling into their beds. Silence fell, with the only noises those of the old house creaking around them under the dying force of the storm.

Suddenly, she spoke. "I'm sorry," she said softly. "You are being kind to me and I am making things difficult. The perfume was my husband's choice. I don't use it any longer but it still lingers on some of my clothing. It always was particularly cloying."

This opened a number of new questions, but Francis resolved to ignore them. He couldn't resist saying, "I would give your clothes a good airing, ma'am, if I were you."

He thought, he hoped, they were done with talk for the night. Now if only he could just forget that she was there at all, he might be able to get some sleep.

It was impossible. His body ached, and he stirred restlessly.

"I'm sorry if the perfume makes you want a woman," she said softly in the dark. "If you wish, you may mount me."

"*What?*" Francis could hardly believe what he had heard.

"I am causing your problem," she said rather shakily. "It is only fair that I ease it."

Desire caught Francis like a vise, but he fought it. He knew her now. She was a whore of the most blatant kind and he'd be mad to give in to her. God knows what price he'd end up paying. "There is no need," he said coolly. "After all, you would not want to risk getting with child, would you?"

"I cannot conceive a child," she said very faintly. "I am barren."

Francis found himself saying, "I'm sorry."

Another weighty silence fell, and then the bed shifted as she turned away from him. "Good night, then."

"Good night." Francis was surprisingly affronted that she had raised and dismissed the question of their joyful consummation so easily. Then he, too, turned onto his side, telling himself he'd had a most lucky escape.

His body would agree with that in time.

Serena huddled in the darkness.

He didn't want her. Dear Lord, what was to become of her if the right sort of men didn't want her? She had four guineas in her pocket and nothing else to offer.

Perhaps her rescuer had done her an ill turn. Perhaps it would have been better to have died in the storm. Dishonor might be preferable to death, but if death it must be, she'd rather a quick death than a lingering one of starvation.

What was she to do?

What was she to do?

Drowning in anxiety, Serena fell into sleep. . . .

A bang in the house brought her sharply awake. She immediately realized where she was, that it was morning, and that the noise had merely been one of the Posts dropping something. There was the pale hint of first light coming through a crack in the heavy curtains, but the room was still dark.

A peacefulness outside the window told her the storm was over. There was nothing to prevent them from leaving, nothing to prevent this man from dropping her at Hursley and driving on.

What was to become of her? Her first panic-driven courage had evaporated and she was terrified of the world. In a few hours she would be alone again, she who had never been alone in her life.

She *wouldn't* return to her brothers, to be sold again.

She doubted she could get to London without help.

Her bed partner was the only man she'd ever met who had been kind to her.

He might be married.

But married men kept mistresses, too.

How was it done?

If she offered herself plainly, would he accept? She'd tried that.

Perhaps she needed to give him a sample of her wares.

Serena swallowed. What she was contemplating horrified her, but surely afterward he would not be so eager to drive away. . . .

She knew what to do. She knew, at least, what Matthew would have wanted her to do. Were all men the same in these matters?

Serena lay there in fearful indecision. She had never so much as kissed a man other than her husband, and now she was contemplating seducing one.

What choice did she have? She was alone in the world with only one currency to offer.

She eased over in the bed to lie against the heat of

him and slid her hand around his torso. She caught her breath in surprise. Lord Middlethorpe was so firm. Matthew had been big and flabby. She ran her hand lightly over the ridged muscles of his abdomen, sensing with delight the life-force within him.

It was the first time she had ever enjoyed touching a man.

He moved slightly beneath her hand.

She froze, half hoping he would wake and discover what she was doing. Then he'd either take charge or put a stop to it.

He settled back into sleep.

Serena sighed and let her hand slide lower.

He'd wake eventually. . . .

Francis was dreaming . . . dreams of forbidden passion such as he had never had even as a youth. He was swirling in a maddening perfume, and a lissome succubus writhed close against him in the dark. A hand touched him intimately, creating a sweet fire that engulfed his body.

He shifted, and his tormentor moved with him. She covered him with luscious delight, trailing silken hair against the skin of his neck, engulfing him in musky perfume, nipping at his hot skin. . . .

He reached out to control her but wool, silk and lace both tangled and evaded him.

The slick hand was replaced by skillful lips and a hot, wet tongue doing incredible things. He muttered, "Dear Lord," and his own husky voice told him he was awake, but in the deep perfumed dark nothing seemed real.

Where the hell was he, and who was he with?

His heart deafened him with its pounding. His every sense was focused on that searing mouth. His body was eagerly accepting an ecstasy beyond anything he had known before.

But . . .

But . . .

Before he could collect the fragments of his mind, the succubus twisted again and one moist heat was replaced by another. It was a slow, tight slide so astonishingly perfect that he gasped a profanity and seized the maddening creature above him before she could escape. She twisted under his hands, but only to swoop down to bite him sharply, painfully, on the neck even as her body slid tightly around him.

He was hurled into pure need.

He rolled, plunging into the pit of pleasure. Sleek legs entwined him in a nest of perfumed cloth. Teeth and nails tantalized his burning flesh with exquisite pain. Mobile hips and subtle secret muscles forced on him a perfect, shattering release.

He lay limp with his head on a silken, musky breast. He felt drained to his soul, yet full of ultimate satisfaction. . . .

Gentle fingers played in his hair.

His brain twitched back into operation.

He had just been seduced.

He'd as good as been *raped.*

With weakened arms, he pushed off her, struggling to collect his exploded wits, to assemble words to express his feelings. *"Why the devil? . . ."*

One silken hand gripped his arm. "Perhaps I desired you, my lord. . . ."

He shrugged her off and surged up to seek her features in the dark. "And if I'd desired you and taken what I wanted in the night, would you have been pleased?"

"You are not pleased?"

The hurt in it reached him, but he was bloody furious. "No, I am not pleased." *He wanted her again. Now.* "I repeat, why did you do that?"

"I'm sorry," she whispered, and he heard tears. "I did not think any man would not . . . I'm sorry."

"What were you doing? Trying to pay me back for a little kindness in whore's wages? Or is there more to it than that?"

She flung an arm over her eyes. "No. Please don't . . . I just . . . just wanted to please you."

He stared at her shadowy shape, confused and angry to be so, distraught to be awakened to a need he'd controlled thus far in his life. He sank his dizzy head in his hands. He had no reason, for God's sake, to feel *sorry* for her.

Her voice was thin when she said, "I just wanted to stop you from abandoning me. I hoped you would make me your mistress."

Francis caught his breath. So it had been a kind of whoring. Not desire, just an attempt to put him in her debt.

"I never intended to abandon you, ma'am," he said coldly. "Despite your behavior, I will still keep my word. I will take you to Hursley."

"I have no reason to go to Hursley." It was a little-girl voice, tremulous with tears.

Francis knew he was being dragged down into quicksand, but he could not reject the unspoken plea.

He could not abandon her. The basest parts of his mind did not want to.

She wanted to be his mistress. Why not?

She's a professional whore, doubtless used by any man with a guinea.

Despite all the evidence, he couldn't quite believe that.

He took control of the situation. "Then I will place you at an inn, ma'am, and you will await me there until I return to assist you."

She turned her head slightly. *"Will* you return?"

"You are going to have to trust me, ma'am, alien though that may be to your nature."

He stood, and in an attempt to destroy the heavy atmosphere in the room, he dragged back the curtains to let in the thin early light. He turned.

She lay absolutely still, but her skirt was disheveled and her bodice had shifted to reveal too much of one tempting breast. Her tumbling hair veiled her face but did not hide the wanton beauty of her features. The light did nothing to disperse her perfume and the smell of sex.

Dear Lord, but he wanted to fall on her and explore her, and do it fully conscious this time.

She turned her huge dark eyes upon him. "And the matter of my being your mistress?" she whispered.

He forced the words out. "I regret that I cannot accept your offer." The regret, at least, was honest.

Her lips quivered like a frightened child's. What the devil was he to do with her? He turned away and began to dress.

She sat up abruptly. "You're leaving?" Fear rang through her question.

Francis ignored it as he realized that his clothing was disarranged. Of course it was, but the thought of her undressing him in his sleep was both infuriating and incredibly erotic.

"*We* are leaving," he said as he buttoned his breeches. "Unless you do not wish to. *I* have no intention of compelling *you*." He made it into a formidable reproach.

"I am truly sorry . . ."

"Forget it," he said curtly. "There's nothing to be said."

With what sounded suspiciously like a sob, she climbed out of the bed. He turned but her head was lowered as she fumbled at her skirts, straightening them and her bodice. She meticulously tidied the bed, then hunched into the black shawl.

As he turned the doorknob, Francis thought there should be more to say between two people who had shared such a shattering intimacy. He could think of nothing that would not move them into areas he was not yet prepared for.

With difficulty, he called to mind Lady Anne, waiting patiently for his return and his proper proposal.

He politely ushered his unwelcome siren out onto the landing and down the plain stairs.

After a taciturn but ample breakfast, Francis and Serena climbed into the curricle and headed for Hursley. The silence stayed with them, for Francis could think of nothing to say, and Serena Allbright had once more become a mute statue.

An erotically perfumed statue.

A man would be mad to turn his back on a woman like Serena. Then he remembered Lady Anne. This was no time to be even thinking of taking a mistress.

"Why were you going to Hursley?" he asked at last.

Her head was lowered within her hood. "Because the road went there."

He would *not* be sorry for her. Doubtless whatever troubles weighed on her, she had brought them upon herself. "Do you have anywhere you want to go?"

"No."

What had he done to deserve this? "Very well. Then you will stay where I put you, and I will come back to see what I can do. But I repeat, I have no need of a mistress."

They drove on in perfect silence.

Hursley proved to be a mere hamlet, offering little in the way of shelter, and so he drove on to Romsey and took rooms there at the Red Lion. In view of the excellence of their clothing and carriage, and an ample supply of guineas, the innkeeper was perfectly willing to overlook their lack of luggage. He appeared to believe the story that they had been caught unawares by the storm and that Mrs. Haile needed to rest to recover from the experience.

Because he was unsure of how long his business in Weymouth would take, Francis paid for board and lodging for two days, and gave Serena a few extra guineas. When he drove away, he was aware of the haunted despair in her eyes. She didn't think he'd return.

She'd probably take up with the first alternative protector who passed by.

The thought of her not being there when he returned almost had Francis swinging the curricle back to collect her, sensitive business or no. Hazy memories of the morning's lovemaking lingered in his mind like her sultry perfume, making him regret bitterly having slept through so much of his first sexual experience.

He might be a virgin—have been a virgin—but he was not ignorant. Talk about sex was open among his friends. He knew that coupling had been truly extraordinary.

He told himself that was all the more reason to put miles between him and Serena Allbright.

Chapter 5

Francis made himself concentrate on his more important business—putting the fear of the devil into Charles Ferncliff.

Did the man actually think that he could frighten ten thousand pounds out of his mother with such a scarecrow? It was true that his mother laid great store in her reputation, but even so it was a strange maneuver.

It was even stranger that Ferncliff had written to Francis. Perhaps the man had despaired of extorting the money out of the mother and thought the son would be an easier touch. A peculiar misconception.

In fact, all the evidence indicated the man was severely unbalanced, and he'd have to be to come up with such a faradiddle.

Francis's mind boggled when even trying to imagine a salacious story involving his mother. Certainly she was a fine-looking woman for her age, but hardly the sort to sneak into the tack room with the groom. Was she supposed to have huddled in the pulpit with the elderly vicar? Made love over the estate records with the steward?

71

He shook his head and turned instead to formulating a satisfying plan of action. And every time Serena Allbright crept into his mind, he firmly pushed her image away.

Rain had followed the wind, and the road was still muddy. In retrospect, it had been a mistake to take the shortcut from Winchester, and not just because of the state of the road. He had become wretchedly entangled as well. . . .

But he wasn't going to think about his siren.

Even when he reached the better surface of the toll road, it was still hard going. Though Francis was anxious to settle with Ferncliff he didn't push the team, and it was late afternoon when he pulled into the Crown and Anchor in the small port of Weymouth. When he inquired after Charles Ferncliff, he was frustrated to be told that the man was out.

A blackmailer could at least have the courtesy to be waiting for his victim.

He took rooms, for he would doubtless have to spend the night. There had never really been any question of returning to Serena today, but Francis marked the delay down to Ferncliff's account and felt even more darkly toward the man.

Perhaps he *would* thrash him.

He ordered dinner, then paced the room worrying at his problem, which was not Ferncliff.

Should he make Serena Allbright his mistress? A simple decision and she could be his. He could return to the Red Lion tomorrow and enjoy her endlessly. He could set her up in London and give her everything she desired.

She'd be a great hit with the Rogues.

The Company of Rogues had been a schoolboy group, formed for mutual protection. Now it was a company of friends, but one with very deep and firm bonds. It had recently become clear that both mistresses and wives would be accepted as part of the group.

But what of Lady Anne? She was the sort of well-bred girl who wouldn't make a fuss over her husband setting up a mistress, but he couldn't feel right about putting her in such a position.

In fact, he couldn't feel comfortable about setting up a mistress at all, especially such a one. Serena was beautiful and skilled in erotic arts, but she could turn out to be wickedness incarnate. After all, what kind of woman ravished a stranger in the night?

His pressing duty was to marry, to provide an heir. His pressing need was to marry so as to swamp this unwanted obsession with a tantalizing whore.

There was another reason for marriage, too, scarce acknowledged until this moment.

Eleanor Delaney.

When his friend, Nicholas Delaney, had disappeared a year ago and was feared dead, Francis had found himself drawn to his wife, Eleanor. Any expression of his feelings had been restrained by the ardent hope that Nicholas would prove safe, and by Eleanor's advanced pregnancy, but the feelings had been there.

Nicholas's safe return, along with the evident happiness of his marriage, had put an end to the foolishness—or should have at least. Francis had been sufficiently uneasy on the matter that he had been avoiding his friend for a year now. He had hoped that his forthcoming marriage would bury the matter absolutely.

He now doubted that marriage to Lady Anne Peckworth would have any effect on his disturbing feelings for Eleanor Delaney. But Serena Allbright had risen in his mind, and Eleanor was fading like the pale moon in the light of the summer sun.

"Plague take it," he muttered. Serena was certainly no candidate for marriage, not the least because she couldn't produce an heir.

"Is the problem really worthy of such language?" asked an amused voice.

Francis swung around. "Nicholas! What the devil . . . ?"

Nicholas Delaney, a handsome blond man with a rather careless style, came in and shut the door. "Received a cryptic missive from your mother. The mere fact of her writing to me at all was enough to bring me hotfoot. What's amiss?"

"From my mother?" Francis echoed, alert to the peculiarity of this turn of events. What on earth could have brought his mother to do such a thing when she had always resented this friendship?

Francis began to wonder whether this whole bizarre adventure wasn't some kind of Machiavellian plot to cut him off from Nicholas. No, that was surely ridiculous. But his mother's behavior was damned fishy.

"From your mother," Nicholas agreed, shrugging out of his greatcoat. "Hope I'm welcome, because I'm not going anywhere tonight."

"Pleased to see you, of course," Francis said abstractedly, "but I'm put out that you've been given a needless journey. I'm here on a simple matter of business. What did my mother say?"

Nicholas tossed over a sheet of paper.

My dear Mr. Delaney.

Francis is traveling to Weymouth, to meet a gentleman at the Crown and Anchor Inn there. I am very afraid of the consequences and believe your presence could be of benefit.

Cordelia Middlethorpe.

"What maggot's in her head now?" Francis asked. "Does she think I can't even handle a half-mad tutor without help?"

Nicholas laughed. "Remembering some of the half-mad tutors from our school days, she might have cause. Remember Simmons? Went after Dare with a horse-whip after one notable exploit. Have you ordered dinner? Yes? Then I'll ask them to double the rations. I'm starved." He opened the door and called for the inn-keeper. In minutes an order was under way and a bowl of hot, spiced punch had been produced.

Nicholas settled in a chair by the fire, glass in hand. "Now, tell me what the pother is about."

"There is no pother," said Francis coolly.

"Ah." Nicholas appeared to accept it, but Francis did not miss the penetrating look in his eye. "Have you kept up with the comings and goings?" Nicholas continued lightly. "Leander is back in England, and I'm hoping he'll make it down here eventually. His property is in Somerset after all. And Miles is in Ireland to deal with some trouble at one of his places there. Smuggling, I think. There's a possibility Simon will be back from Canada soon. Perhaps we can have a grand reunion of the Rogues, the surviving ones, at least . . ."

Francis threw himself into the opposite seat and took a deep drink of punch. "There's no need for idle chat, Nick. I'm sorry if I froze you out, but you don't need to worry over my affairs. It's just that my mother seems of the opinion that I couldn't take the skin off a pudding without your help."

"I'm amazed. I thought she considered me a disreputable influence."

"So she does," said Francis thoughtfully. "It's dashed peculiar. If there's anything in the dinner that I dislike, don't touch it."

Nicholas laughed. "Shades of Lucrezia Borgia! I'm sure even your mother wouldn't go to those lengths."

"Somehow these days, I don't know."

"Parents have a way of disconcerting us, don't they? Being one myself now, I find it quite demoralizing. After all, one day Arabel will think me a fogy with no understanding of life at all."

It was Francis's turn to laugh. "I find that hard to believe."

"So do I, but that doesn't affect the probability of it being true."

They passed some time sharing gossip of friends and family, and by then their meal had arrived, with the message from the innkeeper that Mr. Ferncliff still hadn't returned to the inn.

As they sat at the table, Nicholas said, "This Ferncliff is the reason you're here?"

"Yes." It went against the grain for Francis not to tell Nicholas what was afoot, but he was still suspicious of this whole affair.

"And your business?" asked Nicholas, addressing an excellent oxtail soup. "You see, I am not to be put off, so you may as well tell me."

"It's not my story to share," said Francis firmly.

"Ah. In that case, I'll desist. I thought I'd given up

meddling, anyway." He glanced across the table. "It was just that something in your manner when I arrived made me think it was personal."

Francis winced under this perception. "That's another matter."

"And also not to be shared? Should I be hurt?"

"You don't need my problems."

"You don't need them, either. Share them."

Francis met his friend's eyes, aware of a need and a disinclination to tell all. The disinclination had nothing to do with the momentary resentment he'd felt when Nicholas had appeared, for now, as usual, he felt close to him as to no one else. It was a matter of not knowing what to say.

Nicholas had been out of England a great deal in recent years and didn't know about Francis's sexual inexperience. Francis had no desire to enlighten him. Francis didn't know, however, how his adventure would appear to a man like Nicholas, who had a reputation as an experienced lover.

Perhaps being seduced in the night by a stranger was quite common in some circles.

He put down his spoon. "I picked up a woman on the road yesterday in the middle of the storm and spent last night with her at a farmhouse. I've left her at an inn with a promise to return and help her, but I don't know what to do for the best."

"You intend to abandon her?" asked Nicholas with a faint but forceful hint of disapproval.

"Of course not. But what do I actually do with her?"

Nicholas's lips twitched. "What are the options?"

"Anything, I suppose, from marriage to murder." No, not marriage, he reminded himself.

"Really? Is she ripe for either?"

"How the hell do I know? I'm not even sure I have her real name."

Nicholas raised his brows. "A truly Roguish adventure. Tell me."

So Francis did, even including the strange dreamlike seduction. Nicholas whistled. "Many men would envy you that."

"Would you?" And Thérèse Bellaire hovered in the room between them. That notorious and beautiful French whore had set out to ruin Nicholas, forcing him to serve her sexually in any way she pleased.

"Probably not," said Nicholas soberly, but then a smile glinted. "However, I shall drop pointed hints to Eleanor when I return home."

"That's the point, isn't it?" said Francis. "What kind of woman would do that to a stranger, uninvited?"

"A well-trained whore, I'd say, who wanted to make you her debtor."

"Quite."

"I have nothing against well-trained whores in their place. Do you?"

Francis didn't answer. He was strongly tempted to tell Nicholas that he knew nothing of whores, well-trained or otherwise.

"You're not a married man," Nicholas pointed out. "My guess is that you find this woman damned attractive. Why not take her up?"

"You forget. I'm about to be married."

"Ah. All settled, is it?"

Francis found he was fiddling with a fork and stopped himself. "No. But I intend to speak to the duke at the first opportunity."

"Opportunities been scarce, have they?"

Francis gave his friend a look, and Nicholas laughed with a touch of embarrassment. "Sorry. Bad habit. I'm resolved to give up probing without permission."

"Good." But Francis had to admit that he could have settled his betrothal any time these past few months.

So why hadn't he?

Nicholas interrupted his thoughts. "Which still leaves you with an unwanted seductress to dispose of gracefully. Tell me what you know of her."

"Nothing." But under Nicholas's gaze, Francis said, "She's frightened, though I don't know why. She's beautiful in a way that frightens *me.* I never would have thought that a woman's beauty could be a barrier, but the power of hers is almost off-putting. It's elemental—like the force of that storm last night; it could carry a man away against his will. . . ." He stopped, realizing where his words were leading.

"You don't actually sound as if you want to get rid of her, you know."

Francis rested his head on a hand. "Perhaps I don't."

A log shifted in the grate with an audible crack. "Apart from her frightening beauty," said Nicholas, "—and I can understand that, by the way—and the fact that you are contemplating marriage, is there any other problem?"

"Do I need more?" asked Francis, looking up.

"Probably not, but it's the weight they carry in the balance that matters. What weighs heaviest against her?"

Francis thought about it. "Her frightening beauty,"

he said at last. "She's a siren. A Lorelei. She could lure men to their deaths." Then, made uneasy by his own words, he broke the intensity of the moment by serving them both from the steak and kidney pie.

"To twist Milton's meaning," advised Nicholas, " *Live well: how long or short permit to Heaven.*' You almost make me envy you." He reached for the dish of potatoes.

"With Eleanor as your wife, I doubt that."

Nicholas paused in the act of lifting a potato onto his plate. "Ah. Can we discuss it, then?" He completed the movement and then looked up. "I would like you to be ensnared by this siren if it will bring you comfortably back into friendship."

Francis didn't try to evade the issue. "I have never ceased being your friend."

"But a remarkably absent one."

"I'm sorry. I had a foolish fear that something would grow that I did not want."

"Had?"

Francis raised a questioning brow.

"You used the past tense. Has this fear disappeared?"

Francis evaded the question. "I have a number of things on my mind just now. . . ." He cut into his pie, adding, "I hope you know that I would never . . ."

"Goes without saying. And to be blunt, Eleanor feels nothing for you but fondness."

Francis assembled food on his fork with care. "I know that. I would hate to embarrass her, though, or you."

"You won't. And I promise, at the first hint of plaintive sighs or longing looks, one or the other of us will throw a jug of cold water over you."

They both laughed, at ease at last.

"Will we see you soon, then?" Nicholas asked. "You would be welcome to spend Christmas with us, but I suppose you must be at home then."

"Yes. My mother sets great store by it. But I will visit. . . ."

The conversation was interrupted by the innkeeper popping in to say that Mr. Ferncliff had returned not long since and had ordered his dinner.

Francis immediately rose and took out a gold-mounted pistol, checking its readiness.

Nicholas eyed the weapon with interest. "Need any help?"

"None at all," said Francis, and left to deal with a scoundrel.

The innkeeper had indicated the room but when Francis knocked, there was no reply. He turned the knob and entered, but found the parlor quite empty. Frowning, he opened the door to the adjoining bed-chamber. This room, too, was empty, even of the items one would expect of a guest. A certain disorder suggested that it had been emptied in a hurry.

He ran down the stairs to confront the innkeeper. "Did you tell me the wrong room?"

"No, milord," said the man in some distress. "I've been told just this minute that Mr. Ferncliff gathered his things, paid his shot, and took off like a fox before hounds. I'm terrible sorry, sir, but he'd been here a while, me being busy elsewhere. Seems he read a note waiting for him and that had him away. None of my people told him you were here, milord."

The man pretended to be apologetic, but he sounded mighty relieved. When Francis saw his eyes flicker to the pistol in his hand, he knew why. "Where did he go?" he snapped. "Did he take ship?"

"Nay, sir. There'll be no more sailings today. He has a horse and has ridden off on it."

Francis cursed under his breath and ran back up to his room. "The damned bird's flown," he said as he grabbed his greatcoat. "I'll have to race him down."

"Am I invited?" asked Nicholas, bright-eyed.

"Why not?" said Francis, and headed down to the stables.

There he and Nicholas hired new horses, then set off in the direction taken by Charles Ferncliff, riding faster than the fading light made wise.

Night settled inexorably, however, and soon even rash courage was not enough. They had to admit that it would be madness to go on and that the chances of finding their man were remote.

Francis let loose a string of oaths.

"What harm can he do you?" asked Nicholas, sitting at ease on his horse.

So, as they turned their mounts back toward Weymouth, Francis told him.

"Strange story," said Nicholas. "The man sounds ready for Bedlam, but of little danger."

"But that sort of mischief-maker can cause trouble. I just hoped to frighten him into giving up his game."

"Perhaps you've succeeded."

"Perhaps. But there are some bothersome questions. Who sent him a warning note, and why did he run when he'd asked me to come here?"

"The pistol could have had something to do with it," said Nicholas dryly.

"He decamped before he saw it."

"Perhaps the letter did not so much warn of your coming, but that he'd misjudged his pigeon."

"But who? No one knew I was coming here. The innkeeper said that the letter was brought by a groom. . . ."

"Perhaps friend Ferncliff has an accomplice in your house."

"Damnation."

"At least this has likely put an end to it all. Which leaves you free to pursue the more interesting question of your siren."

"It's doubtless wisest to give her the money to get safely to London, where she can pursue her profession."

"But 'tis folly to be wise, or so the poet says."

"And ignorance is bliss? I never thought to hear you recommending ignorance."

"How true. And I suppose with you contemplating matrimony, it would be unwise to entangle yourself with such a woman."

"Very unwise."

"But if I were you I couldn't feel comfortable with just shipping her off to fend for herself in London with winter coming on."

"I'm sure she'll fend easily."

"Are you?"

After a while, Francis said, "No, damnit. In a way she's like a frightened child."

"Ah." They rode on, slowly and carefully now in the dark. "Then," said Nicholas, "if your siren is agreeable, I think you should take her to your Aunt Arabella."

"Aunt Arabella? Why, for God's sake?"

"I suspect she needs some help."

"Aunt Arabella?" repeated Francis in astonishment. His aunt was a tough single lady who was a great believer in women's rights, especially her own. He had recruited her to help Eleanor during the terrible days after Nicholas's disappearance, and Nicholas and Arabella had a warm, though hard-edged, friendship.

"No," said Nicholas. "I think your siren needs help. Though I'm sure Arabella Hurstman can put her to use."

The rightness of the idea came quickly to Francis. Late November was no time for a woman to be wandering about, no matter how bold she might be, and he wasn't at all sure Serena Allbright was bold. He *wouldn't* feel easy in his mind just putting her on the coach to London.

He also knew that he was reluctant to send her to London for another reason. She would soon find a protector there, and he hadn't entirely made up his mind on the matter of making her his own mistress.

Aunt Arabella would take her in and care for her, but would put up with no nonsense. Given a week or two to think things through, Francis would be clearer in his mind as to the wisest course.

"Taking a candidate for *carte blanche* to live with one's female relatives is not really done," he pointed out.

"Your estimable aunt," said Nicholas dryly, "will at least ensure that you pay her well."

* * *

When Francis drove up to the Red Lion the next day he still did not know how he felt, except that he was crashingly anxious to see Serena again.

He and Nicholas had spent the evening sharing stories and catching up on their friendship without the subject of Serena being raised. They had parted this morning with a promise that Francis would visit the Delaneys at Redoaks as soon as possible. Francis was feeling happier today than he had in almost a year; he hadn't been aware until now of how he had cut himself off from Nicholas, and how much he had missed him.

And that, he supposed, he could lay to Serena's credit. He knew that his interest in her had begun to break his unwanted obsession with Eleanor Delaney.

Which brought the disturbing admission that his courtship of Anne Peckworth had not made a crack in it.

He had pushed his team, worried that Serena would have disappeared as magically as she had entered his life, but when he turned into the inn yard she was there, stroking a fat marmalade cat. She turned at the sound of the curricle, wide-eyed and nervous. He didn't know of whom she was afraid, but at least it wasn't him. As soon as she recognized him the fear faded, and she flushed with something close to joy. It made her beauty remarkable. It unmistakably stirred his heart, along with some other portions of his anatomy. . . .

She walked over, smiling. "Welcome back, my lord. I hope your business went well."

He leapt down. "Not particularly." He made himself speak coolly. "But I have time to see to you before I take it further. Are you ready to leave?"

Her smile faded at his curt tone, but she nodded.

As she moved toward the curricle, her perfume reached out again to entrap him even in the open air. He frowned. If she really hadn't used it recently, she must previously have been in the habit of drenching herself with it.

Well, that was a habit that could be broken.

Then he realized what direction his mind was taking and steeled himself not to lower his guard.

Francis settled accounts with the innkeeper and then they were on their way again.

His companion said nothing for a while, but then asked, "Where are we going?"

He realized she was showing great trust in him, and was touched. "To an aunt of mine who has a cottage up near Marlborough, in a village called Summer St. Martin."

"An aunt!" she exclaimed. "But surely, my lord . . ."

"She'll take you in until we can decide your future." He was stiffly unable to put their possible plans into words. "Unless, that is, you have some alternative to offer."

"No, I'm sorry. I can't think of anything. I am virtually penniless."

"What of your dead husband?" he queried skeptically.

She lowered her head. "He left very little, and I cannot use it."

"Why not?"

"I cannot tell you that."

His jaw tightened. "If you trust me enough to come

with me, Mrs. Allbright, why cannot you trust me enough to tell me the truth?"

She turned to meet his eyes. "I wish I could." She appeared completely honest.

"At least tell me if I have your true name."

She flushed. "I gave you my maiden name, my lord."

"Why?"

"I prefer to forget my marriage." It was said with eloquent simplicity.

"Then why not remove your rings?" he taunted.

Her color deepened, and to his surprise, she immediately slipped them off. "I don't know why I didn't do that before. It's just been so long. . . ." She looked at them. "I suppose I could sell them."

"You could," he agreed, intrigued against his will. "I'll do that for you, if you wish. It's not a business for a woman."

"Thank you," she said, but she put them in her reticule. Well, she'd have to be a total fool to trust him that far.

"Now," he said firmly, "why don't you tell me your true story."

"No," she said, equally firmly.

"There must be *something* you can tell me, ma'am. Where is your family home?"

"Near Lewes."

He flashed her an irritated look, noting the remarkably firm set of her chin. "Do I have to wangle it out of you word by word? I need to know what were you doing, Mistress Allbright, wandering around in a storm almost penniless."

She turned to face him. "You *need?* What right do you have, my lord, to demand my life history?"

"I believe you have given me a right to be interested, at least."

She flushed at that attack, but did not look away. He found the anger in her eyes combined with their erotic promise to tangle his wits. She looked as if she were considering particularly exotic ways to torture him . . .

"Very well, then," she said at last. "I will tell you what I can. I was forced into my marriage, my lord, when I was very young. When I was widowed I thought myself free, but I discovered that my brothers intended to compel me into another similar match. I ran away. It was doubtless foolish, but they have the means of forcing me, I am sure."

It was such a strange story that he wondered if she were addicted to novels. "Would another marriage really be so tragic?"

"Yes," she said flatly.

"Yet you offered to be my mistress."

"That would be different."

He glanced at her in surprise. "Preferable?"

She was staring straight ahead now. "Yes."

"Why?"

Slowly, her eyes turned to his. "I would not be bound by vows before God."

It was the most bizarre thing he'd ever heard. She was admitting that she would prefer not to be bound to one man only, but implied that she would take those vows seriously if forced to make them.

If it came to setting her up as his mistress, he'd have to make a few rules clear. He would expect a mistress of his to be as exclusive as a wife—at least for as long as the connection lasted.

Anyway, the story was damned fishy. A respectable widow, no matter how unhappy her marriage and how desperate her situation, would not have seduced him last night with such skill. Francis didn't need extensive sexual experience to know that.

"Did your husband leave you nothing?" he asked.

She answered easily. "My jewels and a small amount of money, but I was forced to flee my family home without them. I cannot imagine how to get them from my brothers now. Anyway, they have already lost the money at cards or dice, and the jewels are bound to follow. They are addicted to wagers," she said simply.

Francis was vaguely acquainted with some men called Allbright, though they hardly moved in the same circles as he. Big, uncivilized men always to be found at sporting events. Still, if true, that made her birth fairly respectable.

If true.

He began to question her about her childhood and her family, trying to make it sound like casual conversation. In reality, he was looking for a slip that would suggest she was not as gently born as she claimed to be.

Nothing came up to disprove her story, but something actually seemed to confirm it.

"So you attended Miss Mallory's school in Cheltenham?" he said. "You must know Beth Armitage, then." This should sort matters out, he realized. Beth had been both pupil and teacher there, and was now wife to a fellow Rogue, Lucien de Vaux, Marquess of Arden.

"Yes," she said, with the first genuine smile of the

89

day. "I remember her well. She was a year older than I, but we were friends. I heard she married the heir to a dukedom. I was quite surprised, for she was rather a bluestocking and a trifle radical in her opinions."

"Still is," he said, relaxing. Serena clearly knew Beth. "She and her husband fight about such matters regularly."

"She fights with her husband?" Serena said blankly.

"Spiritedly."

"I'm surprised he permits it."

"I don't think he has much choice other than to gag her. . . ." Francis's mind was not on this. He was pondering a whole new level of complication in his once-orderly life.

What would Beth have to say about a fellow pupil becoming a Rogue's light-o'-love? Convention said she'd disapprove, but there was no telling with Beth Arden, who believed that a woman's right to freedom was more precious than any social rules.

After all, despite opposition from all quarters, Beth had formed a firm friendship with her husband's ex-mistress.

Serena was relieved when Lord Middlethorpe let the inquisition lapse, for that was what it had been—a careful inquisition. She thought she had passed muster, which wasn't surprising since she had been telling the simple truth.

She wondered if she were any closer to being offered the position of mistress. Despite a great deal of trepidation, she hoped so. She really didn't want to be taken to his aunt. Experience had shown Serena that women, especially straitlaced spinsters, disapproved of her on sight.

She equally didn't want to be left alone again.

And memories of the feel of Lord Middlethorpe's body told her she wouldn't find being his mistress totally unpleasant.

The traitorous thought entered her head that she wouldn't find being Lord Middlethorpe's *wife* totally unpleasant, either. When thinking of the horrors of marriage, she had always imagined a man similar to Matthew. Lord Middlethorpe was almost his opposite.

He was handsome and cultured, and seemed kind, moderate, and forbearing . . .

But, she reminded herself, she knew only too well that men could pretend to be kind when it suited them, then be anything but once a woman was in their power.

No, no, not marriage. Not even to him.

She reminded herself that she was barren. That protected her from marriage to most men, for they wanted children. The only men who would consider marriage to her were Matthew's debauched friends who only sought a wife as a bound plaything.

Serena turned her mind anxiously to the problem of how to persuade Lord Middlethorpe to set her up as his mistress rather than take her to his fearsome aunt.

Though the day was crisp and clear, the roads were still muddy, becoming veritable quagmires in places. It soon became obvious that despite pushing the horses and changing for good teams, they would not make Marlborough that night.

"We will have to stop on the road," said Lord Middlethorpe.

"Yes." Serena wondered what opportunities this night would bring. She certainly could not repeat yesternight's boldness, but perhaps there would be other ways to tempt him. Her instinct still told her that he was attracted to her.

They left the highway to find an inn in the village of Fittleton. It was a simple place, but it could provide two bedrooms and a private parlor, which was all they needed.

Two bedrooms. Serena understood the message of that. Again he had claimed they were man and wife, but he had taken two bedrooms. . . .

As Francis stood in his solitary room, he felt very proud of himself. In taking two rooms, he was behaving nobly in the face of great temptation. The allure of making love to Serena—and this time awake and with his wits about him—was humming through him like a fever.

But he would protect both himself and her.

They ate in the shared parlor, and careful conversation was much spaced by painful silences. Neither felt able to touch on important or personal subjects.

When the meal was over, Serena rose to go to her room. Francis stood up politely, on the whole pleased to have her disturbing presence removed before his willpower collapsed.

She paused at the door. "I . . . I wanted to say, my lord, that you need not be concerned that I will . . . of a recurrence of last time . . ." Her cheeks had turned an exquisite pink and Francis found it rather hard to breathe.

"I'm sure," he managed stiffly. "Sleep well."

She slipped into her room.

Francis slumped back into his chair and drained another glass of wine, aware of every nerve in his body clamoring to follow her. Over the meal, the creamy rise of her breasts, half exposed by the low bodice of her gown, had mesmerized him. It would not do, though. Was he to be ensnared against all reason by a mysterious wanton?

Yes, oh yes! screamed his body.

With a groan, he buried his head in his hands.

He heard the door click open, and looked up sharply. She had loosed her hair so it clouded around her in the back-light of her candles, and that devilish gown of hers seemed to draw attention to every beautiful curve of her body.

"What is it?" he asked hoarsely.

"I . . . I thought I would leave the door open." She turned a deeper pink and quickly ducked back into her room.

Francis stared at the open door. She had moved beyond sight, and all he could see was a chest of drawers and a washstand draped with pristine white towels, but the open door was eloquent.

It promised a welcome, a heaven of sensual delights. It also told him that the last night they had shared had not been an aberration. She was, at heart at least, a whore, and he desired her far too much to surrender.

He reminded himself forcibly that he was going to marry a good and virtuous young woman, and it would be nothing less than an insult to simultaneously establish a ravishing beauty as his mistress.

He should abandon this plan of taking her to Aunt Arabella's, for he knew it sprang from his weakness about this woman. Undoubtedly, the wisest course would be to give Serena a purse full of guineas and put her on the London coach.

But he knew he wouldn't.

Chapter 6

They arrived in Summer St. Martin at midday. Serena climbed down from the curricle and approached the solid stone house called Patchem's Cottage with all the enthusiasm of one approaching the gallows. Why was she even agreeing to this?

Because, coward that she was, she was terrified of all the alternatives.

Lord Middlethorpe knocked on the black-lacquered door, and a middle-aged maid opened it. Her homely face immediately brightened. "Why, my lord! Come you in!"

In moments, an older lady was out in the small hall. This one was scrawny, vigorous, and bright-eyed. "Francis. What a lovely surprise!" Then she saw Serena and her brows raised. "In trouble again, are you?" She shook her head as she ushered them into her parlor, commanding, "Tea, Kitty."

The maid hurried off, and Serena entered the small room warily. Arabella Hurstman was not the stiff-lipped spinster Serena had expected, but an ageless, vital woman. She still terrified her.

"Sit down," Arabella said brusquely to Serena, pointing at a chair close to the fire. "Make yourself at home." Then she turned her sharp eyes on Lord Middlethorpe again. "Not another of your friend's wives, I hope."

Serena looked at her benefactor in astonishment and could swear that he colored. "Of course not."

Arabella sat down, ramrod straight. "Saw the notice in the papers that Charrington's hitched. He's one of you Rogues, is he not? Seemed too much of a coincidence."

"I only just heard he was back in England," said Lord Middlethorpe. "I wasn't aware that he had any plan to wed. Doubtless there'll be something in my post at home. I presume Nicholas didn't know or he would have mentioned it."

"Been hob-nobbing with King Rogue again, have you? Doubtless that accounts for your predicament."

Despite this tart barrage of comments, Serena could see that Miss Hurstman was very fond of her nephew, and he equally fond of her. She wished, though, that she understood all this about rogues.

"Aunt Arabella," said Lord Middlethorpe, seizing control of the conversation, "I make known to you Serena Allbright. She is in need of a place to rest, being at outs with her family. I hope you can find it in your heart to look after her for a few weeks."

Thus prompted, Arabella Hurstman looked at Serena closely for the first time. "Lord love us," she said. "It shouldn't be allowed!"

Serena felt herself flare with guilty color. "I'm sorry . . ." She made to rise, but the woman pushed her firmly back into her chair. "Don't take offense, child!

I'm just taken aback by your looks. They must be a great trial to you."

This amazing understanding caused Serena to break into volcanic tears in the lady's arms. She vaguely heard Miss Hurstman calling for Kitty and dismissing her deliverer. Then, having cried herself into exhaustion, she was tucked up in a warm bed like a babe. It was only later that she realized that Lord Middlethorpe had left without her thanking him.

A part of her was sad, but on the whole she was relieved. By some miracle she had been granted sanctuary, a place of safety where she could rest, and think, and regain her balance in the world. She was deeply, deeply, grateful to the man who had brought her here, but no longer wanted him as protector in any sense of the word. She wanted nothing to do with men at all.

Serena did not even think about Lord Middlethorpe again during those first days. She just allowed Arabella—as Miss Hurstman insisted on being called—and Kitty to tend her and slowly draw her into the daily tasks around the cottage. They asked remarkably few questions.

At last, however, Arabella faced Serena over the tea table. "Time for you to tell me your story, gel, so we can decide what to do for the best."

Serena stared at the tea. "I really don't want to."

"Bite the bullet. You'll feel better later."

Serena looked up rather resentfully. "I suppose surgeons say that as they are about to hack someone's leg off. And in just that tone."

"Doubtless." Arabella was unrepentant. "And they're right. Well? Or do I have to get an ax?"

Serena sighed. "My real name is Serena Riverton.

My husband was Matthew Riverton. You won't know of him, but—"

" 'Course I know of him. Randy Riverton. Disgusting fellow. What were you doing married to him? He must have been old enough to be your father."

Serena was stunned by this brisk acceptance. "I . . . I had no choice."

"Every woman has a choice, gel, does she have the courage to use it."

"Not at fifteen," retorted Serena.

"Fifteen," said Arabella, and Serena would swear she paled.

"Yes."

"Oh, you poor child."

Serena felt tears threaten for that child. "Yes."

Arabella cleared her throat and poured more tea. "I see. And he died recently, didn't he? So what's your problem now, gel? Ain't you a rich widow?"

"No." Serena found her handkerchief and blew her nose. "Matthew squandered most of his money trying to buy his way into Society, and before I knew what was happening, my brothers had their hands on the rest." She looked up sharply. "I know that was doubtless feeble of me, too, but euphoria had turned my wits. I never thought . . . I never expected that they would . . ."

"Would take over and abuse you? You don't know men, dear. They always take over given half a chance, and a good many of them will abuse." She pursed her thin lips thoughtfully. "Doubtless your money could be regained by the courts . . ."

"I suppose so," said Serena, toying with her cup. "But there was little enough—about three thousand pounds—and I know legal bills can eat up money. Also," she added hesitantly, "I'm afraid of them. My brothers, I mean. I know they aren't supposed to be able to force me into another marriage, but I fear they could. I'd rather they not know where I am."

"Very well, then," said Arabella, as if it were of little account. "You must stay here. I could do with the company. Of course, it's a dull life for a beautiful young woman . . ."

"It's perfect," said Serena sincerely, beginning to hope, seeing a lifetime of peace and security spread before her.

"For now, maybe," said Arabella skeptically. "And, of course, we'll have to see what Francis has to say."

"I have no particular claim on his kindness," said Serena quickly.

Arabella frowned. "He has no right to dictate my life," she corrected. "Say it."

Serena gaped, but saw that Arabella was in earnest. "He has no right to dictate my life," she said faintly. "But . . ."

"Say it again."

Serena opened her mouth. "If he doesn't," she said, "then neither do you!"

Arabella grinned. "Good girl. I knew you had a spine in there somewhere. It just needs a bit of exercise. The first thing, though, is to provide you with some clothes."

"I only have four guineas."

"I made sure Francis left you some money. There's twenty pounds or so."

"I can't use his money," Serena objected. "If I do, I *will* have to allow him to dictate my life."

Arabella looked at her. "Are you really only worth twenty pounds, body and soul?"

It was an absurd notion. "No, but . . ."

"Francis gave me that money for his own good reasons, gel, and you owe him nothing."

For an appalled moment Serena wondered whether Lord Middlethorpe had told his aunt about her shameless behavior, and this was his way of paying her off. But that could not be.

It was, however, doubtless a sop to his conscience and Serena was glad of it. She knew she had been very wrong in what she had done, but realized a man—a good man—would feel some debt. If this money had freed him of that burden then she was pleased.

Serena spent some of the money on cloth for two plain dresses, and a little more for the village seamstress to make them up. Mrs. Pritchard also made her some much needed underwear and nightwear.

Mrs. Pritchard would have liked to have made the items rather fancy, but Serena insisted on an almost schoolgirl simplicity and when she put on the first gown, she was glad. The simple, functional round-gown had ample cloth in the skirt and a high neckline. The fullness allowed her to wear pockets underneath, which Matthew's gowns had not, and that was a convenience. The modest style appealed to her greatly, but even more appealing was the fact that it carried no memories, and no trace of her old perfume.

Her fur-lined cloak was still tainted, and so she took Lord Middlethorpe's advice and hung it out each day in the fresh air hoping that eventually the aroma would be gone. For the meantime, she was happy to wear

Arabella's second-best cloak, a simple country one of red wool.

She took to dressing her hair in a severe knot with no curls allowed to escape. She didn't fool herself that she had become plain, but felt considerably more normal. She threw herself with delight into the village's preparations for Christmas.

Preparing for Christmas was something Serena had not done since her childhood—since before her marriage—and it gave her great joy. She arranged seasonal greenery on mantelpiece and shelf, and spent much time down at Saint Martin's church decorating it for the festivities. The people of the village accepted her easily as a young friend of Miss Hurstman's.

She even began to feel strong enough to plan her future. Despite the appeal, she knew she couldn't stay with Arabella forever. But now that people were accepting her, she thought perhaps she could obtain employment. Not as a governess, for she knew it would not work for her to be in a household where there were men, but perhaps as a companion to an elderly lady. Arabella would give her a reference, and so would the vicar here. Arabella might even know some suitable lady.

Once the weather improved in the spring Serena would set out to be independent, but for the moment she would enjoy herself. Serena was truly happy for the first time in her adult life.

Until the morning when Arabella, slightly pink, said, "I never thought that you might be needing monthly cloths, my dear, such matters being long past for me, thank heaven. There is plenty of white flannel in the linen cupboard. Help yourself."

Serena stammered her thanks, and Arabella clearly took her unsteadiness as embarrassment, but it was not so. Serena was realizing that her courses were overdue. A count back told her that they were a week overdue. She had heard that shocks could upset these things, but in a life that had contained many shocks, she had always been as regular as the church clock.

But she *couldn't* be expecting a child.

She was barren.

After a moment's thought, the panic eased. She couldn't have conceived. Matthew's physician had said she had a deformity of the womb and in eight years of marriage there had never been any sign of conception. It clearly was just a matter of her adventures disordering her. Serena joined in Arabella's plans for charity baskets for the village poor, silently thanking heaven for her barren state.

If she were with child, she had no idea *what* she would do.

As Serena gave thanks for her barren state, Francis sat in White's addressing a rather dull dinner. He'd spent the weeks since he'd left Serena trying to track down Charles Ferncliff, for he was not convinced that the man would abandon his mischief. He'd had no success.

He'd discovered Ferncliff was a younger son of Lord Barrow of Derbyshire, but discreet enquiries of that family had discovered that they believed him still to be employed by the Shipleys. Some enquiries around Weymouth had uncovered nothing of use. During his short stay, Mr. Ferncliff had spent all day just riding about. His excuse had been an interest in Anglo-Saxon remains, for heavens sake.

What could that be a cover for? Theft? Most available Anglo-Saxon remains were things like church walls and stone crosses. Hardly suitable for carrying away to sell.

Today Francis had received a letter from his mother assuring him that she had not been troubled by the man further. Moreover, she had urged him to take up the matter of Lady Anne again, for the duchess was tactfully inquiring about his silence. Finally, Lady Middlethorpe commanded her son to be at the Priory for Christmas.

He supposed his mother was right on all counts. Clearly Ferncliff had been frightened off, and Anne would be wondering what was going on. He was appalled that he had not so much as written to her parents to explain his absence. If he set off tomorrow, he could stop at Lea Park for a couple of days and still be home in time for Christmas.

But what of Serena? Since he'd heard nothing to the contrary, he assumed she was still in Summer St. Martin. A woman like that would hardly remain there forever, though. He should send more money—a handsome amount of money—and make sure Arabella understood that Serena was to be allowed to decide her own fate. Serena would doubtless head for London as soon as the weather improved, and find herself a protector in no time. . . .

Alternative plans insinuated themselves into his head.

It would be so easy to arrange. He would hire a small house here in London, then furnish it and equip it with discreet servants. That done, he would drive down to Summer St. Martin. He need only say, "I would like you to be my mistress," and she would join him. They would be happy for all eternity.

He shook his head. Such a course would be wrong on all counts.

He hoped his obsession with Serena was simply that she had been the first. To fight it, Francis had been tempted to visit a brothel. He had not gone through with it, though. Well-used whores still revolted him, no matter how skilled, and he doubted such a casual coupling would make a dent in his feelings.

What was more casual than a chance-met woman seducing him in the night?

But, against all reason, it had not been casual.

He had been tempted to turn his enquiries from Ferncliff to Serena Allbright. He should be able to discover her full story with ease. He knew, however, that to know more of her would make his life more difficult, not less.

He wanted to wipe her out of his life entirely, but if he did that, then one day he would meet her on the arm of another man, and he could hardly bear the thought. As it was, his nights were made restless by longings and tortured dreams. . . .

"That was a heartfelt sigh," said a voice at his elbow. "The fish doesn't agree with you?"

Francis looked up to see Sir Stephen Ball, M.P. by his side, and he gestured to his friend to join him. "Just a dilemma, Steve."

Sir Stephen took a seat with his usual careless elegance that had gained him the nickname of the Political Dandy. He was rapidly making a name for himself in the House of Commons with the power of his convictions and his witty speeches—always delivered, however, in a sardonic drawl.

He was pale, blond and handsome, with a face already marked by cynical humor at the age of twenty-five.

"Dilemma a Rogue can assist with?" Stephen asked as he summoned a waiter to bring an extra glass.

"No. And certainly not one for the House." Francis put Serena firmly aside and concentrated on Ferncliff. "Are there any clever ways of finding a man who don't want to be found, Steve?"

"Not usually. If he's willing to avoid his home and his usual haunts, it would be sheer luck that turned him up."

"That's what I feared." Francis filled his friend's glass.

"What's the fellow done?"

"Threatened to spread some malicious nonsense about my mother. There's been no recurrence, but I'd like a moment alone with him just to be sure of it. I have to leave for the country tomorrow, however, without finding a sniff of him."

"Any reason to think he'd be in London?"

"No," Francis admitted. "It's just that the place is like a lodestone. Attracts all the villains sooner or later."

"True enough. I'm staying in London over Christmas. Give me a name and I'll keep my ear to the ground."

Francis felt an irrational reluctance but said, "Ferncliff. Charles Ferncliff."

"Charles Ferncliff!" exclaimed Stephen. "I can't believe it."

"You know him?"

"I've met him. Brilliant fellow. Takes tutoring jobs while he works on a book about Anglo-Saxon culture. More interested in barrows and old poetry than modern-day matters."

Strangely, it fit. "His studies have turned his brain, then, I assure you. Took a grudge against my mother because she didn't approve of his rough and tumble ways with his charges. Threatened to start some nasty rumors about her if he wasn't paid off."

"Good God. Poor man."

"I'm more concerned for my mother," Francis pointed out.

"Well, of course, but it must be some sort of sickness. I can believe the bit about rough and tumble. Even though he's a brainy type, Charles is a great one for a jape and an excellent sportsman. But the rest . . ."

"How old is this man?" Francis asked. "I'd assumed he was younger than us."

"Good Lord, no. Mid-thirties at least. As I say, he only takes these tutoring jobs to finance his studies, and makes sure they're in an interesting location. One that has Anglo-Saxon remains."

"And we have an Anglo-Saxon church, and a hill that was probably the mound for a manor house. . . . It fits, but it's damned peculiar. As you say, it must be a sudden sickness. Shades of the king."

"Lord, I hope it's not as bad as that," Stephen said. "But then, even the king harms no one but himself. As I know Ferncliff, however, I'll certainly be able to spot him if he shows."

"I'd be grateful. And if he really is afflicted, see if you can straighten him out, Steve. I bear him no grudge if that's the case, but I can't have him distressing my mother."

" 'Course not."

The young men then set to gossip, particularly about Leander Knollis, who had made a surprising marriage to a nobody but who—according to Stephen—seemed well content.

"He was through London earlier in the month with his bride," said Stephen, rising. "Seems to me it's time the Rogues had a full-blown reunion."

"I think Nicholas had some such thing in mind."

"Good. Enjoy Christmas. Regards to your mother et cetera." With that, Stephen took his leave, leaving Francis with yet more thoughts of marriage.

Three Rogues married. It was obviously the fashion, and he'd best get on with his. He wondered how soon Anne would agree to be wed. She'd probably think of May or June, but he'd rather it were sooner. Much sooner.

Next week? His awakened body was becoming an inconvenience.

He'd see if he could talk Anne and her parents into a winter wedding. January, perhaps. Once married, he'd have no more thoughts of Serena Allbright.

A part of his mind laughed.

As he finished his meal, Francis resolutely turned his attention to the strange case of Charles Ferncliff. The man didn't sound at all as he had imagined him. He'd thought him a young, clerical type.

For some reason, the whole business was beginning to look damned fishy.

With a mysterious siren in Wiltshire, an eligible lady in Hampshire, an unpredictable mother at home, and an unlikely villain eluding him everywhere, Francis was beginning to feel fit for Bedlam himself.

The next day Francis drew up before the great portico of Lea Park, determined to take control of his life by offering for Lady Anne Peckworth. He couldn't avoid the fact that he was uneasy about it. Before turning in at the gates, he'd felt tempted to drive by. After all, he hadn't forewarned the Arrans of his arrival, so he wouldn't disappoint anyone. . . .

He reminded himself that it was past time to settle down and start his nursery. As he leapt down from his curricle, however, he impulsively decided not to stay the night. He would talk to the duke, put the question to Anne, then drive on to the Priory, using the proximity of Christmas as his excuse.

Excuse?

The word meant nothing, he assured himself. Just that he must be home for the pre-Christmas festivities. His mother set great store by them. If he couldn't arrange for an early wedding, he'd come back after Christmas for a long visit. Or invite Anne to the Priory.

As he approached the great doors, he was aware that his heartbeat was much faster than usual, and that it wasn't being driven by love.

He was ushered into a warm family saloon and greeted by the duchess, a clever woman who had never had any claim to beauty. "Middlethorpe, how kind of you to stop by, but I'm afraid Anne still isn't up to visitors."

"Visitors, Duchess?" he asked blankly. "Is she ill?"

"You didn't know? We sent word two days ago to the Priory. Chicken pox. She caught it at the village school. She will take these duties so seriously." She twinkled at him. "She really wouldn't want you to see her just now, I'm afraid. She's *very* spotty."

"I suppose not," said Francis numbly. Chicken pox. These days, nothing seemed to go according to plan. He suddenly determined not to be thwarted. "Is the duke at home? I would like to speak to him."

The duchess gave him a shrewd look. "Unfortunately not. He's in Scotland, though due back soon. Why don't you return after Christmas? You will doubtless find us all here and hearty, and of course you will be welcome to make a long stay."

Francis surrendered to fate. "Yes, of course, Duchess." After directing his best wishes be sent up to Anne, he took his leave and headed for the Priory.

What peculiarity would he find there? Would his mother have finally decided to move a piece of furniture?

Not bloody likely, he thought as he tooled his team toward home. The Priory was like a mausoleum to his father; nothing was ever changed there. Even such a simple matter as new hangings for his bed had caused his mother grief. He supposed her devotion to his father's memory was admirable, but life went on and things must change.

Thorpe Priory, however, would be just as it had always been, and his mother would have it perfectly prepared for Christmas.

Why did the thought depress him so?

Because his mother's style of Christmas—Christmas

as it had been in his father's time—was simply not to his taste.

Holly, fir, and rosemary would be arranged in precisely the same places as they had always been, bound with red ribbons so much like in other years they could have been the same. The special red perfumed candles would stand ready in the hall to be lit to greet the villagers when they dragged in the Yule log on Christmas Eve. The villagers would stay to sing traditional songs at the Big House, and be treated to mulled cider and mince pies from Lady Middlethorpe's own hands. Lord Middlethorpe—himself, now—would give each caroler a crown as they left.

All exactly as it had been for thirty years or more.

The villagers would all be warmly grateful, and Francis recognized that it was an important tradition for them, but for years he had been feeling chained by this ritual. He was always envious of those simple folk who were returning to a rollicking good time in their cottages.

On Christmas Day the childless vicar and his wife would eat their dinner at Thorpe Priory.

On Boxing Day he and his mother would give all the staff their Christmas boxes containing sensible new clothing.

It had been more jolly when his sisters were at home. Last year Aunt Arabella had come for Christmas and enlivened things a little, not the least of which being when she directed her challenging wit at her conventional younger sister. But of course, Arabella would not come this year. She had Serena to keep an eye on.

It would be just Francis and his mother, and dearly though he loved her, it was going to be dashed dull.

As he turned with precisely judged speed onto the familiar country road leading to Thorpe, Francis wondered what Serena and Arabella would do on Christmas Day. Knowing his aunt, it would be a great deal more entertaining than his schedule.

He supposed, even if he were not willing to absent himself from his home at Christmas, he could break the pattern and invite some guests. Some of the Rogues, for example.

He laughed out loud, gaining a strange look from his groom. He could imagine his mother's reaction to that violation of her orderly tradition.

By the time he turned into the arrow-straight drive at Thorpe Priory, edged with arrow-straight poplars, Francis was feeling both lonely and depressed, a most unusual state of mind for him. The sight of his classically beautiful home, pure white in the thin December sun, did not raise his spirits at all.

Like an acidic splinter, he remembered that Anne thought the Priory perfect and would want to preserve it just as it was.

In fact it *was* perfect, he told himself. Most of the authorities on such matters agreed. His father had razed his ancient, rambling house and hired the finest architects to build this Palladian masterpiece.

But, he thought savagely, Thorpe Priory's a damned stupid name for piece of classical perfection.

Perhaps he just didn't appreciate classical perfection.

He liked the warm hominess of Nicholas's Redoaks, or the coziness of Lucien's cottage *ornée*, Hartwell. Even Lea Park, allowed to grow over three hundred years, was more to his taste than the house he had inherited.

Neither his well-trained staff waiting by the door nor

the perfect decorations in the chilly marble hall made him feel welcome or at home.

This was ridiculous.

As he was divested of his outerwear, Francis resolved that as soon as Christmas was over he would do some hunting. Though he was not addicted to the sport, there would be plenty of jovial company in Melton, and some of the Rogues, too. Stephen would be there for part of the time, along with Con Somerford, Viscount Amleigh. Miles Cavanagh would certainly be there with a new string of his superb Irish horses to show off. It would be surprising if Lucien de Vaux didn't put in an appearance, despite being recently married. He was hunting mad.

That prospect raised Francis's spirits so that he was able to be suitably cheerful to his beaming servants.

It only occurred to him later that he had left Lady Anne out of his immediate plans. He told himself that she would need some weeks to fully recover from her ailment.

One of his first actions was to question his butler about the household servants, for he was still uneasy about the letter that had warned Ferncliff off in Weymouth. Griffin assured him that they had hired no new household staff within the year and that all the staff were reliable and honest.

"And what about a gentleman named Ferncliff who was in the area, Griffin? Are any of the staff friends of his?"

"The gentleman who was tutor to Lord Shipley's sons, milord? I am not aware of any of the staff knowing him in a way that would be above their station."

Stranger and stranger. And Francis had heard a

tone of respect in Griffin's voice. Any opinion the butler held of Charles Ferncliff was good.

Perhaps some madman was using Ferncliff's name, but the only way to discover that was to find the real Ferncliff.

Francis didn't meet his mother until they sat down for dinner, for she swept in at the last moment murmuring something about a kitchen calamity. Once the soup was served, he dismissed the servants for a while so they could speak in privacy. "I hope there's been no further trouble, Mother."

"None at all," she said brightly. "You must have handled it superbly, dearest one."

"I didn't handle anything. The man slipped through my fingers at Weymouth, and I've not caught a sniff of him since."

"Oh, well. He has clearly thought better of his foolishness, then."

Something in his mother's manner was not right at all. "I'd call it rather more than foolishness," Francis said, watching her carefully. "Stephen Ball is of the opinion that he must have run mad."

"Mad?" said Lady Middlethorpe, staring.

"Stephen knows the man. Says he's brilliant and an all-around good fellow."

"Doubtless a fellow Rogue," she said sourly, but a flush rose in her cheeks.

"Hardly likely. Apparently, he's a good ten years older, for one thing. You described him as a young man."

"To me, a man in his thirties is young. . . ." Lady Middlethorpe pushed away her scarce-touched soup.

113

"He has clearly decided to leave me alone, which is all that matters. Shall I ring for the next course, dear?"

"Very well." But Francis looked down the length of the table that could have seated ten, thinking what a damned silly way this was to be having a conversation. Why had he never thought so before? Because before he'd not felt the pressing need to see his mother's expression somewhat better.

When the butler and footman returned, Francis stood and walked down to her end of the table. "Griffin, lay me a place here, please."

As the butler hurried forward, his mother looked up in surprise. "Francis, what on earth are you doing?"

"Growing tired of bellowing down the length of the table, Mother."

"We were not bellowing. It is perfectly possible to conduct a conversation along a table without raising one's voice. Your father and I—"

"Must have had superior hearing," said Francis, taking his seat. "I fear I need to be closer."

Lady Middlethorpe opened and shut her mouth. "It looks most peculiar," she said at last.

"I'm sure the servants are deeply distressed." Francis glanced around and caught the footman grinning. He winked at the man.

"It must be as you wish," said his mother frostily. "You are the master here."

Francis accepted a serving of beef. "Please don't resent a few minor changes, Mother. I will not turn the place upside down."

"Of course, I do not resent anything," she said, but still coolly.

Now that he was close, Francis could see that his

114

suspicions were correct. His mother was rather the worse for wear. Delicate use of cosmetics could not hide the fact that she was pale and had shadows under her big blue eyes. Now as not the time to get into it, but he feared that damned Ferncliff—or whoever was claiming to be Ferncliff—had not left her alone. She was doubtless lying, still trying to protect her delicate son from the big nasty man.

'Struth.

Francis launched aimlessly into talk to pass the meal, only realizing after a while that he was speaking of the Rogues. Normally his mother would have stopped the topic with a caustic remark, for it had always infuriated her that he had formed such an attachment to the group, particularly to Nicholas Delaney. As Nicholas had said, it was extraordinary that she write to him, even if she thought Francis about to be slaughtered.

Now, however, she smiled vaguely, even making a few encouraging comments as he spoke of his friends. He decided on an experiment.

"Met Nicholas a few weeks back," he said. "In fine form now he's settled. I'm going to spend some time down there in the spring."

"I'm sure that will be very pleasant," she said with no hint of sarcasm.

"He's talking of a grand reunion. I thought we might hold it here."

"If you wish."

Francis began to wonder if it was his mother whose wits had been turned.

As soon as the meal was over and they were alone in the small drawing room, he said, "So, there have been no further messages from Ferncliff?"

"None at all." His mother poured him tea, but the spout knocked against the delicate china cup in a most untypical piece of carelessness.

"If he is mad he could be dangerous," Francis pointed out as he took the cup.

"All the more reason to ignore him, dear."

"That is foolish, Mother. If he is mad, he must be confined before he does further damage."

She looked up sharply. "Oh, no!"

"Why the devil not?"

"Language, Francis!"

He was on the verge of blistering her out of her slippers with his language, but controlled himself. "Why not?" he repeated.

She looked down and replaced her cup and saucer on the table. Francis saw that a few drops had been spilled into the saucer. By a shaking hand?

"Those places are so terrible, Francis," she said. "We hear such things. I would not want *anyone* to be confined in chains and filth."

"He is upsetting you, Mother," said Francis firmly. "I do not believe for one moment that the letters have ceased."

He put down his own cup and rose to his feet. "I think you are lying because you fear I will be hurt. Well, I am hurt. I am hurt by your lack of faith in me. I am a grown man. I am a dead shot with a pistol and well able to take care of myself with my fists. I no longer need to be protected."

She was staring up at him in astonishment, and not a little apprehension. "Francis . . . I did not . . ." He saw her collect herself. "There have been no more letters." But her eyes shifted betrayingly.

116

"Good God, Mother!" he exploded. "Do I have to have your mail searched?"

"No, Francis, please! It is not worth all this pother."

"Of course it is. You look haggard. This man is hurting you, and who knows to what lengths he will go?"

She suddenly hid her face with her hands. "Francis, please. You are hurting me more than he."

"For heaven's sake!"

She looked up, even more haggard. "I ask you to forget all about this. It is causing me terrible distress. You may not want me to be afraid for you, but I am a mother and cannot help it. Leave it, please, and get on with your courting of Lady Anne."

"I cannot attend to one with the other outstanding."

She stared at him in genuine astonishment. "What has one to do with the other?"

Francis realized that the answer was, nothing. Except Serena, whom he would not have met if he had not been on the road to Weymouth. He had a vision of his life if uninterrupted. He would be engaged to Anne and everything would be orderly.

But what in God's name would have happened to Serena if he had not befriended her? The possibilities chilled his soul.

"Well, Francis?" Lady Middlethorpe insisted. "What possible connection is there? Lady Anne has reason to be hurt by your neglect."

"I am not neglecting her. I stopped at Lea Park yesterday fully intending to speak to her, but she has chicken pox. They wrote here with the news."

"Oh, of course. How could I have forgotten? How is she?"

You have forgotten, thought Francis, because your mind is tied in knots trying to save me from Ferncliff. "She will be fine, but I must give her time to recover. I thought I'd do a little hunting first."

"Francis, no!"

"Good Lord, Mother, Anne isn't going anywhere. I've spent the last month traipsing around the country after your demented tutor . . ."

"Not *mine.*"

Francis ignored that. ". . . and I fancy a week or two enjoying myself with my friends. Is that so terrible?"

Lady Middlethorpe seemed suddenly very weary. "Very well. I am sorry this business has cut up your peace and put you so out of temper, Francis, but I did tell you from the first to leave it be. If you must hunt, I suppose you must." She rose to her feet. "Do write a note to Lea Park, though, to explain your absence."

With that, she left the room, drooping reproachfully.

Francis stared down at the fire, aware that he *was* out of temper, which was very unusual for him. He should trust his mother's good sense; he should put the matter of Ferncliff out of his mind; he should send more money to Serena and reaffirm the fact that he had no personal interest in her; he should write a letter to Lea Park making his intentions perfectly clear.

Then, when he came back from the Shires, he'd have no choice but to talk to the duke and settle his marriage.

As a plan of action, it had no flaw at all.

But he didn't follow any of it.

* * *

Once Christmas was over, Lady Middlethorpe waved Francis on his way with a smile that hid deep misgivings. Her life seemed to be sinking further and further into a mire of deception. Her wanton foolishness had made her miserable; now it appeared that she had thrown Francis's life into turmoil, too.

If she had not summoned Francis back in November, he would be safely betrothed to Anne. He had said as much. Now she sensed a reluctance in him. In addition, he was now headed for the hunting field where men not infrequently died. She would have forbidden it if she had been able, but such days were past. In fact, recent events seemed to have brought about an alarming change in her son.

He was now clearly beyond her command.

And what was she to do about Charles? Lady Middlethorpe returned to her boudoir, eyeing the silk-covered chaise with both dislike and longing. She unlocked a drawer and removed a bundle of letters. Francis had been correct in thinking that there had been more. She read the latest, which had arrived but days before her son.

Your young firebrand seems to be pursuing me all over the country, Cordelia! I have had to go to ground in a damnably out-of-the-way place to get any peace. He's even been to my family seeking news of me. You had better talk sense to him or I will stop avoiding him. If he's intent on shooting me, on his head be it, and on yours.

Another lie. She had been so desperate to prevent a meeting between Francis and Charles that she had told Charles her son intended to shoot him on sight. *"Oh, what a tangled web we weave, when first we practice to deceive."*

The situation was growing so dangerous. She should

119

have had the courage to tell Francis the truth, but how could she? *My dear boy, I have been lying to you from the start and vilifying an innocent man. Not only is Charles Ferncliff not a blackmailer, he is the man I allowed to . . .*

She glared at the offending chaise as if her sin were all the fault of the piece of furniture. Then she wandered over and trailed a hand over the slightly nubby silk, remembering the feel of it against her skin.

She and George had never made love anywhere except in a bed. Oh, it had been very nice, but there had been none of the dreadful rapture edged with danger. . . .

She snatched her hand away. "Stop it!" she hissed to the chaise. *"Stop it!"*

She grabbed the miniature of her husband that she kept on her desk and held it to her heart, then moved it away so she could look at the gentle face of the man she had so deeply loved. Dear George. How could she have betrayed him? He had been such a good man, and Francis was like him in so many ways.

Lady Anne was a very lucky young woman.

Chapter 7

On his way to Melton Mowbray and the hunting season, Francis had to pass quite close to Summer St. Martin. He could think of any number of reasons to stop, not the least of them being to visit his favorite aunt, but he did not. It would be too dangerous to his equilibrium to see Serena again.

Arabella had sent a couple of witty letters, both of which conveyed the clear impression that the two women were rubbing along surprisingly well, and that Serena was healthy and happy. The only solid piece of information in the letters was that Serena's brothers had cheated her out of three thousand pounds left by her husband. Francis gained the clear impression that he was supposed to do something about that. Heaven only knows what.

He was pleased by the obvious accord between the women, but a little surprised. Was Serena Allbright really contentedly putting up preserves, mending sheets, reading novels, and taking long country walks?

If she was, he thought with sudden alarm, he'd go odds all the males of the area were gathering around

Patchem's Cottage like tomcats round a queen in heat. He almost did then make the detour to claim his siren, but he forced himself onward.

He was going to marry Anne Peckworth. Serena Allbright, with her beauty and courage, vulnerability and erotic expertise, was no longer any concern of his.

Let her take a bucolic lover if she wished.

Francis was not far out in his reckoning. Serena's appearance in Summer St. Martin had certainly created a stir . . . a stir that Arabella Hurstman watched with interest.

She was as intrigued by her guest as was Francis, and as unsure about the future. The idea of a girl of fifteen being forced into any marriage appalled her, but marriage to such a man as Matthew Riverton . . . Well, there should be a law against such things, and Arabella was considering various ways of making sure there would be.

But, innocent victim or not, eight years of such a marriage must have an effect. Arabella had learnt that much of Serena's sultry appearance was misleading, but she certainly couldn't be considered any kind of innocent. The question was, was her mind damaged beyond hope of normality?

Arabella was sure she had detected feelings between the beautiful young woman and her favorite nephew. She would like nothing better than to see them amount to something, but only if Serena was capable of being a loving, decent wife.

Each day brought reassurance. Serena behaved like a perfect lady.

A point in her favor was that she made absolutely no attempt to attract. In fact, her plain, high-necked dresses and severe hairstyle seemed to be attempts to mute her appeal.

It could be that the young woman had a complacent knowledge that she had no need to make efforts, but Arabella didn't think so. She had seen enough pretty girls making the most of their looks and throwing out lures, to know that such a course would be unusual. No, one would have to say that Serena had no desire to attract male attention or admiration and was doing her best to fade into the background.

It did not work, of course, but Arabella could not hold that against her.

Patchem's Cottage had suddenly become of great interest to the young men of the area. In fact, any location where Serena happened to be—in the church, visiting the poor, or in the tiny village shop—immediately became a lodestone for men as if a bell had rung.

It was all perfectly safe, for in the village, under the eyes of people who had known them all their lives, none of the men was going to take one step out of line.

So, if Serena was a lady, what did the future hold?

Cordelia's letters implied that Francis was showing interest in one of Arran's daughters, but in that case, what was he doing befriending a sultry creature like Serena? A marriage to Matthew Riverton's widow could not compare to an alliance with the Arrans. In fact, thought Arabella with a chuckle, it would doubtless turn her sister Cordelia's hair gray.

A fig for that! Arabella's main concern was Francis's happiness, though she would like to see Serena happy, too.

One evening in late January, as she and Serena sat together sewing, Arabella said, "I expect we will see Francis here any day."

Serena looked up, with more alarm and pallor than Arabella expected. "Do you truly think so? I thought he would have forgotten about me by now."

"Hardly likely," said Arabella dryly. "I doubt there's a man has ever set eyes on you and forgotten about you, gel."

Serena colored. "I do not seek to attract attention, Arabella."

"Know you don't, but you do. And Francis will be back. What plans have you made?"

The girl looked stricken. "Of course, you wouldn't want me here forever. . . ."

"Would, in fact," said Arabella gruffly. "Very pleasant to have around. But it's not natural, a young thing like you."

"I know."

"You want to hide here, but that's no solution."

"You've hidden here all your life," said Serena rebelliously. "Why is it different for me?"

"Hidden?" Arabella snorted. "Nonsense! Took a great deal of courage to decide I wouldn't marry, that I'd live here on my own. Offends people greatly that I like to make my own decisions, take responsibility for my own actions. I expect you wish to do the same."

Serena sighed. "I have been thinking about it. The only respectable position open to me is companion, so if you will help me to such a position, I will begin to take care of myself."

No mention of marriage, or of Francis, Arabella noted. "A suitable plan, though I will miss you, my dear. Now, I'm sure if I put my mind to it, I can think of an employer who will appreciate your kind heart."

Arabella applied herself to the task. She was reluctant to speed Serena's departure, but she didn't think this aimless life actually suited her guest very well. Serena was looking a little haggard these days. So Arabella wrote some letters, but when no ideal replies arrived, she did not send out another batch. Instead, in February, she raised an alternate plan.

"Perhaps we ought to take you somewhere more sociable, gel, before you settle into a life of drudgery. Bath, perhaps, or Tunbridge Wells."

"No!" exclaimed Serena. "My brothers!"

"You can't hide all your life, gel! I assure you, with me by your side, they won't be up to mischief. You deserve a little holiday, and you need to meet other young people, other young men."

"There is no point in matchmaking, Arabella," Serena said stonily. "No one is going to want to marry me."

"Every male who sets eyes on you wants to marry you."

Serena flashed her a cynical, all-too-knowing look. "No, they don't."

Arabella felt herself turning red. "They'll pay for it with marriage, then."

She saw Serena shudder. "My husband paid thirty thousand guineas for it."

"Oh, my dear . . ." Arabella found herself bereft of words. Years ago, she had deliberately turned her back on ignorance, and certainly didn't consider herself naive, but sometimes a look in Serena's eyes made her feel as innocent as a babe.

125

"Has it turned you off marriage, dear? Not that I ever thought much of the institution," she continued trenchantly. "Form of slavery, if you ask me, though most women seem eager for the shackles. Of course, there's children to consider. There don't seem any way to stop men and women from making babies, and we wouldn't want to leave the innocents to be victims . . ." To her alarm, she saw tears swell in Serena's beautiful eyes, hidden a moment later by a trembling hand.

"Oh, Lord, what have I said now? Here now, gel, don't start crying. . . . I won't bully you anymore . . ."

Serena pulled the hand away. "Arabella, I . . . I think I'm . . . with child!"

Arabella was struck dumb. Of all the many disasters she had imagined, this—amazingly—had never occurred to her.

"Whose?"

"I don't want to say."

"Can you say?" Serena's look of shocked hurt almost had Arabella in tears. "Oh, I'm sorry, child. Don't look like that. But you have to tell me. . . ." Then it struck her. "Good God. It's Francis's, isn't it?"

Serena's face gave the answer.

Arabella surged to her feet. "The *wretch!* To treat you so, then abandon you with never a word."

Serena leapt up, too. "Oh, no, Arabella, you don't understand!"

"Do I not?" Arabella's eyes spoke of battle. "I understand perfectly, and that young man will be back here to do his duty!"

"No!" shrieked Serena.

Arabella put her hands on her hips. "What do you intend, then? To make that poor innocent child a bastard?"

Serena put her hands over the slight bulge of her abdomen, looking horrified.

"That's your choice, gel. Marry the father or curse the child."

Tears burst out and trickled down the young woman's cheeks, then fell to stain the brown wool of her dress. They did not detract from her beauty at all, though. She gave a shuddering sigh as if her heart were breaking. "If Lord Middlethorpe is willing to marry me," she whispered, "I will agree."

Arabella bit back the caustic words that came to mind. "Excellent. Now sit down and take care of yourself. Drink some milk or something. I'm going to write a letter."

Francis was at last enjoying himself.

Lucien de Vaux, Marquess of Arden, had not allowed marriage to change his winter habits and was keeping open house at his father's magnificent hunting box on the outskirts of Melton. The Duke of Belcraven's "box" had twelve bedchambers and all the luxuries one could hope for.

The guests came and went—Stephen Ball, for example, took his position as member of parliament very seriously and frequently returned to London on affairs of state—but there was a nucleus of eight: Francis, Lucien, his wife Beth, Con Somerford, Miles Cavanagh, Miles's extraordinary ward Felicity, Hal Beaumont, and his mistress, Blanche Hardcastle.

It was a household that raised a lot of eyebrows, even among the male society of the hunting season.

A gentleman did not generally admit a woman of loose morals into a house that contained his wife, but in this case the matter was worse. Blanche Hardcastle, the woman of loose morals—who would have leveled anyone bold enough to so describe her—had been Lucien de Vaux's acknowledged mistress for four years before his marriage.

Blanche and Beth Arden were the greatest of friends and shared a passionate interest in women's rights. They frequently took a united stand against the wary marquess and his friends.

Hal Beaumont was assiduously trying to persuade the beautiful actress to marry him. She was firmly refusing, though it was clear to all that she loved the one-armed major deeply.

Francis was accustomed enough to this strange situation to no longer be surprised, but he *was* surprised that Miles had brought his twenty-year-old ward over from Ireland to join the ménage. Melton at hunting season was hardly the place for an unmarried lady, anyway.

"Daren't leave her at home," said Miles with a shake of his head. "She's run wild, and there's no one there to handle her anymore. Add to that she has an enormous fortune, and some scoundrel would be after her for it."

"You could have stayed there and sorted out her affairs."

"And miss hunting season? Devil take you for a blasphemer, Francis! Now look, you must be seeking a bride. Wouldn't you like to take on Felicity? She's a pretty enough thing and enormously rich."

Francis declined the offer. Felicity Monahan was a black-haired, black-eyed hellion. Her story wasn't being told, but she was a mass of resentment and anger. She had only been restrained from violence at one point by her guardian tying her to a very solid library chair. Beth and Blanche were working a certain amount of magic on the girl, but with their radical philosophies and ardent belief in women's rights, Francis had to wonder into what all the resentment would be transmuted.

He just gave thanks that this woman wasn't his responsibility.

He did manage to have a word with Beth Arden about Serena while strolling through the winter-bleak garden.

"I met someone who says she knew you in her school days," he said. "Serena Allbright."

"Serena," said Beth in pleased surprise. "I haven't heard of her in years." She sobered. "She left school quite young."

"Did she? How young?"

"She was only fifteen. How is she now?"

"Beautiful."

Beth gave him a look. "Is that all you men ever think of?"

He held up an apologetic hand. "Be fair, Beth. It's hard to think of anything else when first setting eyes on her."

"Doubtless true. But no benison to her. When I heard Riverton was dead, I felt great relief."

"Riverton?" asked Francis, bemused.

"Her husband."

Francis felt as if he'd been struck in the gut. "You mean, *Matthew* Riverton?"

"Yes. Didn't you know? She was taken out of school to marry him. Aunt Emma, who owned the school, was distressed. I gathered even then that he wasn't a pleasant man, but . . . it wasn't until I married that I realized quite why Aunt Emma was distressed."

Francis eyed her. "You may want to rephrase that for Lucien's hearing."

She colored, but laughed. "Don't be foolish. Lucien is a great joy to me, but I can imagine what marriage must be like to a man one doesn't care for. And from reading books Lucien would rather keep hidden, I know a great deal more. And she was only fifteen."

"God, yes," murmured Francis, sickened by the thought of Serena's treatment when still a child. He had two younger sisters and could easily envision them at that age—short skirts and pigtails, and the teasing beginnings of an interest in men; an innocent interest, though. How could a father give such an innocent to a man like Riverton, even in marriage? Perhaps especially in marriage. Francis was beginning to see why Serena rejected the very thought of another husband.

"So," asked Beth, "how is she?"

"Well enough," said Francis vaguely. "I gather her brothers have managed to take over what was left of her husband's wealth, though."

"Have they indeed?" said Beth with a militant light sparking in her eyes. "Then we must do something about that."

"Beth," said Francis, "you don't want to get involved."

"What utter nonsense!" Beth marched off to confer with Blanche and Felicity.

When Francis reported this to Lucien, the marquess sighed. *"A Monstrous Regiment of Women.* Doubtless I'll have to do some breaking and entering again." Beth's rescue of another schoolgirl had resulted in the Rogues doing a little burglary the year before. "Perhaps we should summon Nicholas if there's going to be that kind of fun."

"If there's anything to be done, I should do it."

"Have a personal interest, do you?" asked Lucien curiously.

"Of course not," said Francis, but knew his expression was betraying him, and Lucien's quirked brow emphasized the fact.

Feeling like a naughty child, he confessed, "I've left the woman with Aunt Arabella while I think what to do."

"Among what options?" asked Lucien warily. "I think Beth might be interested."

Francis didn't give again the flippant answer, marriage to murder. He picked up a book aimlessly. "I can't marry her, Luce. She can't have children."

"That's a shame."

The subject was dropped, perfectly understood. Lucien, too, was an only son with a responsibility to his line.

Francis admitted for the first time that he might have wanted to marry Serena Allbright if she had been able to give him an heir.

No, not Serena Allbright. Serena Riverton.

Randy Riverton's widow.

God, his mother would have an apoplexy, and the

Peckworths would never speak to him again. Thank heavens he couldn't be tempted to that folly.

Of course, there was still the option of making Serena his mistress, an option it seemed she would prefer. Probably, it could be managed discreetly. But then he was distracted by the logistics among the Rogues. It had become clear that they were willing to accept both wives and mistresses as members, but a wife and a mistress at the same time?

That would stretch even this liberal group's tolerance to the limits, not to mention Anne's and Serena's.

He realized he could imagine Serena in this irregular household, but not Anne.

Anne, however, was just the sort of wife he wanted.

What he really wanted, he decided bitterly, was to drown his sorrows in brandy and stay thoroughly soused for a six month.

The next day there was a meeting of the Quorn. All the men settled down to a hearty breakfast, full of the high spirits suited to perfect hunting weather.

Until Beth announced, "Serena's brothers are here in Melton. They'll doubtless be at the hunt today."

Lucien raised his brows. "Shall I ride them into a thicket for you, light of my life?"

"We want their money, not their lives," she pointed out.

He grinned. "I always knew you had the instincts of a highwayman."

"Oh, yes," said Felicity, dark eyes flashing. "Let's hold them up!"

"Stubble it," said her guardian, and she subsided, but with a blistering look at him.

Lucien was observing his wife in amused resignation. "Heaven help us all, but do you have a plan?"

"No," she admitted.

"Thank heavens."

"Yet."

He groaned but was laughing.

"I'll take care of it," said Francis flatly. "I'll just discuss the matter with them, face to face."

"Not altogether wise, old man," Con Somerford pointed out. "You have no rights, and they'd be bound to ask your intentions. Unless you want to marry the woman, a direct approach would be disastrous."

"Damnation," said Francis, then muttered, "Sorry, ladies."

"Oh, heavens, Francis," said Beth cheerfully. "Do not be worrying about such things in this company. Keep your mind on the problem. The fact is that Serena's brothers have cheated her out of her rightful property, and it must not be allowed. To be a penniless woman is very dangerous. It would," she mused, "be helpful to know the precise amount. One does not wish to take more than one should. . . ."

"Doesn't one?" asked the irrepressible Felicity, causing her guardian to shake his head.

"About three thousand, I understand," said Francis.

"Take?" echoed Lucien. "Beth, all joking aside, I am not going to allow you to be involved in criminal activities again. Particularly now."

"*Allow?*" Beth gave her husband a dark look. "I knew you were going to turn silly over this."

"Silly!"

"Very silly. A mere matter of procreation will not stand between me and—"

"Beth!" thundered her husband. "You will recall we haven't even mentioned the matter."

"Oh," she said, blushing.

Hal Beaumont grinned. "Do we gather the duchy has a chance of another generation?"

"You do," said Lucien. "So my marchioness will cease her meddling."

Beth opened her mouth, then clearly decided on discretion. "Very well, my lord marquess, what do *you* intend to do about this patent illegality?"

"Hell, I'll pay the woman the few thousand."

"That is *not* the same thing."

"She'll never know the difference."

Francis interrupted. "*I* would know, and I approve no more than Beth. Serena's brothers deserve to suffer."

They pondered the problem for a while, coming to no satisfactory point until Miles Cavanagh laughed. When asked for an explanation, he said, "Tom and Will Allbright care for gambling, horses, and women, in that order, and they're not too bright about any of them, though they're neck-or-nothing riders. Why not take them on, two out of three?"

"How?" Francis asked.

"You know Banshee?"

Francis shuddered. "Yes." Banshee was one of Miles's new horses, a wicked gray with a mind hell-bent on destroying anyone who tried to ride him. He was ugly, looking as if no part belonged to another, but he was also surprisingly fast and had amazing stamina.

He was a hell-horse, but he'd be a prize hunter if a man could control him and survive the ride.

Miles grinned. "During stables this Sunday, it shouldn't be that hard to set up a wager between Banshee and one of the Allbright's nags. They have a couple they're proud of. I'll win, and there you are."

On Sunday, the hunting fraternity amused themselves by admiring one another's horseflesh, making bets and sometimes purchases.

"Problem is," said Con, "that the Allbrights would have to be imbeciles to underrate any horse of yours, Miles, and they're surely not that stupid."

"Yes," said Francis. "And this is my business, anyway. I'll ride him. In fact, I'll buy the horse first just to make it aboveboard. How much do you want for him?"

"Fifty."

Francis gave him a look, but said, "Done."

Miles grinned at Felicity Monahan. "There, *alanna*. Didn't I say I'd get fifty for him? You owe me a cake baked by your own fair hands."

Felicity glared, but then burst out laughing. "Miles Cavanagh, sometimes I have to like you, you wicked man. What a thoroughly underhanded scheme. You are a rogue of the first water!"

"We all are, my dear," said Miles. "Every last one of us."

On Sunday afternoon, a large proportion of the hunting fraternity gathered just outside Melton to watch the race between Tom Allbright on his big roan, Whiskers, and Lord Middlethorpe on a most peculiar gray named Banshee. The betting was heavily against the gray. Middlethorpe was a sound rider but no miracle worker. The horse showed no promise and was vicious besides. He'd already taken a bite out of one unwary spectator.

Francis eyed his partner in crime warily. Banshee glared back and bared his teeth, kicking out in the hope that someone might be behind.

This morning, when the men had toured the various stables around Melton, Banshee had been marked as his and had been the subject of considerable amusement. When the Allbright brothers had strolled by and made a scathing comment, however, Francis had taken offense. Words had grown heated and the matter had quickly come to a wager and a race, just as he intended.

It hadn't been quite as simple to escalate the wager to the thousands he wanted, but the brothers had allowed their greed to take control. Anyone could see that Banshee had all the appearance of a disaster. The wager finally stood at three thousand guineas.

"Having second thoughts?" sneered Tom Allbright as he came over to shake his head over the hell-horse. "Too late now."

"Too late for you, too," said Francis. "He's faster than he looks."

Allbright guffawed. "He'll have to be!"

It suddenly occurred to Francis that the Allbright brothers showed no sign of concern about their sister. It was possible that they had Runners out looking for her, but somehow he doubted it. They had apparently taken her small fortune and washed their hands of her, leaving her to fend for herself in a harsh world.

He smiled at Banshee. "Ready?" he asked Allbright.

"Ready and raring, Middlethorpe. First to Cottesmore Church, right? I hear the innkeeper in Cottesmore makes a fine brew. I'll sample it as I wait for you." He strolled off, laughing, toward his well-behaved roan.

Francis took a deep breath and approached his horse. He'd ridden the brute twice since the idea had been mooted, and he had the bruises to show for it, but he could manage Banshee. It was just that mounting the gray was the greatest challenge.

Miles came over to help the struggling grooms. He deflected teeth by thumping the horse on the nose, then grabbed a foreleg, holding it up. Off balance, the gray ceased its madness for a moment and Francis swung into the saddle. Once settled, he nodded to Miles and the handlers to let go.

The gray kicked, then swung to try to take a bite out of his rider. Francis gave him a sharp cut with the whip. Banshee immediately froze into a statue of outrage. Francis grinned. One thing he'd learned about the hell-horse was that he behaved better with a rider on his back than without, especially if the rider was resolute. Banshee was actually fairly well schooled, as one would expect of any horse from Miles's stables; he just had a vicious temper and resented the human race.

He was also, Miles had assured Francis, rabidly competitive. Banshee would tolerate no horse being before him. It made him difficult as a hunter, for the Master and the huntsmen generally thought they had a right to be before the field, but it was a useful quality in a race.

Francis raised his whip to Allbright and saw the man's eyes narrow at the sight of the silent horse.

Francis pondered for a moment the effects surroundings could have on a physical feature. Both the Allbright brothers had eyes rather like Serena's—dark and tilted. In their red, puffy faces, those eyes looked like malignant currants.

Perhaps eyes were the mirror of the soul.

What, then, did her huge dark eyes say about Serena?

He gingerly touched his leg to the horse's side, urging him forward. Banshee was clearly in two minds about cooperation and took only a hesitant step forward. Francis saw Allbright smirk at the awkward movement.

A number of other horsemen had decided to join the race, though it was accepted to be between Francis and Allbright. Lucien was there, and Con, and Will Allbright. Lucien was riding his big black stallion, Viking, even though he did not hunt the horse for fear of injuring him. Francis knew that Lucien was riding him in the race because that magnificent horse could outrun anything on the field, and he wanted to make sure of fair play.

The race almost didn't start.

Lord Alvanley, who had agreed to act as starter, chose to wave a red spotted handkerchief, and Banshee took grave exception. First he shied wildly, almost unseating Francis, then he set his ears back and went for both handkerchief and holder. Francis had to use the full power of the harsh bit in the horse's mouth to persuade him to stop.

Then the handkerchief dropped and they were away.

After a fashion.

Banshee again objected to the fluttering red and white and made a determined effort to go sideways instead of forward.

Francis thought he'd have to use the whip again, but the gray suddenly realized there were other horses ahead of him. He put out his head and raced hell-for-leather forward.

They were off!

Banshee was certainly fast but had all the elegance of a warped cartwheel. Each stride sent a jolt through Francis, and there would be ten miles of this. God, would Serena ever appreciate what he was doing for her?

He pulled up hard to steady the horse for the first jump. To his surprise, Banshee obeyed and cleared it beautifully. "Good lad!" Francis shouted, elated. It seemed the horse had intelligence enough to accept a rider's guidance if it suited him.

They thundered by some slower members of the field, but the leaders, including both Allbright brothers, were well ahead.

The race was over ten miles, though, so starting speed was not of great importance. Endurance was. Tom Allbright's horse was a hunter and thus bred for endurance, but Francis trusted Miles that there wasn't a horse born with the staying power of Banshee.

Francis wondered if *he* had the staying power. He tried to ease the pounding on his seat and spine by standing now and then, but he couldn't hold that for long. The jumps were a relief—a blessed moment of smooth passage through air, then a landing like a ton of bricks and the pounding all over again.

Slowly, they worked their way up the field, though,

passing more than one horse and rider that had parted company in the grueling ride. Francis tried to pull Banshee back occasionally to pace him, but the horse simply seemed intent on overtaking everything in the field.

Lucien rode up alongside on his big black. "Going well!" he shouted.

Banshee's ears went back. That was all the notice given before the horse whipped his head sideways and went for Viking's throat. Francis hauled hard on the bit, using legs and hands to control the damned beast, feeling as if his arms were going to be torn from his sockets. Lucien fell back, cursing.

Francis sensed his horse tense to buck and used the spurs. Banshee shot forward. In a moment it was as if nothing had happened, and the horse was eating the distance between him and Will Allbright's chestnut.

"You're a spawn of the devil," Francis muttered as they surged past the younger Allbright, "and in a right and proper world, you'd be dog meat tomorrow. But win this race, my lad, and I'll look after you."

It occurred to Francis that he was acquiring some strange dependents, but he didn't much care. He was very much looking forward to presenting Serena with her stolen money.

He came up with Tom Allbright at a little past halfway as they galloped through the village of Teigh. His opponent looked shocked to see him and whipped his horse to greater speed. Banshee merely produced more speed as if it were limitless. What heart the horse had.

Francis, however, was in trouble. Each jarring stride was agony and further weakened his legs and back. It would be ironic if he was the problem in this race by getting thrown. If Banshee determined to throw him, he wasn't sure he could stay on.

Now there were no horses ahead, Banshee allowed Francis to hold him back a little, which was a relief to his body and his conscience. Francis had no desire to have the animal drop dead under him. Some distance away, Tom Allbright was also taking the opportunity to rest his horse a little.

Francis relaxed, but he relaxed too soon.

With no one ahead of him, Banshee was distractible. A plover firing up from a covert had him veering off at right angles and almost unseating his rider. Francis blistered his ears and hauled on the reins. The contest was about even until the hell-horse realized Whiskers was in front. Immediately, he was off like a white devil, with Francis just trying to stay on his back.

Once even, he slowed again.

Damnation. There was no way to make the horse build a lead, and the ending was going to be very dicey.

Unless . . .

He glanced around. Sure enough, there was Lucien, keeping pace a cautious distance away, watching for tricks by the Allbright brothers.

Francis waved him on.

Lucien didn't seem to understand.

Francis waved again, desperately.

Then Lucien grinned and saluted. He urged his horse on and the magnificent stallion surged ahead of the field.

Banshee gave a noise like the screech of the creature he was named for and produced an amazing burst of speed, hurtling after the black ahead. Francis just clung on for dear life as his hell-horse thundered toward Cottesmore.

There was a crowd there, waiting to see the result. The cheering, waving bedlam was enough to spook any animal, but Banshee paid no attention at all.

Lucien glanced back and pulled his horse slowly in. Banshee surged past at the lych-gate of Cottesmore Church, then—blowing as he was—did a saucy little dance and kicked his heels at the arrogant animal that had tried to steal his race.

Viking looked aristocratically unimpressed.

Francis burst out laughing. "Oh, you devil!" he said to his horse. "I could almost get to like you. Almost," he muttered, as his aches, pains, and bruises began to make themselves felt.

The crowd showed a tendency to gather around the victors, but Banshee soon showed them the error of their ways. Francis didn't dare dismount just yet, as the horse would be a great deal more unmanageable then.

So he waited in solitary splendor, like a damned equestrian statue, as Tom Allbright drove his foaming horse to the finishing point.

"Damn you to hell!" the man snarled. "I saw that! Arden paced you!"

"Nothing in the rules against it. By the way, I wouldn't get too close, or Banshee'll take a lump out of your horse. Or you. He's not fussy."

Allbright backed up, only inches ahead of the gray's bared teeth, then swung around to the observers. "Arden paced him in! I wouldn't have challenged that great black brute!"

There was a murmur of distaste at this unsporting behavior. The marquess walked his horse over to Allbright. "Are you suggesting I did something out of line?" he asked, with all the blue-blooded arrogance of which he was capable.

Allbright paled. "Not at all, my lord. Just that Middlethorpe followed you in."

"Nothing to stop you following, too," Lucien pointed out quite amiably. "Excellent race. Have to thank you, sir, for setting it up. Sundays can be so dull."

"Yes, of course," Allbright muttered as some remnants of sense took over. His eyes still burned with rage, however.

Francis began to get the delicious feeling that Allbright couldn't pay. That was a bonus he hadn't counted on. He wished he was off this damned horse to enjoy it.

With relief, he saw his grooms coming forward and was able to surrender Banshee to them. Dismounting was painful, and even standing straight was a challenge. He made his way over to Allbright. He'd have liked to have strolled arrogantly, but various parts of his body made that impossible. He managed to walk with dignity . . . just.

"Thank you for the race," he said benignly. "We'll settle this evening, shall we? Would you call on me at Arden's place?"

A brick-red color settled in Allbright's coarse face, more from anger than embarrassment. "Don't have that sort of money on me, my lord," he choked out. "I'd rather settle at Tatt's. I'll be in Town a week on Tuesday."

It was quite normal for racing debts to be settled at Tattersall's in London, but not during hunting season when the men were fixed in Melton. Francis would be within his rights to object, but he didn't mind letting the Allbrights sweat for a few days.

"Of course," he said, enjoying the thought of Allbright doing the rounds of the moneylenders. Then he had an inspiration. Serena must have acquired some jewelry during her marriage, and he'd go odds her brothers had taken that, too. "If you find it hard to come by the cash," he said idly, "I'll take it in kind."

"Kind? What kind?"

"Land, jewels . . ."

He saw the idea sink into the man's thick head. "Ah, jewels . . . Well, I do happen to have some trinkets. Belonged to a female relative. Should appraise about right."

Francis was hard pressed not to level the man, who clearly felt no qualms at misusing his sister's only property. He took comfort in the thought of Tom's fury when he discovered that the "trinkets" had been returned to their rightful owner. One way or the other, Francis would make sure he found out.

"Very well, then," said Francis. "Tatt's, a week Tuesday. At ten?"

Allbright grunted agreement and pushed his way out of the area. Francis savored the moment. He would return Serena's jewels to her, adding the three thousand from his own pocket with her none the wiser. She'd be in transports of joy. The thought of Serena in transports of joy was enough to distract any man.

Lucien surrendered his mount to his grooms and came over to Francis, grinning. "Are you in quite as much pain as you appear?"

Francis was aware of a profound disinclination to

move. "Probably more. That horse was never designed to be ridden."

"Ah, the things we will do for a woman. With great foresight, and after a hint or two from Miles, I arranged for a carriage to be here to transport you back home."

"Thank heavens," said Francis sincerely. "I don't want to put leg across horse for days. Weeks. Years . . ."

Lucien laughed. "You'll feel better shortly. My head groom, Dooley, has a rare hand with massage and unguents."

Chapter 8

Dooley did indeed have a rare hand with massage and unguents, which is not to say that the process didn't hurt like the dickens. As Francis groaned and cursed under the pommeling fingers, he wished Serena Allbright . . . no, Serena Riverton . . . knew what he was suffering in her cause.

Serena Riverton was enough to make him curse as it was. By birth she was not really suited to be a mistress, and he dreaded to think what Beth would say about such a situation.

By marriage, however, it was a different matter. Sir Matthew Riverton's widow could be considered more of the demimonde, despite a church service. It would depend on what role she had played in his life. If, as was generally the case, she had been left in the country while her husband debauched himself in London, then it was not too bad. If she had been part of his notorious life, then she was ruined.

Francis racked his brain, but could only dredge up snippets of information. He thought he remembered hearing that Riverton boasted of having a well-trained wife, leaving no one in any doubt as to the skills she was trained to use. He had also heard that he hosted wild parties at his Lincolnshire home during the hunting season. If that was his only country home, it didn't look good.

All in all, Francis thought, it was as well that Serena was barren. It removed any temptation to do something stupid.

Tough, calloused fingers were suddenly replaced by strong, soft ones. Francis jerked up and around, cursing as his back objected, to see Blanche Hardcastle had replaced the groom in attending to his naked body. "What the devil . . . !"

"Lie back down," she said comfortably. "I'm not after your virtue, but I'm skilled at a more subtle kind of massage than Dooley. I don't know why you men think torturing sore muscles will make them better. This won't hurt as much but will do just as much good."

Francis collapsed back down again, for her strong, firm manipulations of his thighs and buttocks did feel healing. After a while, she began to massage him with smooth, sweeping movements of her oiled hands, so that his abused body relaxed.

"Is this an obligatory skill for a mistress?" he asked lazily. "If so, I should have sought one sooner."

"A useful one. The crude think of only limited ways for one person to serve another in an intimate way, but who wants to be crude?"

"I envy Lucien."

"Perhaps you should pity him," she teased. "He has given me up for another."

"Hard to believe."

She pinched him. "There's no need to be polite. Anyway, I'm sure he will have taught Beth such skills by now."

"Taught her to serve him as he wishes?" Francis asked, bothered by Beth's comments days before, bothered, too, by lurid imaginings of Serena's life with Riverton.

"Taught her a range of pleasures," said Blanche. "Did you think this went one way? Lucien enjoyed massaging me as much as he enjoyed being massaged."

Francis couldn't help but envision massaging Serena and being massaged. He was grateful he was lying on his stomach so the consequences were not obvious.

He tried, but could not imagine Anne Peckworth being on either end of a naked massage.

"Blanche," he asked, "why would a woman want to be a mistress, not a wife?"

"Are you referring to me? I am sunk too deep to become respectable."

"That's nonsense," he said, though he knew there was some truth in it.

"So you weren't referring to me. Who then?"

"It doesn't matter."

"Serena Riverton?" she asked shrewdly.

He knew his silence was answer.

Blanche's hands continued to make soothing magic over his body. "To be a true mistress to a good man is to have a lot of freedom. To be a wife to a bad man can be a slavery as terrible as that of the worst whorehouse in London. I'm sure Riverton was a bad man."

"Why?" Francis wanted Blanche's angle on this, for she knew more of the underbelly of Society than most.

"I never knew him, but one hears things. He was a

man who constantly desired novelty. In matters of sex, it eventually becomes impossible to have novelty without hurting or debasing someone. I gather he soon discovered hurting and debasing people to be to his taste. Of course, many men behave one way with their casual women, and another with their wife."

She lapsed into silence and Francis closed his eyes, trying to consider Serena's situation without actually thinking of some of the things she might have done.

He discovered it was actually very simple: It was impossible to let her walk out of his life. He'd worry about her all his days.

He desperately wanted her as his own. She wanted to be his mistress.

So be it.

And he was a good man. He vowed she would find no man more gentle, understanding, and generous than he. If she wasn't barren, he told himself, he *would* marry her despite the problems.

As it was, it would be perfect if he could just be discreet. And even if it should become known, Lady Anne would know how to ignore such a matter.

No. He dismissed that sophistry. If it became known, Anne would be hurt no matter how well she handled it, so it simply must not become known.

He suppressed a groan. Such things always became known.

He remembered Nicholas suffering agonies when trying to juggle a mistress and a wife, and he had hated the mistress, and only kept her as a service to his country.

He remembered Nicholas saying he found it impossible to go from his mistress's bed to his wife's. Francis knew in his heart that he, too, wasn't the kind of man who could go blithely from his mistress's bed to his wife's, particularly when he cared for both women.

But he *couldn't* marry Serena.

And he *couldn't* let her go to another man.

"You're very tense," said Blanche, applying pressure to his shoulders. "Is Serena Riverton such a problem?"

"Of course not," said Francis. There was no point in asking advice on such an insoluble matter.

Blanche gave one last sweeping stroke and moved away to wipe oil from her hands. "I'll massage you again tomorrow. You should feel more comfortable in a day or two."

Francis couldn't imagine ever feeling comfortable again, in body or mind, but he sat up, making sure the towel covered him decently. "Thank you."

"It was a pleasure to soothe the gallant victor." Blanche frowned slightly in thought, then said, "I gather Serena Riverton is barren. I know it would go against your code not to produce an heir, but is continuation of the line really worth such pain?"

He hit back instinctively. "You think Lucien should have married you?"

"What makes you think I can't have children?"

"Why didn't he marry you, then?"

Her lips quirked wryly. "For many excellent reasons, the main one being that he never wanted to. Lucien never loved me."

"I don't love Serena Riverton."

"Then let her go to another."

With that she left, and Francis considered her excellent advice.

He wished he had the strength to take it.

The letter from Aunt Arabella arrived the next morning. It was curt and not informative, except in so far as commanding Francis to present himself at Patchem's Cottage *immediately*. It was all too like the one from his mother that had started the unraveling of his life.

His first thought was to dash off in fear that something terrible had happened to Serena, but nothing of that nature was implied at all.

In fact, he'd swear his aunt was cross with him.

The only reason he could imagine for Aunt Arabella to be angry with him was if Serena had spun her some lying tale. He was tired of terse, uninformative letters. He was tired of being entwined in female machinations. He ached from head to foot and didn't think he'd had a restful night's sleep since he'd first met Serena.

So Aunt Arabella could damn well wait.

He lounged around the house for two days, being waited on by ladies and servants, and massaged by Blanche. He began to regain his freedom of movement but failed to find a solution to his dilemma. Solomon would doubtless recommend that he be cut in half to be shared between the two ladies. He feared they'd both need the same parts, however, though for different purposes.

By the third day, Francis couldn't put it off any longer, and he left Melton to drive to Summer St. Martin.

* * *

Despite the curtness of Arabella's note and his many misgivings, Francis was aware of delighted anticipation as he approached the village. He warned himself that Serena's beauty could turn out to be a trick of his memory, her golden appeal prove to be mere gilt.

He should want it, for then he'd be free.

He didn't want it. He had decided, whatever the cost, to make her his mistress.

He intended to enjoy her and protect her rare quality. He would establish her in comfort, make sure she had everything she required, and protect her from all harm. He couldn't wait to prove to her that men could be gentle and caring.

He couldn't wait to make love again.

To her.

He couldn't wait to return her property and tell her that he had won it for her.

He decided that he wouldn't wait for Allbright to produce the jewels. He would explain about the race and give Serena a draft for three thousand guineas. He'd surprise her with the jewels later. That would make two occasions upon which she would be very pleased with him.

His heart beat faster as he drove into the village, every second closer to Serena. He swung into the lane where Aunt Arabella lived, but drew to a frustrated halt at the sight of a crowd blocking the way. An archery butt had been set up there, and three young men were taking turns shooting at the bull.

What a damnable time and place to hold a contest.

Then he noticed that though a number of people were gathered to watch, one person sat in pride of place on the wall at one side, like a lady watching a medieval tournament. It was Serena, and it wasn't hard to guess that she was in some way the cause of this competition.

What, he wondered caustically, did the winner get?

Even so, his mind was tangled by the sweet sight of his siren. She was every bit as beautiful, every bit as special as he remembered.

But different.

Today she was bundled in a simple red woolen cloak, the hood tossed back to leave her head free. Conventional wisdom said that scarlet would not go with deep red hair, but each glowed in the reflection of the other. That hair was no longer in wanton curls, but swept neatly into a tight knot on the top of her head. The severe style did not detract from her charms at all, though he wanted to loosen it and drown in its silken weight.

She laughed at a comment, cheeks aglow, eyes sparkling. She looked young and happy in a way he had never dreamed possible, and as ravishingly beautiful as any women in silk and jewels. The only frivolous thing about her, however, was a white ribbon fluttering from the clasp of her cloak.

An arrow hit the edge of the bull and she cheered, clapping like a child.

She looked like a mere schoolgirl.

Then people began to notice him and turn.

Serena looked, too.

Francis handed the reins to Kipling and swung down, feeling a chill that had nothing to do with the weather. A look of horror had passed over Serena's face at the sight of him.

He wasn't welcome?

Who had taken his place?

Suddenly furious, he stalked over and seized a bow from a startled contestant. He sighted on the target and sent an arrow whistling into the very center of the bull.

"Well," he asked, turning to Serena, "do I win?"

"I think so," she said faintly, attempting to smile.

He smiled, too, though he could feel the effort hurting. "What, then, do I win?"

She reached up to loose the white ribbon with trembling hands and offered it, fluttering in the breeze.

"How touching." He took it, not knowing what to make of any of this. "Is the entertainment over, or is there more?"

Her eyes were huge and apprehensive. "It's over, I think. It was just an impromptu."

"Then perhaps I could have a word with you in private."

"Of course." She managed a smile and kind words for her disappointed admirers, then led him up to the cottage.

"Is Aunt Arabella in there?" he asked. The last person he needed at the moment was his meddlesome aunt.

"No. She's visiting Mrs. Holt."

He allowed her to lead him into the house, trying to control this mad fury of jealousy. He had never been prey to such feelings before, but now they raged in him. He wanted to set hands on her and shake her. He couldn't abide the thought of her giving her favors left, right, and center.

He looked at the ribbon that he'd wound tight round his finger. For heaven's sake, it was a ribbon, that was all. Why was he in such a state?

She turned in the parlor, clutching her cloak tight about her. "I'm sorry." Tears welled in her eyes and he felt an utter cad.

He reached for her. "Don't Serena. I'm sorry, too."

She evaded his grasp. "But it wasn't your fault," she said brokenly. "It was mine, all mine. . . ."

"Serena, there's no need for all this drama. You acted unwisely, perhaps, but no real harm is done. I had no reason to be angry."

She was staring at him. "But you *were* angry?"

She looked so young and frightened that he could not be stern with her. "Not anymore," he said gently. "Now, Serena, I want to talk to you about our future before Aunt Arabella returns. Then we can present a united front."

She stared at him in a strange manner; he'd never imagined that even her eyes could grow so huge. Perhaps she no longer wanted his *carte blanche*. That was a source of anguish. Had she perhaps received another offer, a respectable one? The knowledge that he could not top that offer ate into him. Wanting some kind of contact with her, he reached out and helped her off with her cloak. After a moment she released it.

The gown revealed was nothing like her russet wool masterpiece. It was a simple fawn cotton, simply made. It was high at the neck, long in the sleeves, and gathered so as to conceal most of her figure. It was very demure and, surprisingly, it suited her. He didn't know what to make of her anymore. She sat neatly in a chair, her disturbing eyes fixed on him, looking like a schoolroom miss awaiting a rebuke from her father.

He was to propose an immoral liaison to this creature?

But, knowing what she could be, he wanted her, here and now. . . .

Francis took a stand near the glowing fire, feeling the heat on his legs and a flush in his face. He gazed down into the flickering flames and steeled himself. "I realize that it has been some time since we spoke together, Serena. You seem to have settled here quite well." He cleared his throat. "I wonder if you have . . . have made any plans about your future." He looked up soberly. If she had a chance of marriage, it would be unfair to stand in her way. "Plans that do not include me."

She seemed startled. "No. I'm sorry."

Francis let out a breath he had not been aware of holding. "There's no need to apologize." To his surprise, the words were hard to say, but he managed. "I have come to ask you to be my mistress."

She was not pleased. He watched her turn white, watched as her eyes grew even more enormous. Then red flooded her face like a wave, and he caught an expression of deep hurt before she looked down. "I . . . I don't think I can do that anymore."

He felt strangely as if he should apologize, and then annoyed to be so put in the wrong. "It was your suggestion, if you remember."

"Ye . . . yes, but . . ." He saw her swallow.

"Goddamnit, Serena, will you kindly decide what you want!"

"What she *wants!*" snapped Aunt Arabella, marching into the room like a battalion, armed with an umbrella. "What the devil do you think she wants, you reprobate?"

"*Reprobate!* What story has she being telling you?"

Francis heard himself shouting, bemused that he was driven to such lengths.

"The truth. Or do you deny it?" Arabella took up a belligerent stand behind Serena, like a wizened guardian angel in a very large black bonnet.

"How can I deny anything unless I hear the charges?" Francis asked icily. "I've just offered this lady what she begged for a few weeks ago, only to have it thrown in my face."

Arabella moved around to face Serena. "You refused, child? Why?"

Serena looked up, eyes flickering between them both. Francis saw the terror that had been in her eyes when he'd first met her, and felt sick to be the cause of it.

"Serena, don't," he said, taking a step forward. "Don't be afraid. . . ."

Arabella turned to poke him with her umbrella. "If she's afraid, she's afraid of you, and not surprising. Do you know yet who her husband was?"

"Yes."

"Then it's hardly peculiar that she's nervous of accepting another offer of marriage, is it? Give her a moment and she'll come round."

Francis took a deep breath. "I have not offered marriage."

Arabella straightened slowly and fixed him with a fearsome glare. "Are you trying to buy her off, you wretch?"

"Not precisely," said Francis, badly off balance. The conversation didn't make sense, and it wasn't a normal occurrence for any man to try to set up a mistress under the eyes of an elderly spinster relative. Aunt

Arabella was highly unconventional, but even so he was not sure he would come out of this with a whole skin. He'd depended on a simple fact—that Serena wanted this as much as he.

"He's offered me *carte blanche,*" said Serena, with cold clarity. She suddenly rose to her feet and faced him, looking taller than she was. "I would much rather you had not come, my lord. I know you were not to blame, and I would have accepted it if you had washed your hands of me, but . . . but not this."

"Carte blanche!" Arabella loosed it like a war cry.

"This woman," shouted Francis, and realized he had actually flung out a hand to point like a bad actor in a melodramatic play, "begged to be my mistress, and—"

But he caught himself on that accusation. He could not accuse her of that before others.

"That," said Arabella formidably, "was doubtless a petition made out of fear and before she realized she was with child."

Silence fell. Francis stared at Serena, and she met his eyes, chin high.

"Is this true?" he asked quietly as the world shifted around him and he tried to find a footing.

"Yes." Her anger turned to confusion, and she looked between him and his aunt. "Didn't you know?"

"You said you could not conceive."

"I believed it to be true." She clasped her hands tightly. "I'm sorry you were not told, my lord. I do not insist on marriage, but you must see that I can no longer be your mistress."

"What, then, would you do with the child?" He still

felt as if he were in a very bad play. Was it comedy or tragedy?

She lowered her eyes. "I hoped you would support it."

"But you will not be my mistress? Why?"

"Good grief, you numbskull," snapped Arabella. "How could she? Is she to live with you, with a child—possibly a son—at her knee, and know that it has lost its rights? How is she to explain it to him one day? 'Yes, this is your father, dear, but it did not suit us to marry.'"

Francis found his eyes had traveled to Serena's stomach, but there was nothing to see under the loose gown. He was not sure how much there should be to see, anyway. What would it be? Three months, he supposed. He had to ask. "Can you be sure it is mine."

Arabella made a noise but Serena turned on her. "You asked the same question." She turned back to Francis. "I have no way to prove it, of course, but since my husband's death nearly six months ago, I have been intimate with only one man—you, my lord. There is no doubt in my mind."

Francis turned again to look into the fire, but found no answers there, just disturbing questions. He turned back. "Aunt Arabella, I wish to speak with Serena alone."

Arabella looked down her nose, but after a moment, she harrumphed and turned to go. But she turned back to Serena. "I'll be in the garden, child. If he upsets you, call." With a final glare at Francis, but a glare weakened by concern, she stalked out of the room.

Francis studied the puzzling enigma who was turning his life upside down and inside out. He wished she were still in her bold russet dress and surrounded by her whore's perfume. He'd be surer of his way, then.

"If I got you with child," he said, "you can hardly hold me to blame."

She had been pale, but color invaded at that—awkward patches of it in her cheeks. "I don't."

"If," he said, watching her closely, "you had found yourself with child—by a servant, perhaps, or a married man—you might well have sought to make a better prospect think it his."

She looked up sharply. "No!" But then her eyes became unfocused as she thought. "I suppose a more clever woman than I might indeed have done such a thing." She looked back at him, frowning. "But surely, my lord, I would have had to be mad to wander the country roads in November on the off chance that a suitable man might come by."

Francis had no response to that.

"And," she added firmly, "if you'll remember, I was very reluctant to join you in your carriage, and it was you, not I, who told the Posts that we were married."

"But it was you who proposed a sexual liaison," he countered, "and you who pursued it even when I refused."

She nodded. "I admit it, but I cannot see that you can think it a premeditated plot."

Nor could Francis, but he was still feeling trapped.

On the other hand, if she really was carrying his child, it went against all his instincts to let it be born a bastard.

He walked over to Arabella's big leather-bound bible. "Come here."

161

Serena came to stand nearby, pale, anxious, and looking so damned young.

"Put your hand on the bible," he said, "and swear that you are with child."

She did, her hand small and pale against the dark leather. When she would have moved, he trapped her hand there. "And swear that it is mine."

She looked up into his eyes and said firmly, "The child in my body is yours, my lord. I swear it on the Holy Book."

Her hand was so cold beneath his.

So be it. Francis faced the tangled future bleakly, but was aware of a distant hint of delight. "Then we will marry tomorrow."

"Tomorrow?" echoed Serena faintly.

"There is no time to lose," he said dryly. "If I leave immediately, I can acquire the license from the bishop today and return tomorrow."

She swallowed. "You will need my real name."

"I know your real name, Lady Riverton. I trust you will be ready."

He realized he still had her hand trapped on the bible, and let her go.

She was pale as a sheet, but she answered firmly. "Yes, my lord, I will be ready."

As soon as he left, Serena sought out Arabella. "Why didn't you *tell* him? I thought you had told him."

Arabella sniffed. "It hardly seemed a thing to put in a letter. Anyway, I have little faith in men. He might have made himself scarce. He's hardly rushed over here."

"He didn't know there was reason."

"I assure you, I made the matter sound urgent enough. So, is he going to do the right thing?"

"Oh, yes." Serena paced the small garden. "But I wish you had told him, Arabella." She turned suddenly. "Am *I* doing the right thing?"

" 'Course you are. You're going to bear his child, and the child deserves to be legitimate. If Francis has any problem with it, he should have thought of it before he took advantage of you."

Serena froze. This was the moment when she really should tell Arabella the truth, but she couldn't. She couldn't. Except in moments like this, she managed not to admit the truth even to herself. She hadn't really done that to a stranger. She hadn't really caused him to make her pregnant, so now he was going to marry her, even though he didn't want to. . . .

She could see the attraction of throwing herself in the nearest river, and might have done so if it hadn't been for the precious life within her.

Suddenly, she was in Arabella's arms, though the older woman was far too brusque to be good at hugging. "There, there," Arabella muttered as she tapped Serena's back. "It'll all work out. Do you think I would marry you to my favorite nephew if I didn't think you'd be a good wife?"

Serena struggled with her tears. "I'm terrified."

"No need of that," said Arabella. "Wherever you go, gel, I'm going with you."

On the drive, then hanging about the bishop's palace, waiting for paperwork to be completed, Francis had plenty of time to think. Not that thinking did him any good.

The cold logical part of him said that this all could be a clever trick by a scheming wanton, but his heart told him Serena had sworn the truth on the bible. No matter what she was, she was carrying his child.

Among the many reasons for his decision to be celibate had been an abhorrence of creating children promiscuously. It was impossible that he turn his back now on his own child, impossible that he not give it his name.

But he was perfectly aware of the ramifications. His mother was going to be appalled. Anne and her parents were going to be shocked and hurt. There was going to be a lot of gossip, particularly when the child was born and people counted back. It was possible Serena would not be well accepted. She was, after all, Matthew Riverton's widow, as well as a late-wed bride.

He wasn't even sure what kind of wife she would make and whether he would ever feel easy about trusting her. He remembered all too well that she wasn't in favor of faithfulness and had demonstrated her wantonness to him.

The only blessing in his thoughts was that the Rogues would accept her; it was part of the creed. And if she showed any faults, Beth Arden would do her best to correct them.

He was aware of a strong desire to take Serena to meet Nicholas, and see what his friend thought of her. Well, why not? He'd planned a visit.

A clerk came out with the license and took the money.

Francis left with one positive thought in his head.

Thank God for the Rogues. He was going to need them.

Chapter 9

Serena tossed and turned the night away, seeking some course other than the one before her. She was nothing but a burden to Lord Middlethorpe, one foisted upon him by her own wicked behavior.

And what of his family? she wondered with a shudder. Arabella had told her of his widowed mother, a very high stickler with an elevated notion of the importance of the Haile family. There were also three sisters, all married now. The sisters sounded pleasant enough, but they were bound to wonder at the irregularity of this marriage.

She rolled over and buried her head in her arms. She had no choice. For her child's sake, she had no choice.

Through bouts of fractured and uneasy sleep, Serena made it to the first pale light of dawn, then rose to walk around the misty lanes, trying to wear out her nervous energy. When she returned to the cottage, she found Arabella in an agitated state.

"I didn't know what to think!" the older woman exclaimed. "I thought perhaps you'd run off!"

"Now, why would I do that?" asked Serena dully, and sat to face the eggs prepared for her. She hadn't been sick as so many women were, but she had little appetite.

For once, Arabella didn't nag at her, and Serena managed with a little toast and tea. "When do you think he'll be here?"

"By noon, I would think. As you are of age and have lived here for the required number of weeks, there should be no problem acquiring the license."

Serena mangled her toast. "I wish there were some other way."

"Well, there ain't," said Arabella trenchantly. "And though I gave Francis the edge of my tongue, you deserve a cut of it, too. Unless you want to claim he raped you, which I would never believe, then you are as much to blame as he. If you find the situation not quite to your liking, you have no reason to complain."

Serena felt her face flame. Why did it occur to no one that the man might be the victim? "I had better dress, then," she said, and escaped.

She had only the one fine dress, the russet wool in which she had fled her brother's house so long ago. It was stained around the hem from its adventures but still showed its quality. It also had the shaped, low-bodiced design her husband had chosen for her. As she picked it up she smelled the trace of perfume that lingered, despite airing. Surely it was faint enough now to be innocuous, and she wanted to look her best for him today.

He'd called it a whore's perfume, but he'd confessed to the effect it had. She wanted that effect. What else had she to offer?

She put on all her old clothes—silk underclothing, fine wool on top—but then added a plain cambric chemisette to make the bodice decent. In the flyblown mirror in her room she considered herself, seeing the old Serena for the first time in months.

And yet, it wasn't the old Serena. Something had changed other than the new life within her. Nor was it the girl she had been when she had been taken away from Miss Mallory's. That Serena had been excited at the prospect of marriage, but a little sad at leaving behind her friends and her opportunity to play the lead in the upcoming theatricals.

A child.

A poor, betrayed child.

The Serena looking back from the mirror now was a new creature. Would this Serena fare better than her previous incarnations? She was older and wiser—older and wiser enough to be terrified.

Serena put her hands over the slight swell of her womb. She must do this for her child. And at least now she had Arabella as friend and companion.

Arabella could not hover over the marriage bed, though.

With trembling hands, Serena brushed out her long hair and gathered it up in a looser style than she had favored recently, letting some curls escape around her face. She remembered the newly hired maid who had arranged her hair so skillfully before her first wedding; the maid who had turned out to be as much a guard as an attendant.

She remembered the delicious white silk gown provided for her to wear—sheer and almost transparent except for the many layers, and decorated with finest embroidery. When she'd put it on, she'd felt like a fairy princess and danced around her room for joy. Matthew had ripped it off her that night, a symbol of her innocence now his to do with as he wished.

She covered her face with her hands as memories of the horror that had been her first wedding night swooped down on her. She had survived her years of marriage by tearing apart mind and body, but here in Summer St. Martin she had begun to put herself together again.

She was stronger now and more resolute. But she was also more vulnerable to pain.

There was *no* similarity between Matthew and Lord Middlethorpe. She had to believe that.

They were both men, her doubts taunted.

Serena leapt to her feet and hurried downstairs, hoping the doubt-devils would not pursue her. She would go out and walk. She reached for the red wool cloak, then changed her mind and put on her sable-lined one.

She walked briskly about the village, and as she went people waved and exchanged greetings. Her heart eased. She had made a place for herself here, a normal place. Certainly, her beauty had singled her out, but because she had behaved as if unaware of it, it had not been a disaster. She knew that even the young men vying for her favors were just playing a game. None, thank heavens, had lost his heart to her.

She had proved to herself that she could live a normal life. She would do so in future. With God's help, she would prove to Lord Middlethorpe that she could be an excellent wife. She set off back to the cottage, much lighter in her heart.

At the sound of a carriage, she stepped to the side of the lane, but then realized and turned.

Lord Middlethorpe leapt down, eyes intent, and came over to her.

"You look as you did when first I met you," he said soberly. "Frightened."

She could not deny it.

They stood for a moment, silence pressing in, then he said, "I'll walk with you back to the cottage." He waved his groom to drive the curricle ahead, and extended his arm.

Serena had no choice but to place her hand upon it.

They strolled along in unnatural silence. Serena was perfectly aware of a number of eyes upon them and a number of correct assumptions being made. She saw, too, how the women looked at her companion.

Appreciatively.

She found herself wishing that he were shy, pudgy, and awkward. It made her feel guilty to know that she had trapped such a prize.

At last he spoke, sounding a little strained. "I stopped at the vicarage. Reverend Downs will be ready to perform the service in half an hour."

Serena wanted to say, It's all right. We don't have to do this. I've thought of an alternative.

But she hadn't.

"What will happen afterward?" she managed to ask.

She had never thought of Lord Middlethorpe as particularly large before, but in his caped greatcoat and high beaver he seemed massive beside her. She felt fragile and vulnerable.

"A meal, I suppose. Then we will go to Thorpe Priory. It is only twenty miles and we should be able to make it before dark. Unlike our previous journeys, the weather is fine and the roads in excellent condition."

Serena's heart thumped. She was to be pitchforked into his home today? "Arabella intends to come with us," she said.

"I am supposed to fit four and baggage into my rig?" His voice was sharp with irritation, and she flinched.

"I don't know, my lord. I, at least, have very little baggage."

They covered the rest of the walk in silence.

When they arrived at the cottage, however, Lord Middlethorpe gave his groom instructions to ride into Marlborough and hire a traveling chaise for a journey to London.

"London?" Serena asked. "But, my lord . . ."

"London," he said shortly. "I'm sure you have purchases to make, and it would hardly be fair to you or my mother to break the news by turning up unannounced. I will write and forewarn her."

Then Arabella appeared and plans were made. She approved of the trip to London and reasserted her intention to accompany them. She gave orders to her housekeeper to prepare a substantial meal, then set out with them for St. Martin's church.

To Serena, it all seemed dreamlike and impossible. She could not really be about to marry a man she had spent less than a day with.

But she was, and she had to.

As they approached St. Martin's church, Serena was at least glad she would be married in this old church. Her previous wedding had been in the drawing room at Stokeley, a place with no spiritual atmosphere at all. St. Martin's was charming and rich with the atmosphere of seven hundred years. In her weeks in the village, Serena had come to know it well. She had prayed well there, and for her it was a holy place.

The kindly vicar was waiting for them, beaming, obviously convinced this was a romantic affair. A number of villagers, sensing what was afoot, slipped in to attend.

Reverend Downs gave a brief but playful homily, making much of the gallant hero who had claimed the fair lady by an arrow straight to the heart. Then he conducted the ceremony.

Serena's new husband had obtained a simple gold band to slide onto her finger. He said his vows without hesitation. She said her vows clearly, hoping she would be able to keep them without destroying herself.

Lord Middlethorpe turned to her, and she couldn't miss the troubled shadow in his eyes as he kissed her briefly on the lips.

Serena said an extra prayer that somehow this marriage would be a source of joy to him.

Reverend Downs insisted that the couple step into the vicarage for a moment for a congratulatory glass of Madeira. Francis made no objection, giving some coins to one of the villagers with the instruction that they all go and drink to the new couple's health at the Duke of Marlborough Inn.

The vicar and his wife could not help but indulge their curiosity about this match, but Lord Middlethorpe handled it easily.

"My wife and I met some months ago, sir, and became close, but the death of her first husband was too recent for her to make decisions on a second marriage. Once she agreed, however, I was in no mind to wait."

The vicar chuckled. "I can quite see that, my lord. Permit me to say that you have acquired a treasure. Your wife has created quite a stir during her weeks amongst us. But she has created great joy, too. A genuinely kind heart. She will be missed."

Serena felt tears prick at her eyes, for sincerity rang in Reverend Down's voice. She smiled at the man. "I will miss Summer St. Martin, too, vicar. You have all been very kind to me here."

He beamed. "You're not hard to be kind to, my dear Lady Middlethorpe. But I am pleased to be handing you into the care of Lord Middlethorpe. His aunt speaks much of him, and all of it good. Not one of these rackety young bucks we hear too much of."

Then they were on their way back to the cottage, Arabella discreetly walking a little distance behind.

Serena glanced up at her husband. "I had not fully realized that I would be Lady Middlethorpe. Is there anything I should know about it?"

"It shouldn't be a great burden," he said coolly. "It is not a high title, like countess or duchess."

"What duties will I have?"

"None you do not care for. My mother handles everything. Leave this for now," he said rather impatiently. " *'Sufficient unto the day is the evil thereof.'* " Then he winced. "I did not intend that quite the way it sounded."

Serena could not help but be hurt, though.

There was a lavish spread at the cottage. Arabella and Lord Middlethorpe did justice to it, but Serena did not. She picked at a slice of tongue.

"Serena," said Arabella testily, "you must eat. You'll make yourself ill."

Serena looked at the meat distastefully and picked up a slice of bread and butter. She glanced at her husband, thinking he might command her to eat something more sustaining, particularly when it might be his son and heir at risk. Though he frowned a little, he said nothing.

She would eat, she told herself, when things were just a little more settled. At the moment, the thought of food made her stomach rebel.

Her possessions were packed, so when Lord Middlethorpe's man returned with the coach and four, it was a matter of moments to put their luggage into the boot and be off. Postilions were now in charge, and Kipling was left to take the curricle home. He was also carrying a letter to Francis's mother informing her that she was now the Dowager Lady Middlethorpe.

Serena had to be happy not to be there when that news arrived.

As they bowled out of Summer St. Martin, Serena sat stiffly in her seat, both glad and sorry to have a third person on this journey. She was anxious to learn more of her husband, to find out how he would behave toward her, but she was also very afraid.

"Went off well," said Arabella gruffly. "Nice simple wedding. Don't care for these grand affairs. You'd think some people were staging a theatrical rather than exchanging vows."

Lord Middlethorpe looked across at Serena. "How did this compare to your first wedding, my dear?" There was an edge to the question, and she knew he was taunting her.

Was he going to turn churlish now that she was trapped?

"It was very similar," she said, hands tight beneath the cloak. She felt the smooth band on her finger, subtly different from the one it had replaced.

Suddenly, she opened her reticule and pulled out her two old rings. "Take these, please," she said, and passed them to her husband. It was a gesture of trust, and she hoped he took it as such.

Not that it mattered anymore. All her possessions were his to do with as he wished. Including her body.

He looked at the rings. "What do you wish me to do with them?"

"Dispose of them suitably." She was referring to his offer to sell them, but to her astonishment, he lowered the carriage window and hurled them into the hedgerow.

"Here!" screeched Arabella. "Have you run mad, Francis?"

He slammed the window shut again. "I'll give Serena the value of them."

"So I would hope, but if you've a mind to toss such baubles around, toss 'em my way. I have many uses for their value."

He flashed her a cynical look. "You have plenty of money, too."

"No harm in a little more."

Serena wondered what on earth had possessed him to throw her rings away. She had to admit that if they hadn't stood between her and starvation, she might have done the same thing, but *he* had no cause to be disgusted by them.

"Speaking of money," said Arabella militantly,

"when we are in London, I intend to instruct my man-of-business to draw up settlements to ensure Serena's welfare."

Serena made a sound of denial, but her husband said, "Of course. But my man will draw them up. Yours can go over them if you don't trust me." Then he pulled out a paper and passed it to Serena. "There is also this. It is for your own use, to do with as you wish."

She found it was a draft for three thousand guineas, signed with his name.

"What is this for, my lord?" she asked with a touch of horror. Payment for that one wicked act? What was a high-class whore worth? She did not know.

"I wish you to call me Francis," he said sharply.

Serena looked up, wanting to say, And I wish you to be kind to me. But she knew she did not deserve kindness.

"Francis, then," she sighed. "What is this draft for?"

"It is not *for* anything. It is your money obtained from your brothers."

"But how . . . ?"

"A wager," he said tersely.

"My goodness," said Arabella, "that was well done. It would have been deuced awkward, dragging it through the courts. But what of Serena's jewels?"

"I don't want them," Serena said.

"Well, you should want them," said Arabella firmly. "Any jewelry given to you during the marriage is indisputably yours. We'll consult a lawyer."

"You will do nothing unless Serena wishes it," said Francis.

Serena touched Arabella's hand. "I am completely satisfied with the money."

Arabella gave a snort of disgust.

Serena, however, was overwhelmed with relief that she would never have to see those ornaments again. If necessary, she would have taken them and sold them to survive, but this was much better. She tucked the draft neatly into her reticule, then listened as Arabella and Francis had a very businesslike discussion of marriage settlements.

Serena had known nothing of the settlements of her first marriage, and the present discussion confused her. To her, marriage meant confinement in the country with everything purchased for her. All this talk of pin money, together with arrangements for household accounts, was new and frightening. In fact, in these matters she was still an ignorant fifteen-year-old.

Lord Middlethorpe looked at her. "Is this agreeable, Serena?"

"I think so," she said, hiding her fear and ignorance. "If there are to be documents, perhaps I could look at them."

"Of course you should look at them," said Arabella sternly. "Keep your wits about you, gel. Turn out to be a widgeon and I'll wash my hands of you."

Conversation lapsed after that. Serena gazed out the window at the bleak winter landscape, worrying about new responsibilities.

Even though her mother had died when she was eight, she had never been encouraged to deal with household management at home. Her father had hired a housekeeper who took care of everything. With adult wisdom, she had come to realize that Mrs. Dorsey had doubtless earned her wages in Sir Malcolm Allbright's bed as well, but she had kept Grove House in good order.

At Miss Mallory's, household management was a subject dealt with in the later years, which she had missed.

At Stokeley Manor she had been mistress in name, but as she had been given no money, the title had been hollow. The servants had run the place according to Matthew's orders. They had not consulted her at all except in such minor matters as what she would like for her meals.

Now she was to be put in charge of her husband's properties, which included at least a town house and his estate. Lord Middlethorpe said his mother would continue to take care of everything, but would the dowager wish to, and if she did, did Serena want that? Growing in her mind was the bold notion that she would like to run her own household, and run it well.

As the light began to fade, more immediate concerns grew in Serena's mind. Soon she would be alone with Lord Middlethorpe as his wife for the first time.

What would he want of her?

Under her cloak, she began to tremble. She desperately wished she could avoid the coming night.

She could plead the child. She had to cough to stifle a burst of wild laughter at that unconscious parody of the reason a convicted woman could give for not being hanged.

After she had forced herself on him once, however, Lord Middlethorpe—Francis—would hardly be sympathetic to any modest qualms on her part tonight.

Perhaps the inn would be crowded, so that a private

room for Arabella would be impossible to procure. She prayed for it.

Soon they drew up at the Bear in Esher, a pleasant, solid inn that Serena regarded with deep disquiet. It was spacious and did not look like the sort of establishment to run out of rooms in February.

Her belief was proved true. Francis had no difficulty in obtaining a suite of rooms consisting of two bedrooms and a private parlor.

Soon they were in the latter, with a large table being laid for their meal. Arabella went immediately to hold her hands out to the welcoming fire and Serena joined her.

Arabella moved aside. "Come closer, gel. You're looking chilled. All right, aren't you? You seem to be taking this business like a trooper, but don't hold back if you're feeling not the thing. We can make arrangements."

Serena stared at Arabella but then realized that she was referring to her pregnancy, not her wedding night. "I am quite well," she said. "Just a little chilled, and perhaps a little weary."

Francis came over without his greatcoat. "Can you dispense with your cloaks yet?" he asked, then eased them off and laid them aside. "I've ordered a bowl of punch. That should warm us all. Tomorrow's journey will be short as we only have a little over ten miles to go."

"I have never been to London," Serena said.

"Have you not? Then I will take pleasure in showing it to you." It was said courteously without warmth. "And you will doubtless wish to make many purchases."

"I could send to my brothers for my clothing," she offered hesitantly.

"No." His voice was rather sharp. "It will be more pleasant to start afresh."

Serena agreed wholeheartedly with that. She thought she might be able to have an intelligent conversation with her husband if Arabella weren't there, but situated as they were it was impossible. And she would not be without Arabella for the world.

The innkeeper came in with a large, steaming bowl of punch, and they all sat down to enjoy it. In a little while Serena felt her tension ease.

"So," she said, "tell me how you won three thousand guineas from my brothers, my lord."

A mischievous grin lightened his face. It was the first time she had seen him smile in such a way, and it suited him. She smiled a little herself, for she could see he was quite proud of himself.

"It was all on account of a hell-horse called Banshee," he said, and told them the story.

Serena actually found herself laughing. "That was truly noble! Oh, how I wish I had been there to see Tom's face. He must have been furious."

"I fear he was," agreed Francis with a distinct twinkle. "Serves him right. I almost wished I'd managed to palm off the horse on him as well, but he'd have fed him to his dogs, and the beast deserves better than that."

"What will you do with him, then?"

"Lord knows, for I never want to ride him again. I suspect he'll live a life of leisure, eating my grass and believing he's won the game after all."

"You'd keep a horse you will not ride?" Serena asked in wonder.

"He served me well," was his only reply.

By that time their meal had arrived and they set to. Aware of eyes on her, Serena managed to eat the soup and a little of the rare beef, but she refused the apple pie.

Without asking, Francis peeled an apple and sliced it onto a plate for her. "Eat it," he said.

Her first marital command. Serena sighed and chewed her way through the apple.

Arabella suddenly stood. "Well, I'm for my bed. These old bones don't travel well anymore."

Francis raised his brows at this unlikely statement, but he made no objection and politely opened the door to his aunt's room. "Good night."

"Good night," said Arabella. She looked at her nephew as if she might add something else, but she didn't.

Francis came back toward the table. "Are you finished?"

It was time to face her fate. Serena stood. "Yes, thank you."

He took her hand. "It would please me if you would eat a little more. You have to think of the child."

She looked up at him. "I will. My appetite was quite good until . . . until recently. It is just that matters are so unsettled."

"Matters are quite firmly settled."

She flinched at the edge in his voice. "No they are not. I feel adrift."

"I suppose I feel adrift, too," he admitted. "But our course is settled." He touched the ring on her finger.

"There is a family betrothal ring. I will have it for you soon."

Serena wanted to protest, as if she had no right to it.

Dear Lord, if only she had not been taken by that mad impulse in the Posts' bedroom.

But in that case, Francis would have washed his hands of her. Oh, he would have made some arrangement, but she would have played no part in his life, and that would have been a shame. . . .

"Perhaps you would care to retire."

Serena's mouth dried as she recognized the command.

"If you ring," he continued, "one of the inn's maids will come to assist you."

Serena went to the bedchamber thinking that at least he did not intend to rip the clothes off her. Of course, ripping well-made wool would not be an easy business. . . . Her mind was skittering around, seeking to avoid the central matter.

The maid assisted Serena out of her garments and into the plain flannel nightgown. Serena realized then that she should have tried to obtain some more appealing nightwear. There had been no time, but would he realize that? An alternative occurred to her, but she would not, could not, await him naked.

The maid brushed and braided her hair, then tidied the room and left.

Serena reviewed herself anxiously. Remembering Matthew's rage whenever he found her in bed with her hair braided, she undid the plaits and spread her long hair around her shoulders. She wiped her damp and trembling palms on the heavy cloth of the nightgown and climbed into the warm bed, heart thumping.

Really, it was absurd to be so terrified. It was beyond belief that her new husband ask anything of her tonight that she had not already endured. And yet she was deeply frightened. She was aware of too many horrible possibilities, aware that supposedly civilized men could show another side entirely in the privacy of the bed.

At least on her last wedding night she had been ignorant. . . .

Unable to bear sitting up, Serena slid down beneath the covers and worked at calming her scurrying heart.

Her husband came in. He scarcely glanced at her, but her eyes tracked him as he went behind the screen to undress and wash. She studied each sound he made, as if it were a clue to a puzzle. Eventually, he emerged in a nightshirt and joined her in the bed. He left the candles burning.

Memories of another occasion came back like a brutal wave. How could she have been so wicked?

"I am so very sorry," she whispered, staring at the bed canopy.

"Sorry for what?"

"For all of this. If I'd not . . . if I'd trusted you not to abandon me . . ."

"What's done is done," he said flatly. "For the child's sake, you must stop worrying."

"I'll try."

"You could also look at me, perhaps." His voice was sharp.

She swiveled her eyes nervously. He was lying on his side, looking at her. "Of course."

"Devil take it, Serena, you've presumably achieved your aim, so why these tragedy airs?"

"Achieved my aim?"

"Me. Marriage. A title. You've done very well and I won't hold it against you, but I'm damned if I'm going to be made to feel like a brute over it."

He thought she'd seduced him with this in mind? "I didn't—"

"Spare me. You most certainly did."

She felt the color flood her face. "I said I was sorry, and I am. For me as well as for you. The last thing I wanted was to be married."

His expression conveyed total disbelief. He swooped down and captured her lips in a kiss.

Serena stiffened, shocked by the sudden intimacy after his disbelief, and by the anger in it.

She struggled, but he captured her hands and she found she had no recourse against his strength. His lips demanded more and more of her, and his body pressed on her. Her old defenses rushed back and she surrendered, pulling her mind away from what was being done to her body.

He broke the kiss. "Serena?" He sounded concerned. "I'm sorry if . . ." But then a touch of irritation entered his voice. "If you're going to pretend to be delicately offended, forget it. You're no virgin bride."

She blinked up at him, returning cautiously to her body. "I am not offended, my lord. Do what you want to do."

"On a rag doll?"

Serena studied him anxiously. "You frightened me."

The anger faded, or at least was shielded. "I'm sorry. I don't like lies."

"I was not lying."

"Forget it," he sighed. "It's spilt milk." He picked up a strand of her hair and fingered it gently, studying it as if it were of great worth. "It is softer than I thought it would be. . . ."

"I hope it pleases you. I hope I please you."

"How could you do otherwise?" But it was flatly said.

Serena did not know what to do, and the panic of it was swelling in her chest like a pain. She was an expert at submission and at a host of erotic skills, but she did not know what to do.

She did the one thing that seemed safe.

She had long ago lost any inhibitions about her naked body, only hating the sense of vulnerability that it brought. Now that they were together and he had not changed into a monster, she was no longer afraid of being naked.

She wriggled out of her nightgown. As her head emerged and she shook her hair back, she saw the heat in his eyes and relaxed. It would be all right.

She knelt up and presented herself to his gaze. She was supposed to be beautiful and she prayed he found her so. Matthew had been very interested in her breasts. They had always been full and in the past weeks had grown a little fuller. She glanced at Francis anxiously and saw the intent look in his eyes as they explored her.

"You are exquisite," he said, but guardedly.

He put out a strangely tentative hand and cupped one breast, testing the weight and texture of it. The very hesitancy touched Serena deeply. She had never experienced anything quite like it. She leaned into his touch a little and remained there, letting him do as he willed.

He raised his eyes to hers as the roughness of his

thumb brushed over her nipple. She caught her breath and saw his eyes darken in response.

He gently pushed her down onto the bed, sweeping back the covers so that she was completely exposed. Then he took off his own nightwear, so that he was as naked as she. Serena looked at him and marveled, realizing how little she knew of the male form.

Matthew had rarely stripped for his pleasures, but then Matthew's body had been better hidden.

Her new husband was as beautiful as the ancient gods. His lithe, well-muscled torso flared up to broad shoulders. In a strange way he looked bigger naked than clothed. Her gaze passed over his genitals but did not linger there. He was made like other men and such things held no fascination for her. She noted, however, that he was already well aroused. There was both relief and threat in that. There would be no need of extraordinary measures to stimulate him, but there would be no putting off his release.

To her surprise, he made no immediate move to seek his ease. Instead, he began to explore her with eye and hand, as if each curve of flesh, each edge of bone, were a new-found miracle. His touch was pleasant, but the rapt expression in his eyes was more so. She felt worshipped.

His hand came to rest, at last, over the gentle swelling of her womb. "Do you feel anything yet?"

"No."

"When you do, I want to know. I want to know about this child before it is born."

On instinct, she covered his hand with her own and held it there. "It *is* yours," she said.

"I know."

"How do you know?"

He looked up into her eyes with a faint smile. "I don't know how I know, and that's the truth. Do you not like being kissed?"

She was unprepared for the question. She thought of lying but knew her expression had given her away. "I haven't."

He dropped a light kiss on her lips, then let his mouth drift down to her breast. "What about here?"

The playful gentleness of his lips on her skin confused Serena. She thought she'd experienced everything that the marriage bed could encompass, but she had never experienced this slow, gentle exploration.

The experience was not entirely pleasant. She had no idea what her part was in this and was terrified of making a mistake. The quickest glance showed her that he was ready for her now, more than ready. Why the delay? What did he need from her?

She was hardly paying any attention to what he was doing, though the play of his lips was causing her some physical agitation. Then his head traveled down over the mound of her belly, paid homage to her navel, and kissed at the juncture of her thighs. "Do you like this?"

She knew what he was asking and again thought of lying, but the least she could give him was truth. "Not really. But you can," she added earnestly. "I don't mind."

He sighed and took one of her hands in his, easing it. She only then realized that she had clenched it into a fist.

Fool, she berated herself. *Fool!*

He released her hand and resumed his restless exploration of her body. His hand trembled a little, which was hardly surprising. He must be desperate. What did he *want?*

He slid up suddenly to look into her eyes. "What do you like, then?" he demanded.

She had no answer to that peculiar question.

His voice sharpened. "Come on, Serena. Give me a hint. This isn't a game *I* like to play."

She looked down and saw how darkly erect he was. No wonder he was angry. Unable to think of anything else, she reached for him. He slapped her hand away.

"What do you want from me?" she wailed. "I'll do anything."

He groaned, and without another word he pushed her legs apart. In his passion he was clumsy; she put down her hand to guide him and adjusted her hips skillfully to greet him, immensely relieved that they were finally at the point.

His whole body shuddered as he filled her. His eyes closed and he made a sound that was part sigh, part groan. Again his reaction was unlike anything she had seen in Matthew, but it did not crush her joy. This business she knew, and knew well.

She matched his thrusts, watching him carefully, using her muscles and her hands to increase his pleasure. When she'd watched Matthew it had been with disgusted wariness, hoping only to avoid his anger. With Francis it was a pleasure that came close to his ecstasy. She was astonished at how sweet she found his need.

She saw his release coming on him and tightened to slow it, to draw out the moment for herself as well as for him.

His eyes shot open, half pleading, half wondering.

They froze like that, gazes locked and entranced, until she released him to achieve his end.

He cried out and collapsed upon her, trembling and running with sweat. This time there was no bitter leave-taking. Serena stroked his damp curls gently, lovingly, and soothed his raptured body. She couldn't believe how much she had enjoyed pleasing this man, and how much she wanted to do it again.

She would not mind how often he made demands of her, for she finally knew the sweetness of the marriage bed.

Slowly, languorously, he eased up, nipping at her breast as he did. He smiled at her, stroking her tangled hair off her face, but then a frown touched his sated eyes. "What about you?"

"Me?"

"What of your pleasure?"

"I liked that very much." In turn, she stroked his damp ebony curls back and smiled. "Truly, Francis. That was lovely."

The frown did not lift, but he merely dropped a butterfly kiss on her lips. "We'll have to work on it, but not now. I have never been so sweetly exhausted in my life."

He rolled, carrying her with him so she was snuggled in his arms. For a moment she stiffened with shock, for she had never experienced such a thing. But she allowed him to mold her firmly to his body so they melded there, one flesh, in a way quite different from coupling but in many ways sweeter.

Serena felt the fine contours of his body against hers, alive with youth and health, slick with the sweat on him. She could hear his heart beating steadily, could smell an aroma that blended sweat and sex but was amazingly pleasing. Such smells before had nauseated her, but now they were like perfume.

His hand moved gently over her back, bringing a delight such as she had never known, for it spoke to her of tenderness. She began to feel a trace of something new in this man's arms.

She had no name for it, but it was good.

Francis sensed when his wife drifted into sleep, but he continued his lax exploration of her silken back.

He was finding exhaustion didn't last very long, but he'd be a monster to demand more lovemaking now, especially from a woman who gained so little pleasure from it. He frowned down at her, wondering what he had done wrong or left undone. Theoretical knowledge was all very well, but the complexity, the wonder of the truth, left him feeling like a child.

A wondering but apprehensive child.

Though he had chosen to avoid casual sex, he had never seen any virtue in ignorance. Nicholas had once remarked that in a time and place where brides were supposed to be innocent, it was a man's duty to be both knowledgeable and wise. Francis had taken the message to heart and educated himself about erotic matters. In addition, talk among the Rogues was frank and he had gained by that.

He obviously had not gained enough. Perhaps he would have been wiser to seek out some experienced woman—someone like Blanche—and take lessons. It was clear he was doing something wrong.

Even in his passion, when his control had broken, he

had been aware that she had not been with him but had been ministering to him, ministering to him with exquisite skill. That might be what a man wanted of a whore; it wasn't what he wanted in a wife.

Chapter 10

Serena awoke late to the sound of bells and realized it was Sunday. Sunlight streamed through a gap in the curtains, and the mantel clock told her it was gone nine o'clock. Her husband was still beside her, just opening his eyes.

She considered him cautiously. "I am not usually such a slugabed, I assure you."

He smiled. "Perhaps I am."

Heartened, she smiled back. "For some reason, I do not believe that. I suppose we should attend church, though."

"Assuredly."

Serena found she was feeling unusually happy. Not deliriously so, for the future was still full of uncertainties, but happy to have a solid foundation for her life, that foundation being this man.

He wouldn't abandon her. She knew that now.

And she didn't think he would abuse her.

He caught a tendril of her hair and wound it around his finger. "I think perhaps we both needed a good rest.

I have been traveling for days, and you must have been in some anxiety."

She looked down at his strong brown hand. "It has not been easy."

"I would have come more quickly if Aunt Arabella had been specific."

Serena decided not to tell him why Arabella had been vague. He would be hurt, for he was a good man. She was unaccustomed to good men but was perfectly willing to learn.

He released her hair. "Since you are the one unaccustomed to being a slugabed, I think you should rise first."

She eyed him. "Why?"

"I want to ogle you."

At his mock leer, she laughed and sprang out of bed to stand before him. "Ogle, sir. Soon I will look like an inflated bladder."

"I don't think so," he said absently as he studied her. "Lord, but you're beautiful. You are perfectly formed. . . ."

She interpreted the look in his eyes. "It is not so late . . ."

He flushed, as if caught in some crime. "Yes, it is. Arabella has probably been up for hours. Stop tempting me, wife, and put on your shift at least."

Confused, Serena pulled on her short silk shift and glanced at him. "Better?"

"Only a little," he said dryly, climbing out of bed.

As he walked to the chair upon which he had placed his clothes, Serena stole the chance to study him. He turned and caught her at it, but smiled slightly. "And do I please you?" he asked.

"You are beautiful," she said, and meant it. He was all lithe elegance and long, strong muscles, and he moved with exceptional grace.

He colored slightly. "Hardly that. I'm a skinny sort of fellow."

"I don't think so."

Clearly embarrassed, he turned away to dress.

Serena found she was victim to an almost overpowering compulsion to fondle his muscular buttocks. She saw them disappear into his drawers with great regret.

This was most peculiar.

She sighed and turned to attend to her own dress.

They maided and valeted each other, and though nothing was said, Serena thought that they both found pleasure in serving and being served. Such little things, but so important.

She had never wanted Matthew's attentions of any kind.

Francis brushed out her hair with all the gentleness of a good maid, and Serena almost purred like a cat.

"Like that, do you?" he asked softly, watching her in the mirror.

She could not deny it.

"I will learn," he said. "I will learn what makes you melt, Serena, and melt you thoroughly."

She almost protested, for she was not consciously withholding anything from him, but she sensed what he meant. Unfortunately, she knew that the surrender he wanted was not, could not be, deliberate. As he gave her the brush and she began to fasten up her hair, Serena wondered if she were capable of being the kind of wife Lord Middlethorpe wanted, or whether Matthew Riverton had killed that woman during those eight years of slavery.

When they emerged for breakfast, Arabella gave them both a searching look but said nothing. As Francis had expected, Arabella had already eaten, and so they did not dawdle over their breakfast. Afterward, they walked over to the handsome church and attended the Sunday service, and then they went on their way.

The journey to London was soon accomplished.

As they passed through the rural outskirts of the city, Serena gazed out the window in fascination and trepidation. She saw vast market gardens being prepared to grow food for the masses of people who lived in London. She saw rows of smart new houses swallowing up farmland. She saw manufactories making the thousand and one things needed by people here and elsewhere.

Soon they were in the city proper. It was an exciting place but frightening, not just because of its size and bustle, but because it was the place where she would have to act as Lady Middlethorpe. Moreover, she suddenly realized, it was just the sort of place where she might meet someone who had known her as Matthew Riverton's well-trained wife.

Only a handful of men and a few of the demimonde had been invited to visit Stokeley Manor, but those men had mostly been of the upper ten thousand—the sort with whom Matthew had wanted to curry favor. She suspected that they ranked somewhere after nine thousand nine hundred ninety and would not be considered at all respectable, but it was possible she might meet one of them here. If such a man gossiped about what had gone on at Stokeley, Society would turn its back.

All in all, mother-in-law or not, Serena would much rather have been arriving at Francis's country home. Instead, the chaise drew up in front of 32 Hertford Street, a handsome, stuccoed, double-fronted house with gleaming windows and a polished brass knocker on the door. This told Serena that Francis must have sent word ahead that he was expected.

To confirm her belief, the black lacquered door swung open and a number of servants emerged to minister to their master. They showed no apparent surprise at the existence of a new Viscountess Middlethorpe.

The interior of the house proved to be as pleasant and well maintained as the exterior. The spacious hall was tiled, and sprinkled with tasteful ornaments and paintings. A handsome wide oak staircase rose in front of her, then broke into two sinuous curves. She was gently steered past curtsying and bowing servants up those stairs.

Arabella and Francis were chatting of minor matters, but Serena was absorbed by the massive portrait that loomed over the central landing where the stairs divided. It showed two stately people who could only be Francis's parents twenty or so years ago.

His father appeared quite pleasant; there was something about the expression in his brown eyes that reminded Serena of Francis. His mother looked dauntingly gracious. Her beauty came from a rather fearsome projection of good bones and color, and even in oils on canvas, she was alarming.

Serena was frozen there. Francis gently pulled her

onward. "Monstrous, isn't it? It needs to be hung in an enormous chamber where one only need view it from a distance.

"They look a fine couple."

"I suppose so. My father was more energetic than he appears there, but it is quite like my mother. She still looks much the same after twenty years."

Serena shivered and thought that at least she would recognize her if she saw her—which would give her the opportunity to run and hide under the stairs.

Within moments they were in a beautiful drawing room with white painted walls and a vaulted ceiling. Though there was a charming air of informality, Serena judged it to be the kind of informality that is long thought on and carefully preserved. She'd never dare to move a vase here.

"This is a lovely house, my lord," she said as she gingerly took a seat in a chair upholstered in rose-patterned silk.

"Francis," he correctly gently. "I am pleased you like it, for it is now one of your homes."

"Yes, of course," she mumbled, trying not to quake. It was dawning on her that this room—in fact, the whole house—had been created and cherished by someone. That someone had to be Francis's mother, and she was going to hate having an intruder become mistress here.

Especially when the intruder was Randy Riverton's widow.

When the butler and a maid brought in a tea tray and a stand of cakes, Serena made herself take charge of it and do the duties of the mistress of the establishment. If she didn't, she would fail entirely.

"Good gel," said Arabella quietly. "Begin as you mean to go on."

As soon as she had finished her tea, however, Arabella announced that she intended to go out and visit some old friends. Francis overrode some objections and insisted that she take a footman.

When Arabella had left, he showed Serena their bedchambers—two lofty rooms with an adjoining door. To cover her nervousness, Serena asked, "Is Arabella in danger that she needs an escort?"

"Probably not, but I don't care to have her wandering about London unescorted. She doesn't come here often." He restlessly opened and closed an armoire. "You will need a personal maid, I suppose. Arrange for one of the maids here to attend you until we find you one."

"And what of me?"

He turned. "I beg your pardon?"

"Will I need an escort, too?"

"I certainly do not want you wandering about unescorted," Francis said rather sharply. In a milder voice, he added, "Whenever possible, I will be your escort, but if not, you must command one of the maids or footmen."

Serena understood perfectly. In these matters, then, her second marriage was not to be much different from her first. She was forbidden to go about freely, when and where she wished.

"I wish to hire my own maid," she stated firmly.

"Of course. The best way would be to request one of the agencies to send around some candidates. Dibbert, the butler, could see them first if you wish."

"Very well." Serena had no idea how these things

were done, but this time she wanted a maid who would not be a warden.

"We do not keep a carriage in London," Francis continued, "as my mother has not been in the habit of spending much time here. You have merely to send to Villier's Livery for an excellent one to be placed at your convenience. Dibbert can handle all such matters."

"Very well."

They lunched alone together, eventually relaxing into ordinary chat, then Francis took her off to explore the nearer parts of London. They strolled down to Piccadilly, past Green Park and into the area called St. James. Serena was astonished to find a boating pond in the middle of St. James's Square. Though there were a few hardy souls rowing on it, Francis laughingly refused to take part on a chilly day in February.

In St. James's Park he pointed out where the Chinese bridge had been, which had so spectacularly burned down during the premature peace celebrations in 1814, and bought her a syllabub from the dairy there.

Serena watched the dairymaid squeezing milk, warm from the cow's udder, onto wine, sugar, and spices, and she ventured a protest. "I am not sure I will care for it, Francis."

"It is just the thing to build up a woman's strength."

Serena was just beginning to feel resentful when he grinned. "Don't worry. If you hate it, you don't have to eat it. It's considered a delicacy by many, though."

The milk had curdled to make a kind of pudding. Serena screwed up her face as she took the first taste, but then relaxed. "It's very nice!"

He laughed, and for a moment looked carefree.

When she had finished the dish, they wandered through the park to Whitehall and watched a parade of troops there. Serena was enjoying herself tremendously, but Francis looked at her and said, "I think I'm tiring you out."

"It's been great fun."

"Good. But we'll take a hackney home. It is growing dark, anyway." On the way home, he directed the driver to take them along Pall Mall so Serena could admire the gaslights that were just being summoned to life.

"How wonderful," she said, fascinated by a gaslighter at his work. "We live in an age of marvels, don't we?"

"Yes, we do." When Serena turned, however, he seemed to be looking at her. She saw desire, but more than desire. Could he be growing just a little fond of her? She was growing more than a little fond of him.

Impulsively, she touched his hand, and he turned it to hold hers.

Over dinner, Serena told Arabella of their adventures, then afterward they all played cards for a while. Serena soon embarrassed herself by yawning, however. She cast an anxious look at her husband, for she had sometimes pleaded tiredness to Matthew in hopes of avoiding an intrusion in her bed.

It had never done any good at all. In fact, it had made him angry.

Francis didn't seem annoyed. He merely smiled and suggested that she go to bed. When he chose to escort her there, she wondered about his intentions, but he left her with a gentle kiss on the cheek. Serena wished she could urge him to her bed, but she truly was exhausted. She was not usually so feeble, so she had to assume that this was the effect of carrying a child. If she was not to anger her husband, however, she would have to be careful not to become so tired in future.

When Serena went downstairs the next morning, she found Francis and Arabella at breakfast. "My goodness," Serena said anxiously, "you make me feel such a sluggard. I do promise to do better—"

"Good Lord, Serena," declared Arabella. "A woman in your condition is allowed to rest."

Serena sat and ate a hearty breakfast. As the days passed and her husband remained kind and courteous, her appetite was reviving.

When she had finished, Francis said, "If you are up to it, Serena, I think we should make some purchases for you."

"Must we?"

He raised a brow. "Your wardrobe is hardly adequate for a fashionable life."

"But if we were to be unfashionable . . ."

"We would soon be bored to tears. Unless we stay indoors entirely, we are bound to encounter members of Society."

That was exactly what Serena was afraid of. Ah, well, if she had to face disaster, she might as well do it in fine feathers. She made no further objection, and they were soon on their way in the hired, but elegant, barouche.

Serena had never bought any of her own clothes except for a few simple personal items. As a girl, first her mother, then the housekeeper had arranged for them; as a wife, Matthew had sent her clothes from London as the mood took him. Consequently, she entered the discreet modiste's establishment very nervously.

Madame Augustine D'Esterville proved to be a lively Frenchwoman who was delighted to have a wealthy customer at such a dead time of year and ecstatic to have a beautiful one.

Francis cut short the woman's raptures with the information that Lady Middlethorpe was in an interesting condition.

"Hélas!" exclaimed Madame.

Serena started.

"We are, of course, delighted," said Francis coldly.

The modiste flushed. "Of course, milord. I meant only that it was a shame that London will enjoy Lady Middlethorpe's beauty for so short a time this year. And, milady," she continued to Serena, "to dress you will be pure joy, and I will allow ample material in the skirt for your convenience. And next year, you come back to me and we create a sensation, yes?"

Serena smiled politely, but to herself she said, Not if I have any say in the matter. Once safe in the country, she intended to bury herself there for the rest of her life.

Serena was measured and eyed and then presented with a bewildering array of fabrics and designs. At first she was hesitant, but then discovered that she did have a clear idea of the sort of garments she wanted—elegant but very discreet.

As a consequence, she and the modiste had a few genteel disagreements.

Madame Augustine ventured that milord might prefer a slightly lower bodice to this particular dress. It was the fashion.

Serena insisted that it remain exactly as she had specified.

Madame recommended a soft and clinging fabric.

Serena chose the more sturdy one.

The modiste shrugged with Gallic fatalism. "With your looks, milady, you could wear sackcloth neck to toe."

Francis took no part in the selection and merely waited patiently. The astute Madame D'Esterville had copies of the sporting papers and the *Monthly Magazine* available for her customer's escorts, and he appeared happy to peruse them.

When Serena was finished, Francis took her off to purchase some made-up items: chemisettes, neckerchiefs, scarves, gloves, and bonnets, as well as drawers, stays, and stockings. These were mostly only for immediate use. Better ones were ordered to be made especially for her.

Serena had to admit to finding pleasure in the novelty of visiting different emporiums and making selections for herself, but she eyed her patient escort curiously. "I would have thought you would find this tedious."

He smiled slightly. "It is not the most exciting business, but I have a mother and three sisters. I am accustomed. Ah, this is more appealing."

It was a jeweler's that had caught his eye. He led Serena in to purchase a fine silver brush and comb, fillets for her hair, pins, bracelets, pendants, and a jewelry box to keep them in.

Serena was delighted, but she noted that none were particularly expensive.

He caught the thought. "There are plenty of grand ornaments at home. These are just for fun."

"Fun," said Serena, fighting tears over the pretty bounty placed before her. She had not realized until then just how extraordinary it was that she had never had any normal jewels other than her rings.

Since Serena only had a couple of pairs of plain slippers and her half boots, a shoemaker was found who could promise a number of pairs of silk slippers, one by tomorrow.

"No riding, I suppose," said Francis regretfully.

"I don't know how, anyway," she said.

"You don't know how?" he echoed. "That we can rectify in time."

A future opened before Serena like a beautiful vista. She had known they were starting a life together, but until this moment she had not thought of next year, and ten years, and twenty. She looked at her husband as he considered some perfumes in a perfumer's. What would he be like at forty? At sixty? She thought his fine-boned elegance would age well.

Was it possible that she would be by his side to see it?

He turned and raised a brow to see her staring. "You should choose, I think," he said. "Perfume is a personal thing."

"But I would wear it for you. Which do you favor?"

He touched one vial. "This one."

Serena tested it and decided to be honest yet again. "No. It is too flowery for me."

She investigated others and then found the one she

203

liked. It was soft and subtle, but more spicy than flowery. "I like this one," she said.

He put a little on her wrist and raised it to breathe in the fragrance. "God, yes," he breathed. "That's perfect." And his eyes told her he wanted her, then and there.

Serena had always regarded male desire as the enemy, something to be avoided at all costs. Now she was discovering that it was rather pleasant to arouse desire in Francis, and that she wouldn't mind satisfying that desire.

The assistant was happily wrapping a purchase of perfume, creams and soap in her chosen fragrance. Serena faced her husband. "You were afraid I'd choose something like that other perfume, weren't you?"

"Yes."

"I hated it."

"Good." He smiled and lowered his voice. "You know I want you, don't you? Want you here and now."

She could feel color in her cheeks, in part from her alarm at what he might actually want to do. "Yes . . ."

"I am going to restrain myself. I am not even going to take you straight back home and ravish you. After all, I am going to have to develop great self-control, or I'll be a husk in a week."

And Serena giggled, the first time she had ever giggled about sex.

Once out of the shop, Francis asked, "What would you like to do now?"

Serena tried to judge what he would like but

couldn't, so she said, "I enjoyed what we did yesterday—just exploring the city."

"Very well, but not so much walking. We don't want you so tired again." Then he looked rather self-conscious and she had to stifle another burst of amusement. "We'll drive by the Tower," he said briskly. "If you'd like, we could visit the Mint."

She wondered if it were her wifely duty to demand sex so as to ease his conscience. But the night would be soon enough. "Can we really?" Serena asked. "I would like to see how money is made."

"By luck or hard work, I think," he commented dryly.

"And how would you know, my lord?" she teased.

He laughed. "Just you wait. Being of the peerage is no sinecure, as you'll find out."

They proceeded to Tower Hill in good accord.

Once in the Mint, Serena watched wide-eyed as a machine flung out one hundred glittering coins a minute. "Good heavens. What do they do with so much money?"

"The government uses it to pay its debts, and then we all use it to do the same."

"But where does it come from?"

"Gold and silver mines around the world." She would have asked more questions, but he put a finger to her lips. "Don't look too closely at the concept or it'll disappear like a fairy treasure."

Serena thought perhaps happiness was like that. She was happy at this moment, but it did not bear close scrutiny.

"How strange money is," she said as they strolled

on. "Important and yet silly. After all, bank notes are just pieces of paper. They are worth nothing."

"Words are worth nothing, unless backed by good faith."

His words and tone lingered in her mind all the way back to Hertford Street. Serena wanted to ignore that hint of trouble and cling to her fragile happiness, but it was not in her nature to choose to be blind.

When they were alone, she challenged him. "Do you doubt my good faith, Francis?"

He gave her a somber look but answered frankly. "I don't know. You seem to keep part of yourself contained, away from me."

"We have only been wed two days," she protested. "And before that, we scarce knew each other at all."

"True." But his somberness did not lift.

Serena saw her happiness disappear as she had feared it would, swallowed by his very reasonable doubts. She pleaded a need to rest and went to lie on her bed, half hoping that he would come and let her give the one gift she had to offer.

He did not, and she recognized wryly he would never intrude upon her when she had pleaded tiredness. He was too much a gentleman. A gentle man, she mused. A precious treasure, that. Everything was so complicated, so different from what she had known.

Life would be a good deal simpler if her husband were not so kind and sensitive, but she could not regret those qualities.

When they gathered for dinner that evening, Arabella announced that she intended to leave Hertford Street the next morning to stay with her friend Maud for the rest of her time in London.

"Goodness, Aunt," said Francis dryly. "Are you confident, then, that Serena is safe in my male clutches?"

"Puppy!" snorted Arabella. "I'll still be around, won't I, if she needs me."

"I wouldn't worry," said Francis. "She's a Rogue by marriage, and I've already written to tell Beth Arden of this development."

Serena noted the name with surprise, but said nothing. She was afraid to hope.

The three of them talked desultorily of economic and political affairs for a while, and then Arabella again managed an excuse to retire early, as she had on their wedding night.

As Francis rose to open the door for his aunt, he said, "I am growing alarmed at your sudden lack of stamina, Aunt. Would you like me to obtain a restorative tonic for you?"

"If you find one, take it yourself. You'll soon need it, I suspect."

At the sudden rise of color in her husband's cheeks, Serena ducked her head to hide a grin. Arabella was a gem. If only Francis's mother were like her.

Serena was not at all reluctant to contribute to her husband's exhaustion, however, and soon announced that she, too, felt ready to retire. She was careful *not* to mention tiredness. Francis went up with her to her room and even entered.

Serena waited, thinking he might want to begin their amours from this point, perhaps by undressing her. He did nothing, however, and so she went into her dressing room and summoned her maid to help her prepare for bed.

She wished he had begun to make love to her immediately, for now she found some of her nervousness returning. She had to face the fact that Francis had not been entirely pleased with her behavior on their wedding night. Unfortunately, she wasn't sure how to improve upon it. She could writhe and moan for him, but it seemed so deceitful.

When the maid had finished her work, Serena studied herself in the mirror. At least she had a new nightgown now. Having been bought ready-made, it was not a special garment—better ones had been ordered—but it was of finer lawn than the one she had worn before, and prettily trimmed with lace and ribbon at the high neck and cuffs.

The door opened and he came in. Serena tried not to show how startled she was. Despite his kindness, every time he did something the slightest bit unusual she tensed for an unpleasant surprise. It was not fair of her.

He was fully dressed, but must have been to his own room, for he now had a glass of brandy in his hand. He looked at her, and something in his expression sent a tiny shiver of unease across her shoulders. Serena tried to tell herself that it was her own disordered sensitivities, but could not.

Something was wrong.

The maid had already brushed her hair, but now Serena sat at her dressing table and picked up her brush again, nervously seeking a way to break the silence. "You mentioned Beth Arden," she said. "You mean Beth Armitage?"

He came over and took the brush, then began to

brush out her hair himself. "As was, yes. Her husband is a friend of mine."

His gentle action was at odds with a tension in him.

"Does that mean I will meet her?"

"I have no doubt of it."

The dark edge to the comment could not be ignored. "You do not approve, my lord?"

He let out an impatient breath. "Serena, stop looking at me like a puppy expecting to be kicked. If I even thought of forbidding you and Beth from meeting, she'd have my head."

Nervous in the face of his anger, Serena said quickly, "What is all this about rogues, my lord? It sounds very wicked."

"Not really." Despite his tension, his brush strokes were slow and gentle. "We were a schoolboy group, gathered to present a united front against bullies. Now we are just friends, but if any of us has a problem, he knows he can go to the others for help. Nicholas—he was our leader—when Nicholas married he decreed that wives would be members, too. Thus far we have Nicholas's wife Eleanor, Lucien's Beth, and Leander's new bride, though I haven't met her. And perhaps Blanche."

Serena picked up anxiously on that. "Why perhaps Blanche?" Was there a wife who wasn't accepted?

He made a few more sweeping strokes down the length of her hair. "Blanche Hardcastle is a mistress, not a wife." He tossed down the brush and moved away. "Nicholas would have my guts. Of course she's a Rogue."

"Oh." Nervously, Serena began to divide and plait

her hair, still watching him in the mirror. "Would I have been a Rogue as your mistress?"

"Yes. Though I'm not sure what would have happened when I married." He paced the room restlessly.

Serena turned to stare at him in astonishment, a sick feeling invading her stomach. "Did you plan to marry?"

He froze and glanced at her. "A man such as I must marry."

"I mean, did you have immediate plans to marry?"

She thought he would not answer, but he sighed. "There will probably be talk, so you may as well know. I was on the point on proposing to Lady Anne Peckworth."

Serena felt as if she'd been punched in the stomach. She'd never even considered this possibility. "Oh, Francis, I'm so sorry."

"I told you to stop saying you're sorry."

"But—"

"No. It's done. It's over. Anne will soon find another husband. She's the daughter of a duke and possessed of a very large dowry."

Serena turned back to the mirror, but she saw it through a film of tears. How could she bear this? *I'm sorry,* she said, but she said it silently, and continued mechanically to plait her hair. She saw him drain his brandy glass.

She rose wearily to go into her bedroom. He blocked her way to the door. She tried not to mind the way his eyes roamed over her—it was his right—but tonight there was an expression in them that she could not like.

"You look like a damned schoolgirl," he said.

Serena looked in the mirror and her heart sank. He

was right. She had picked this garment because it appealed to her, but she saw that it was all wrong. It was like the ones she had worn at Miss Mallory's before her first marriage.

And why had she completed the picture by plaiting her hair into two childish braids? Perhaps it had been the talk of Beth Armitage. This had been how they had looked as they sat on their beds in the night, sharing hopes and secrets. . . .

"I'm sorry," she muttered, and hurried to the dressing table to unravel her hair. Her hands shook slightly and her lips trembled. Now she'd angered him . . . and after he'd been so kind to her. And she'd ruined his chance to marry the woman of his choice.

"I don't suppose it matters."

The door clicked as he closed it behind him. He had gone to his own room. Would he come to her tonight? Did she want him to?

Serena stilled her frantic hands and rested her head on her knuckles.

He didn't want to be married to her, and she didn't want to be married to him—not like this, at least. She wanted to be innocent again, which was why she had bought this ridiculous nightgown.

She wanted to be fifteen again and excited about the school play. She wanted to flirt with young men like the ones in Summer St. Martin. She wanted to drift slowly into innocent love.

She wanted to join a husband in the marriage bed with some sense of wonder left, able to explore the possibilities of delight together. Instead, there was nothing he could show her that she did not know, and that she did not have reason to hate.

Not true, she told herself, straightening her spine.

Last night he had shown her the delights of tenderness and of giving.

But he'd wanted to marry Lady Anne Peckworth, she thought bleakly. All that tenderness should have been for her.

Serena dragged loose the bow at her throat, opening the neckline of the nightgown as far as it would go, then shook her head to spread her hair around her. Having done the best she could, she pushed wearily up from the bench and went to get into the bed.

She hadn't really expected him to join her, but he did, dressed this time in a long blue banyan with apparently nothing beneath it. She had judged wrongly again; she should have removed her nightgown entirely. Nonetheless, she found her heart pattering with a mixture of anxiety and tangled anticipation.

He put out the candles and tended the fire, his movements sure and deft. Serena decided she could gain endless pleasure from just watching her husband. He slipped off his banyan, but she only had a glimpse of his body before he joined her in the bed. Instead of touching her, he lay on his back in silence.

Minutes passed.

Was this normal? Serena had never in her life shared a bed with a man without some sort of sex. Not even, she thought wildly, when the man was a chance-met stranger.

Was she supposed to do something? She could sense a tension in him, pulsing over toward her through the air. She could not bear it. She reached out to touch him soothingly.

He moved suddenly. He covered her, pushed apart her thighs, and entered her in one rough movement.

Serena tensed in shock. He froze and muttered something. Immediately, she relaxed and welcomed him. She willingly offered her skills and gripped his buttocks to show that he was welcome. Of their own volition, her fingers flexed on his taut muscles there, massaging as he began to thrust into her.

He took his pleasure in silence, without a touch of mouth or hands, then, after a shuddering moment, rolled off her and turned away. "Good night," he said.

"Good night," said Serena into the dark.

Chapter 11

The next morning, Serena awoke late and alone. She had spent a good part of the night sleeplessly pondering matters, which had become worse rather than better.

He loved another.

It was one thing to marry a man who did not love you and whom you did not love. There was still hope in that. It was quite another to marry a man who wished he had wed elsewhere. There was no escape, however; nowhere to hide. As he had said, there was no point in crying over spilt milk.

She vomited, though, that morning. It was the first time, and Serena rather thought it was her misery, not her pregnancy, that had caused it.

She would have liked to hide in her room but that would achieve nothing, so she rang for a maid and dressed to face the day.

She found Arabella alone in the breakfast parlor, reading a newspaper. There was evidence that Francis had eaten there not long before.

Arabella laid aside her paper. "How are you, child? You're looking peaked. Not doing too much, are you?"

Serena sat and took a piece of cold toast. "No."

"Heavens, gel. Ring for some fresh food!" Before Serena could protest, Arabella did so.

"I'm not hungry, Arabella."

"No matter how small your appetite, it will be improved by warm food and fresh tea." When Dibbert came, she ordered it, then looked at Serena searchingly. "Francis didn't look too perky, either. Have you two had a fight?"

"Why would we fight?"

"Never known young people to need a reason to fight. Is he treating you well? I won't leave if you don't want me to, you know. Thought you'd do better on your own."

"There's no need for you to stay."

"Devil take it," snapped Arabella, "you're as bad as he is!"

Serena looked up at that. "Where is he?"

"Out. Said something about Tatt's." At Serena's questioning look, she added, "Tattersall's Repository, near Hyde Park Corner. They sell horses there, but the men use it as a meeting place. Settle gambling debts and such."

"Oh."

A maid came in with a laden tray and put out fresh toast, eggs, and tea under the supervision of the butler. "Anything else, milady?" he asked.

Serena looked at the daunting challenge before her and sighed. "No, thank you."

Yesterday, she remembered, her appetite had been quite good. That was because Francis had seemed content. Now she had to force down a slice of toast and a little of the eggs.

Misery was eating at her, and she had to deal with it. "Arabella," she said at last, "what do you know of Anne Peckworth?"

"Ah," said Arabella. "That's what has you in the dismals, is it? She's the second daughter of the Duke of Arran."

Serena cradled a cup of tea for warmth. "Does Francis love her?"

"How would I know? One thing's for sure: He's not likely to set her up in competition to you, is he, and she's even less likely to succumb. Quiet, properly behaved young lady, she is."

The opposite of me, thought Serena dismally. And even if both Anne and Francis were pattern cards of propriety, the young woman could be competition in his heart.

"I gather he was about to offer for her hand," Serena said.

"Quite possibly. My sister's been pushing for it for a year or so. She and the duchess are close, and Anne's just the sort of quiet gel she'd think would suit Francis."

"She should know."

"Ha! Cordelia don't know much about such things, if you ask me. She never really sees Francis. She sees the woebegone little twelve-year-old who'd lost his beloved father and found himself a viscount."

"You don't think he and Lady Anne would have suited?"

Arabella rose. "I don't know anything about it. Well, I'm off, then. But remember, if you need me, I'm only a few streets away."

* * *

There weren't many men in Tattersall's subscription room at this time of year, but Francis found Tom Allbright there, ready to pay. Serena's beefy brother was sitting at a table downing porter from a quart pot. When Francis joined him, he pushed over a package and a sheet of paper.

"I've had the jewels valued, Middlethorpe, and this lot comes to just over the three thousand, as you'll see. Trust you're satisfied."

Francis sensed something in the man, something like malicious amusement. He glanced at the paper, but it was from a reputable jeweler. Where was the trick? It was inconceivable that Allbright descend to outright cheating in a matter like this; he'd end up blackballed.

"Perfectly satisfied." Despite the words, Francis was not satisfied. He'd like to do violence to the burly man. Here was someone charged with the care of Serena, and he'd clearly done a bad job of it. She could be dead under a hedgerow by now and the Allbrights would not give a tinker's damn.

As Francis stood, he anticipated with pleasure Allbright's reaction when he found Francis was married to his sister and that he had indirectly returned her jewels to her. He laid some groundwork. "I'm recently married, Sir Thomas. Perhaps some of these pieces will please my bride."

Allbright raised his jar of ale. "Congratulations, my lord. Perhaps they will."

But Francis did not miss the spark of pure malicious amusement in the man's eyes.

As he left Tattersall's, Francis hefted the package thoughtfully. It weighed the right amount and displayed the jeweler's seal. He had intended to return home and give the package to Serena—it might be some reparation for the way he had treated her last night—but now he hesitated.

He was still appalled at what had happened the night before. Yes, he had been angry with her—angry over Anne and angry that Serena seemed to be playing tricks with him—but he had intended to show his disapproval by not joining her in bed at all. For some reason, he had changed his mind and gone to her. He had intended, however, to sleep with her without intimacy, to show her that he could not be manipulated by his needs.

Instead, his body had taken over, and he had used her without any thought for her pleasure or feelings. He had the horrifying fear that if she had resisted, he would have forced her.

He did not know how he was to face her and had hoped the jewels would help. Now he had his doubts. It might be wister to inspect the package first.

He headed to White's.

It was a dull, chilly day, and that suited Francis's mood exactly. He wished to hell that Nicholas was nearby. Nicholas was the one person he could perhaps confess his total ignorance to—ignorance of how to put knowledge into practice while caught in this maelstrom of hot need. On his wedding night, he'd thought he would explode holding back, trying to please her. Last night had been worse.

He couldn't help a spurt of irritation, however. If only Serena would behave in some way that made sense, it might help.

At the Posts' farm, she had been erotic delight personified—and look where it had landed them. On their wedding night, she had seemed as nervous and unsure as a virgin. Now she was playing the part of an untouched schoolgirl and making him feel a villain for wanting her.

The next stage was probably a vow of eternal chastity!

And then there were the times when she watched him like a terrified child. . . .

Certainly, her first marriage can't have been pleasant, but was that any reason for her to act so with him?

He'd like an unforced smile in bed, like the one they'd shared in the perfumer's, laughing about his lust. Was that too much to ask?

He'd like an unforced touch. Not one of her skillful manipulations, but a tender, uncalculated touch, perhaps a gentle kiss.

She didn't like to be kissed.

What the devil was he to do about a bride who didn't like to be kissed?

Even as he fulminated, he knew that a good part of his irritated state of mind was because he knew the heavens were going to fall in on them at any moment.

He'd sent word to his mother with Kipling, and a letter to Lea Park to inform the Arrans of his marriage. The ducal family would presumably treat the matter with frosty disregard, but his mother wouldn't. She'd either keep silent until they went to the Priory, or post to Town to vent her outrage upon them here.

Because of this, he'd also sent a letter to Melton to inform the Rogues there and to ask for support, for Serena as much as for himself. Beth Arden would be a comfort for her.

Despite temptation, he hadn't sent a message to

Nicholas. It was, after all, February, and no time to be traveling with a family, and he knew Nicholas didn't like to leave his wife and child behind. Francis fully intended to go to Somerset anyway, once the first storm had been weathered.

It was as good a bolt-hole as any.

As he entered White's, he was pondering various strategies for getting over the battlefield intact, which was why he didn't spot Uffham in time.

"Middlethorpe, old fellow! How nice to see you."

Francis stared at Anne's brother blankly, wondering what the devil to say. The young man clearly hadn't heard the news.

"Anne's fit as a fiddle, you'll be pleased to know," Uffham went on obliviously. "We'll be seeing you soon, eh?"

Francis took a deep breath, gestured Uffham into one of the small private rooms, and closed the door.

"Something up?" asked Uffham, still unsuspecting.

"Yes," said Francis, carefully placing his package on a table. "The fact is, Uffham, I'm married."

Lord Uffham looked at him, his pleasant face bewildered. "You can't have married Anne out of hand, can you?"

"My wife is called Serena. We were married two days ago."

It still took a moment to register. "Good God! You . . . you *cur!*"

Seeing what was coming, Francis stepped back and raised a hand. "Think a moment, Uffham. Your family would not want a fuss over this."

With visible difficulty, Uffham swallowed the desire

221

to call Francis out. "Does Anne know?" he asked coldly.

"She should. I wrote as soon as the knot was tied."

Uffham's eyes widened. "Good God, Middlethorpe, *why?* Poor Anne will be brokenhearted, and I thought. . . . I thought you cared."

"I did care, but perhaps not enough. Serena is increasing."

Uffham reddened. "I see. Anne had a fortunate escape, in my opinion."

"Probably true."

Uffham left the room without another word. Francis took a deep breath. That had not been pleasant, but at least he'd managed to forestall a duel. That would be the final bloody straw.

A rap on the door brought him out of his blue-devils. He couldn't imagine why anyone would intrude here—unless Uffham had thought better of it and was sending his seconds.

He strode over and swung the door open sharply.

Lucien de Vaux raised his brows. "Uffham said you were alone in here."

Francis laughed briefly with relief. "As long as you're not his second, come in."

As soon as the door was shut again, Lucien said, "Second? Why the devil would he want to call you out?"

"Because I've as good as jilted his sister."

"Ah. But that sort of affair would hardly help."

"I think I persuaded him of that. It was just that he hadn't heard, so it came as a bit of a shock."

"It came as a bit of a shock to me, too. I sensed that there was something between you and Serena River-

222

ton, but . . . I didn't think you'd marry where you couldn't get an heir."

"She's pregnant," said Francis. " 'Struth. Perhaps I should put it in the papers! Lord Middlethorpe wishes to announce that he has married Serena, formerly Lady Riverton, because she is three damn months pregnant with his child."

Lucien rang a bell. When a discreet servant answered it, he ordered brandy. When it came, he poured two glasses, giving one to Francis. "Is that the only reason you married her?"

Francis knocked back a fair amount of the spirit. "I was as good as promised to Anne Peckworth. I don't suppose I'd have backed off without this gun to my head."

"But do you regret it? If you hadn't been courting Lady Anne, would you have minded the gun?"

"You're beginning to sound like Nicholas," Francis said bitingly. "But you're not nearly as good at it, so don't bother."

"Christ Almighty," said Lucien. "Next you'll be calling *me* out, and I'm only trying to help."

Francis pushed fingers through his hair. "I'm sorry. This is not one of the high points of my life, Luce, and I still have an interview with my mother, and possibly with Anne's father, to get through before I see a glimmer of light." He looked at Lucien. "Do I gather Beth's here?"

"After receiving your startling news? We're all here, staying at Belcraven House. Except Hal and Blanche, of course. They're at her place."

"Thank heavens. I'm hoping Beth will support

Serena a little. This isn't going to be easy for her, either."

"Of course. In fact, why don't you dine at the Palace tonight." The Rogues had always called the grand ducal mansion the Palace.

"Beth won't mind?"

"She'd have your head for imagining it. In fact, she suggested it. In case it hasn't occurred to you, not only are your Serena and Beth school friends, but they are going to be mothers at about the same time. Now, there's a bond to make a weak man tremble."

That even summoned a laugh from Francis. "Thank heavens for the Rogues."

"Amen."

As they moved to leave the room, Francis picked up his package, then remembered his purpose in coming to the club in the first place. "Hold on, Luce. I just want to check this."

"What is it?"

"Serena's jewels, provided by Allbright in payment of his debt. I was going to go and place them victoriously in her lap, but now . . ."

"Now?"

"There was a look in his eyes I didn't like. If he's fixed a joke of some kind, I don't want her to find it." He broke the seals and unwrapped the package.

Each item of jewelry was in its own soft pouch, and he spilled out the first one. Then another. Then another, until the whole glittering collection was spread over the table.

There was undoubtedly at least three thousand pounds worth of precious metals and gems here, but no wonder the Allbrights had been willing to part with

4 FREE BOOKS

TO GET YOUR 4 FREE BOOKS WORTH $18.00 — MAIL IN THE FREE BOOK CERTIFICATE T O D A Y

Fill in the Free Book Certificate below, and we'll send your FREE BOOKS to you as soon as we receive it.

If the certificate is missing below, write to: Zebra Home Subscription Service, Inc., P.O. Box 5214, 120 Brighton Road, Clifton, New Jersey 07015-5214.

FREE BOOK CERTIFICATE
4 FREE BOOKS

ZEBRA HOME SUBSCRIPTION SERVICE, INC.

YES! Please start my subscription to Zebra Historical Romances and send me my first 4 books absolutely FREE. I understand that each month I may preview four new Zebra Historical Romances free for 10 days. If I'm not satisfied with them, I may return the four books within 10 days and owe nothing. Otherwise, I will pay the low preferred subscriber's price of just $3.75 each; a total of $15.00, *a savings off the publisher's price of $3.00.* I may return any shipment and I may cancel this subscription at any time. There is no obligation to buy any shipment and there are no shipping, handling or other hidden charges. Regardless of what I decide, the four free books are mine to keep.

NAME

ADDRESS _____ APT

CITY _____ STATE _____ ZIP

( )
TELEPHONE

SIGNATURE _____ (if under 18, parent or guardian must sign)

Terms, offer and prices subject to change without notice. Subscription subject to acceptance by Zebra Books. Zebra Books reserves the right to reject any order or cancel any subscription.

ZB0294

GET
FOUR
FREE
BOOKS
(AN $18.00 VALUE)

ZEBRA HOME SUBSCRIPTION
SERVICE, INC.
120 BRIGHTON ROAD
P.O. Box 5214
CLIFTON, NEW JERSEY 07015-5214

them. It would be hard to sell them at anything near their true value.

To begin with, the arrangements were crude and tasteless. It was strange how gold, sapphires, rubies, and pearls could be made to look tawdry, but here they had. Sometimes the designs were frankly lewd, as with a large baroque pearl that was shaped exactly like an erect penis. Mostly they were just vulgar. It was impossible to imagine a lady wearing them in public.

He picked up a ruby and emerald band that looked like nothing so much as the collar for a pampered dog. When he saw the gold chain attached to it, he realized that after a fashion that's what it was. What he had taken to be a bracelet was actually one of a pair of manacles. . . .

"Victory for the forces of light?" asked Lucien, and moved closer.

Francis made a movement to cover the collection, then realized it was pointless. Lucien read him, however, and sobered. He sifted silently through the glittering pile. "They'll be worth quite a bit broken up," he said at last.

"Yes." Francis was cold with rage at this evidence of a bondage he could scarcely even imagine.

Lucien swept them carelessly into the larger pouch. "Dump 'em on a discreet jeweler and have some better ones made up. Now, will we see you at the Palace this evening?"

"Yes," said Francis, his mind still full of the jewels. "Thank you, Luce."

"Think nothing of it." And Francis recognized that the instruction was directed at more than the invitation, but he couldn't follow it.

He'd accused her of looking like a frightened puppy, and her first husband had given her a dog collar.

He'd told her he wouldn't whip her, and among that collection there had been a jewel-handled whip.

He'd taken her silently in the dark as if she were a thing, not a person, and her first husband had clearly used her as a thing, not a person.

He left the club and headed home, not at all sure what to do.

On his way back to Hertford Street, he passed a young lad hawking a puppy. He'd never seen anyone doing such a thing before, but the lad—who looked about ten—was carrying a covered basket and calling, "Puppy! Puppy for sale. Fine, healthy puppy!"

On impulse, Francis stopped and said, "Let me see."

The lad's face brightened and he pulled back the cloth to reveal a dozing bundle of golden fur. The puppy immediately woke and scrabbled at the sides of the deep basket, tail wagging furiously. It looked to be about ten weeks old.

"Why are you selling it?" Francis asked.

"We've only this one left, sir. Da says he'll drown her if she's still home tonight. She's a bit small, see, so she got left, but she's healthy and friendly."

"What are her parents?" He tickled behind the floppy ears of the puppy, who certainly did seem of an amiable temperament.

"Her ma's largely spaniel, sir, but we don't rightly know about the da."

Pure mongrel, in other words. It was a crazy impulse, but Francis wanted a gift to take home to Serena, and the jewels were clearly not suitable. "How much?" he asked.

The boy glanced at him cannily, but then said, "To be honest, sir, I'll give her away to a kind home. I'll have to charge you threepence for the basket, though, if you want it. It's ma's."

Francis took the basket and gave the lad a crown. "For your honesty. Don't worry. She'll have a good home."

The boy's eyes grew huge. "Thank you, sir! God bless you!"

Francis went on his way, carrying the basket and assured that he had at least made one person happy today. When the clouds broke and sun slanted through to brighten the street, he took that as a sign of higher approval.

He envisaged presenting the puppy to Serena and being rewarded with transports of delight. Being of a practical nature, however, he also envisaged the puppy immediately soiling her gown in its excitement. For that reason, instead of going to his front door, Francis approached his house via the mews, heading for the garden, where the puppy could relieve itself. With any luck, it had reached some understanding of these matters.

As he walked down the carriage lane, he encountered an abstracted gentleman coming the other way. The man clearly had weighty matters on his mind, but when he glanced at Francis he halted as if about to speak. Then he shook his head and continued on his way.

Francis turned to watch the man stride off. Was he going mad, or had that man looked startled to see him? He was sure he didn't know him. He was a good ten years Francis's senior, very tall, and robust. He had broad shoulders under his greatcoat and ruddy good health in his cheeks. . . .

Francis shrugged. He surely had enough tangles in his life without searching for mysteries where none existed. He went into the garden of his house and let the puppy out.

Once Arabella had left, Serena spent the morning exploring her new home. She found that Francis's mother had a bedroom and boudoir here. Francis, on the other hand, had kept—and possibly still did—a set of bachelor's rooms elsewhere and rarely used this house.

She wondered if he would keep those rooms now and to what use he would put them.

This house, however, was clearly his mother's, which was a depressing thought.

When Serena saw the sun come out, she rang for a cloak and went out to explore the garden at the back of the house. It was large for a town garden, and had been cunningly designed to give the impression of rural privacy. The paths wandered around hedges and arbors, so that at times she felt she could be in a large park. At this time of year some of the bushes and hedges were without leaves, but in summer Serena decided it must be completely charming.

She came across a gardener preparing a flower bed, and he touched his forelock.

"This is a lovely garden," she said.

"Aye, milady, that it be. All laid out by her ladyship near twenty years ago, it were."

Serena smiled and walked on, but the thought depressed her.

In February there was not much growth, though far back in the garden, where the sun was strongest, she was charmed to see a mass of golden and purple crocus scattered through with delicate snowdrops. She crouched down to admire them more closely, even taking off her gloves to touch the delicate petals. She was almost startled into toppling over when a voice exclaimed, "Damnation, Cordelia!"

She scrambled to her feet and turned. The big, ruddy man froze. "My pardon, ma'am. I thought you were Lady Middlethorpe."

"I am Lady Middlethorpe, sir." Serena edged away. The secluding hedges could now prove to be a hazard. She glanced behind and saw a gate in the wall, presumably leading to the mews.

"What?" the man's look sharpened. "Middlethorpe has married, then? You must be Lady Anne."

Serena felt herself go painfully red. "No, sir. I am Serena, Lady Middlethorpe." His familiarity with the family was easing her fears, however. "Who, pray, are you?"

"Ferncliff. Charles Ferncliff." Almost absently, he gave her an engraved card with his name upon it.

"Well, Mr. Ferncliff, if, as I gather, you wish to speak to my husband's mother, I am afraid she is still in the country."

"I thought with the knocker on the door . . ." he muttered. Then he fixed Serena with a keen eye. He was a handsome, vigorous man with a look of intelligence and honesty, and despite his strange behavior, she could not remain too nervous.

"As you suspect," he said, "I have important matters to discuss with Lady Middlethorpe. The Dowager Lady Middlethorpe," he corrected. He suddenly laughed. "I doubt she'll like being a dowager. There's hope yet. Do you know if she is expected in town?"

"No, sir, I do not. If you wish to speak to her, however, it is no great distance to Thorpe Priory."

He shook his head and grinned. "Once she hears of this, she'll be here." He bowed. "My very best wishes to you, Lady Middlethorpe, and my congratulations to your husband."

Then he was gone.

Serena pondered the strange encounter, then decided there was no sense to be made of it all. She had to wonder what sort of woman Francis's mother was, though. She would not have thought that the stately lady of the portrait was the kind to have dealings with Mr. Charles Ferncliff, particularly clandestine ones in the garden. She realized that she still had his card in her hand and slipped it into the pocket of her gown. She would ask Francis about all this when he returned.

If he returned. Of course he must, and yet she was irrationally afraid that he had left her forever.

She went sadly back to the house. In Summer St. Martin she had grown used to being busy, but this establishment was too well managed to really need her care. She found herself sitting in the drawing room with nothing to do but worry.

Francis was surprised to find Serena sitting alone in the drawing room. He'd forgotten, damn it, that Arabella was leaving and that she would be without company. She didn't know a soul in Town other than her brothers. He'd have to take better care of his wife.

He found himself nervous about his gift, however, for it was beginning to look like a foolish, maudlin gesture. She might not even like dogs, and a puppy needed a lot of care. At least the animal had relieved itself in the garden, but it had been quite reluctant to return to the basket.

As he entered the room, Serena leapt nervously to her feet, eyes wide on the basket. "Oh, hello. What on earth is that?"

Did she look afraid of him? "It's a gift. If you don't like it, we can make some arrangement for it. . . ." He placed the basket on a table.

Serena approached slowly. His heart ached at how clearly she distrusted surprises. He wanted to heal her hurts and to teach her joy, but he wasn't sure if he knew how. He remembered how she had looked that day in Summer St. Martin, sitting on the wall and cheering on her mock suitors. She'd been happy then, but her happiness had fled with his arrival.

She glanced up at him nervously, then eased back the cloth. Immediately, a little wet nose pushed at her hand and the puppy scrambled to be out.

"Oh!" Hesitantly, she gathered the bundle of golden fur into her hands. The puppy sniffed and clambered, almost falling from her grasp in its excitement. Its little tail was wagging frantically, twitching its whole body. "Oh, you sweet thing. You're adorable!"

She looked up at that moment, and Francis could almost think she addressed those words to him. His heart did a strange, anatomically impossible, somersault.

"Do you like her, then?" he asked.

Serena glowed. A glowing Serena was a rare and wonderful sight. "She's beautiful! Thank you!"

She held the puppy to her chest, murmuring sweet sillinesses to it, laughing when it licked at her chin.

"She has already proved her worth," he said, and pulled a pair of gloves out of his pocket. "Yours, I think. She found them in the garden and insisted I take care of them."

Serena beamed at the puppy. "How clever you are!" She took the gloves and sank to her knees, dangling them for her new pet.

Francis subsided into a chair and simply watched as his wife played, recognizing that she played as one who has forgotten how to play but is perfectly willing to be reminded.

And a puppy, it appeared, was an excellent trigger for the memory.

She was on the floor now, letting the animal run around, but the puppy seemed as fascinated by her as she was by it. It burrowed into skirts, tugged at a slipper ribbon, and frequently returned to worry at the gloves. Serena laughed and lay back, whereupon the puppy clambered over her chest and nuzzled down her bodice. She giggled and kissed it, then squeaked when it tangled in her hair, which had slipped from its pins to dance around her face.

Francis slid lower and watched with deep, warm satisfaction. Something good was coming out of this day, and the future already looked more promising. . . .

Just then the door burst open and his mother swept in, swathed in furs and righteous indignation.

She stopped dead.

Serena sat up sharply and held the puppy protectively close to her breast.

Francis sighed. It had been a pleasant few moments. He rose to his feet. "Hello, Mother."

Lady Middlethorpe's maid was behind her, but the dowager shut the door in the woman's face. "Francis, how *could* you!" Her eyes sliced through Serena.

"Mother, I make known to you my wife, Serena. If you're not prepared to be civil to her, you may as well leave now."

Serena was hastily scrambling to her feet, straightening her skirt and trying to confine her tousled hair.

The dowager blistered her with a look. *"Serena Riverton!"* But then Francis's words seemed to sink home, and she took a deep breath. "Tea. I need tea." She flung off her fur cloak and sat rigidly in a chair.

Serena popped the puppy back in its basket and hastened to ring the bell. When the maid came, she ordered a tea tray.

Francis let his mother glare at him. She was the least of his troubles. "Francis," she said at last, "I need to speak to you in private."

He turned to Serena and smiled. "You'd better let her get it over with, love."

He saw Serena start at his use of an endearment, though it had fallen without effort from his lips. She gathered up the basket and prepared to leave, but then turned to her mother-in-law. "It wasn't his fault," she said earnestly "Truly, it wasn't."

"Serena!" Francis had to be sharp before she made a disastrous revelation, but he hated the frightened glance she cast at him. She swallowed and retreated from the room, basket clutched in her arms. He understood her fears much better now, and he desperately wanted to follow and reassure her.

"Really, Francis," said his mother as soon as the door closed. "You must be demented. And she's a total hoyden as well. She was on the floor, showing her garters!"

"Only to me, Mother," he said mildly.

"And what of Anne?"

He looked down at his boot. "I am sorry about that. But she'll do as well or better elsewhere."

"The duke and duchess are going to be most upset."

"I'm sure they are."

"Why could you not at least have married the woman in a decent fashion?"

Here we go again. I definitely should put it in the papers. "Because she's increasing."

Lady Middlethorpe gaped. "Do you mean . . . ? While you wre paying decent court to Lady Anne, you were . . . ? *You wretch!*"

"I'm sure you're right."

The tea tray came. As his mother seemed disinclined to act, he made the tea and poured it for her. She was very genuinely shocked and he couldn't blame her.

She drank the whole cup down. "Francis, I find this hard to believe of you."

"Thank you."

She stared at him. "Can you not tell me why? I thought I knew you, the kind of man you are . . ."

This was proving to be far more difficult than he'd expected. He could cut his mother off, simply refuse to answer her questions, but that was hardly fair. But he could not tell the truth.

234

"I thought I would be well suited by Anne, Mother, but . . . It was in November, when I went to settle that Ferncliff business. I met Serena, we acted unwisely, and there were consequences. In honor, I could do nothing else but marry her. I ask you to be kind to her."

His mother's shock was profound. She grew positively haggard. "In November . . . Oh, no."

"Serena is three months pregnant," he confirmed. "The situation will be obvious when the child is born."

His mother stared at him with a look of tragedy in her eyes.

"Mother, it is not quite as bad as that," he protested. "There will be talk, but these things happen."

"But you and Anne would have been *so* well suited."

Francis knew that if there were to be peace in his house, he would have to put an end to this. "Mother, I love Serena."

"Do you really, my dear?"

"Yes."

"And she loves you?"

"I believe so." Gads, and he'd always been such an honest fellow. Frank by name, frank by nature, Nicholas had once teased.

His mother stared thoughtfully into space. "Is love enough, do you think, with all else weighed against you?"

"I pray it is. But it is not quite so bad as that. . . ."

"It most certainly is," she retorted with a return to her usual forceful manner. "The Arrans are going to be deeply offended, and there must be grave doubt as to whether anyone of consequence will acknowledge her. Matthew Riverton's widow!"

"Her family are solid gentry."

She flicked him an icy look. "The Allbrights have been louts for generations. I knew this girl's father. We had best all remove to the Priory tomorrow."

"I'm afraid that is not convenient."

"What, pray, is the purpose of staying here? There are few people of importance in Town, and you do not have the social connections to launch a dubious wife!"

"We are to dine tonight at Belcraven House. Beth Arden is a friend of Serena's."

Lady Middlethorpe stared. "The Marchioness . . . ?" But then the surprise turned to disgust. "Oh, one of the Rogues. And *she* was a penniless schoolteacher before she trapped Arden to the altar." She sighed. "You are my son, however, and I will not let you suffer because . . . I suppose I will have to stay and take a hand in matters before you make a greater mull of it all."

With that salvo she marched out.

Francis collapsed into a chair, head in hands. He was tantalized by visions of what might have been. He could have married Anne Peckworth—a decorous marriage after at least a month or two of betrothal. They would have been surrounded by universal approval and good will. She would have behaved with shy decorum in the marriage bed, and at least nine months would have passed before the birth of the first child.

It was an idyllic vision.

But Francis stood and made himself put aside such thoughts. The course was set, and it was just a matter of getting over it as lightly as possible. No scandal lasts forever.

He went to acquaint Serena with their plans for the evening.

* * *

"Dine out?" said Serena. "Oh, but I do not have a suitable gown yet."

Serena was using that as an excuse. She had not missed the dowager's reaction and feared she could expect the same from all she met. As an Allbright, she was not good *ton;* as a Riverton, she was beyond the pale. She had been pacing her room taking comfort in the fact that her simple country clothes made any mingling in Society impossible. Now that his mother had been faced, surely they would go immediately into the country.

"Your blue will do. It won't be a formal affair."

"At a ducal mansion!"

"It will still be just the Rogues." He picked up a delicate figurine, then put it down rather sharply. "Trust me about this, Serena. There is nothing to fear. I am sorry about my mother. . . ."

"Oh, don't! She has a right to be shocked."

"Yes, I suppose she has. Thank you for being so understanding." He looked at her somberly. "And I want to talk about Anne."

Serena made a movement to stop him. The last thing she wanted was to discuss his lost love. He firmly grasped her hand. "Serena, I did not—and do not—love Anne Peckworth. You must believe that."

She searched his eyes and thought she saw truth. "But you wanted to marry her."

"Yes. She would have been a suitable bride. I am very fond of her and her family. Perhaps love would have come. I hoped so."

Serena hoped the pain of each sentence was not

showing on her face, for he was trying to be kind and honest. Perhaps love will come for us, too, she thought, but without great hope. She was *not* suitable, and he must detest her family. "Thank you for being so honest," she said.

"I will always be honest with you, Serena. May I expect the same in return?"

"Yes, of course."

He touched her cheek gently. "Then I think we will do very well." She thought he might kiss her, and despite her dislike of the messy business, she would have welcomed it, but he moved away. He glanced at the puppy, sound asleep in the basket. "And you like her?"

"I love her. I have called her Brandysnap, Brandy for short. Do you think that silly?"

"Not at all. And she at least appears to have her functions under control, which will make life easier."

"Not entirely," said Serena with a wry smile. "She has soiled this gown a little. I must change in a moment. But she did look appropriately contrite."

He smiled at that. "A well-brought-up young lady overcome with excitement. I think you will need some help with her, though. There is a kitchen boy here who could probably be persuaded to care for her when you cannot—judging from the longing looks I caught on his face as I was letting her run in the garden."

Serena hid her face by bending over the puppy. You are a truly good man, she thought. You are honest, you stood up for me without hesitation to your mother, you notice a kitchen boy's dreams. You deserve better than this debacle and I want to give you better. I wish I knew how.

"That sounds excellent," she said.

She collected herself and turned, grateful for once that she had been trained to dissimulation in a hard school. "What time are we to go out this evening?"

Chapter 12

Serena spent the time before they were to leave trying to think of sensible ways to improve matters, but with little success. She knew nothing about Society life.

She had gone from school into prison, and she did not know the world at all. She did see, however, that her husband would be miserable if they were socially ostracized. How was it to be avoided once it was known that she was the relict of Randy Riverton? The wedding announcement would reveal that, but even if that hazard was avoided, it would only take one encounter with a man who had visited Stokeley Manor to create a scandal.

As Matthew's wife, she had never been forced to take part in the public displays of bed-work that had amused his guests so, but she had been made to watch. In the later years of her marriage, it seemed to excite Matthew to make her uncomfortable.

She had been forced to perform "attitudes," as made famous by Emma Hamilton, and sometimes lewd ones, skimpily dressed. It had depended largely on whether Matthew had been pleased with her or angry. After he had been told she was barren, he had been angry more often than not.

She looked back on that existence now as a bad dream, but one that still shadowed her present life. Cowering under that shadow, she had little faith that a meeting with Beth Armitage would help her. Beth had stayed safe at Miss Mallory's school until leaving to marry. She could know nothing of the life Serena had lived, and would certainly not understand.

Nor did Serena feel at ease about meeting Francis's friends. She was about to be pitchforked into a group of people who would side with him, who would see all the evils of his situation and blame her.

As the carriage rolled into one of London's finest squares, she wondered how much Francis had told his friends. Surely he wouldn't have told all. But how else had he explained his actions?

The carriage drew up at the majestic steps of a great house on Marlborough Square. The footman went to ply the knocker, then opened the carriage door and let down the steps. By the time Serena and Francis were approaching the massive doors, a small army of servants had appeared to attend to them.

They were ushered into a magnificent marble and gilt entrance hall. Serena stared, having never seen anything quite so grand in her life. It merely intensified her fears, and she stayed close to Francis's side.

As soon as her cloak was off, however, she was warmly and informally greeted by a handsome woman she still easily recognized as Beth. "Serena! This is of all things wonderful!" She linked arms. "We are going to have such fun and become sickeningly maternal together. Speaking of sickening, have you been? No? I haven't, either, but I do feel queasy at times. . . ."

Serena was swept up to a cozy saloon and introduced to a startlingly handsome blond man. Thus Serena found herself shaking hands with the heir to a dukedom, found her hand being kissed by the heir to a dukedom . . . kissed with sensual expertise both on knuckles and palm. "I am a connoisseur of beauty," he said with a devastating twinkle in his blue eyes. "You are *very* welcome, Serena."

For some reason she could not take offense, but she blushed.

"Luce!"

Serena caught the sharp anger in her husband's voice and snatched her hand away guiltily. Was her cursed beauty going to destroy this friendship, too?

The marquess and his wife turned to her husband in surprise. "Homage to beauty is my way, Francis," said Lord Arden lightly. "If you want to stop me, you'll have to shoot me."

"Oh, no," said Serena. "Please! I'm sure it was all my fault. . . ."

"Don't be a widgeon, Serena," said Beth cheerfully, and went over to kiss Francis warmly and thoroughly on the lips. "There. Now all's fair."

The tension lessened, but Serena was immensely grateful when another man strolled in the open door. "Bride and groom present?"

This rakish specimen with ginger-gold hair spoke with a trace of an Irish accent. He came over. "Welcome to the Rogue's Palace, my dear. I'm the one who provided the horse that won back your treasure. May I claim a kiss for it?"

He didn't wait for permission but kissed her soundly. Serena flashed her husband an alarmed look, but he seemed to have regained his equilibrium.

"Serena, make known Miles Cavanagh to you and"—Francis glanced at the door—"his ward, Felicity Monahan."

The dark young woman who'd been standing by the door walked boldly in. "They're a devil of a bunch," she said. "If it weren't already too late, I'd warn you off."

Soon there were five strangers there, for they were joined by Sir Stephen Ball, who was blond and wry. It was a cheerful, chattering group unlike any Serena had ever known, though it did bear a faint resemblance to the parlor at Miss Mallory's during a bun-fest.

The humorous talk was of the Princess Charlotte's latest, and most likely, suitor.

"A fine figure of a man," said Miles of Prince Leopold, "even if he is another impoverished German come to batten on the Crown."

"The next monarch cannot marry someone with too strong an interest in his homeland," Beth pointed out. "History shows us how disastrous that can be."

"This one has no interest at all," replied Miles with a grin. "For interest, one requires capital, you see."

They all chuckled at that.

Serena had relaxed enough to confess some ignorance. "A prince without capital?" she asked. "Is he not rich?"

It was Stephen Ball who answered. "Leopold is the third son only of a very minor principality. On his last visit, he stayed over a grocer's shop on the Marylebone High Street. This time he is lodged at the Pavilion in

Brighton. It really would appear that his goose is cooked."

"That sounds as if you pity him," Serena remarked.

"That depends," said Stephen with a grin, "on whether the goose is his pet or his dinner."

Serena decided to pick up that conversational ball and tell them about Brandy.

"A puppy!" Beth exclaimed. "How sweet. Lucien, do you think . . . ?"

"Anything you desire, as always," the marquess drawled. "But a lapdog, Beth?"

She grinned. "Wolfhounds must be puppies at one stage."

He grinned back. "Now, there's a thought."

"Typical of the idle rich," declared Miles. "Wanting wolfhounds in a country that has no wolves."

"Dear Miles," sighed Felicity, "I wish you would drop this pose of proletarian politics. You are disgustingly rich and will one day have a title."

"Ah, but I'm Irish, my dear, and that wipes out all the rest."

"No politics," said Beth firmly. "See, dinner is served."

Over the meal Serena fully relaxed. It did seem that these people at least were willing to accept her without reservation. She remembered Francis saying that as the wife of a Rogue she was a Rogue. It seemed to be true.

It was completely novel to her to be among such a relaxed group of men and women, but she thought that in time she could come to like it very well indeed.

She could not be comfortable, however, with the flirtation going on. All the men flirted with all the women as a matter of course, and Beth and Felicity seemed completely happy to flirt back. Serena thought Felicity sometimes went beyond the bounds of playfulness, but no one seemed to take offense. All the same, Serena's nerves were jumping. She was terribly afraid of causing trouble and constantly watched Francis, trying to judge his reaction.

As a result she could eat little and felt the beginning of a headache.

Beth Arden suddenly rose. "Serena, unless you have a taste for port and brandy, why don't we go and have tea."

Serena was only too happy to follow this plan, but as they left the room, she glanced back and saw the door close on Felicity there with four young men. "Beth . . . Lady Arden . . ."

"Oh, Beth, please." Beth led the way up the sweeping stairs.

"Beth, then . . . Do you think it wise to leave Miss Monahan unchaperoned with the men?"

"Felicity will get up to no mischief. Miles seems to have the way of handling her, even if he does occasionally choose rough measures."

That hadn't been quite what Serena had in mind, but she could imagine rough measures and shuddered. And Mr. Cavanagh had seemed such a pleasant gentleman. Did Beth think nothing of such things?

Perhaps her marriage had not been so strange after all. Perhaps she had been peculiar for finding it horrible. . . .

Beth was chatting about the house as they walked along a corridor. Serena hardly listened as she fought an internal battle. By the time they arrived at the small saloon, she had lost and had to speak.

"Beth, I cannot think it right to leave Felicity down there with those men."

Beth stared at her in genuine perplexity. "But Miles is there. He is her guardian."

"But . . . but *anything* could happen."

A glimmer of comprehension entered Beth's eyes. "Serena, those men are Rogues. Now, I wouldn't go so far as to say that any one of them alone might not do something wicked, but when together . . . It just seems that the nobler side must win."

Serena sat. "I don't understand any of this."

"Rather different from what you've experienced before, I would think."

"Totally."

"Don't worry about Felicity. The truth is that's she's an unrepentant hoyden and would much rather be down there talking horses and hunting than up here talking husbands and babies."

A footman and maid brought in the tea tray and were dismissed.

"This is a magnificent house," said Serena. Her words were true, but she hoped they sounded more complimentary than she felt. It was too magnificent. She was just delighted not to have to live in it. Even this small room carried a weight of plasterwork and gilding that was quite oppressive.

"Ridiculous, isn't it?" Beth said dryly. "Even Lucien finds it so at times, and he was born to it. And wait until you see Belcraven Park."

"How do you make yourselves comfortable here?"

"We don't spend a great deal of time here. Our true home is Hartwell. It's quite a simple place down in Surrey. But as we don't keep London quarters, when we're in Town, we use the Palace. It's a kindness, really," she added. "The duke and duchess rarely come to London, but the house is kept up in case they do. The staff here grow rather bored."

"I would think keeping this monstrous place in order would be work enough for an army."

"Yes, but if no one uses it, it must seem pointless work. Now, tell me, how are you settling in as a married woman?"

Serena wasn't ready for confidences yet, and so the talk was of Summer St. Martin, and gowns, and households. Eventually, she did touch on mothers-in-law, however.

Beth pulled a face. "Francis's mother is a bit of a dragon, isn't she? No, that's not fair. She's very pleasant, really, but overprotective of him and inclined to be superior. I gather it was a great shock to them all when Francis's father died."

"And there's his sisters, too."

"Oh, you don't need to worry about them. Diana is in Paris with her husband, who is a diplomat, and Clara is positively entrenched in her husband's Scottish estates. Amy, the youngest, is married to Peter Lavering, and he is an honorary Rogue. You'll like them, but since the birth of their first child, they're content to stay in the country."

Serena decided it was time to take Arabella's advice and bite the bullet. "Francis's mother was shocked by his marriage, though, and I gather he was generally expected to offer for Lady Anne Peckworth. His marriage to me is bound to cause talk, and once it is realized that I . . . that I am prematurely with child, there will be a scandal, won't there?"

"There will certainly be talk," Beth admitted. "Scandal, though? Sudden marriages do happen."

"But what of my background? My family is not well-thought-of, and with reason. Even *I* don't think well of them. And my first husband was notorious."

Beth put down her dainty cup. "I admit, there could be a problem there. It depends on how people decide to take you. The *ton* is fickle."

Serena looked at Beth directly. "What I am asking is, is there anything I can do to improve the odds? I will do anything. I owe it to Francis to try to make a comfortable life for him, and I'm sure he would hate to be a byword."

"I don't think you *owe* him anything," said Beth rather severely. "However, you will both be more comfortable if completely accepted. Let me think. . . ."

After a moment, Beth said, "Francis hasn't announced the wedding yet. When he does, the notice will have to include your previous name. It's tempting to give it as Allbright, but I doubt Francis would agree; he's a stickler for honesty. Anyway, someone would be sure to know."

"Is it hopeless, then?"

"I don't think so. As Ovid says, the best defense is usually to attack. We'll have to talk to Lucien. He's much better at these social maneuvers than I am, but I think if we can get you accepted by enough important people before the news breaks, it might work. It is much harder to break a connection already established than to refuse one."

"But how could I be accepted by important people?" Serena asked.

"My dear," said Beth dryly, "you are already ac-

cepted by us." She laughed. "Oh, don't look so morti-
fied. I think it absurd, too, but the fact is that as Marquess and Marchioness of Arden, and future Duke and
Duchess of Belcraven, Lucien and I are among the
highest of the high. The duke and duchess will support
us, I'm sure, if I can only persuade them to come to
Town. What is more, the Rogues can recruit quite a
few other leaders of Society. If you are willing to brave
the lions, I think we could give it a try."

That predatory image was all too close to the way
Serena felt. "What if I meet someone who . . . who
knew me as Matthew's wife?"

"Is it likely?"

"I didn't meet many people, and few were of the *haut
ton*. There was one lord—a Lord Deveril . . ."

"He, at least, is dead," said Beth with a degree of
satisfaction. "If the rest were lower in status than him,
the chances of you meeting them are remote. Deveril
was not accepted. If you do meet any such people, cut
them."

Serena clasped her hands. "Lord, but it terrifies me.
I'd much rather live in the country."

Beth said nothing, just looked at her.

Serena shook her head. "You used to do that at
school, too, you wretch. I know. Hiding would do no
good. Very well. By all means let us charge Society
sword in hand. I just pray there is no bloodshed."

Beth immediately set in to making plans. "If we're
going to fire you off, it will have to be before you and
I become noticeably large. Thank heavens waists are
still high."

"Waists always will be high."

"I doubt it. The move downward is already taking

250

place. To be honest, that gown you have on is years out of date. Have you not noticed that stays are becoming more substantial, too? I fear we are seeing the demise of rational dress."

"A return to stomachers and panniers?" Serena queried. "Women will never put up with that again."

Beth made a wry face. "Nothing is too foolish for fashion. One day I will have the courage of my convictions and take to wearing trousers."

"Beth!"

"Well, why not? But let us not be distracted; we certainly don't want to fire you off in pantaloons. We are aiming for total respectability." She found some paper and a pencil and began making notes. "I wonder if it is fair to ask Leander to come up. An earl would help, but he is newly wed. Then there's Nicholas. It doesn't seem quite right to plan a Roguish enterprise without him. I think," she mused, "I could persuade the Duchess of Yeovil to give us her countenance. Her son was a Rogue. He died at Waterloo."

She saw Serena's glazed look and laughed. "Let's talk about Rogues, and all will become clear."

"Francis did say that they were a group of close friends."

"Rather more than that. It is more like a family, but a family such as few of us have. It is simply unthinkable that any one not help the others, except possibly in matters illegal. Only possibly," she added with a grin. "We indulged in a little housebreaking last year."

"Francis, too?" Serena was not sure what she thought of these overgrown schoolboys.

"Francis was given a safe, watching brief. I remember he was rather put out, but Nicholas pointed out that he and Steve were our only members of Parliament present, and if anything went wrong, we could need some strings pulled."

"It sounds positively conspiratorial. And who is this Nicholas?"

"Hasn't Francis said anything about Nicholas Delaney?" asked Beth with a quick, startled look.

"He mentioned him. He is married, yes? And I think . . . Is he the one Arabella referred to as King Rogue?"

"Probably. But more importantly," Beth said gently, "Nicholas is Francis's closest friend, and vice versa."

"Oh." Serena could see that Beth was astonished that she could be married to Francis and not know this, and in truth she was hurt. It pointed out clearly the superficiality of their relationship.

"I'm sure you'll meet him soon," said Beth, a little too gaily, "and then you'll understand about Nicholas. He can't be explained. Suffice to say that the families of the Rogues are generally grateful that he saw fit to gather the group together."

"Why?"

"They recognize what a redeeming influence the Rogues exert. Lucien, for example, has only been saved from unbearable arrogance by the group. Without them, he probably would have been surrounded by toadeaters and spoiled beyond redemption."

"It's extraordinary," said Serena, "but I can imagine the appeal."

"Yes," said Beth thoughtfully. "If I'd been as farsighted as Nicholas, I would have formed such a group at Miss Mallory's. We might not have prevented your marriage to Riverton, but you would never have been abandoned."

Serena shook her head. "I was permitted no letters, no friends."

"Oh, I'm sure there are ways. But that is in the past. Now you are a Rogue and we are all dedicated to your happiness."

Serena stared into the fire. "Beth, I'm not sure I know what happiness is."

Beth put down her cup and reached over to take Serena's hand. "I know, but you will. Of all the Rogues, Francis is the kindest and the gentlest. It is clear that he cares for you, and I know he can make you happy."

Serena felt tears brimming. She wished she could confess her terrible sin to Beth, but it was impossible. "He didn't want to marry me," she said. "He wanted to marry Lady Anne Peckworth."

Beth dismissed that with a wave of her hand. "What's done is done, and I doubt Lady Anne would have made a good Rogue."

There was no time for more, for the rest of the party joined them. Beth immediately announced the plan for an attack upon Society. Serena saw Francis flash her a look, but he said nothing, joining in the discussion of appearances at the theater, the opera, and some carefully planned entertainments.

Eventually, however, he came over to sit beside her. "Did Beth bully you into this?"

"Not at all," said Serena firmly. "It was as much my idea as hers."

He frowned slightly. "I don't want you to wear yourself out."

Serena projected tremendous enthusiasm. "Heavens, a little gadding about Town will be a pleasant change after the quiet life I've led."

"I see. But at the moment you are looking a little tired."

Serena admitted that, for she was feeling weary.

"Perhaps we should leave, then," he said.

"If you wouldn't mind . . ."

"Not at all. We can return tomorrow to make more of these exciting plans."

In the carriage heading home, Serena wondered if she were imagining the heavy atmosphere. "Is something wrong, Francis? Do you not feel it wise for me to try to be accepted?"

"No, it is a good idea and with any luck will probably work."

She searched for another problem. "I'm sorry about the flirting. I could think of no way to stop it."

He shook his head at that. "That is my problem, Serena, not yours. It will just take me a little while to grow accustomed to having a wife. Anyway, I trust the Rogues. I'd trust any of them alone with you in a bed."

Then awareness of his words flushed them both with color. Could *she* be trusted in that situation?

He turned his head to look out the window. "We didn't order you any fine gowns, and there wouldn't be time for them to be made, anyway. I wonder if Beth has any to lend you."

"Oh, I couldn't!"

"I know you would prefer your own, but there is no time."

"I don't mean that. I mean, I cannot take Beth's gowns. I am some inches shorter. They would be ruined."

"I doubt that will matter to her. She and Luce aren't overly fond of grand occasions, but they have to play their part now and then, and so she has the clothes for it. What gowns she has, though, certainly won't be worn this Season and perhaps not the next. The future Duchess of Belcraven cannot wear dresses two years out of date."

Serena could hardly imagine this point of view, but when she considered the magnificence of Belcraven House, she suspected it was plain truth. "If she truly doesn't mind, I would be very grateful."

"And I must arrange for jewels for you. The heirlooms. My mother—"

"Oh, please don't ask her to give them up!"

He turned. "They are yours, Serena. In trust, of course . . ."

There was something disquieting in his eyes that Serena couldn't fathom. "I won't pawn the family diamonds, Francis," she joked.

"Of course not."

But he sounded so serious. Did he really think she was not to be trusted with his family heirlooms?

When they arrived back at Hertford Street, he escorted her courteously to her room, ensured that she had all she required, and left her there. It was clear he would not join her.

Serena allowed the maid to prepare her for bed and lay there in sleepless misery. If her husband didn't trust her, and didn't desire her, what hope was there for them?

* * *

Francis went to his own room, fighting and winning a battle with lust. Lord, but he was turning into a monster. Not only did Serena not really enjoy sex, but she was tired, and yet he still wanted to use her to slake his own needs.

To bolster his willpower, he took out the jewels and spread them on a table, contemplating them. Until he could be sure he would treat Serena with more respect than her first husband, he would not touch her. What was he to do with these things, though?

It was a kind of theft to dispose of them without her consent, but that was what he would like to do. He did not want to discuss them with her. His instinct, in fact, was to throw them away, as he had thrown her rings into the hedgerow, but that would be folly.

They would have to be sold, but he did not at all care to take them to a jeweler himself. He would have to find a discreet agent for the business.

With a sigh, he shoved them back into the pouch and put it in an unlocked drawer. If they were stolen, it would in many ways be a relief.

He warmed himself by the fire, nudging a coal farther toward the heart of the blaze, then grimaced at the mark on the glossy surface of his kid slipper. He had little patience for London Life. It was all artificiality and deception, and it meant wearing glossy shoes that showed every mark.

It would appear Serena had a taste for it, however. He supposed it wasn't surprising when she had been kept in the country all her life. He would indulge her. The plan to take Society head-on was a good one, in fact. He had been pretty well resigned to enduring scandal and waiting a year or two for it to blow over. This plan, if it worked, would be better.

Was it unreasonable, though, to see in it yet more of his wife's adroit planning?

Damn it all. All he wanted was a simple life!

Then he laughed. Francis remembered sitting over breakfast at Lea Park feeling aggrieved because his life was so boring. He was well served.

For a moment he allowed himself to wonder which path he would have chosen if he had been given a choice back then. It was bewildering, but he had to admit that he would likely have chosen the path that led to Serena.

That thought was unwise, however. He was suddenly aware of her lying in the bed so close by, his wife, his by right, all soft curves and secrets, warm and perfumed. . . .

But he couldn't, wouldn't, give in. In time, with patience, he would bring her to desire him as he desired her. . . .

He shook his head. All these years he'd thought himself such a virtuous fellow for resisting the lure of loose women. Now he found that if he'd practiced the manly arts more assiduously, he might be in a better position to cope with his marriage.

He looked for some other focus for his restless mind. That damned Ferncliff. Steve had mentioned this evening that he thought he'd caught a glimpse of Ferncliff one day last week, though not close enough to catch the man. Ferncliff was responsible for this whole bloody mess, and if he was in London, Francis wanted to speak to him. With the help of the Rogues, surely the man could be flushed from the covert and dealt with. He'd see to it first thing in the morning.

Now all he had to do was get through the night. He settled to letting the brandy decanter help him.

As a consequence of the brandy, Francis woke late and with a sore head. He did not want breakfast and thought it wise not to see Serena, so he left the house and walked to Marlborough Square to consult with the Rogues about Ferncliff. He found the resident Rogues at the breakfast table supplemented by one—Hal Beaumont. Hal and Beth were in a spirited discussion about Blanche's refusal to enter Belcraven House.

"Damnit, Beth. She says it ain't proper, and there's no way I or Lucien can change her mind. Try if you can."

"It's ridiculous. Hello, Francis," said Beth. "Would you faint to see Blanche here?"

Francis sat down and cut into this debate ruthlessly. "I need some help."

Everyone instantly paid attention. "What?"

He explained the bare bones of his problem to those who did not know, then said, "I want to find Charles Ferncliff if he's in London. How do we go about it?"

There was a brief practical discussion in which Beth and Felicity joined, and then ducal servants were sent out. They were each to hire two more people they could trust, then fan out across the city with Francis's description in hand. They would check by name, too, but the man might be using a false one.

All hotels, inns and clubs would be visited, and discreet word—and promise of reward—left at chop-houses. Even if Ferncliff had private lodgings, it was likely he would need to eat out.

When the hunters were dispatched, Lucien looked at Francis. "So, what are you going to do when you catch him? Covering up a murder would stretch even our abilities a trifle."

Francis flushed. He knew his demeanor when talking of Ferncliff probably did predict violence. It wasn't entirely logical, but he blamed the man for turning his life upside down.

"Ask him some questions, that's all."

Lucien raised his brows but said nothing more on the subject. Instead, discussion turned to the planned visit to the theater this evening. It would be the first move in the assault upon Society. Francis raised the subject of clothes and found Beth was delighted to give some over to Serena's use, agreeing that she would likely never wear them again.

Eventually, the group broke up, and Francis knew he must return home, and that he was reluctant. He both longed and feared being with Serena. As he waited for his coat, he faced the fact that he could not trust himself to be with her without losing control of his desire. He could imagine all too easily abusing her on a table or against a wall.

He was waylaid by Beth and drawn off into the magnificent library. Glass-doored shelves held the wisdom of the ages bound in red Moroccan leather. Francis wished that wisdom would leach out into him. He was in water that was far too deep, and he was drowning.

"Francis," said Beth directly, "Serena is in low spirits. She seems to think you'd rather be married to Anne Peckworth."

Oh, God. He knew Beth's intentions were good, but he didn't need this now. "Perhaps I would," he said shortly.

She stared at him. "Then why . . . ?"

"Damnit, Beth, she's with child."

"But why?" she asked simply. "If you'd rather be married to Anne Peckworth?"

"What a clever question. Tell me if you discover the answer." Francis swung on his heel and slammed out of the room. He seized his coat from the waiting footman and escaped into the street.

Beth stared at the door in amazement. Francis *never* lost his temper, and it was almost impossible to imagine him engaging in a mindless coupling while in love with another woman. But what other explanation was there?

She took the problem to Lucien, discovering him in his small study attending to some correspondence.

"I don't know, Beth," he said. "And he ain't telling. But it was clear in Melton that he cared about Serena. I don't think mindless coupling comes into it. In fact, Francis has always been notably restrained in such matters. He probably thought he wanted to marry Lady Anne until he met Serena." He smiled mischievously at her. "She is enough to distract any man, after all."

Beth poked him in the chest. "Be distracted, my lord marquess, and you'll regret it. Not least because such behavior would upset Serena."

He tugged her down onto his lap. "Mmmm. And what wonderful ways would you find to punish me, ruler of my heart?"

Beth draped her arms around his neck. "I would read Mary Brunton to you all night long."

"No, you wouldn't."

"I wouldn't?"

He touched the tip of her nose with the tip of his tongue. "I'd distract you."

Beth chuckled. "I fear you would. I did not used to be so easily distracted. You have quite ruined me, sir."

When her husband would have ruined her even further, however, she pushed him away. "Wait, Lucien. I am very concerned about Francis and Serena. I wish I knew what was wrong. Do you think he really would rather be married to Anne Peckworth?"

He accepted her mood and lounged back, hands no longer touching her. "I can see that it offered certain comforts. But on the other hand, Serena offers remarkable advantages. . . ."

"Lucien!" Beth warned.

"Let me distract you, then." His hand crept up her side.

She captured it. "No. And now I come to think of it, what happened about that wager? Did Francis ever get her money?"

Lucien's hand ceased its struggle to be free. "Ah. A matter best ignored, love."

"Do you mean Allbright didn't pay?" she demanded. "And you are all willing to let him get away with it? Well, I'm going to—"

"No, you're not," said Lucien firmly.

Beth recognized that he was serious. "Why not?"

He sighed. "Beth, can we perhaps have just one subject that isn't plumbed to the depths?"

"What on earth can be so terrible about a debt? The man either paid or he didn't."

"He paid in kind. With jewelry."

"As long as he paid . . ." Then her eyes narrowed. "If Tom Allbright had jewelry, I assume it was Serena's."

"Yes."

"But Lucian, that's not fair! He paid his debt to her with her own jewels."

"Francis is not debating the point."

"Has Serena even been told? I will—"

"No, you won't. Beth, I doubt Serena ever wants to see that jewelry again."

"Why not? If it is ugly, it can be reset."

To her alarm, he pushed her off his knee and walked away.

"Lucien?"

She thought he wouldn't answer, but then he said, "It is ugly. It is also vicious."

"Vicious?" Beth asked disbelievingly.

He turned, almost angrily. "Very well. You will insist on knowing everything, won't you? You are about to learn how fortunate you are in having married me, Madam Wife." He counted off on his fingers. "Item: one jeweled collar and chain. Item: jeweled shackles. Item: one jeweled-handled whip . . ."

Beth ran over and grasped his eloquent hands. "Don't! Lucien, don't." She looked up into his angry

262

eyes. "She was just *fifteen!*" She went instinctively into his arms.

He held her tight. "I know, love. I know. It doesn't bear thinking about."

Chapter 13

Serena chose to breakfast in bed, reluctant to encounter either her husband or his mother. She wondered if her low spirits were the result of her pregnancy or her situation. She certainly had enough to be miserable about, but if anything, her situation should be improving. She would not bear a bastard, nor would she and her child starve, and her husband was a kind and generous man. Despite this happy state of affairs, her spirits seemed to be sinking lower and lower into a bottomless trough of despair. It was all because of Francis's discontent.

She could not even think of happiness when he was so clearly unhappy. There was a great deal she could not mend—she could not give him Lady Anne for a wife, for example—but there were things she could do. She owed it to him to make their life together work.

Pondering her problem, Serena washed and dressed, then rang to have Brandy brought to her in the drawing room. As a gift from her husband, she was especially precious to Serena.

The scrubbed kitchen boy proudly brought up the

basket. "I took her out in the garden just a little while ago, milady," he announced.

"I'm sure that was a good idea."

"And I made her a rag ball." He proudly showed her the object.

"That was very kind of you."

The lad showed a tendency to linger, and Serena suspected he was already beginning to think of the dog as his. She dismissed him firmly and settled down to enjoy the lovely creature.

Brandy appeared happy to see her but not inclined to be cuddled. She was much more interested in the ball, chasing it around the room and under the furniture. When it wedged under a pedestal stand, she worried at it, little rump sticking out and wagging.

Despite her cares, Serena was laughing when Beth was announced. Beth starting laughing, too, at the sight. Soon both ladies were down on the floor with the puppy, trying to get the ball out.

Francis's mother stalked in. "What on earth? . . ." A picture of elegance, she stared at them, then simply turned and walked out.

"Oh, dear," said Serena, forced back to the cares of the world.

Beth chuckled. "She probably thought we were maids misbehaving." She turned back to trying to rescue the ball.

Serena thought of running after Francis's mother and begging her pardon, but abandoned the notion. It would probably do little good. She rather thought winning over Francis's mother was a lost cause, but how they were all to live together at Thorpe Priory was hard to imagine.

Beth's fingers found a trailing scrap of cloth and pulled it free. Then she tossed it across the room and the puppy scampered after it with glee. Beth just sat there on the carpet, hair escaping its pins. "She's adorable. I must have one."

"A wolfhound?" Serena queried, leaning back against the pedestal. It felt just like their school days, and she wished for those innocent times again.

"Why not? I don't care, and Lucien has a low opinion of what he calls lapdogs."

Serena glanced at Beth. "Your husband is very grand. I could almost be frightened of him."

"He's a fiery creature," Beth agreed, "but sound at heart. He's very like his stallion, Viking. Superbly bred and trained, but still a stallion."

"Why did you marry him?"

Beth met her eyes calmly. "Why did you get pregnant?"

Serena blinked with surprise at the neat parry. She must not forget that Beth had always been very clever. The obvious answer to both questions was "for love." It wasn't true in her case. Was it in Beth's?

"Do you love him?" she dared to ask.

"Yes," said Beth, adding in a prosaic voice, "To the point of insanity. It is, at times, a damned nuisance." She pushed herself to her feet. "Now, are you ready for the theater tonight? It will be a chance to show your face."

Serena wanted to gush enthusiasm but knew her face betrayed her. "It is necessary," she said flatly.

"Yes. There's no point being mealy-mouthed about this, Serena. For the plan to work, people must meet you and like you before talk begins. It will be much harder then for them to shut you out. But Francis can only wait a few days before announcing the marriage formally."

"Which will mean announcing my former name."

"Quite."

Serena captured Brandy and hugged her for comfort. The puppy was beginning to tire and seemed content to be stroked. "Beth, about Matthew's cronies . . ."

"I'm sure there is nothing to worry about. We are going to be moving in the highest circles. . . ."

"You don't understand," Serena interrupted. "They will have seen things . . . Matthew used to . . ." Her mouth didn't seem able to form the words.

"It doesn't matter," said Beth briskly, too briskly. There were patches of color in her cheeks. "Such people carry no weight at all. Now, I have brought some gowns for you. I think they will fit except for the height." She grinned. "You are definitely better endowed in the chest than I, though I seem to be expanding daily. Why don't we go to your room?"

Serena abandoned her warnings and hoped Beth was right. She suspected that no one would understand her life at Stokeley Manor, and she didn't want to enlighten them.

Beth had brought her maid with her, along with a number of boxes. Soon Serena's room was a mass of gorgeous fabrics. Beth picked up a yellow gown and held it against her friend. "I thought this color would suit you," she declared triumphantly, "and since the skirt is plain, it will be easy to alter the hem. Put it on and Redcliff will pin it."

Serena suppressed an urge to object and allowed the

maid to assist her into the lovely gown. It consisted of an underdress of heavy textured silk in a dusky golden yellow, with two shorter overdresses in paler shades. The lower one was of fine sarcenet, the upper of delicate gold-shot lace.

Serena stared at her image in the mirror, stunned by the beauty of the creation. Every movement had it shifting like water, glimmering in the candlelight. "It's too beautiful. . . ."

She was ignored. "It'll need a few tucks around the waist, milady," said Redcliff, applying some pins. "If you were to lend Lady Middlethorpe your bronze zephyr shawl to wear as a sash, it'd likely hide any rough work."

"Excellent, Redcliff," said Beth, who was on her knees, adjusting the hem. "The underskirt must come up three inches, but I think we can leave the outskirts, since there is so little time. Can it be done by the evening?"

"Surely, milady."

The dress was whipped off and carried away, and another—a green—was brought out for consideration. Serena didn't see how Beth could bear to part with such beautiful gowns. "These dresses will be ruined for you," she objected.

"Don't give it a thought. That yellow never looked half as good on me as it does on you, so I think I only wore it the once." Beth looked shrewdly at Serena's still-dubious face. "If you are feeling at all guilty, you must come and inspect my wardrobes one day. They are full to overflowing with clothes I will never wear more than once or twice. It is ridiculous, but it is the price of high rank. At least we employ a great many people in the making, and since I even pay extra to ensure that the seamstresses have good light in which to work, my conscience doesn't trouble me too much."

She was obviously telling the truth. Serena fingered a cream and brown confection. "Then I can only say thank you. I have never owned gowns as lovely as these." In the back of Serena's mind was the memory of her exquisite wedding dress, but that had soon been tarnished by unbearable memories.

She was snapped out of her thoughts by a growling sound. She chased down Brandy, wondering how a tiny puppy could be making such a threatening noise. Just as she spotted the dog, Brandy launched herself at Beth's bonnet, which had fallen to the floor.

"No!" shrieked Serena and grabbed, but Brandy came up with the feathered ornament on the brim of the bonnet firmly between her small teeth. "Let go, you bad girl! Let go, I say." She forced the small jaws open and rescued the bonnet.

Beth was laughing. "She looks so proud of herself! I fear you have a bird dog there."

"Beth, I'm so sorry. She's broken one of the feathers."

Beth took the bonnet and placed it on one of the spindles of the dressing table, well out of reach. "It is of no matter, I assure you. Isn't it strange, though, how such instincts are inborn?"

Serena rang for the lad to come and take charge of Brandy before the puppy did even more damage, and then she submitted to yet more fittings. She was hard put to join in with the cheerful chatter, however. A new weight had descended upon her. No wonder Francis was so dismayed by his situation. Not only had he lost his chosen bride—and even if he didn't love Lady Anne, he did not deny that she had all the qualities he desired—and been plunged into scandal, but his children would have the Allbright blood.

Serena herself had never felt part of the Allbrights, for she took more after her mother in looks and temperament. She had to accept that it was possible, however, for her children to turn out to be very like Tom and Will.

Lady Anne Peckworth doubtless carried no such undesirable traits within her.

"Now," said Beth, "what of jewels? I have plenty of those, too."

Serena returned to the matter in hand, the only one that seemed within her control. "Oh, no. Francis bought me a topaz necklace and earrings yesterday that will surely do."

She and Beth inspected the items in the jewelry box, removing a filigreed gold bracelet. "I have some ivory pieces that would go well," said Beth, and would not be gainsaid. "I will send them over. Think of it as armor, Serena. People will take you as they find you. If you look wealthy and confident, they will accept you as such."

"But I'm not at all confident, not at heart."

"Perish the thought. I never feel like a marchioness, but I've learned to act the part." She gave Serena a very warm hug, as if she understood some of her anxieties. "You are not to worry," she instructed firmly. "You are a Rogue now, Serena. You are safe from *the terror by night, the pestilence that walketh in darkness, and the destruction that waiteth at noonday.'* Trust us. Yes?"

Serena could do nothing but nod.

Beth left, but her words lingered. They had the force of a command. Serena understood them, but she felt like a starving waif peeping into a banqueting hall. The feast, however, was not food but security. She saw it, she could smell it and almost taste it, but she was not sure it was really for her.

She was not sure that she deserved it.

Francis returned, and she could not penetrate his courtesy to find the truth. They talked of the gowns, of the Rogues, and of the puppy. He laughed at Brandy's predatory ways and was as amiable as anyone could wish, but in some way it was not real. Serena could only assume that he was masking his unhappiness and disappointment.

Was this to be the pattern of their lives?

The dowager joined them for luncheon and was equally polite, though in a far more chilly manner. When she agreed to join their theater party, it was with a daunting air of sacrifice. When the dowager left to visit a friend, Serena had to ask, "Francis, will your mother live with us?"

"Freezing you, is she?" he asked without offense. "It is a problem. We could take alternative quarters in town but there's little option in the country, and I'm afraid my mother is deeply attached to the Priory. She and my father built it, you see."

"Built it?"

"From the ground up. My father inherited a Tudor manor house which had first been a priory. I gather the old house really was falling down—deathwatch beetle and everything. They decided to build anew. The planning and construction took the first five years of my parents' marriage, and I suppose there is a part of them both in it. My mother loved my father very deeply."

"I see," said Serena. She did, but the future was daunting.

"I keep hoping that she will marry again—she's still a handsome woman—but I doubt she could bring herself to leave the Priory, or to replace my father."

"I will do my best to live with her in harmony," Serena said. *Anything for you, my dear.*

An awareness stirred within her, an awareness of how much she wanted to touch his heart. . . .

"Perhaps it will help when the child is born," he said, as if from a distance.

Will it help us, too? She wished she dared touch him, invite him. Good heavens, it was the middle of the day. She rose to her feet. "I think I should rest."

Then she was aware that she was using tiredness as an excuse to hide from him, when she knew it was as good as slamming her bedroom door in his face.

"A good idea. We will be out late tonight." He rose to escort her to the door, but captured her hand and raised it for a kiss. It was not a simple kiss of courtesy, but somehow heated. His other hand cherished her waist, her hip, then pulled her closer.

Serena looked up at him, her nerves leaping with a combination of hope and anxiety. He looked so somber. What was he thinking?

"I think we should practice kisses," he said huskily. "to see if we can find some you like." His hand had come to rest on her bottom, pressing her against him. She could feel his hardness. For whatever reason, at this moment he desired her.

"Kiss me," he whispered:

What did he mean by that? Serena slid her hands behind his neck to lower his head to hers, kissing him gently on the lips. He pulled her hips against his restlessly.

"More," he said.

She opened her lips a little against his, then brought her tongue into play teasingly.

Abruptly, he slanted his head and melded with her mouth hotly. He moved a few steps so she was pressed against the wall and one hand came up to knead at her breast. His hips pressed against her. She took his tongue and sucked it, moving her hips against his encouragingly. *Oh, yes, my love, let me do this for you.* . . . .

Suddenly, he broke free. He stepped back, eyes wild and heated. "I'm sorry," he said tightly.

She moved toward him. "It's all right. . . ."

He swung away. "Just leave, Serena."

Serena fled, fighting tears. Did he hate this marriage so much that he could not even bear to take his ease in it?

Francis buried his face in his hands. God, what was he to do? Another moment and he would have been taking his wife there against the wall like a street doxy in an alley. He paced the room, struggling with himself desperately.

Serena's face as she had turned to flee him was imprinted upon his mind. He'd terrified her. She needed tenderness, and all he seemed able to offer her was maddened lust.

He called for his coat and strode out of the house. The only safety was to be away from his wife.

He knew he would be welcome at Belcraven House, or he could go to one of his clubs, but such company did not appeal. Instead, he went to Scarborough Lane, to the house of Blanche Hardcastle.

Her maid was a little startled to see him, but admitted that her mistress was at home and took him into the parlor. Francis wondered what the devil he was doing here. Hal could be here. If Hal wasn't here, his visit could look peculiar.

Blanche came in, dressed in white as was her habit. "Hello, Francis. What can I do for you?"

It was as if she could read his mind. "I need advice."

She sat down and gestured for him to take a seat. "About your wife?"

"Yes. Is it so obvious?"

She smiled gently. "It is bound to be complicated."

"An understatement, I assure you. Will Hal mind me being here?"

"If he does, he'll get his marching orders," she said. "I'm no man's chattel."

"Is that why you won't marry him?"

"I thought we were to talk of your problems, not mine. But no, that isn't the reason. Love binds without laws. But love also trusts."

"Trust," he sighed. "I suppose trust takes time."

"It takes time to root. It has to be tested, I think. But it can come quickly."

"And if trust is broken?"

"Then it takes time to mend. Is that the problem?"

Francis realized that he had little reason to distrust Serena. Her first action had been unwise, but he could understand it. There was really no evidence that she had done anything else questionable. "Not really," he said.

"Then it must be sex."

He could feel himself flushing.

Her eyes flashed with knowing humor. "Why else would you seek out me rather than one of the Rogues?"

"Does it seem an insult? I'm sorry."

"Of course it doesn't. It's a simple fact that I've taken a great many men to my bed and made it my business to learn the art of it. I would rather have been born a lady of leisure and lived in perfect virtue, but I wasn't and I haven't. It was either a life of squalor or use the gifts God gave me, and I regret very little that I have done. Now, what can I do to help?"

Francis leaned back in his chair and the words came out more easily than he had expected. "I was a virgin until I met Serena."

"Ah." Then she smiled. "That's lovely."

"Lovely!"

"Yes." She twinkled a smile at him. "Don't ever let this past your lips, but I suspect Lucien was a virgin when I became his mistress."

"Lucien!"

"You see, all those merry schoolboy tales you shared were probably mostly just that. Tales." She smiled into the distance and said, "He was nineteen and so beautiful, *I* would have paid *him* if I'd been able to afford such a creature. I think when he offered to make me his mistress, he was just playing the game, doing what was expected. He was quite shocked when I agreed, though he hid it well, even then. If not the first, I was certainly the first to join with him with care and leisure. I felt very honored. I also felt a responsibility. I think I trained him well." She looked back at Francis. "Does Serena know?"

"No. I doubt she'd think it so marvelous."

"Why not?"

"She doesn't like it. Lovemaking."

"She refuses you?"

"No . . . she . . ." Francis rose restlessly to his feet. "I don't know. Perhaps she is normal. How would I know? She doesn't seem to enjoy herself. She seems to be tense. . . . I am clearly doing something wrong."

Blanche rose, too. "Do you want to share my bed, Francis? Is that why you came here?"

He turned sharply. "God, no."

"Good. I am faithful in my own way. I could find you another woman, though. A good one."

"No. Is that the only way to learn?"

"I don't know. I'm sure Serena's experiences in her marriage were not pleasant. . . ."

"So am I."

He was more reluctant than he had been over his own ignorance, but he told her about the jewels.

"Ah. Poor girl. But if she welcomes you, that says a lot. Do you take the time to give her pleasure?"

He could feel the damnable color flood his cheeks again. In a way he resented Blanche's questions, but he would put up with them for both Serena's sake and his. "I have tried. She seems to like some things but never stops thinking, damn her."

"Perhaps her first husband punished her if she stopped thinking."

He looked at her, arrested. "Do you think so?"

"It is very likely. He was an older man, and sometimes such men do not find it easy to couple. He probably taught her ways to help him and punished her if he failed."

"What can I do, then?"

"Make love to her and show her that you will not blame her for any shortcomings."

"Even if she does not get full pleasure?"

"Of course. To expect that from her is a kind of burden, don't you think? But don't do anything she does not like."

He took another restless turn. "Sometimes my desire is too great. I cannot be as careful as I want."

"Francis, are you avoiding her because of that?"

At her tone of amused reproof, he turned. "I am only thinking of her."

She put her hands on her hips. "Lord above. Such unselfishness is likely to kill you both! It will just make matters worse. Take your pleasure in a mad storm if you must, but then give her pleasure afterward."

"I tell you, I can't."

"I didn't say orgasm. I said pleasure. Hold her. Stroke her. You could massage her."

"Massage her?"

"As I did to you in Melton."

Francis was feeling rather dazed. "I see. You think this best?"

"I think abstinence will solve nothing. If the intensity of your need bothers you, though, there are ways to relieve it. I'm sure you know them."

He was blushing again, damn it. "I don't know if I'll ever be able to face you again after this."

She laughed gently. "Yes, you will. Serena is your wife, Francis, and I cannot believe that she finds you repugnant. She will be happy to serve you in bed, if that is all it is, but I think she will welcome the closeness that comes of it, too. In time, there will probably be more, but don't make her response a challenge for her. She has had enough, I would suspect, of bedtime challenges."

"I think you are right. Your advice, however, fits so neatly with my desires that I suspect it."

"Don't. I always put a woman's cause before a man's."

Francis left the house and wandered the streets, not seeking companionship, trying to decide if Blanche's advice was sound or not. He had to believe her final statement, though. She thought such a course would be better for Serena as well as for him.

He knew Serena was unhappy. He could sense it. Their present situation was not ideal, with his mother's antagonism and the stress of entering Society, but there was more to it than that. Perhaps some intimacy would be helpful.

His desire, of course, was to rush home and drag his wife into the bedroom immediately, but the very intensity of the need gave him pause. The nighttime would be better.

Francis had not returned by the time Serena had to start preparing for the evening. She took her bath, and then her maid assisted her into her underclothes and arranged her hair. The maid proved skillful but claimed that Serena's hair was perfect to work with. Whatever the cause, she worked the deep red mass into an artistic masterpiece of curls and tendrils, finishing it with an aigrette of creamy lace and russet feathers.

Serena decided she had best not go anywhere near Brandy looking like this.

She considered the attractive arrangement uneasily. It was second nature for her now to play down her looks, and this style did anything but. It emphasized her eyes and the length of her slender neck. Did it make her look bold and wanton?

She remembered Harriet Wilson. "A cocked gun pointed at the heart of this man's world." In this situation, was a gun a good or a bad thing?

She addressed the maid. "Please see if Lord Middlethorpe is in his rooms. I wish to speak to him."

The surprised maid draped a wrap around Serena, then went off to inquire. Francis was home. He came in and the maid discreetly disappeared. He was in shirt sleeves and his collar stood open, for he had not yet arranged his cravat.

He halted just inside the door, far away from her. "You are unwell?" he asked with reserved concern, but his eyes were not reserved.

Serena stood nervously. "No." She was finding herself alarmingly distracted by his appearance. His state of half-dress was exceedingly attractive.

Roguish was exactly the word that came to mind.

"You wanted something," he prompted, frowning slightly.

Serena collected her wits. "I just wondered if I was going to look right. Beth's lending me a dress. It's very fine. With my hair like this . . . will I look too bold?"

He smiled. "My dear, you look beautiful, not bold.

And I doubt Beth has a dress in her wardrobe that could make you look unsuitable."

Serena discovered that she wanted, quite desperately, to be held in his arms, but he was on the far side of the room and showed no sign of moving closer. "I want to look right for you," she said earnestly. "I know this evening is important."

"Important for you, too, surely. You want a position in Society."

She clutched the negligee to her. "I have lived without Society all my life, Francis. I could be content in a cottage in the country."

"It is a charming fancy, my dear, but I doubt it. And I would not care for it. I am fond of my comforts."

"I was happy in Summer St. Martin."

"Then I am sorry to have dragged you away."

That wasn't what she had meant. She took a few more steps toward him.

"Serena," he said flatly, "if you come any closer, I am likely to throw you on the bed and ravish you. It will undoubtedly mess up your hair and make us late for dinner."

She stared at him, not knowing what to make of such a declaration. "Please," she said, intending it as agreement.

He shook his head and produced a smile. "I was joking, my dear. You look beautiful. Now finish dressing or we will be late." And with that, he was gone.

Serena returned to her dressing table feeling shaken. Had that been a joke or not? Did he really want to ravish her? She was aware of a number of ways he could ravish her without disturbing her hair at all. Nor would they take very long. So why had he not?

She glared at herself in the mirror. She was sure that in some way her beauty was to blame for her wounded marriage, as it had been to blame for just about all the problems in her life.

It was a cocked gun, however. If she couldn't use it to seize her own happiness, at least she could use it to take Society by storm.

Her own happiness. Her husband's heart.

She caught her breath at that. Was she truly, truly going to aim for the moon?

What else could she do when she loved him?

Her mind wandered over her feelings like a blind person exploring a new and unknown object. Yes, she thought it was. She thought it was love. The care she felt, the tenderness, the desire to fight for him and for his happiness; it was the awful power of love. . . .

A tap on the door brought her maid back with the gown. "The hemming's a bit rough, milady," she said, "so try to keep it up away from anything that might snag it." She flipped the gown onto Serena and fastened the buttons at the back. "But the length's dead right. My, but it does look pretty on you."

Serena looked in the mirror and knew it was true.

The glowing yellow gown was perfect with her coloring. It made her skin more delicate and her hair richer. The neckline was wide, but unlike all the gowns Matthew had bought for her, it was also completely decent.

The maid quickly wrapped a long bronze scarf around the high waist and knotted it to hang down one side. Serena put on her topaz set, the bracelet, and then the ivory pieces Beth had sent. There was a carved arm band and a heavy pin that she used to anchor the scarf.

The maid had also brought a cloak to match the dress. It was ivory velvet lined with yellow silk.

Serena knew that she looked the very picture of a Society beauty, and for once in her life there was nothing suspect about her fine clothes.

She dismissed the maid with warm thanks, then used the perfume Francis had bought for her. What would her beloved think?

Knowledge of love made her raw, so that the fine silk of her shift grated against her skin and her curls weighed heavy at her neck. She knew her breaths as a newborn must, each one a painful wonder. She almost hesitated to face him now, as a saint might fear to face a glowing God. . . .

Serena gathered her courage and knocked on the adjoining door.

He opened the door himself. He was dressed now in dark evening clothes, snowy linen, and discreet jewels. His valet was nowhere to be seen. She saw his lips part on a breath. "You are very beautiful," he said, and his eyes told her he spoke the truth. But there was something almost agonized in his look.

She searched for his reaction. "But do I look right?"

"Yes, of course you do. You will be a sensation." He raised her chin and kissed her gently, finger and lips like fire. "Don't worry. With the Rogues behind you, you are as invincible as Wellington."

She gripped his arms, intending to make more of the kiss, but he gently disengaged. "We mustn't ruffle your finery, must we?"

As they left the room, Serena knew that her Waterloo was not Society, but her husband's heart.

Francis's mother awaited them, dressed in elegant

dark blue. With her slim build and fine bones she somehow made Serena feel blowsy, but she seemed determined to be pleasant. She complimented Serena on her appearance and kept up a flow of light conversation all the way to Belcraven House. Clearly, the dowager had decided that in her son's cause she could do anything.

In that, thought Serena, we are in agreement, my lady. She deliberately pushed the frightening new knowledge of love to the back of her mind and concentrated on her task.

At the ducal mansion, Serena found that their party contained four extra ladies.

Sir Stephen Ball had brought his sister Fanny, a vigorous and much respected bluestocking. Con Somerford, Viscount Amleigh, had turned up and brought his cousin, Lady Rachel Ibbotson-French. Her husband was apparently a highly respected diplomat currently sorting matters out in Italy, and Lady Rachel was also a member of the influential Greville family.

To Serena's delight, Arabella was present and had brought her friend Maud, who turned out to be the formidable Dowager Countess of Cawle.

Even Serena had heard of the Dowager Countess. From her mansion on Albemarle Street—which she refused to give over to her son and his wife—she had been a ruler of London Society for thirty years. Not for her to hold great routs, or dispense vouchers for subscription assemblies or opera balls; the Countess of Cawle merely observed and listened and occasionally passed judgment.

From her reputation, Serena had expected a crone, but Lady Cawle was a full-figured woman and still handsome. If she was of an age with Arabella, she must be in her late fifties, but her smooth skin and big eyes made her look less. She was not a follower of fashion, however. She took up a whole sofa because she insisted on wearing the full skirts of her younger days, with a waist at its natural level. On this occasion, the spreading skirts were in sage-green with black silk ruching.

When Serena was introduced to her, the countess gave the briefest of nods, but her deceptively sleepy eyes missed nothing. Serena quaked in her shoes, not able to believe that this woman would countenance her for a moment.

Throughout the meal, the dowager ignored her. But then all the lady's attention was upon the Marquess of Arden, who was flirting with her shamelessly. Despite the age difference, it did not seem at all ridiculous, and Beth appeared to find it amusing. Serena wondered how she would feel if Francis flirted with every lady he met. She suspected that she'd be as mad as fire.

This seemed to prove that she was at heart a country bumpkin. Serena was grateful to be seated between Francis and Miles, and relatively comfortable, even if most of the light conversation was left to the Irishman. Francis must be very worried about the evening to be so tense.

When the ladies went apart, Serena suspected that her time of comfort was over. As she had feared, she was beckoned to the countess's side. "Sit, gel," Lady Cawle said in a tone very like Arabella's. "So, you're Riverton's well-trained wife."

Serena's color flared and she bounced up from the seat she had just taken.

Lady Cawle did not blink. "Run, gel, and I'll wash my hands of you."

The matter hung in the balance for a long moment, and then Serena took a deep breath and sank back down into the chair. "Good," said the countess as if without interest. "Pity you're so beautiful. People will think the worst. There is a universal desire to find fault with a beautiful woman."

"Perhaps they should," said Serena, swallowing.

"Should they?"

Serena looked at the woman, who exuded all the warmth of a marble statue. "What do you mean?"

"Have you done anything of which you are ashamed, Lady Middlethorpe?"

Serena knew she should lie, but the night at the Posts' farm rose up in her mind like a label of sin. She lowered her head. "Yes."

Amazingly, the countess chuckled. "So I should hope. I'd never have believed you if you'd said no. But are you ashamed of your life? I am not talking of what has happened to you but of what you have done."

Serena frowned at the puzzling woman and considered the question. "No," she said at last. "I can think of many things I would change, being older and wiser, but I did the best I could at the time."

"Good. I have a soft spot for young Middlethorpe. If I'd had the chance, I would have stopped this marriage, of course, for it won't be easy, but as it's done, I'll try to smooth your way. You, gel, will do your part by *believing* that you're as good as any of 'em. It's mostly true. Cower, and I'll have no more of you. Do you understand?"

Serena felt bludgeoned. "Yes. But what if—?"

"No ifs. No buts. Stare 'em down. Never flinch. Men don't make a cavalry charge with hesitation in their hearts. Make no mistake, this is an assault."

Cocked guns. Waterloo. Cavalry charges.

"People die in cavalry charges," Serena pointed out.

"So they do." There was no trace of sympathy or hesitation in the countess's voice.

"You would have made a remarkable general," said Serena, and it was not entirely a compliment.

"I think so. I'm ruthless enough. You would have made a dreadful one. If I'm any judge, though, you'll make a good wife and mother, given a chance. It's as well you are not dressing boldly, for it's the women we have to win over. The men will all just envy Middlethorpe, but that will make it harder to win over their wives. You're what every man wants, you know. A decent woman who can act the whore."

"I'm not—"

"Which are you not?"

Serena shut her mouth resentfully.

The countess fixed her with eyes that no longer appeared lazy at all. "Are you willing to charge Society without flinching, young woman?"

Serena wanted to tell the witch to go to hell, but she said, "Yes."

"Lady Arden," the countess called across the room, "I shall be attending the theater."

Serena hadn't known it had been in doubt.

She was dismissed and escaped to sit by Lady Rachel, who seemed capable of an endless stream of superficial chat. Serena supposed it was an admirable diplomatic skill. As she let the words flow over her, Serena worried about the countess's words. *A decent woman who can act the whore.* She supposed that did describe her perfectly, but what then of Francis? She wasn't sure he believed her to be a decent woman, and he didn't seem to want her to act the whore.

Soon Arabella drew her away. "How are you faring, my dear? You are looking very grand. I gather you stood up to Maud. Good for you. It amuses her to terrify people."

"I would have thought she could find something better to do with her life."

"Tush, tush. Don't show your claws, dear. Maud works quite hard at being the Guardian of Society. She don't concern herself with the majority of the fashionable throng, but she watches the fringes. And Society watches her. Many a worthy person has gained the entrée through her, and many a scoundrel has been routed. She can sense petty malice and deception like a hound on the scent."

Serena cast a puzzled glance at the countess, who had seemed to approve of her, all in all. "She is extraordinary," she said. "I confess that I am surprised you two are such friends."

"Are you? Women choose their own ways to challenge life. I chose to do without men. Maud preferred to use them. But at heart we're like two peas in a pod. Of course, she was always pretty and I was not, which may have had a lot to do with our choices."

Serena glanced at Arabella curiously. Would Arabella have wanted to marry? Nothing, it would appear, was ever simple or quite what it seemed. It did make life extremely difficult.

Soon the men joined them, and the whole party left for Drury Lane. They all traveled by coach except for the countess, who invariably used her own sedan chair, with her own chairmen and escort. Moreover, as there was a hint of drizzle in the air, she commanded the chair be brought right into the house for her to enter.

At the theater, eight of them sat in splendor in the ducal box, while Miles, Felicity, Fanny, and Stephen Ball cheerfully settled in the lively gallery, intent upon doing their best to spread gossip.

Certainly, there were many glances at their box, for though it wasn't a busy time of year, the theater was well attended, and people in a ducal box must be of interest, especially once it had been discerned that two of the inhabitants were the marquess and marchioness. Beth was playing up to the occasion in a splendid tiara and high necklace of diamonds.

The presence of the Dowager Countess of Cawle also attracted attention and whispers.

Serena saw an increasing number of looks at herself—the unknown. Francis sat beside her and paid her a great deal of attention; the truth must be obvious to all. Serena raised her chin and smiled at him, at anyone else who spoke to her, and out at the rest of the audience. And though it hurt her face, she relentlessly smiled throughout the evening.

She rather thought she could have enjoyed the performance if she hadn't been so intent on smiling.

There were three intermissions, and at each one Serena, Beth, Francis, and Lucien went out to promenade. Serena walked on Beth's arm, in the manner of an old friend. Each walk was a constant stream of introductions, but they always moved on before people had time to ask questions.

The looks were curious, sometimes admiring, occasionally jealous, but never suspicious.

It was not nearly as difficult an event as Serena had expected, but still, by the end of the performance, she was exhausted.

After the theater, the marquess conveyed them to Emile's for a fashionable supper. There, a whole new range of people stopped by the table to pay their respects and to be introduced to the unknown. The choice of lady-sponsors proved to be genius. The intellectuals stopped because of Fanny, the diplomatic and government set because of Lady Rachel, and the social butterflies because of the countess and marchioness.

Serena continued to smile. She thought the expression had become fixed and quite possibly resembled a grimace rather more than a look of happiness. She did note, however, that though there was much admiration directed at her, and one or two intrigued looks at Francis, no one seemed to realize that she was Randy Riverton's widow.

Yet.

She was constantly alert for a face she knew, but saw none. Perhaps Beth was correct, and her husband's cronies simply didn't move in these circles. But at some point Francis would have to announce the wedding in the papers, and all these smiling people would know who she was. Who she had been.

She was worried enough to confess her fears to the countess as they made their farewells.

"No, my dear," said Lady Cawle quite kindly. "There will be talk, but as long as you behave as you did tonight, no one will dare to make trouble. They have already accepted you, you see, and cannot admit to have made a mistake. And anyone who makes trouble will risk offending some very important people, including me."

On impulse, Serena kissed the woman's powdered cheek. The countess was startled, but then laughed. "I can see why Arabella has taken a fancy to you, gel. Be good to Middlethorpe." With that command, she entered her ornate chair and was borne away.

Serena would be delighted to be good to Middlethorpe, if only he would give her the chance.

Everyone seemed elated with success, but Serena just felt fortunate to have survived. This time. It was all to do again tomorrow.

When they arrived home at three in the morning, Francis escorted her to her room. "It all went well, I think," he said.

"I hope so." To her dismay, she yawned. But what else could anyone expect? She had never been in the habit of staying up late.

"You are tired. Tomorrow I'm sure Beth will want to gad about to show you off in as many places as possible. Don't do more than you wish."

"I won't mind." Though he appeared composed, something was humming about him, humming between them. Her head and her heart wanted him to make love to her, but her body wanted to go to sleep.

He entered her room with her and took her hands. She thought his trembled slightly. She felt as if he were about to say something, something of significance, but he merely raised her hands and brushed them with a kiss. "Sleep well, my dear."

And he was gone.

Serena looked at her big bed, where she apparently

was to sleep alone again. She was exhausted and in no mood for bed-work, but it would have been lovely to have shared the bed with him.

Francis went to his room and got drunk again. He was sure Blanche's advice was good, but he still couldn't bring himself to rut upon a tired woman. Tomorrow. Perhaps even a morning visit to his wife. Yes, he thought, pouring more brandy. In the morning. Serena in the sunlight, drowning in her hair . . .

When he woke up, however, it was afternoon and he felt worse than the day before. On dredging his sodden memory, he realized that his valet must have had to put him to bed. He groaned with more than the throb of his head.

If he went on at this rate, he'd be a wreck.

It was as well that Serena was already out of the house, apparently in the company of Beth.

Chapter 14

Serena was finding that Francis's prediction had been correct. The assault on Society was to continue, but now in an entirely feminine way.

She had awoken at the decadent hour of eleven and taken her breakfast in bed. Along with the tray was a note warning her that Beth would arrive at noon to collect her.

First they had gone to Belcraven House to inspect Beth's wardrobe. Serena was astonished at the quantity of gowns there, and she accepted a few more.

After a luncheon, Beth and Serena paid a morning visit to the countess and were granted twenty minutes of her time. There were a number of other ladies present who accepted Serena without question. But then, Lady Cawle, Arabella, and Beth managed to deflect any attempt to question Serena about her origins.

Then they went to Hookham's, where they browsed the shelves and—almost incidentally—encountered any number of people who were delighted to make the acquaintance of the new Lady Middlethorpe.

Serena could see that Beth's sponsorship was almost a foolproof entry to Society. No one would lightly risk offending the future Duchess of Belcraven.

As they drove on to Gunter's, she said as much to Beth.

"It's true," said Beth. "And while I still hate the power of rank, I have come to see that attitude to be as pointless as hating the wind for blowing. Instead, I try to find ways to use it for the best."

They had arranged to meet Lady Rachel at the pastry shop, and she had brought her brother, Sir Jeffrey Greville, as escort. This witty gentleman was apparently known to half of London, and a whole new range of introductions interrupted their refreshments.

As they emerged onto the pavement, Serena shook her head slightly. "I feel as if I have been introduced to the whole of London!"

"Not quite. But a good part of it," admitted Beth, surveying the crowded street. "The important part. How busy it is today. See, the coach is down the street, unable to come closer. Horror of horrors, we will have to use our legs!" They shared a grin as they made their way toward the crested carriage. Beth's perturbed footman was hastening forward to escort them.

"As if," murmured Beth, "we were in danger of assault in a few yards of rather busy pavement . . ."

It was no easy matter to make progress, however, for the fine weather had brought a good many ladies and gentlemen out of hibernation, and many of them seemed as intent on sauntering and chatting as on purchasing. In addition, servants on errands threaded their way through the crowds.

Two ladies came out of a linen-draper's shop, and

Beth and Serena stopped to allow them to cross in front to enter their coach. The older lady noticed them and paused with a pleasant smile. "Lady Arden. Somewhat busy today, is it not?"

"Indeed it is, Duchess. A burst of premature spring weather has us all in a frenzy, like March hares. . . ." At the end of this chatter, something in Beth's tone changed, and Serena looked at her, wondering if she were taken ill.

"Beth? . . ." she said.

The duchess looked between them, mildly curious. Duchess of what? The duchess's companion was a young woman whose good looks were given dignity by an aura of neatness and composure.

The duchess moved to fill the awkward silence. "I don't believe you are acquainted with my second daughter, Lady Arden. Anne, make your curtsy to the marchioness, my dear. Poor Anne has not been well. We are going to spend a few weeks in Bath."

"How nice that will be, Lady Anne," said Beth, still in that strange voice. Serena clearly heard her sigh before she said, "May I introduce my companion, Lady Middlethorpe?"

When Lady Anne's face went sheet-white, the truth finally dawned on Serena. This pretty, dignified young woman was Francis's Lady Anne. She appeared fragile, for she was of slight build with pale blond hair, and the shock made her appear more so. Now, however, her pallor was drowning under a wave of pink embarrassment.

Serena could feel the same hectic color in her own cheeks.

The duchess was also red, but red with anger. At any

moment there was going to be a truly disastrous scene. Serena wondered desperately what one was supposed to do in this situation. Just walk on? Apologize? *Lady Anne, I am so sorry for stealing your future husband. . . .*

Then Lady Anne held out her gloved hand. "Lady Middlethorpe, I'm pleased to meet you." It was said rather woodenly, but it was said.

Deeply grateful, Serena touched her gloved fingers to those offered. "And I you, Lady Anne. I hope you enjoy your stay in Bath."

Lady Anne managed a flicker of a smile. "I don't suppose I shall enjoy the waters." She looked around vaguely. "We are blocking the pavement, I'm afraid."

The duchess came to life and nodded curtly. "Lady Middlethorpe. Lady Arden." Then she swept her daughter into their carriage and it rolled off, but not before Serena had noted that Lady Anne walked with a slight but noticeable limp. It somehow made everything ten times worse.

"I'm sorry. . . ." Both Beth and Serena said it together, then shared an appalled glance.

They continued on toward their coach. Serena was fighting tears and knew she must not shed them here. She already felt as if the whole street had been witness to that scene, even though there was no sign of anyone else having noticed.

"What an awkward business," murmured Beth shakily. "But really, what could we have done?"

They climbed into the carriage with relief. "Nothing, I suppose," sighed Serena. She swallowed hard. "Lady Anne seems a lovely person."

"She certainly did well just then," agreed Beth.

Serena sniffed back the gathering tears. "I can see w . . . why Francis w . . . wooed her."

Beth took her hands. "Serena, stop this! If Francis had truly wanted to marry Anne, he would never have made love to you."

Serena covered her face and wept.

Beth ordered the carriage to go directly to Hertford Street. As soon as they entered the house, Francis was there. "What happened?"

Beth had her arms around Serena. "We met the Duchess of Arran and Lady Anne."

He turned pale. "Here in Town?"

"We hardly drove down to Wiltshire, now, did we?"

"Don't snap." He took Serena into his own arms and held her tight. "What happened?"

"Nothing," Serena said, trying to free herself from his embrace, an embrace she did not deserve. An embrace she had *stolen* from a better woman . . .

Ignoring Beth, he swept Serena into his arms and carried her up to her room. Once there, he laid her on her bed and gently removed her bonnet. "What happened?" he asked again. "You didn't become this upset over nothing."

Wearily, Serena sat up. She found her handkerchief and blew her nose. "Truly, nothing happened. We were all incredibly well behaved. Lady Anne went out of her way to smooth over the awkward moment."

"Yes, she would."

Serena blew her nose again to cover an unworthy spurt of irritation. Lady Anne clearly was exactly the sort of wife Francis wanted and deserved, and she was the most miserable wretch in creation.

He relieved her of her soggy handkerchief and

dabbed at her eyes with his dry one. "At least you and Anne have met and handled it with civility, so the worst is over. The one thing about all this is that these things only have to be done once. It will all blow over. . . ."

The words escaped. "But you wanted to marry *her!*"

He didn't deny it. "That is in the past. Now, if you are up to it, a jaunt is planned for tonight to the Royal Circus, followed by a musicale at Lady Cowper's. They should both be the sort of entertainments to raise your spirits. Tomorrow, Beth and Lucien are holding their soirée. With any luck, that should be the end of it."

Serena felt bone weary at the thought of this endless social merry-go-round and depressed by his tone. He was clearly finding all this as dreadful as she was.

She made no objection to these busy plans, however, but slid off the bed to remove her spencer. When she turned she saw the look in his eye and recognized it. Welcomed it.

When she realized Francis wasn't going to do anything about the way he felt, Serena was totally confused.

Did he not know that she was willing to serve him?

How could she invite his attentions without seeming bold?

They were just standing there, so after a moment she took his hand and brought it slowly to her breast. It rested there like a captured creature, but then it moved, kneading gently, and he drew nearer.

Abruptly, he pulled away.

"Do you not want me?" She could *see* that he did.

His jaw tightened. "What I would like," he said rather hoarsely, "is to massage you."

"*Massage* me?"

298

"Yes." Color had touched his cheeks, and he was not looking at her at all. Serena did not know what to make of this. Was it a euphemism? For what? Still, she would allow him just about anything without complaint.

"If that is what you want," she said. "What do you want me to do?"

"Take off your clothes." Then he moved forward with an abruptness that stole his normal grace. "Let me help."

He turned her around and made short work of her fastenings, despite some clumsiness in his fingers. Together they took off her cambric gown, her stays, her petticoat, and her shift, so that she was left in only her cotton stockings and drawers.

Nudity did not distress Serena, but she felt the vulnerability of it and watched him warily. He was somber, like a man studying a disquieting piece of sculpture, but she could almost feel his gaze passing over her like a finger of fire.

"How perfect you are," he said softly, but made no move toward her.

"If I please you, I am pleased." *What do you want? I can see that you are growing hard. Do you want me to fall to my knees and take you in my mouth? Do you want me to bend over the desk so you can take me from behind? Do you want to tie me up? What do you want?*

"Shall I undress further?" she asked at last.

"No. Not yet." He stirred, but only to delicately remove the pins from her hair and finger-comb it loose around her shoulders. The brush of his hands on her sensitive scalp had her lids drifting shut with pleasure. He smoothed her hair softly over her back and then down the front, over her collarbone to her breasts. Her skin was tingling, restlessly wanting more.

She looked at him, full of wonder. He gathered a handful of her hair and raised it to his mouth for a kiss.

Of necessity, that brought her closer to him, so her breasts brushed against the roughness of his woolen jacket in a gentle abrasion that stole her breath.

When he raised his head from her hair, his lips were no great distance from hers. His head lowered, angling against hers. . . .

Then stopped.

He moved away.

Serena remembered telling him she didn't like to be kissed. She caught at his sleeve. "Kiss me, Francis. I would like you to kiss me. . . ."

He allowed her to pull him back, then slid one hand around her neck beneath her hair. His lips lowered again, and his lids shielded the hot darkness of his eyes.

He was gentle. He was too gentle. His lips barely touched hers, though she could feel the heat of his restraint.

Serena stretched her arms around his neck and forced him closer, deepening the kiss. He seemed to almost resist, but then his lips parted and their mouths blended for one sweet moment. . . .

Then he pulled free.

"Enough of that," he said with strained lightness. "Lie on the bed. I want to take off the rest of your clothes."

Serena was acutely disappointed, but her hopes ran high. She obediently lay on the coverlet on her back.

He deftly removed her beribboned drawers and her stockings. He did not touch her in a lascivious way. In fact, he did not touch her at all if it could be avoided. What on earth was all this about?

His eyes wandered over her, and she could see each breath he took. His need was almost more than she could bear. She raised a hand slightly, inviting him.

He frowned then and turned to fetch a big linen towel. "On this, I think. We don't want to soil the brocade."

This was careful planning indeed, thought Serena, but wondered why they did not just get between the sheets. Unless, she thought with sudden anxiety, he had something more unpleasantly soiling in mind . . .

"Right," he said. "Turn over. I'll be back in a moment."

With that, he left the room.

Serena stared after him. After a moment, she obeyed him and lay on her stomach, but with a great deal of uncertainty. In her experience, approaches from behind were generally unpleasant. What had he gone to get? She rested her head on her arms and tried not to think of whips.

She heard him come back and tensed, trying to determine from the sounds he made what might be about to happen. Apart from his footsteps, there was nothing. Then a clink, as if he had put a cup or a bottle down. What could it be?

He touched her and she flinched instinctively, but immediately realized that it was a gentle touch, a warm touch, an oiled touch. She would have twisted to look at him, but he pushed her firmly down, brushed her hair out of the way, and began to rub her back with his oiled hands.

301

Massage. No more, no less. Had anything ever felt as sweet?

His hands were strong and slightly rough, but they were wonderfully soothing as they worked along her spine and ribs. Sometimes they pressed, seeming to find places that wanted to be pressed; sometimes they stroked, smoothing her like a creased sheet under the iron.

"Is that pleasant?" he asked.

"It's heaven," she breathed.

Serena lost sense of time, just growing softer and softer under his hands, softer than it was humanly possible to be. Now he was stroking down her legs. Now he was at her feet.

She felt him move onto the bed and bend her leg so her foot was up. Then he began to massage her foot, giving attention to every bone, every tiny area of skin.

She hadn't thought it possible but she melted even further, dissolving into a warm puddle of contentment. She heard a noise and realized it was her own blissful sigh.

He laughed.

It was the first time she had heard him laugh in such a way and she laughed herself, in so far as anyone can laugh who no longer has bones or muscles left.

Eventually, he stopped, leaving Serena absolutely incapable of movement. He left her, but was back in a moment to wipe all the oil from her back and legs with a soft cloth. Then he pulled back the bedclothes and rolled her under the covers. "Now, rest and be ready for the evening."

Serena was inescapably somnolent, but she looked

up at him with concern. She had expected this to end in sex. "But . . ."

He silenced her with a brief kiss. "Rest."

Then he was gone.

Serena could not fight it. She drifted off to sleep.

Francis washed his hands, feeling like the noblest of sainted martyrs, and in all the pain a martyr could expect. He did not regret his restraint, though. It would have been wrong to drag Serena into sex when she had just had such an upsetting experience, one he felt he should somehow have prevented.

He admitted that he had hoped the massage would lead naturally to lovemaking, but it had been obvious that she was growing sleepy, not aroused. He mustn't forget that she was carrying a child and unused to this busy social round.

On the other hand, that massage had definitely aroused him. It had built the hum of desire that seemed to be constantly with him to an almost unbearable intensity.

He sighed. Perhaps it would be better to avoid massages in the future. At least until their marriage was more normal.

Who'd said the choice was between marriage and burning? Marriage seemed to consist of living in a furnace.

He knocked back a glass of brandy, hoping one burn would kill another, then glared at the empty glass. He was going to turn into a souse at this rate. He rang for his valet, Grisholme, and instructed him to take the brandy away. The man looked heartily glad to do so.

Francis paced his room restlessly. It was damnable that Serena had to encounter Anne. Damnable for both of them. He wished he'd not had to tell Serena about Anne in the first place. It had clearly hurt her. He'd had no choice, however. She had to be prepared for just such an encounter as had happened today.

He wondered just how upset Anne was and if any good would be served by talking to her. It would be hard to explain his actions to a delicately reared young lady, but he hated to think that his silence would hurt more than his explanation.

Francis pondered the situation as he paced the room restlessly. He had not written to Anne during their courtship, for that would not have been proper, and now hardly seemed the time to start a correspondence. But matters were hardly normal, and according to both Serena and Beth, Anne had behaved superbly.

In the end, he wrote a letter to Anne, thanking her for her kindness and apologizing to her for his behavior. He enclosed it, unsealed, in a note to the duchess.

He had just dispatched it when he was told Lucien had come to see him. He went down.

Lucien rose to his feet. "There's news of your quarry."

"My quarry?"

"Ferncliff. Remember him?"

"Oh, yes. At last!" Francis reckoned he could burn off a good deal of his frustration in a violent confrontation with the author of all his troubles. Lucien had brought the footman who had made the discovery, and the man was summoned.

"Staying with a scholarly fellow in Little George

Street in Chelsea, milords," said the footman. "Fellow as fits the description, anyhow."

"Is he there now?" asked Francis.

"Saw 'im go in and made haste straight back to Marlborough Square to report, milord. Can't be an hour yet."

A hackney was summoned and Lucien and Francis piled in. The footman climbed up on the box with the driver and guided him to the house.

Francis had taken the time to grab his pistol case and loaded one in the carriage.

"Just give me warning," said Lucien lazily. "Am I going to have to stop you from committing murder?"

"I doubt it." But Francis didn't respond to the teasing tone. "I just want the truth and an end to it all. My life is tangled enough without this."

"I suppose it is." Lucien stretched out his long legs and swayed as the carriage bounced over the uneven streets. "There was nothing Beth could have done to avoid that incident, you know."

Francis turned to look at him. "Of course not. Does she blame herself? Tell her not to. Thank heavens Anne Peckworth has sense and a kind heart, though."

"Yes," said Lucien, but he gave Francis a funny look.

"Luce," he said impatiently, "I would never have considered marrying Anne if she hadn't been a fine sort of girl. I'm not going to try to pretend she's a harpy now, just to suit my convenience."

Lucien raised a hand in a gesture of surrender. "Fair enough. And as you say, it's as well she didn't create a scene. None of us need that."

The carriage jerked to a halt.

Ferncliff's haunt turned out to be a respectable tall house containing gentlemen's rooms. The footman was given charge of Francis's pistol case—less one pistol—and sent to watch the back of the house. Francis and Lucien climbed the stone steps to rap at the front door. It was opened by a tall, stick-thin individual. "Yes, gentlemen?" he asked in the careful accent of an upper servant. He was clearly impressed, but not awed, by their obvious quality.

Francis realized that they did not know with whom Ferncliff was staying. "We wish to speak with Mr. Charles Ferncliff."

"Ay do not have a tenant of that name, gentlemen." The man was now more wary and began to close the door a little.

"On the other hand," said Francis, "we know he is staying here. It is important that we speak with him. A tall, ruddy man of about thirty-five or forty."

The man wavered.

Lucien took a hand. "Be so good as to tell him that Lord Middlethorpe and the Marquess of Arden wish to speak with him." He dressed the words up with a thick layer of drawling arrogance.

The man's eyes widened. "Yes, milord. Why don't you step in, milords. . . . I will make enquiries, milords."

Thus Francis and Lucien progressed as far as the narrow hall. The landlord disappeared up the stairs, and they saw him knock at a door to the right of the upstairs landing.

"You do that so well," said Francis with a touch of amusement.

"Damned rank has to have its benefits. He recognized the description, at least."

"I noted that."

In a short while the thin man returned, looking rather nervous. "Ay'm afraid there is no Mr. Ferncliff 'ere, milords."

"Then whom do you have staying here to fit his description?" Francis asked.

"Er . . . n . . . no one, milords. Truly, you are mistaken."

"I think not." Francis brushed past and ran up the stairs, pulling out his pistol. Lucien quickly followed.

"Milord! Milords!"

The man's protests followed them as they reached the door. Francis rapped on it. Somewhat to their surprise it was opened promptly, and a plump, elderly servant ushered them in with only a weary look at Francis's weapon. "Come in, milords."

Francis flashed Lucien a bewildered glance. Then a voice bellowed, "Get in here, you blasted reprobates!"

"Simmons," they both muttered in amazement, immediately transported back to their school days. Dr. Mortimer Simmons had been one of the most ferocious tutors at Harrow.

They glanced at one another and moved somewhat warily into the parlor. Francis slipped his gun into his pocket.

It was nearly eight years since they had seen Dr. Simmons. He had always been a big man, and now he appeared positively dropsical. He certainly made no attempt to move from his huge chair but just sat there, glaring at them like a red-faced, malignant toad.

"Arden and Middlethorpe," he snarled. "I might

have known! Where's that damned Delaney, eh? Come to a bad end yet? What're you about, eh, disturbing a man's home? What're you about? I'll have your hides! Damn if I won't!"

Francis almost expected to be birched at any moment. Then he collected his wits. "We are looking for a Mr. Charles Ferncliff."

"So?" demanded the choleric man. "So? Does that give you the right to barge into a man's home? Being sprigs of the aristocracy wipes out no crimes with me, sirs, as I've shown you many a time!"

"I believe he is here," Francis persisted, despite a temptation to cower.

"And if he is, Middlethorpe? If he is? What then, eh? Going to search the place?" He jabbed a swollen finger at Francis. "Over my dead body, sir. Over my dead body! You were rogues as lads, the lot of you, and age hasn't improved you. You still need a sound whipping."

The man was whipping himself up to a frenzy, pounding his swollen fists on the arms of his chair. "What are you about, eh, to be hounding a poor man? What are you about? Think because you have a title you can bully your way through life? You'll come to a sorry end, the lot of you. Company of Rogues, ha! Never a truer word. Gallows bait." He fixed them with a glare. "I know who put senna in my cordial, sirrahs. I know."

At that true accusation, Francis felt guilty terror merge with insane amusement.

"Get out of here!" Dr. Simmons shouted, pointing at the door. "Get out of here, you scum of the earth, before I treat you as you deserve!"

Francis and Lucien shared a look, then fearing that the man was going to have an apoplexy at any moment, they beat a hasty retreat.

In the street again, they burst into laughter. "Gads, I was shaking in my shoes!" Lucien declared. "Simmons! Who would have believed it."

"And the senna!" They fell into laughing again, despite the strange looks they were getting from passersby. After a while the laughter faded and Francis leaned against the railings, feeling limp. "I needed that."

"Laughter?" said Lucien with an understanding look. "Yes, but what about Ferncliff?"

"I'm tempted to say to hell with Ferncliff, but I don't suppose I can. We'll have to keep a watch on the place. He can't cower in there forever. I'll stay here. You go back and arrange things."

"Right." Lucien hesitated a moment before leaving. "I know I'm not Nicholas, but if you want to talk about anything, I'm willing to listen."

Francis smiled. "Thank you. And I'm sorry for snapping at you on Tuesday."

"Don't mention it. You could visit Blanche."

"She has already helped me, as it happens." Francis straightened. "Don't answer this if it's intrusive, but do you and Beth massage one another?"

Lucien's brows rose, but he answered. "Yes. Why?"

"Does it usually end in lovemaking?"

"Generally."

Francis wanted to ask whether receiving a massage normally aroused a woman's interest in lovemaking or sent her to sleep, but he felt he had already asked too much.

Lucien shrugged and left, first to tell the footman to keep to his post, and second to arrange for continuous surveillance of the house. In half an hour, Francis was relieved of duty and able to return home.

He couldn't deny that as soon as he entered his house, he thought of going to make love to his wife. When did he ever think of anything else?

His lascivious intentions had him knocking on Serena's door, but he found her with her maid, dressing for dinner. Her hair was already in an elaborate style, and somehow he could not imagine trying to make love to Serena without that marvelous hair loose around them.

He sighed and went off to prepare himself for the next assault upon Society, resolving to at least stay sober in the future.

Serena had seen the look in Francis's eye and interpreted it correctly. She was cross with herself for drifting off to sleep earlier and was determined to put an end to the strange state of affairs. She wasn't accustomed to men who put a woman's feeling and needs first, but she liked it very much. On the other hand, too much consideration would have them living as brother and sister for the rest of their lives. Now that she was sure Francis desired her, she would make certain he knew he was welcome.

She glanced at the clock. Not now, alas. They were due at the Palace to dine.

Chapter 15

The evening passed much like the previous one, though the circus was a more informal entertainment. Serena was nervous that the more mixed audience would contain a disaster for her, but she soon saw that the youthful entertainment would have little appeal to Matthew's cronies. Once she relaxed, she delighted in the juggling, balancing, and equestrian acts.

Over dinner, the Rogues had gained considerable amusement from the account of the invasion of old Simmons's rooms, and they all seemed to have reverted to schoolboyish ways. The circus only seemed to make them worse. Beth had to lecture them firmly before they progressed to Lady Cowper's soirée.

Lucien said, "Yes, ma'am," and kissed her soundly in the street.

Serena and Francis shared a look, then she took her courage in her hands and pulled him to her for an equally sound kiss. His hands tightened at her waist, and for a moment he deepened it. But then control returned.

Serena was a little regretful. She would not mind missing Lady Cowper's soirée.

The event was a great deal more formal than the circus, and in fact only the Ardens, the Middlethorpes, Sir Stephen, and Fanny went on there. Pretty Lady Cowper greeted them warmly.

"Ah, Lady Middlethorpe, London is already humming with your beauty. One of the Sussex Allbrights, I believe." Lady Cowper clearly had no great opinion of the Sussex Allbrights but would not hold that against Serena. Serena wondered what would happen when news of her first marriage broke.

The company was the very highest of Society, some already known to Serena. She knew that it would have been foolish for Francis and her to have rushed home to bed. If this event went well, nothing short of an outright scandal would stop her acceptance.

Then she saw the Duchess of Arran across the room, along with Lady Anne and two men, one older, one young. Probably the duke and one of Lady Anne's brothers.

Did scandal hover? Certainly the younger man glared at them ferociously.

Serena nudged Francis.

"Yes, I know," he said calmly. "It is up to them."

She could see he wasn't as calm as he sounded. She watched him surreptitiously for signs of a broken heart. She didn't detect any, but both he and Anne seemed able to mask their feelings under perfect manners.

What a wonderful couple they would have made. Serena's faith in her attractions was draining away. Perhaps the state of their marriage wasn't because of

Francis's care and concern, but because he felt no desire. . . .

No. She had seen his desire.

But perhaps that was just the mindless lust that men seemed prey to, that sent them to streetwalkers, to any woman who would open her legs.

They all sat to enjoy a harp recital, with a gloomy song that echoed Serena's mood completely.

"For, oh, my love he loves not me,
And I am steeped in misery . . ."

At the end of that ballad the character threw herself into a waterfall.

Serena accompanied Francis into another room for refreshments, thinking that a waterfall was highly attractive. She would be out of her misery and Francis could marry Anne. Only Serena's poor child would be less well off, and even there she could argue that it was spared the sorrows of the world.

As they entered the room, they were suddenly confronted by the Peckworths.

"Good evening," said the duchess with rather strained good humor. "A beautiful performance, was it not?"

"Yes, Duchess," said Francis. "Madame Ducharme is very talented."

"Quite a good company for this time of year," said the duke, a rotund man with a genial face, though his geniality was artificial at the moment.

"Indeed it is," said Francis. "Duke, I don't believe you have met my wife." The introductions were made and acknowledged without incident, and the Peckworths moved on.

"Rode over that rather well," Francis said softly as they moved farther into the room.

Serena could see that he was genuinely relieved, and she squeezed his arm. She thought that having to depend on the kindness of her victims made self-destruction even more attractive, but for Francis's sake she tried to appear lighthearted. And the plan did seem to be working. With all these members of the high aristocracy willing to support them, how could they fail?

Later, however, when Serena had to go to the room set aside for the ladies, she encountered Lady Anne.

Serena greeted the young woman, but warily.

Lady Anne stared at her as if at a conundrum, then said, "Lady Middlethorpe, please can we talk?"

Serena would have liked to refuse, but she thought perhaps she owed the younger woman the chance to berate her. Anne led the way to a small anteroom, that slight irregularity in her step seeming a profound reproach.

Once in the room, Anne turned to Serena with determination. "Lady Middlethorpe, I just wanted to say that there need be no restraint between us."

"Need there not?" Serena asked rather blankly.

"No. Clearly you know that Francis . . . that Lord Middlethorpe had . . ." Color was burning in Lady Anne's cheeks. "Oh, dear, why can I not say this right?"

Serena took Anne's nervous hands. "He had been courting you," she completed.

"Well, yes." Anne's hands squeezed gratefully. "But nothing had been said. Uffham—he's my brother—he seems to think I have been jilted, but *truly* it is not so. I wanted you to know that."

"Words had not been spoken," said Serena gently, "but I think perhaps expectations had been raised."

Anne removed her hands. "A little, yes." But then she raised her chin with remarkable firmness. "Truly, though, I am not nursing a broken heart. I would not have wanted to be married just as a convenience. And that is clearly what I was."

"No—" But Serena had to bite off the denial.

"Oh, yes. I have a handsome dowry, and our families have known each other forever. It was that sort of thing. And I can see why he was drawn by you. You are so very beautiful." This was said with poignant wistfulness.

Serena knew Lady Anne was being honest and kind, but if she had sought a way to heap burning coals on Serena's head, she could not have done better. "Good men do not wed just for beauty, Lady Anne."

Serena longed to tell Anne the truth, but it would do no good at all. In fact, if she guessed aright, Anne was comforted by the belief that Francis's marriage was a great love match.

"I think you are wise, Lady Anne, not to want to marry without love. I am sure true love will come your way in full measure very soon."

Anne smiled a little mistily. "I do hope so. I hope to have what you and Francis have."

Serena summoned what she hoped was a blissful smile. "I wish you a husband you deserve, Lady Anne, for he will be a treasure among men."

When Anne had gone, Serena sat with a thump on a little sofa. How many more of these excruciating moments were there to endure? Would she ever be able to move through a day without an eye open for traps?

She had to admit, however, that the talk with Lady Anne had eased her a little. Unless Anne was the greatest actress in creation, she truly had not loved Francis, not as Serena loved him.

Serena sat there quietly, dwelling on her love. She loved Francis quite desperately. She wanted—needed—his love in return. If only she deserved it.

She fought her tears. It would not do at all for her to return to the company with red eyes.

Francis came in. "Here you are. Are you feeling unwell?"

Serena was dangerously vulnerable. Her heart danced at the sight of him; his voice thrilled her senses. If she could just be here with him for eternity, she would be happy. "No. No, I'm fine."

He came to sit on the sofa by her. "Then why are you here at all? Do you not care for music?"

What did he feel? It was impossible to tell. Did he love Anne? Heaven knows, she was lovable.

"I was talking to Lady Anne," she confessed.

His light smile faded. "About what?"

"You, of course."

"And?" He was very watchful, but giving nothing away.

"And nothing," she sighed. "She merely wished to assure me that you had not jilted her."

"She is generous, then. It was as near as made no difference. Come. The carriage waits. It is time to go."

Serena did not try to continue such an awkward discussion.

When they arrived home, it wasn't quite as late a

night as the last, and Serena, after her nap, was not particularly tired. As they went up to bed she wished she could depend on her husband coming to her. It was not sexual desire that moved her, but the need to prove that Francis desired her, the need to give him something to compensate for all she had taken.

He entered her room with her and said, "Are you tired tonight?"

"Not particularly." Her heart began to speed.

"Then I will return in a little while, if you do not mind."

"No," she breathed. "No, I do not mind at all."

Francis went to his own room, still holding his desire by a tight rein. This time there would be no repeat of that last encounter. He would take it slowly and give her as much pleasure as he could.

My God, though, it was hard when she was so utterly desirable. Tonight he had seen other men look at her with heat in their eyes. He'd received a few congratulations on his marriage that had rung with envy. Young Farnham had declared her a Toast.

Francis wanted to bury his wife in the country and keep her to himself. Then he remembered that her first husband had done just that.

As Grisholme attended him with quiet efficiency, Francis clenched his teeth on commands to hurry. It would be pointless. It would take time for Serena's maid to ready her for bed, and he didn't want to be a subject for yet more servants' gossip.

Lord above, did they spend their evenings below stairs speculating about his intimate life?

When Francis was in his banyan and ready for bed in more senses than one, Grisholme was still in the room, quietly putting everything in order.

The valet had been behaving in this manner for as long as he had been in Francis's employ, but now it seemed like an act of malice. Francis threw himself into a chair by the fire. He rose quickly, however, as he felt something under him. He turned and picked up a pair of lady's pockets by the ribbon used to tie them at the waist.

He dangled them from his fingers and raised a teasing brow at his very proper manservant.

Grisholme did look a little discomfited. "Your apologies, milord. An oversight on my part. An undermaid delivered them from the laundry for her ladyship. They had been sent down by mistake with a gown. I forgot to give them to her ladyship's dresser."

The man's embarrassment at such a dereliction of duty was quite amusing.

Grisholme came over to take the offending pockets, but Francis said, "No matter. I'll give them to Lady Middlethorpe myself." Foolishly, Francis then felt embarrassed that his words could be taken as an announcement of his intent to make passionate love to the said Lady Middlethorpe. He tossed the pockets carelessly back onto the chair.

"Good night, then, milord." At last Grisholme bowed himself out.

Francis took a breath and made himself wait a few moments more. He wished he didn't want to make love to Serena quite so desperately. It would make it hard to be careful, damn it. But careful he must be. He must never bring back memories of her first marriage.

He held out a hand and noted wryly that it trembled slightly.

Perhaps he should have used some other woman to slake his lust so that he could be moderate with Serena, but he couldn't do it. Apart from the fact that it would hurt her if she found out, he didn't seem to desire any woman but Serena. This evening at the musicale, he'd looked at Anne and had been completely unable to imagine the intimacies of marriage with her. He'd glanced at Serena and had desired her instantly.

There was Blanche's other solution, but he'd use that only if he were truly desperate.

He stood sharply and attended to the fire, then he picked up the pockets. He had them upside down, however, and a few coins and a card slid out onto the floor. Muttering with impatience, he gathered them up. Then the name leapt out at him.

Charles Ferncliff!

He stared at the rectangle of white pasteboard in disbelief. What the devil was Serena doing with a card from Charles Ferncliff?

He scanned the card, trying to find some sense other than the obvious. Hell and damnation. It wasn't possible.

Despite his disbelief, scenarios leapt into his mind.

Serena and Ferncliff?

He had been after Ferncliff when he met Serena, but no one could have planned that meeting. He'd met up with Serena because he'd taken a shortcut.

But a well-known shortcut.

Perhaps that letter had not really been intended to send Francis asking questions of his mother, but to send him on the road to Weymouth.

He collapsed back down in the chair and stared at the card as if it could reveal more. Could Ferncliff have started this insane affair in collusion with Serena? Could he have planned to trick him into meeting with Serena so he could be seduced by her and marry her?

God's truth, but no one would believe a plan like that.

What was he supposed to believe, though? He turned the card helplessly in his hand.

What he should do was go to Serena now and ask her about all this.

If there was an innocent explanation, though, there was no need to ask.

And if there wasn't, she'd surely lie.

And if there wasn't an innocent explanation, he wasn't sure he wanted to know.

What he wanted was to enjoy her luscious body . . .

After another long study, Francis flicked the card into the flames and watched it curl and char.

Then, suddenly, he remembered the man he had encountered near here on Tuesday. Tall, ruddy, dark-haired. *Charles Ferncliff.* He'd stake his life on it. He'd had his quarry in his grasp! Had Ferncliff been coming from a meeting with his accomplice?

His lover?

No, surely not that.

Francis wanted answers. His hand went to the bell-pull, but that would bring Grisholme back when the man was doubtless heading for his own bed. It wasn't Grisholme he wanted, anyway. He went downstairs to find—as expected—his butler making the final check of the house.

"You require something, milord?" Dibbert managed to imply that Francis was behaving most improperly by wandering his house in his nightwear.

"Were there any callers to the house on Tuesday?"

The man considered it. "No, milord. Of course, Lady Middlethorpe—the Dowager Lady Middlethorpe—arrived, along with her staff."

"But no one visited anyone here. Or left a card."

"No, milord. It was not generally known then that you were in Town. Yesterday and today, of course, a number of people have left cards."

Francis wanted to interrogate the man about Serena's movements on Tuesday, but that would be to reveal too much. "Thank you, Dibbert. Good night."

"Good night, milord." The butler continued his duties, and Francis returned to his room to pace.

Brandy had found Serena's gloves in the garden. Ferncliff had been coming from the garden. He and Serena had clearly met there in a clandestine manner. What the devil was going on?

He tried to remember that occasion. Had Serena seemed uneasy or guilty? It was impossible to tell. Francis had been awash in his own guilt over his use of her body, and shocked by those horrible ornaments. Upon meeting her, he had been intent on giving her the puppy.

There had been nothing guilty in her enjoyment of the puppy.

He couldn't—wouldn't—believe that she was Ferncliff's lover, but what else could they have been doing together?

Francis leapt to his feet. He wouldn't believe the worst, but now—more than ever—he wanted a word with Charles Ferncliff. Ferncliff was at the heart of the whole plague-ridden mess. Francis had a strong urge to go over to Simmons's rooms now, in the middle of the night, and force the truth out of the villain.

And he didn't give a damn whether it gave Simmons an apoplexy or not.

There was a tap on the door. It opened, and Serena came in rather hesitantly. "I . . . I thought perhaps you wanted me to come here."

She was dressed in a new nightgown, a low-necked garment of filmy silk and lace that hid little. Her hair was a loose deep red cloud.

"Why not?" he said. No matter what else she was, she was his wife and it was his right to enjoy her. Seeing her here in all her available enchantments, he felt his control slip away.

Still, he commanded himself, you must act the gentleman.

She was hovering by the door as if about to take flight. He strode over, swept her into his arms, and carried her to the bed. As he laid her there on the crisp white sheets, he searched her face for reluctance or duplicity and found none.

Perhaps she read something in his features, though, for she raised her arms and said, "Francis, I want you to join with me above anything. Come."

He couldn't even wait to undress her, though he managed not to rip the lovely garment. The top slipped down easily to give him access to her delicious breasts, and the bottom pushed up. She must have removed his banyan, for he did not and yet he was naked.

He tried to hold back but it was like the first time. She took him into her and brought his release on him, so that he exploded into limp satisfaction without any clear recollection of the stages.

The relief was astonishing, but it was followed by annoyance.

Damn it, he'd omitted all the careful pleasuring of her he'd intended. He moved to the side ready to apologize, but she looked radiant with contentment.

She placed a gentle kiss upon his lips. "You must never think I do not welcome you, Francis. Sharing my body with yours is the greatest joy I have ever known."

He had to believe her.

He wrapped her in his arms and offered up a prayer. Please, God, don't let anything come between me and this woman. He put the thought of Charles Ferncliff's card firmly out of his mind.

Serena and Francis slept deeply, but she came to awareness in the middle of the night, to find his hands busy upon her. It was the mirror-image of their first encounter, except that she was completely aware and enthusiastic. Thinking of that, she moved on top of him and pleasured him as she had that first time, but now with his full consent.

She could almost thank Matthew Riverton for teaching her these skills. Every time Francis achieved his satisfaction, Serena felt a wild surge of joyous triumph. She would do it over and over again if she thought he could bear it.

They fell asleep again almost immediately, but she woke to his touch once more, this time in daylight. His fingers traced to the peak of her breast. "Time to attend to you, my siren . . ."

Serena, however, heard the clock strike ten and seized his busy hand. "Heavens, Francis, I promised to help Beth."

He twisted around to snare her wrists. "Beth has more servants than she knows what to do with. I have only one wife. . . ."

She struggled playfully. "Stop it, Francis! That's not the same. She is putting on this entertainment for us, and I should help."

He sighed and released her. He smoothed the hair off her face and there was too much understanding in his dark eyes. "Perhaps that is true. Very well, then. I will let you escape . . . this time."

Serena did escape to her own room and rang for her maid, wishing that hint of discord had not marred a wonderful night. His unspoken surmise was correct, however. She loved his burning desire and delighted in pleasing him, but she feared his careful attentions. She was all too sure she was incapable of the response he wanted.

Chapter 16

Serena walked to Belcraven House, but with a little entourage. Dibbert had insisted that she take a footman, and Serena had decided to take the puppy with her. That necessitated the presence of the excited kitchen boy. She felt quite queenly.

She pondered the night just past and decided that it was good. A barrier had been broken down, and the road to happiness laid open. There was still a great deal of work to be done, however, not the least being in this final establishment of her respectability.

Once at the Palace she plunged into the preparations for a grand soirée, finding it both exciting and educational. She had never taken part in such plans before, for her life at Stokeley Manor had not been remarkable for its entertainments.

Twenty were invited for dinner, and then there would be many more guests for the remainder of the evening. Provisions were being made for both dancing and cards, and for a musical interlude.

As Beth had predicted, the staff appeared happy to

have a chance to show their mettle. The gentlemen, however, were notably absent.

"They'll be hiding out at their clubs," said Beth with a grin. "And truth to tell, they would only be in the way."

"What about Felicity?"

"Lacking a club, she is hiding out in her room. I think I'll force her out. She needs to learn some feminine skills."

In the mid afternoon, a stir was heard in the entrance hall. Beth and Serena, along with a reluctant Felicity, were arranging flowers in the reception room.

"I wonder . . ." said Beth, and hurried out. *"Maman!* How lovely."

Serena followed, to see Beth hug an elegant blond lady. The resemblance to the marquess would have announced the identity of the older lady without introduction, but introduced Serena was, and to the quiet, gray-eyed duke.

The duke eyed Serena with frank interest. "I am always intrigued by what my son's friends will think of next," he said with dry humor. "You are definitely a promising addition to the circle."

Serena noted the marquess's resemblance to his father, too, not in looks but in manner.

Soon they were all seated around a tea table in the duchess's boudoir. Both the duke and duchess maintained a suite of rooms in the mansion for their sole use, which were always in readiness for them.

"So," said the duchess, looking at Serena frankly, "you are something of a scandal, yes?" Her voice still held a trace of the French that was her native tongue.

Serena was beginning to have steadier nerves. "Thus far I am only a novelty, Your Grace."

"I have dragged myself to Town at this time of year for a mere novelty?" asked the duchess with a twinkle. "Come now. This will never do."

"Your support will be a great help, *maman*," said Beth. "Soon all we will need is Prinny to pinch Serena's cheek, and she will be untouchable!"

"Could be arranged," said the duke, "even though he is down in Brighton putting Prince Leopold through the hoops. But are you quite sure you want the Regent dancing attention? He's a damn tedious fellow, really."

Serena had no idea what to say to such a scandalous comment.

Beth chuckled. "Perhaps we will do without the royal cipher. With three dukes and duchesses—present company included—coming tonight, we need little extra cachet." At a query, she said, "Arran and Yeovil."

"The Arrans will come?" said the duchess. "Well done, my dear."

"Lady Anne virtually insisted. She is being splendid."

Serena gritted her teeth. Lady Anne was indeed being splendid, and it was mean-spirited to resent it.

"And the Yeovils," said the duchess. "I must find time to talk to them. It was so sad about poor Dare. And they never even had the solace of interring his body. What a charnal house that battlefield must have been. But at least the war is decisively over now. Who else do you have?"

"The Countess of Cawle," announced Beth rather smugly.

327

"My dear," declared the duke, toasting with a tea cup. "Better than Prinny by far!"

"I think so, but I can't take the credit. Turns out she's bosom bows with Francis's Aunt Arabella."

The duke burst out laughing. "It occurs to me that we should just surrender the management of the country to the Rogues and have done with it."

"Not at all!" cried Beth in mock horror. "Stephen is the only one with any taste for politics at all. The rest of them would turn it into a Bartholmew Fair. Now, if you want to recruit the Rogue's wives and mistresses . . ."

After the tea, Serena pleaded tiredness and escaped back to Hertford Street. She knew in her heart that she hoped to find Francis there and be able to tempt him to a little more bed-work. Even that hateful phrase no longer distressed her, though she thought a better term would be bed-play.

Unfortunately, he had left the house not long after she and had not yet returned.

Francis was with Miles and Lucien at the Red House Club, engaged in a shooting competition. He had put Charles Ferncliff's card firmly out of mind, and though his life was not yet perfect, it was a great deal brighter today than recently. His hand was steady and his aim was always true.

"Damnation," said Miles as he paid over another twenty-guinea bet. "Don't you ever miss?"

"Not today, it would seem," said Francis, reloading his pistol. There were servants present to do the task,

328

but he preferred to handle it himself. "Going to take me on, Luce?"

Lucien drained a glass of punch. "You've relieved me of enough gilt today, thank you. I'll take on Miles."

Francis grinned and went to sit by the punch bowl and watch. At the sound of new arrivals, he looked up and saw Uffham come in with some friends. There was nothing he could do to avoid the meeting, so he just hoped the Arrans' good sense was rubbing off on Anne's brother.

Uffham saw him and stiffened. "Not shooting?" he asked with a sneer.

"Not at the moment, no. Would you care for some punch?"

"I can think of a punch that would suit me very nicely," Uffham muttered under his breath, but perfectly audibly.

Francis pretended not to have heard. He completely sympathized with the man's outraged feelings. He would have felt much the same if anyone had treated one of his sisters so scurvily.

Uffham curled his lip, and he and his friends wandered farther down the shooting gallery to take their sport. Francis was just relaxing when Anne's brother returned.

"Since no one seems to want us to face each other in earnest," Uffham said, "why don't we see who would have died. Just out of curiosity."

"What a morbid form of curiosity."

Uffham's jaw worked. "Afraid to see your fate?"

Francis could see that the man was on the edge of his temper. "By all means let us test our skill, Uffham. We've been playing a stake of twenty guineas. . . ."

329

"No stakes. Just live or die."

"Just rest in peace or flee the country, you mean. Which would you prefer?"

Uffham just glared.

"Best of ten?" Francis asked, carefully neutral.

"One shot each," Uffham countered, "and at the ace of hearts. Closest to the heart kills." Morbidly symbolic, in Francis's opinion. Why was his life continually plunged into this kind of melodrama these days?

Francis made no objection, however, and both men prepared to shoot. Spectators gathered. Francis suspected that the edge to the competition must be obvious even if people didn't know his recent history.

He checked his pistol. "Do you want us to shoot simultaneously?" he asked. "As if this were a real duel?"

He saw with relief that Uffham's normal good sense was returning and he was beginning to feel like a fool. "Why don't we toss for it?" Uffham asked.

They tossed and Uffham won. He lined up the shot with a rock-steady hand and his ball pierced the red heart. A servant ran out and retrieved it for inspection.

"There," said Uffham with satisfaction. "Dead center on the heart."

"Not quite," Francis pointed out. "It's off to one side."

"But deadly."

"Assuredly."

"Then let me see you do better."

"Do you really wish us both to be carried dead from the field?" Francis queried, but he turned to make his shot at his own card.

He considered carefully. There would be a great

deal of satisfaction in defeating Uffham, but nothing to be gained. He sighted on the heart and squeezed the trigger.

"A bull!" someone shouted, and the servant brought the card.

Uffham looked at it. "Devil take it, it's just the same as mine!"

The men crowded around, exclaiming at the coincidence. The two holes could almost be fitted one over the other.

Francis looked at Uffham. "Perhaps we should take it as a sign that this contest is over."

Uffham gritted his teeth, but then grabbed Francis's hand to shake it. "So be it, Middlethorpe. I'll never really understand what happened, but I can't stay at outs with you forever. You're too much of a good fellow."

"Thank you," said Francis, genuinely touched. He drew Uffham away from the others. "Anne will do much better, you know. I realize now that our feelings were not deeply engaged. I would have been good to her, but she deserves better than mere kindness."

Uffham sighed but said, "You're doubtless right. You love your wife, then?"

Francis ducked that one. "Would I be going through all this if I didn't?"

Uffham laughed. "That's a palpable truth, by gad!" He slapped Francis on the back and went off to join his party.

Lucien came over with the two holed cards. "As pretty a piece of shooting as I've ever seen."

"There are times to be grateful for pointless skills."

"Hardly pointless if he'd called you out."

"Completely pointless. If he'd called me out, I'd have had to let him shoot me. I could hardly shoot him when I am in the wrong."

Lucien just shook his head.

Since Francis was not at home, Serena attended to some household matters and then settled down to play with Brandy.

The puppy had just woken from a long rest and seemed particularly energetic. A glance out the window showed that the late afternoon sun was bright, and so Serena took her into the garden. Soon Brandy was exploring the entrancing world of grass, earth, and bushes. There were even birds, which fortunately had the sense to keep well away from an enthusiastic baby hunter.

Serena, too, enjoyed the pleasure of a warm late winter's day, and after the bustle of Belcraven House and the pressures of mingling with Society, the deserted garden was a haven of peace. The evergreen bushes and hedges gave an illusion of privacy, and she could almost imagine that she was far from the city and the cares it brought. Just a few more days, she thought, and then hopefully they could remove to the country.

When Brandy finally tired and began to look for her bed, Serena carried her as far as the kitchens and gave her into the care of the lad. Serena, however, was not yet ready to return to the house. Even though Francis's mother seemed to have given up the reins without complaint, there was little to do there. The servants were all excellent and the place ran efficiently on its own.

She wandered back into the garden.

There was a stone bench in a sheltered spot warmed by the last of the sun. Serena sat there buffered from the cold stone by her thick, luxurious cloak. All the perfume seemed finally to have left it, just as the horrors of her first marriage had left her mind. The sensual delights of the past night still lingered with her, and she began to think that she could, in time, give Francis the surrender he wanted.

If only . . . if only Francis loved her, how happy she could be.

Why should he, though? She had done him nothing but harm. Her beauty and sexual skills would not bring love. If such things touched the heart, men would not use whores and wander away whistling. She could only hope that now that she and Francis seemed to be moving into calmer waters, he would begin to appreciate her other qualities.

She knew she had them. She was kind by nature, and honest, and faithful. Perhaps if she were less faithful, she would have found the courage to flee Matthew years ago. She had felt bound by her marriage vows. She was not scholarly, but nor was she stupid. She could manage a house properly, and she thought she would be a good mother.

Were these enough virtues to win love?

What caused love?

Why did *she* love *Francis?*

Just to ponder such a question was cause to smile with delight. Perhaps more than anything else, she loved him for his gentleness. It was not a weakness, she knew that, just a gentle concern for others. It was a precious quality. He had so many other precious qualities, too. He was intelligent, competent, and trustworthy. Above all, Serena valued trust. She knew without a doubt that she could trust Francis with her life and her children.

But all those things generated liking and respect. What turned liking into love?

His body? He was slender, but she had had enough of big, brawny men for a lifetime. She thought his body beautiful. His features were indisputably handsome, made more so by the personality that shaped them. One did not love for a body, however.

His mind? She did not think she had come to know his mind, yet.

She shook her head. Perhaps there was no making sense of love. It was a treasure, though, and one she wanted to preserve.

She sat for a little longer, praying for guidance and patience, and then rose to return to the house. As she left the arbor, however, someone stepped forward to block her way. Two men.

With a spurt of fear, she recognized her brothers and took a step back.

Then she realized she had nothing to fear. She was married now and beyond their power. She stopped her retreat and raised her chin. "Hello, Tom. Will. You are trespassing, you know."

"Trespassing in our dear sister's garden?" sneered Tom. "Haven't you done well for yourself, Serry? Viscountess Middlethorpe, no less. Why didn't you think to tell your loving family of this happy event, then?"

"If I had a loving family, I might well have done so. What do you want?"

"Ten thousand pounds."

Serena stared at him blankly. "What?"

Tom's eyes were flatly malignant. "Your husband owes us ten thousand pounds, Serry, no matter who he be, and I want it."

She laughed. "Then I suggest you apply to my husband for it."

She could tell that he wanted to hurt her but didn't dare. That knowledge was very sweet. She moved forward. "Now, if you will excuse me, I must return to the house."

She had misjudged. He seized her arm in a cruel grip and pushed her back into the arbor. "Preparing for an evening in a ducal mansion, I hear. Moving in fine circles, aren't you, you little trollop? How will the Duke and Duchess of Belcraven feel when they know you were Riverton's wife?"

She forced herself not to struggle in his grasp, though fear was almost choking her. "They do know."

He was taken aback but rallied. "Do they? But I'll go odds others don't. Middlethorpe hasn't announced the marriage yet, has he? I've been watching the two of you this last couple of days since I twigged the way I'd been tricked. You're hoping to take Society by a bold move, but what if word got around about you, and about the things you've done . . . ?"

She tried to bluff him. "It wouldn't matter. I'm already accepted."

"If you believe that, you'd believe in the pig-faced woman. Just let talk start and see what happens to your precious acceptance. Then, of course, there are those pictures. . . ."

"Pictures?" Serena asked in horror.

"Pictures of you in lewd postures." Now he'd gained

her attention, Tom let her go and pulled out a squashed roll of paper. He smoothed it with his fat fingers. "You can't have forgotten them, Serry." He handed it to her.

Serena stared in horror at the crumpled pen and ink sketch. It showed her lounging on a chaise while a faceless footman fondled her naked breasts. And this was one of the mildest of the bunch. "Where did you get this?" she whispered.

"From Riverton's rooms in Town. I knew where he kept 'em. He showed 'em to me once. Seemed to think it might upset me." He chuckled. "Just got me excited, they did. When he died, I went there to see what I could scavenge—for you, of course, dear sister. The duns were already moving in, though. I only sneaked the pictures out by mixing them with some legal papers. They've given me and Will some merry moments, haven't they, Will?"

Will nodded. "I told Tom we ought to get you to pose like that again, just for us."

Serena stared at them both in horror. "I *never* posed for those pictures!" She ripped the one in her hands in half. "That artist changed everything except my head!"

Tom just laughed. "Now, who's to know that? I could sell them for a pretty penny, Serry, especially now you're such a part of Society. Do you know, there's already a few pictures of you in the print shop windows. You're the latest Society beauty."

Blank terror was welling up in Serena, and she was in very real danger of fainting. "Those pictures aren't real! That trick could be played on anyone! An artist could put the queen's face on a whore. . . ."

"But people wouldn't believe it of the queen. They'd

believe it of Randy Riverton's widow. There's plenty know those pictures tell the truth, no matter how they were done."

"Of course they don't. Matthew was jealous. He never let another man touch me!"

Tom looked a bit disappointed but said, "Be that as it may, Sister, the world'll believe the worst."

It was true. Serena collapsed back onto the bench and sank her head in her hands. "What do you want?" It was an admission of defeat.

"I told you. Ten thousand pounds."

She looked up. "You're mad! I don't have that sort of money! You'll have to apply to my husband." She watched Tom's eyes shift. "And you won't do that, will you?"

"I will if you force my hand," Tom blustered. "He'll pay up to prevent talk."

"He'll call you out, rather."

Tom showed his teeth. "Let him. I'll go odds I'm a better shot than that strip of wind."

Tom was a good shot. Dear Lord, was she to crown her follies by causing Francis's *death?*

"He's a dead shot," she declared boldly, and it was pure bluff.

It found a mark, though. Tom's eyes narrowed uneasily. "Is he, now . . . ? Well, anyway, shooting me won't stop those pictures being made public. Will'd see to it, wouldn't you, lad?"

"Course I would," said Will cheerfully.

"Dear God, but I hate you both," Serena said.

Tom chuckled complacently. "Now, now, no need for that, Serry. I can see you'd have a problem laying a hand on that sort of money right away, but we can be reasonable. Let's say you pay us a hundred here, a hundred there. Middlethorpe's a warm man. He'll not mind you helping your family."

"He'll think I've run mad!" Serena protested. "He knows I detest you. And I don't even have access to hundreds, you fool."

"Watch your mouth, Serry," Tom growled. "You'll find enough to satisfy me, and there's an end of it. If you don't, the pretty pictures of you in the print seller's windows will be replaced by the other ones. Use your wits. There's pin money and housekeeping. Doubtless your doting husband's given you trinkets you could say you'd lost . . ."

"No!" Serena was revolted.

"Speaking of trinkets," Tom went on implacably, "I'll have your jewelry back, too."

This new tack knocked Serena even more off balance. "What?"

"The pretty baubles Riverton gave you. They were tricked out of my hands and I want 'em back. Somehow I doubt you're deeply attached to 'em."

Serena shuddered at the mere thought of those ornaments. "I don't have them. What are you talking about?"

Tom eyed her shrewdly, then a grin cracked his heavy face. "Didn't Middlethorpe give them to you? Well, well, perhaps there's more in his breeches than his drawers after all. He must be keeping them to be a little surprise one night when the novelty's worn off."

Serena didn't want to believe all this, but clever deception wasn't her brothers' strong suit. "Why would my husband have them? Last I heard, you had them."

"He won them from me in a horse race."

"You can't fool me with that. He won my three thousand pounds back."

"And I paid with those jewels. . . . So," Tom said with sudden interest, "Did he give you three thousand pounds, then?"

Serena kept firmly silent.

Tom was not fooled. "That'll be a nice start, won't it, Will? Three thousand in ready cash. Now with that and the trinkets, we might even call the account settled, eh? A bird in the hand and all that. Then our little sister can get on with her respectable marriage in peace."

Serena looked at her brothers with loathing. "I'll give you *nothing*. Not one penny."

Tom's smile didn't waver. "Yes, you will, because otherwise I'll ruin both you and your marriage, and you know it. Think your pretty husband'll want you about when you're a byword?" He kicked the pieces of paper on the ground. "Keep that picture and think on it. I'll be back here tomorrow at this time for the three thousand." With that, he turned and left.

Will grinned and followed Tom out toward the small gate that led into the mews.

Serena gave a little whimper and hugged herself. What now? Dear Lord, what now? She wanted to tell Francis, but what if he did call Tom out and Tom killed him? She had ruined her husband's life; would she now be his death?

She wept, rocking herself. She loved him so and wanted to make his life perfect, but all she seemed able to do was to drag him deeper and deeper into a foul stew. Tonight was to have been the moment of triumph when her place in Society would be established, but it would be a hollow victory with this threat hanging over them. The higher her position, the greater the scandal those pictures would create.

She looked at the torn halves of the one Tom had left and shuddered.

She'd wiped the pictures out of her mind, hoping that somehow they had been lost or destroyed. Matthew had always kept them in London, saying they reminded him of his sweet little wife when he was away from home. She'd hoped he kept them to himself, but apparently he'd shown them to Tom. For all she knew, he had been in the habit of passing them around to his foul friends or had even hung them on his walls!

And now Tom had them.

The thought of her brothers gloating over them made her feel sick.

Serena had been just sixteen when Matthew had brought the artist to Stokeley Manor. He had said Kevin Beehan was to do sketches for a portrait. Serena had lost her illusions about her husband, and was terrified and disgusted by him, but she had not come to realize his true nature yet. She had seen no trap in it.

Even if she had, she admitted with a sigh, she could not have refused. Matthew had a quick and vicious response to any insubordination.

There had seemed nothing about the sittings to object to. The artist had sketched her in a number of poses—sitting, standing, lying; in the house, in the garden, even in the stables. She had seen them all. He was skilled, and the pictures had conveyed a charming, graceful innocence that denied the horrors of her marriage. She had asked for one to keep and had been given it.

She had burned it when she'd seen the final results.

She didn't know whether Beehan had used whores to model the bodies or just his imagination, but he had taken those pictures, stripped most of the clothing off her, adapted the body pose where necessary, and added a variety of men. But in all of them, no matter what terrible things were going on, her youthful face smiled dreamily out of the picture with its characteristic counterpoint of sultry satisfaction.

They had been so cleverly done, however, that people would believe them to be exact representations of fact. She picked up the two torn pieces of paper and matched them together. People would think she really had sat half-naked on the chaise in the drawing room at Stokeley Manor, presiding over the tea tray while that brawny footman caressed her.

She leapt to her feet, crushing the paper in her hands. It wasn't fair! What had she done to deserve her fate? What had she done that her life should be constantly torn from her control and ruined?

Serena was tempted to give up, to stop fighting, to run away and hide. That brought her up short. She could not do that. She carried a babe in her womb that deserved its father and a home. She had a good man for a husband, one who deserved a respectable wife. She had to fight on somehow.

The first step was to tell Francis about this new threat. She closed her eyes at the pain of it. She didn't want to. She didn't want to tell him about the pictures.

He had a low opinion of Riverton, but he had no real idea of the way her marriage had been. The pictures would reveal too much. She had not posed for them, but they laid bare the nature of her marriage. What would he think of her?

She had no choice, however. If she once started to keep secrets, she would die inside. If she started to pay her brothers, they would leech her for the rest of her life, for each payment made behind her husband's back would be more fuel for blackmail. She wiped her tears and gathered her nerve. She must tell Francis and she must do it now.

Serena hurried back to the house and summoned a footman. "Is Lord Middlethorpe home yet?"

Chapter 17

The footman seemed startled at the urgency of Serena's request. "I don't think so, milady. Shall I enquire?"

Let him be in. "Yes, please. I will be in my room."

Francis wasn't at home, though, which as she'd known gave her time to vacillate and lose her nerve. Serena paced her room, tumbling from one decision to the other. Twice she almost threw the crumpled picture onto the fire but stopped herself.

As time passed, the question of the jewels came back to haunt her. Surely Tom must have been lying. But Tom did not lie about things like that; he was not a sneaky deceiver.

If Francis had won the *jewels* as the prize for that horse race, then he must have seen them. Why had he never mentioned them? Did he, as Tom suggested, want to use them as Matthew had used them, to stimulate his flagging desire? Did they excite him?

No. No. Of course, he would not mention them. A gentleman such as Francis would not discuss such things with his wife, even if they were no secret to her.

The more likely explanation was that he had sold them and given her the money.

That was it.

But she had to know.

Serena knocked on the door to her husband's bedroom. When there was no answer she slipped in and, after the briefest hesitation, searched it.

She hoped not to find anything, but she found the jewels without difficulty. Her hands trembled as she opened the familiar pouch. Within, all the jewelry was out of its individual pouches and jumbled together. Could he be in the habit of pawing through it, fantasizing?

Please, no.

Foul memories washed over her, and it was as if she were back in Stokeley Manor and Matthew had just arrived to torment her.

Serena picked up the jeweled handcuffs. The heavy silver bracelets set with pearls and rubies had straps to attach them to the posts of the bed. The metal cuffs were lined with padded velvet, for Matthew had said that he did not want to inadvertently mark her delicate skin. Advertently, of course, he had once or twice whipped her harshly enough to mark her. . . .

She clicked one around her wrist, where it looked very much like a fine bracelet. It was not tight, but well designed to be too small for her hand to pass through. She unclicked it. They were easy to get in and out of if one had the use of the other hand. She threw them down onto the glittering pile. She had hated more than anything being bound, being helpless. She had always been helpless, but when she was tied to the bed or a chair, it was made brutally clear.

If Francis had won these for her, then given her the value of them, he could be said to have purchased them for his own use. She was suddenly filled with defiant rage. She would never be used that way again, not even by the man she loved.

These jewels were hers, damn it, by law and any other right. They were paid for in blood and tears. Serena took the pouch and returned to her room. She wanted to throw them into the nearest sewer, but they might be the price of salvation. If she had to, she'd give them to her brothers. . . .

Someone knocked. Serena hastily shoved the pouch into a drawer and called permission to enter.

It was Francis. "You wanted to speak to me? I have only just arrived home."

Serena stared at him, momentarily bereft of words. Did this gentle, smiling man with the elegant bones and the dark, sensitive eyes really want to do the same things as coarse, brutal Matthew Riverton?

He moved closer. "Serena? Is something the matter?"

"No. Yes . . ." She almost didn't tell him, for at the moment he looked loving and her revelations might ruin everything. She forced the words out in a rush. "I went out into the garden with Brandy and met my brothers. They tried to extort money from me."

His brows rose but he took it calmly. "You refused to give them anything, I hope."

His response steadied her. "Yes, of course. But they are threatening to . . . they are threatening to tell the world about my first marriage if I don't pay them."

He smiled. "That will be a toothless threat after tonight."

It almost choked her, but she spat the rest of it out. "And they have pictures!"

"Pictures?"

Face burning, she picked up the torn and crumpled papers and passed them to him. He took the two pieces and smoothed them out on a table, saying nothing.

The wall clock ticked away the seconds of silence. Too many of them.

"I didn't pose for them, Francis. Matthew sent an artist to make sketches for a portrait. I posed for him for days and the pictures were lovely. But instead of a portrait, he did those! He . . . he left off my clothing. . . . In some he . . ."

He turned suddenly and took her trembling hands. "Don't, my dear. You mustn't distress yourself. We can handle this."

"How?" she wailed. "Truly, Francis, that one is nothing. Some of them are *disgusting!*"

He took her into his arms. "That could happen to anyone."

"But they'll *believe* it of Randy Riverton's widow!"

He pushed her away a little to look into her eyes. "They will not believe it of Lord Middlethorpe's wife, I assure you, Serena. I will see to that."

She shivered. "I knew it. You'll end up in a duel, and all because of me."

His hand caressed her hair. "I'll do my best to avoid it, I promise. You've let them upset you, my dear. Don't. It's a hollow threat, but I'm glad you told me."

"Hollow?" His calm good humor was soothing her, but she could not believe the problem did not exist. "It isn't hollow, Francis. Tom says that even if you kill

him, Will can publish the pictures. What are we going to do?"

He drew her over to a chaise and sat down with her. "Well, we could pay them, I suppose. How much did they want? Let me guess," he said lightly. "Three thousand pounds."

That figure startled her, reminding Serena of a number of problems, especially the jewels. "Ten," she said.

"Ten?" Now he in turn was startled. "Greedy, ain't they? How did they come to that figure?" Then she saw a strangely thoughtful look come over his face.

"That was the amount Samuel Seale had offered for me before I ran away."

"I see." He considered her searchingly. "And if your brothers were willing to deal directly with me, I have to suppose they would have done so. So, you are to be their go-between, are you?" It was as if a barrier were sliding up between them.

"I suppose so," she said faintly, not sure what to make of the change in him.

He leaned back and crossed one leg over the other. One long finger tapped on the back of the chaise. "So they didn't expect you to tell me this, did they not? How, then, did they expect you to acquire such a sum?"

Serena felt as if she were being interrogated. "Th . . . they didn't . . . they . . . they wanted the three thousand pounds you gave me, and then more as I could find it. From my pin money, the housekeeping money, and other similar things. I could not do such a thing," she assured him anxiously.

Preying on her mind was the thought that she had

not mentioned the jewelry. But she could not talk about that with this cold-eyed stranger.

"Of course not. It would take forever. Quite literally. Their demands would be never-ending." Superficially, he was at ease, but his eyes were hard and cold.

"I don't think we should give them any money at all," she said. "But then there are those pictures. . . ."

"Indeed." He rose and gathered up the two pieces of paper. "You are not to fret yourself about this anymore."

"How can I not?" she protested. "Francis, you must tell me what you intend to do!"

He raised his brows. "Must? But surely this is just the kind of matter that a husband should handle for his wife. Particularly for his *enceinte* wife. Put it out of your mind, my dear." He seemed his usual courteous self. He was even smiling. But he was coated with a layer of ice. "I think it is time for us to dress now for the evening."

And he was gone.

Serena closed her eyes in despair. Clearly, Francis blamed her for this latest fiasco, and why not? It was her reputation that put them at risk, and her brothers who were trying to extort money from them.

Ten thousand pounds was an enormous sum of money. Perhaps even Francis could not afford that much.

What could she do to ease the threat both to her reputation and her happiness?

Serena rose purposefully to her feet. The only action within her power was to make this evening work so that her place in Society would be less vulnerable.

She *would* succeed.

*   *   *

As a consequence, though she was smiling, Serena was in a fiercely combative mood when she entered the grand drawing room of Belcraven House that evening. She was prepared to do anything to ensure her acceptance and render her brothers' threats toothless.

She was arrayed in another of Beth's gowns, this time a cream and chocolate creation with a wider skirt and heavily ornamented hem. It had been impossible to shorten such a hem, and so the whole border had been cut off and moved up the three inches. The gown had a stiff and heavy feel that suited Serena's belligerent mood entirely. On her head was an elaborate silk toque trimmed with pearls. She imagined it a helmet and liked the fact that it gave her height.

Frustratingly, there was nothing and no one to fight. The glittering, elegant company appeared to approve of her entirely. Serena was startled, however, to find that her first marriage was now being made known.

Mrs. Stine-Lowerstoft, a rather starchy lady, said, "Understand you were married to Riverton, Lady Middlethorpe. I gather he was quite an unpleasant character. You must have felt fortunate to be left in the country."

Serena agreed faintly and fled to Francis's side. "They know!" she whispered.

He drew her apart. "Yes. Don't worry. It's quite deliberate. This way we can control the information and some of your brothers' guns will be spiked."

"But Mrs. Stine-Lowerstoft seems to think I lived an innocent life in the country."

"You were certainly in the country," he said, and led

her off to chat with another group. She recognized with despair that though he was at his most pleasant, that coating of ice was still there. In an attempt to thaw it, Serena applied her every talent to gaining acceptance from the guests.

It wasn't hard. Most of those invited for dinner had come prepared to accept her. It was clear the Rogues' connections had the full story and were allies. The few others were willing to believe the best.

Serena found herself talking to the Duchess of Yeovil, who was still in mourning for her younger son, killed at Waterloo. Serena expressed her condolences.

"It was very hard," said the duchess, but without any tragedy airs. "We never expect our grown children to die before us, and Dare was such a delight. A scapegrace at times, but a joy."

"He was one of these Rogues."

"Yes, indeed," said the duchess with a smile. "Such a collection, but a warmhearted bunch. He valued them deeply, and sometimes, I confess, I have felt that I had a dozen sons instead of only two." She went on to relate an occasion when Lord Darius had held a shooting party at their Somerset estate.

Serena was genuinely touched by the duchess's memories of her son and enjoyed hearing her stories. Afterward, however, when Francis said, "Well done. You have sealed the Yeovils' support," he made it sound as if she had been scheming.

Serena sighed and applied herself even harder to winning all hearts as her only route to winning his.

She tried especially hard with his mother, but though the dowager was superficially pleasant, there was no thawing her at all. When Serena saw Francis's mother being particularly sweet to Lady Anne, she gritted her teeth and resolved not to resent her gracious rival and her family.

In a sour moment, however, Serena muttered to Arabella that it was almost intolerable to be the beneficiary of such noble charity.

"I suspect the poor feel like that, too," Arabella said unsympathetically, "but it's that or starve."

Serena realized for the first time that Lady Cawle was not present. "Where is the countess?" she asked anxiously. "Has she decided to frown on me after all?"

"Not at all. You made an excellent impression. She will come after the meal. She has some plan in mind but is keeping it as a surprise."

Serena shivered. She did not like surprises at all.

After dinner the company increased rapidly. There were not many grand entertainments at this time of year, so anyone who was in Town had accepted. Lord and Lady Liverpool were in attendance, along with Lord and Lady Castlereagh. Mr. Sheridan made an appearance, though he seemed unwell and was quite clearly drunk.

Quite a stir was created when the Countess of Cawle, in full-skirted gray satin, arrived on the arm of the scandalous Lord Byron. Town was already abuzz with rumor that Byron's wife had recently left his house to return to her family, taking their child with her. The gossip was expanding to encompass his finances and his morals.

At a quiet moment, the countess said to Serena, "He's being dragged through the mire more than he deserves, poor boy, but more to the point, his story can easily eclipse yours."

And so it proved. Those with a mind to scandal found the poet's business—including, as it did, hints of cruelty and incest—far more titillating than Serena's mildly grubby past. She wasn't sure, however, that this balance of interest would hold if those pictures were thrown into the scales.

A trio struck up in an anteroom, and those inclined to dance repaired to the large saloon that had been cleared for the purpose. Francis came to Serena and led her there without any question. She did not mind— the idea of dancing with him was delightful—but his reserve chilled her.

"I am not a terribly good dancer," she whispered. "I have had little practice."

"You will find the country dances easy enough."

So it proved. Serena was a natural dancer, that she knew, and had always excelled at it whilst at school. The steps of the simpler dances soon came back to her. She was finally relaxing and beginning to enjoy herself, when a stir by the doorway froze her in mid step.

Disaster! That was her immediate thought.

Did the raised voices and exclamations reflect shock and horror?

Who was it?

One of Matthew's familiars come to disgrace her?

Her brothers with a batch of lewd pictures in hand?

With a start, she realized her reaction must have spoiled the dance, and Serena turned to apologize to everyone. She found, however, that Francis had disengaged them from the line dance, which was cheerfully continuing without them. Looking around, she saw that many of the guests were undisturbed by whatever had happened.

She clutched Francis's arm. "What is it?"

"Nicholas," he said, almost to himself, and steered a rapid course toward the disturbance. It resolved itself into a handsome man and woman in the center of a group of Rogues. Serena knew this must be Nicholas Delaney, the one Arabella had called King Rogue.

Relief turned her knees to jelly as terror had not, and she held even tighter to Francis's arm. He hardly seemed aware of her, however, so intent was he on the new arrivals. From what she'd heard, she assumed he was delighted to see his friend, and yet he did not seem to be.

"Nicholas," he said. "What the devil are you doing here?"

The blond man raised a brow but did not take offense. "Heard rumor of a party."

"From Somerset?"

"No, from Lauriston Street when we arrived." Nicholas smiled at Serena and detached her from her death grip on Francis. He raised her hand for a kiss. "I hope you are Francis's bride. You'll make a very welcome addition to the Rogues."

"Serena, I make known to you Mr. Nicholas Delaney, who appears to be poking his nose into other people's business again."

Nicholas merely smiled. "My best friend has married. I wanted to meet his bride. Speaking of which, meet mine." Serena was introduced to Eleanor Delaney, a good-looking auburn woman with a remarkable air of serenity. Did nothing ever ruffle this couple? How nice it must be, she thought with a touch of bitterness, to have life always flow along smooth paths.

Nicholas Delaney's voice snapped her out of her

thoughts. "Another set is starting, Serena. Will you partner me?"

After an anxious look between the two men, Serena allowed herself to be led back onto the dance floor.

"Don't look so worried," Nicholas said. "Francis is not angry with you or me."

"Can you be sure?"

"Oh, yes. But someone will have to tell me exactly what is going on. Will it be you?"

"No." Then Serena wondered if he would take offense at such a bald denial.

All he said was, "Good."

They danced for some time without further conversation. He was a good dancer, though not as graceful as Francis. Serena found herself trying to puzzle out the few things Nicholas Delaney had said, and felt as if she were faced with a conundrum.

As they stood together for a part of the dance, she said, "Why good?"

He picked up the conversation without difficulty. "Most matters between husband and wife are best kept confidential. If you need to talk, however, you can always come to me or to Eleanor. We may not have answers, but we are both good listeners. So is Francis normally."

They swung again into movement and completed their part of the dance.

When they were still again, Serena defended Francis. "To be a good listener, one has to be a little detached, I think."

"But would one wish to discuss secrets of the heart with someone who does not care? *'Oh, if thou car'st not whom I love, Alas, thou lov'st not me.'* Do you love him?"

The question was launched like a missile. Serena turned away and refused to respond, but she feared he had read the answer on her face.

They completed the set without further talk.

At the end he said pleasantly, "Thank you. I don't think I have ever danced with a more beautiful woman, and I have danced with many of great attractions. A beautiful woman who tries to hide it," he added, "is like a tall person who stoops."

"I am not trying to hide my beauty, Mr. Delaney. In fact, I have gone to some effort to make the most of it tonight."

He was leading her back to where Francis was talking to the Ardens and Eleanor Delaney. She thought he would make no response, but then he said, "A railed garden cannot be fully appreciated, no matter how carefully tended."

Serena wanted to hit him without entirely being sure why. If Francis was irritated to see Nicholas Delaney here, she was in complete accord with him.

For the next set, Serena danced with the marquess. She noted that while he seemed to flirt with every lady, even the dowagers, he no longer flirted with her. *Did* she have railings about her? As they made a pass together, she asked, "Why do you flirt with every lady but me, Lord Arden?"

He raised his brows. "Because I thought you did not care for it. I will with great pleasure if you want. But not," he added, "if you are trying to make Francis jealous."

Serena stepped into the next movement, embarrassingly aware that he had pinpointed her unacknowledged intention. She was heartily sick of all these astute observations.

Though this evening was turning out to be successful in terms of their strategy, it was tying her mind in knots.

When the event finally drew to a close and the guests had all left, the Rogues gathered in the untouched library to review the affair. Beside the Ardens and Middlethorpes, there were the Delaneys, Stephen Ball, Miles Cavanagh, Felicity, Con Somerford, and Hal Beaumont.

"A perfect end to a perfect campaign," said Hal with a smile at Serena. "The Cream of Society have now accepted you. You'd have to really appall them to undo that."

Serena flashed an anxious look at Francis, but he didn't seem about to reveal the existence of the pictures and her brothers' threats.

"Quite clever," said Nicholas, "to introduce Serena in this way. Whose plan was it?"

After a brief hesitation, Serena said, "Mine. With help from Beth."

"I congratulate you. So, tomorrow the notice appears in the papers, I gather."

"Yes," said Francis. "That should bring a swarm of congratulatory callers. After a couple of days of that, I hope we can escape into the country. I was thinking of visiting Somerset."

"Excellent. We can travel back down together. We left Arabel down there, so we will not stay long." Nicholas rose and assisted Eleanor to her feet. "Since we traveled for a good part of the day, however, I think we deserve our beds."

When the Delaneys had left, the others not staying at Belcraven House took their leave, too.

Riding home in the carriage, Serena could not ignore a shadowy tension emanating from her husband. It seemed different from the chill that had settled on him earlier and she probed for the cause. "You seemed angry to see Mr. Delaney, but he appears to be a pleasant man."

"He is. I was not angry to see him."

"Are you angry at me, then?"

"No."

That seemed unlikely. "I'm sorry about my brothers. . . ."

"Their faults are no concern of yours."

Serena remembered her fear that her children would have something of the Allbrights about them, and she shuddered. "Will we really travel with the Delaneys to their home?"

"Not if you do not wish to. We can go to the Priory if you would prefer."

Serena would prefer that he not be angry. They swayed as the coach took a corner and it would have been easy to lean against him, but she did not. "I think everything went well," she said.

"Yes. Excellently."

Silence settled and she could think of nothing more to say.

At home, Francis escorted Serena to her room and it was clear that tonight he would not share a bed with her. It was also clear that he would not share his thoughts. When he turned to go to his room, Serena stayed him with a hand on his arm. "Francis, we can't pretend my brother's threat does not exist. Tonight was all very well, but if those pictures surface, it could undo all."

"There is no need to concern yourself, Serena. I will take care of it."

"Tom said he would be in the garden tomorrow afternoon. What am I to do?"

"Nothing," he said sternly. "Do not by any means keep that appointment. Think, Serena. Your brothers will not use those pictures except as a last resort, for that would give them revenge but no profit." He dropped a formal kiss on her cheek. "Put the matter out of your mind. Good night."

Serena watched the door close behind him and hissed with annoyance. Disaster and shame were hanging over her head, and she was to put the matter out of her mind! Men, even good men, could be infuriating! She rang sharply for her maid.

As the woman readied her for bed, Serena could not get her brothers out of her mind at all. She wouldn't put it past them to publish those pictures out of simple spite.

In fact, she suddenly realized, there was nothing to stop them from making one or two of the less offensive pictures public and then demanding the money to avoid publication of the rest. Francis would have to pay, but Serena would still be tarnished, if not ruined entirely.

A good man wouldn't think of this ploy, but she was an Allbright, so it was perfectly clear to her. She had to explain this to Francis and try to make him understand the way an Allbright's mind worked. As soon as her maid was gone, she went to the adjoining door and knocked. There was no response. She opened the door cautiously and peeped in. Francis's bed had been turned down, and he had clearly prepared for the night. Where was he?

After a moment, she returned to her own room. She supposed there might be any number of matters needing his attention, even at two in the morning, and she could hardly wander the house searching for him.

Her insight would have to wait until tomorrow.

Fearing that yet again Serena would come to him and he would be unable to resist, Francis had taken refuge in the library. He simply could not think it right to make love to a woman whom he suspected of extortion.

It was all very well for love to be blind and for him to ignore the fact that his wife carried the card of a man who was trying to blackmail him for ten thousand pounds. It pushed even his limits to put on blinkers when she came up with another reason to demand the same sum, this time involving her brothers.

All his instincts told him to trust Serena, but it was a simple fact that men could be fooled by a beautiful woman. He couldn't afford to be. The honor of his house was at stake.

He had to accept that there was a clear possibility the child Serena carried was not his but Ferncliff's. It was also possible that the picture she had shown him had been sketched yesterday. There might not be any more of them.

What he was to do about all this was a different matter entirely.

He would not again succumb to drink, and so he took down a volume of Plato and tried to deaden his mind with the effort of Platonic translation.

Chapter 18

When Serena arose the next day, she discovered that Francis had already left the house, apparently to visit his friend, Nicholas Delaney. She supposed her thoughts concerning her brothers' plans could wait, though she fretted about what to do if Francis didn't return by the afternoon. If he thought to handle Tom by ignoring him, it would be a serious mistake.

Serena was also somewhat hurt that Francis had not taken her with him to visit the Delaneys, but she was not surprised. At the moment, in his eyes she was an Allbright. She truly wished her mother had committed adultery!

It was perhaps as well that she was distracted by a minor crisis in the household. A pound of tea had disappeared from the tea chest. Dibbert had apparently taken the matter of the missing packet of oolong tea to the dowager, but that lady had instructed him to call on Serena for adjudication. Serena rather suspected that the dowager hoped she would not be able to cope.

Serena was glad of a distraction and sallied down into the kitchen to handle the supposed theft.

All the tea was apparently kept locked in a chest in the pantry, but as Mrs. Andover, the housekeeper, proved, the lock could be forced with the blade of a knife. Mrs. Andover was accusing no one but clearly had her suspicions of the cook, Mrs. Scott.

Serena noted evidence of a feud there, and from the appeals both women were making to a harassed Dibbert, she suspected that he was the bone of contention.

The cook, Mrs. Scott, seemed intent on pinning the blame on a terrified kitchen maid who had only been hired the month before. The maid's wails brought in the young gardener, who came staunchly to the defense of little Katie. This clearly upset the younger upstairs maid.

Serena noted that perilous triangle.

Affairs of the heart below stairs were almost as complicated as those above!

Mrs. Scott was clearly on the side of the upstairs maid, and she shrieked at having the gardener's muddy boots on her floor. In moments, the household was in an uproar.

Serena silenced them all and made enquiries worthy of a Bow Street Runner. She soon discovered that the oolong was less favored by the servants than the black tea, and that it was only since the recent arrival of the family that it had been used. The missing packet had been the second of two, and its loss had only been noted this morning when it was needed.

"This tea," said Serena, "could have disappeared at any time during the past few months."

"Someone would have noticed it were missing, ma'am," said the cook.

"Who generally went to get the tea from the chest, Mrs. Scott?"

"Katie," said the woman with a glare. "I'd send her to Mrs. Andover for the key."

"I didn't take it!" the girl wailed.

"She didn't take it!" the gardener shouted.

Serena waited for silence.

"Now, it is my decision that after such a time, it is impossible to discover who is guilty. A new tea chest will be ordered, one with a sturdy lock, and you, Mrs. Andover, will check the contents every night. In that way there will be less chance of baseless suspicions being thrown about."

"Baseless suspicions indeed," muttered the cook.

The gardener started forward. "Here, you old bi—"

"Silence!" Serena stared around at them. "There will be an end of this. It will not be spoken of again. However, Katie, if you are not happy in your post, I will see if I can find you another as good in another household."

The girl's eyes flickered anxiously between the cook and the gardener, and then she mumbled that she was all right, really. The gardener flashed Serena a bitter look, however, and she thought that her kind intentions might cause trouble from him in the future.

She wasn't sure if she had handled matters all that well or not.

Serena escaped back to the gracious world of the main body of the house, wondering what dramas would continue to be played out down below before she was called in to adjudicate again.

Would Dibbert favor the housekeeper or the cook?

Would Katie succumb to the handsome gardener's wiles, and would he marry her?

Or would he return to the upstairs maid, who had clearly been his former favorite?

She sighed and shook her head. Though important to those involved, these problems did not compare to the ones facing her.

The morning papers had contained the formal announcement of the marriage of Viscount Middlethorpe to Serena, Lady Riverton. Unless that news deterred them, she and Francis could expect a great many callers in the afternoon, come to offer their good wishes. She could only hope that Francis would be here to greet them.

At four o'clock her brothers would return to the garden, expecting to receive the jewels and three thousand pounds. When she was not there to meet them, she did not know what they would do. Perhaps Francis had all this in hand, but until he told her what he planned, she could find no ease in that.

By midday, Francis still had not returned home. Serena was becoming very nervous that he might forget their callers as well as her brothers. She told herself firmly that he would not let such a thing slip his mind.

It only belatedly occurred to Serena that her two causes for concern clashed. If she and Francis were to be engaged all afternoon with callers, how on earth *was* Tom to be handled? Perhaps she should send her brother a note to explain, but she knew that was just the sort of thing Francis did not want her to do.

Damn him. Where *was* he?

To distract herself, she took the puppy into the garden again. It was far too early for her brothers to turn up unless they were keeping an eye on the place, so she wasn't breaking Francis's interdict on meeting them. On the other hand, she had to admit she would be rather relieved if they did appear. She could explain about this afternoon and placate them until tomorrow.

As she walked out into the sunshine and put Brandy down to play, she was astonished to see Francis's mother coming toward her. Lady Middlethorpe did not strike her as the sort of woman to wander in winter gardens.

Lady Middlethorpe stopped, as if alarmed, but then continued on. "A lovely day for February, is it not, Serena?"

"Yes, Lady Middlethorpe." Serena had half her attention on the puppy, who showed an inclination to venture out of sight.

"If we are to Lady Middlethorpe each other, life will be unbearable. You call Arabella 'Arabella.' Call me Cordelia."

Serena blinked at the dowager. "Very well, Cordelia." It did not slide easily off her tongue.

The dowager frowned into the distance. "There are so few people to call me Cordelia anymore." Her eyes flicked back into focus and she scanned Serena. "Your hair is escaping its pins." She continued on into the house.

Serena hastily tidied herself. How did the dowager—Cordelia—always appear so pristine?

Serena stared after her mother-in-law, recalling the man she had met in the garden—Charles something-or-other—who had wanted to speak to Cordelia. He had entirely slipped her mind with all that had been going on, but could Cordelia be in the habit of meeting *men* here?

As she tried to imagine such a thing and failed, Serena saw Brandy wriggle under a hedge.

"No, Brandy! Come back!"

Brandy thought this a marvelous game and, after a moment, so did Serena. For many minutes they played chase around the garden. Serena didn't care a snap that she was not acting like a viscountess or that her hair was escaping its pins. She was laughing as she dashed around a yew hedge and collided with a man coming out of the very arbor in which she had sat the day before.

For an alarmed moment, she thought it was Tom, but then she recognized her mistake. It was Charles somebody-or-other. "Why, whatever are you doing here?" Even as she spoke, she could guess. The dowager *had* been keeping a tryst!

The man seemed as startled as she. "Lady Middlethorpe . . ." he steadied her then let her go, seeming to be at a loss for words. Then he muttered, "Be damned to it," and continued in a clear voice, "I came to meet Lady . . . with the Dowager Lady Middlethorpe. I see you are shocked."

"Yes, a little . . ."

"Is it so shocking," he asked sharply, "for two people to be in love?"

"Well . . . no."

"But it is if they are of great age. I, young lady, am only thirty-eight."

"But . . ."

"And Cordelia is only forty-six. We are, neither of us, in our dotage!"

"Mr. . . . oh, dear, I have forgotten your name."

"Ferncliff. I gave you my card."

"I have no idea what became of it. Mr. Ferncliff, I am not shocked by your age. I am shocked that any lady and gentleman should meet clandestinely in the garden. It is not proper."

His anger lessened and he gave a sound of exasperation. "I know that, Lady Middlethorpe. This imbroglio is not of my designing. In fact, it is likely to drive me mad, if it does not first lead to my untimely demise."

Serena gave him a look. "I have no faith in stories of people dying of a broken heart, sir."

"Have you not?" he said with some amusement. "But a pistol ball will do the job."

"A *pistol*. Who do you think would shoot you?"

"Perhaps that young firebrand you call a husband."

"Francis?"

"Indeed. He has been pursuing me around the country for months, often with pistol in hand."

Serena sat down on the stone bench with a thump. "Mr. Ferncliff, you must be mistaken. My husband is a gentle, understanding man."

"His understanding does not appear to extend to men who aspire to his mother's hand in marriage, especially men of no great worldly means. Besides which, I am afraid you are deluded, dear lady. He may behave with gentleness to you—and all credit to him— but I have it upon authority that Lord Middlethorpe has been a rascal since his tender years. He is part of a gang of vicious reprobates."

"You mean the *Rogues?"*

"Precisely. Mohocks would be a better term. Cordelia has lamented his connection to these people, and now I have heard of them from other quarters."

Mohocks had been gentlemanly ruffians of the century before who had made the streets of London unsafe for decent people. Serena could see no connection to Francis and his friends. "But really . . ." Serena trailed off, unable to handle this peculiar angle of reality. But which angle, she had to wonder, showed the truth? "Mr. Ferncliff, I am acquainted with some of the Rogues, and they all seem pleasant men."

"I gather they are dashing."

"If you are implying that I am a foolish miss whose head is easily turned, sir, nothing could be further from the truth. Enough of this. Are you sure that my husband objects to your courtship of his mother?"

He laughed shortly. "Very sure."

"But I know he would like her to remarry."

"Doubtless, but to a man of more substance than I. I am a scholar, Lady Middlethorpe. I have a small independence—very small—and am never likely to improve upon it. I have no interest in such matters. To be frank, I would never consider marrying a woman who could bear children, as I would be completely unable to raise them as I would wish."

"I can quite see that my husband would not want his mother to live in poverty."

"There is no question of that. Cordelia has a handsome jointure." His lips twisted. "You see, immediately you assume that I am after her money. So does he. It is not the case. I am completely happy with my simple life. I merely acknowledge that she would not be. But if we are to have a substantial house and a number of servants, if we are to travel and entertain, it will have to be on her money."

"But I can see why my husband might disapprove, Mr. Ferncliff. It is precisely the sort of thing a dutiful son is *supposed* to disapprove of."

"He has every right to be suspicious, Lady Middle-thorpe, but any rational man would wish to meet the suitor in question and discuss the matter. Middlethorpe merely pursues me, gun in hand. The ridiculous situation has gone on long enough. Cordelia says that her son will not tolerate the connection, and she will not marry me if it will anger him so much. I am determined to speak to him at least once to see if I can drive some sense into his head."

"I certainly think that is wise," said Serena. Mr. Ferncliff's image of Francis was so different from her own that she had to believe a meeting would help.

"But how to arrange it?" he demanded. "Cordelia becomes distraught at the very mention of it and refuses to bring it about."

"There must be any number of ways one gentleman can arrange to meet another."

"Certainly, but when a man has twice sought me out with a pistol in his hand, I am inclined to be cautious. Will you be my go-between, Lady Middlethorpe?"

Serena stared at him. "Between you and Francis?"

"Yes."

Serena felt many misgivings. Matters between her and her husband were not sound enough to permit the adding of new strains, and if she appeared to be a suppliant for someone he considered an enemy . . . "I don't know if I can, sir."

"It is not so hard, surely."

Serena stood. "I don't know. Tell me where you can be reached, and I will contact you if I can arrange a meeting."

"I have rooms at the Scepter Inn not far from here, but under the name Lowden." He pulled a somewhat battered gray bob wig out of his pocket and sat it on his head, crowning it with a three-cornered hat. "See to what extremes I have been driven? Middlethorpe seems to have managed to raise the whole of London to search for me!"

"Oh, dear," said Serena. There was such anger involved that she did not know what to do for the best. "I will see what I can do, Mr. Ferncliff."

When Ferncliff had left, Serena realized she had forgotten the puppy. With a cry of distress, she ran out into the open garden calling Brandy's name. When she found no sign, she opened the gate and looked out into the mews lane. Could the tiny creature have gone as far as the street? She imagined the puppy dodging hooves and wheels. "Brandy!"

She was about to return to the house to start a search when she heard a frantic yipping. She called again, and Brandy wriggled under a gate of a nearby garden and raced over gleefully.

Serena swept her up. "Oh, you bad girl. You're covered in mud! Where have you been?"

Quite possibly, Brandy was wondering the same thing. The puppy's ecstasy suggested that she had been thoroughly lost.

Serena headed back to the house, scolding all the way.

"Serena!" She saw Francis coming toward her. "Where on earth have you been?"

"Brandy went exploring. I thought I'd lost her."
Something in his expression alerted her to her appearance. Her hair must be all over the place, and Brandy had thoroughly muddied her gown.

He did look disapproving as he gingerly took the weary puppy from her. "She's covered you with mud and we have guests."

"Already?" Serena exclaimed in dismay.

"Just Nicholas and Eleanor. There's no need to fuss."

Just Nicholas and Eleanor. Serena's nerves tightened. "If you can take Brandy to the kitchen, I'll change my gown."

"Very well."

Serena hurried off feeling her stomach knot. She didn't know why the thought of another meeting with Nicholas Delaney made her nervous, but it did. He seemed just the sort of person to guess that she'd been meeting her husband's enemy in the garden and that, for the moment, she didn't intend to tell her husband about it.

Serena changed quickly into a fresh gown and had her maid tidy her hair. Surveying herself, she knew with despair that even with the greatest care, she would never have Cordelia's elegant gloss. Her figure was too round and her hair just seemed to have a mind of its own. Cordelia never had a hair out of place.

Cordelia couldn't stay so neat in a lover's embrace, though, could she? Were Ferncliff and Cordelia lovers? It seemed impossible to imagine Francis's mother in a sexual tangle, but she had certainly been a lover once, with her husband.

Serena dismissed the maid and took a moment to

371

ponder her dilemma. Ferncliff could be a wicked liar. But Cordelia *had* been out in the garden for some reason.

One obvious course was to speak to Cordelia herself, but the mere thought dizzied Serena. *Cordelia, I want to talk to you about your lover. . . .*

Nor could she see how to raise the subject with Francis. *Francis, I want to talk to you about your mother's lover . . .*

And there was still the problem of what to do about her brothers, who would be angered not to find her waiting, loot in hand.

Don't worry, he'd said.

Hah!

Serena went down to the drawing room, to find Francis already there with their guests. Nicholas and Eleanor Delaney seemed just as pleasant and composed as they had been last night, but Nicholas still made Serena very nervous. There was something in his eyes—a quickness, a perception—that made her feel transparent. There were a great many things that she did not want him to know.

The talk was general—politics, crops, social matters, and the weather. The prospect in all seemed rather gloomy.

"Good heavens," said Francis. "Let us talk of more pleasant things. How is Arabel?"

"Now, really, Francis," said Eleanor. "Are you referring to our pride and joy as a 'thing'?"

"Heaven forbid! How is she?" Francis turned to Serena. "Arabel is Nicholas and Eleanor's daughter."

It was Nicholas who replied, and no one could miss the fondness in his voice. "Doubtless displeased with us. Arabel is of the firm opinion that she rules creation. She is, of course, a benevolent despot, but we decided she must be shown her place and left her behind."

"Does she throw tantrums, then?" Francis asked.

"Of course not. But she enjoyed the company of Leander's two and has made it known that she would like brothers and sisters. We have pointed out that they would be younger, not older, but she is undeterred."

Serena listened to this whimsy with bemusement. "How old is your daughter, Mr. Delaney?"

"As old as Methuselah. She is fourteen months."

"And she *talks?*"

Eleanor laughed. "Don't let Nicholas bamboozle you, Serena. He maintains that he can understand every babble, but I think he just interprets them to suit himself. *He* wants a bevy of children."

Her husband smiled at her. "True."

After some more general talk, Francis took Nicholas away to look at some estate papers. When the two women were alone, Eleanor said, "You are quite correct. We have been given the opportunity to be private in case you wish to talk to me. Don't let it disturb you. It is just Nicholas being clever."

Serena eyed Eleanor Delaney. "Why would I want to talk to you, in particular?"

"I have no idea. Francis and Nicholas have been closeted most of the morning, though. They are very close in a way that frequent absences cannot affect."

"I have been told that. Francis has hardly mentioned Mr. Delaney, however."

"I can't say Nicholas talked much of Francis in our early days. But Francis was of great help to him—was his anchor, in fact—in bad times. We would like to help if we can."

"Why would we need help?"

"Do you not?"

Serena just shrugged.

Eleanor said, "I was probably already pregnant when we married."

Serena stared at her, startled by the admission and curious. "Probably?"

"We did not wait to be sure. It is not a matter generally advertised, and a difference of a few weeks in a birth is not scrutinized."

"Not as a difference of a few months will be."

"Quite. I just wanted you to know that I have some understanding of what an uncomfortable situation it can be."

"Being prematurely pregnant is not nearly as uncomfortable as being Matthew Riverton's widow, I assure you."

"But being Matthew Riverton's widow is surely better than being Matthew Riverton's wife. See," Eleanor said with a twinkle, "we have a case of unrelenting improvement."

Despite everything, that startled a laugh out of Serena.

"I remember at one point," said Eleanor thoughtfully, "wondering what had happened to the wages of sin, as I seemed to be gaining a great deal by my fall from grace."

That was a delicate probe indeed. "Do you think I am *reluctant* to be happy?"

"I don't know. Sometimes we don't feel we deserve what fate gives us, and then we fight the gift. Fate has given you one of the best men I know as a husband. Along with him, you have a position in Society and a comfortable degree of wealth without all the paraphernalia poor Beth has to endure. You will have a child—"

"I am fully aware of my blessings," Serena interrupted. "I am just terrified that they will be turned to dross." Surrendering at last, she told Eleanor about the pictures. "And I can't believe that Francis is even *thinking* of paying them the ten thousand pounds, but I'm not sure he isn't. And he won't tell me."

"It may seem worth the money to give you peace of mind."

"I'd never be at peace again," Serena declared. "My brothers would just take it as encouragement."

"True. I'll speak to Nicholas about it in case Francis did not. I, too, have an unpleasant brother, but the Rogues are good at handling that kind of person."

With a shiver, Serena remembered Mr. Ferncliff's opinion of the Rogues. "What happened to your brother?"

"I have no idea. He went abroad."

Serena did not find that very reassuring. "Would you say the Rogues are dangerous?"

"Oh, yes, if they think their cause is right."

The discussion ended there, however, for Nicholas and Francis returned just ahead of the first callers, Arabella and the Countess of Cawle. The Delaneys soon left, and while none of the other guests stayed very long, the stream was continuous and glittering. Lord and Lady Cowper, the Duke and Duchess of Yeovil, the Earl and Countess of Liverpool, the Duke and Duchess of Belcraven . . .

Serena caught sight of the clock and noticed that it was four. She looked around, hoping to see that Francis had slipped away, but he was calmly talking to the Duke of Belcraven. Wasn't he going to do *anything?*

Or had he handled the matter by having her brothers killed?

Beth, who was disguised in her best marchioness manner, came over and said, "Don't look so frantic. Everything is going splendidly. You are doing magnificently."

Serena couldn't confess her thoughts. "I feel like an automaton. I smile, I nod, I smile."

"Horrible, isn't it? But it will soon be over."

"Beth," said Serena urgently, "are the Rogues bloodthirsty? I mean, would they kill if they thought it necessary?"

"They aren't exactly a unit. But yes. After all, Con, Hal, and Leander were soldiers, and I gather Nicholas has been in dangerous situations. Don't worry," she assured Serena brightly. "They won't hesitate if violence becomes necessary. I have to leave." She kissed Serena warmly on the cheek. "We'll have a better time to talk tomorrow. Stop looking so worried."

Serena wanted to scream, but she had to turn to smile and nod at Lady Buffington. As the lady chattered, Serena wondered whether the Rogues could actually have slaughtered her brothers. No great loss, but she couldn't feel comfortable about it. What really concerned her was the possibility that Francis could intend to slaughter Charles Ferncliff if he got his hands on him.

Ferncliff appeared to be an innocent party.

An hour later, the stream of guests finally dried up,

leaving just Francis, Serena, and Cordelia in the drawing room.

Serena collapsed into a chair. "I feel wrung out."

Francis moved a footstool under her feet. "You did very well. That should be the worst of it. You are now firmly part of the *haut ton.*"

Cordelia looked unruffled, though she had worked just as hard as Serena over the past few hours. "Yes, Francis, I think we can take it as given that Serena is accepted despite her unfortunate past. I will therefore return to Thorpe tomorrow. I think I told you that I will dine with Arabella and the countess tonight." With that, she left the room.

Serena frowned after her. "Francis, would you mind if your mother married again?"

He chuckled. "Going to play matchmaker? I can see that life would be easier for you without my mother underfoot. By all means, if you can."

He had misinterpreted her, but it was an opening to discuss the subject. "I suppose you would be very particular as to whom she married."

He lounged in the chair opposite her. "Me? No. It is nothing to do with me."

"But surely, if she expressed the intention of marrying the stable boy you would have to object."

He laughed out loud. "The mere idea is ridiculous."

"But what would you do?" she persisted.

"Good Lord, Serena. Is this some sort of party game? Of course, I'd put a stop to it. She'd have lost her wits."

Where, then, is the border line? Serena wondered. "Is there a type of man you would not want her to marry?"

He frowned at her, perhaps suspiciously. "You're serious about this, aren't you? Let me see. Obviously, I wouldn't want her to marry a bounder, the sort of man who would mistreat her or gamble away her money. I'm not entirely sure how I would stop her, though."

"Perhaps your disapproval would be enough."

"I'd hope that her own good sense would do the trick. Serena, enough of this. I'm afraid my mother does not wish to remarry. She was truly and deeply devoted to my father."

"I don't doubt that, but time changes things. . . ." Serena wanted to stay on the subject of acceptability. "What about rank? Would you object to her marrying a commoner?"

"No, as long as it wasn't the stable boy."

"You're not taking this seriously!"

"No, I'm not, and nor should you. My mother will marry if she wants to, and it's nothing to do with us."

Serena was by now completely baffled. She turned to the subject of her greatest anxiety. "What of my brothers, then? If you left them to cool their heels in the garden, Francis, their anger will have been roused. They could do anything."

It wasn't until her words caused a change that she realized that for a few moments they had been in a state of amity. Now he had withdrawn behind that chilly barrier. "I told you to leave the matter to me."

"How can I? *Did* you do anything about this afternoon?"

"I want you to put the matter out of your mind and trust me."

Serena heard the words, but her anxiety did not let

378

them register. "It is a sword hanging over my head, Francis! I don't think you understand Tom. He's cunning, but he's also vindictive and stupid in his rages. If he's pushed far enough, he could publish those pictures out of pure spite."

"Could he?"

"What's more, I've been thinking about this. If I were him, I'd give just a few of the less damaging ones to a printer. They'd be enough to create a lot of unpleasant talk without really ruining me. That would force your hand."

"That's what you would do, is it?"

"That's what *Tom* might do. How could you handle that?"

"I'd kill him."

Serena practically jumped out of her seat. "You'd shoot him in cold blood?"

"With pleasure, but I suppose I'd have to call him out."

"Oh no, you *mustn't!*"

"Why not?" There was a sharp edge of suspicion in his voice.

"I could not bear to see you hurt over me."

He stared at her a moment, then rose. "Come with me."

Bemused, Serena followed him. He seemed in the strangest mood. He went to his study and took a gleaming inlaid case out of a locked drawer. He removed a silver-mounted pistol and loaded it with easy familiarity. "Come along."

"Where are we going?" she asked as he led the way into the garden.

"To ease at least one of your fears."

Once out of doors he looked around. "Damnation, there's hardly a straight vista in any direction.

"I think it's a lovely garden. What are you about?"

"It's a charming garden." He went past the first hedge. "Ah. See that early daffodil in bloom beneath the tree."

"Yes." It was a good twenty yards away and only visible through the skeleton branches of a deciduous bush. What is more, the sun was beginning to set and the light was poor.

He raised his hand, sighted, and fired. The yellow bloom fell.

"Oh, how *terrible!* How could you?"

After a moment, he burst out laughing. "You are supposed to be overcome with admiration for my marksmanship and stop worrying about me."

Serena looked again at the fallen bloom. "I suppose it was very clever, but it's a terrible waste of a flower."

"There'll be more. In weeks, the place will be full of them."

"There are always more people, too. Would you kill a person as easily?"

"Of course not."

"Would you kill a person at all?"

He frowned at her intense tone. "If I had to, of course. It would be my duty. But I never have, Serena. Are you worried about your brothers?"

"Are they all right?"

"I certainly haven't hurt them. I'd hardly expect you to fret about them, though."

"I don't," she said, then realized that sounded terrible. "Oh, heavens, I just don't want you to kill them. For one thing, it would cause a terrible scandal."

"I won't kill them, I promise. Let's hope they know my reputation with a pistol and cause no trouble—"

They were interrupted by the young gardener rushing from the back of the garden. "Who fired that shot?" He came to a halt. "Oh, milord. Sorry, milord."

"I'm sorry, Cather. I was just exhibiting something to Lady Middlethorpe. There's a fallen daffodil back there. I think my wife would like it."

With a rolling-eyed look, the young man went off to retrieve the flower.

Serena said pointedly, "I'm glad it won't come to violence. I don't like violence."

"There we are in accord."

She turned to face him. "But you won't pay my brothers the money, will you?"

"You don't want me to?" he asked curiously.

"No."

"Are you sure?"

"Of course I am."

He studied his pistol for a moment, then looked up at her. "What if I were to give you the money to give to them?"

She stared at him. "That wouldn't change anything."

"Wouldn't it?"

Serena thought this conversation was going to drive her mad, but by then the gardener was back with the flower. He gave it to her, looking as if he felt a fool to be handing over such a battered bloom.

"Thank you," said Serena, wondering quite what she was supposed to do with one daffodil that had only a few inches of stem on it. She shrugged. "I suppose I had better put it in water, and I am getting chilled out here without a cloak."

Francis smiled. "I'm sorry. I never thought. By all means, go in and warm up."

Serena felt as if they were both speaking in foreign languages and achieving very little indeed, but there was nothing to do but go.

Francis watched his wife return to the house, wondering what the devil was going on.

Then he realized the gardener was still by his side, fidgeting.

"Yes, Cather?"

"Er . . . begging your pardon, milord, but do you think you could ask milady to shut the gate when she uses it? Otherwise, dogs get in, you see. Unruly-type dogs."

"Of course. I was not aware she was in the habit of going out into the mews."

"Went out this morning, she did, in search of her little pup, milord."

"Oh, of course." Francis was not paying close heed to the conversation. He was still absorbed in the one with Serena. He simply didn't think his wife was actress enough to pretend such disinterest in getting her hands on the money. No doubt it was as she said, and her brothers were trying to squeeze money out of her any way they could.

He prayed it be so.

The gardener spoke again. "And perhaps word could be given to others, milord. There seems to have been a fair old coming and going through that gate the past week."

Serena's brothers. "It might be better to put a stout

lock on it, Cather. The few servants who have business using it could be given keys."

"Aye, I'll do that, milord."

"See to it, then." Francis turned away, but the man's words registered and he turned back. "Who exactly has been using that gate recently?"

"Well, milord, such as I've seen—there was her ladyship this morning, and those two men she spoke to yesterday. Then there's the other man as comes in to speak with Lady Middlethorpe."

"Other man?" Francis felt the chill start at the back of his neck.

"Aye, milord. A hardy sort of fellow. Been here three or four times, he has."

Francis wanted to ask more but didn't dare. "Thank you."

Francis returned to the house feeling as if he had been knocked on the head. He was sure Cather, for good reasons or bad, had intended to impart that information. Perhaps the gardener simply didn't like all this coming and going in his garden, or perhaps he didn't like seeing his employer cuckolded.

But if Cather was to be believed—and it was hardly likely that he'd lie about such a thing—Serena had been meeting Charles Ferncliff in the garden here, and more than once. What innocent interpretation could he put on it?

Chapter 19

No matter how hard Francis tried, he could find no comfortable explanation for his wife's behavior.

He was very inclined to go to her now and throw her guilt in her face, but he was afraid of doing and saying far more than he should. He'd like to throttle her, the lying jade.

He wished he could lay this all before Nicholas, but he hadn't told his friend about his suspicions and was reluctant to do so now. None of this could affect the fact that he and Serena were married. He had a natural reluctance to let his friends know he'd been such a fool.

What of the child she carried?

Francis went into his study and slumped into the chair behind his desk. He could guard her and make sure she behaved in the future. He could bear it all if he could only be sure the child was his.

He'd been sure once. When he was with Serena, he'd swear in blood that she was incapable of duplicity. Was that reality or a siren's power to turn his wits?

He remembered her neatly laying out what an Allbright would do with those pictures—a plan of action that would not have occurred to him.

She was an Allbright.

Life couldn't go on like this. He was going to have to discover the truth and lay it before Serena. Perhaps they could still find some way to make a life together.

First, however, he must find Ferncliff and put a stop to his games. If he could find out anything about the fathering of Serena's child at the same time, then all well and good.

Next he would move against the Allbrights. He'd sent them a curt note, telling them not to bother coming to the garden today and that he would contact them tomorrow.

If they really were after ten thousand pounds, they would soon realize they wouldn't get it. If they didn't stop their games, he'd ruin them. They already lived on the fringes of Society. If Francis and the other Rogues moved against them, they'd never hunt the Shires again or gamble in a reputable establishment.

And if Tom Allbright made any trouble at all, Francis would call him out and cripple him. It would be an immense pleasure.

What if the Allbrights denied the extortion, however? That would bring him back to Serena trying to get the money for her lover. The man who might be her lover . . .

Unless Ferncliff was blackmailing her, too, he thought with sudden hope. Now there was a thought.

But what was she trying to hide that was worth ten thousand pounds?

Francis sunk his head in his hands and groaned. He was assuredly going to go mad.

A knock on the door brought his mother. "Is something wrong, my dear?"

Francis pushed himself to his feet. "Nothing in particular, Mother. Did you want something?"

"Merely to confirm that I will leave for Thorpe first thing tomorrow. Do you have any business you want me to attend to?"

"No, I don't think so. Serena and I will doubtless be there in a few weeks time and will stay until after the child is born."

"Of course. It could be the heir, and the heir should be born at the Priory."

"Quite."

The dowager put on a stern look. "Francis, I cannot ignore the fact that you and Serena are experiencing some problems. I want to advise you that honesty is by far the best policy, and deception only leads to greater grief."

Francis could have laughed. "So you have always said, Mother."

She sighed. "I also want to say that I know it is not at all easy to stick to the honest line at all times."

Francis was rather surprised that his mother was willing to bend her standards a little, even in an attempt to reassure him. "No, it isn't easy, and I'm not even sure it is at all wise. Are there not some truths that are too painful to confront?"

"Do you think that is so?"

"Almost certainly."

"But what happens to those lies over time? Surely they just grow and fester."

"I don't know," Francis sighed. "I just don't know."

His mother came over and laid a hand on his arm.

"I want you to know that I like your bride, Francis. She is not what I would have chosen for you, but she has a good heart and considerable courage. Don't let foolishness and pride come between you." She kissed his cheek and left.

Foolishness and pride. That was hardly relevant to the deepest kind of deception, but he was pleased his mother had mellowed. If he could salvage anything from his marriage, then there was hope.

And she was right. If he was to salvage anything from his marriage, he must lay bare the exact truth.

He left a message saying he would return for dinner at seven, then went out to check on the hunt for Ferncliff.

Approaching Belcraven House, he met Lucien on his way to Nicholas's and accompanied him there. He found Hal and Steve there, too, and in this location, the group included Blanche.

She said, "You haven't brought your wife? I wanted to meet her."

"Then you should call."

"Francis, have sense. When you're trying to conceal the poor girl's past, the last thing you want is someone as suspect as I."

"You'd be less suspect," said Hal without heat, "if you married me."

"Nonsense," said Blanche.

"*And* you'd be able to visit the houses of our respectable friends."

"I doubt it. Francis's mother wouldn't welcome me, for a start."

"She's mellowing," said Francis. "I think you should marry Hal, too, for what it's worth."

"We all do," said Nicholas, "but poor Blanche is too shy to commit herself."

Blanche threw him a scathing look, but Francis was amused. Nicholas had kept his distance from Hal's tussle to get Blanche to the altar; if he decided to take a hand, things could get interesting.

Nicholas's attention had shifted to Francis now, however. "Why didn't you tell me Serena's brothers were trying to extort money from you?"

"From her," Francis corrected. "How did you find out?"

"She told Eleanor."

Francis flicked a look at Eleanor. "I wonder why."

Eleanor answered that. "I think, to explain why she wasn't in a state of delirious joy. I'm afraid I was into 'count your blessings.' "

"And she couldn't find any to count."

"No," Eleanor said gently. "She knows she has many, but she can't help but be concerned about the problems, too. I think it would be a kindness to remove them."

"Exactly what I had in mind," said Francis briskly. "I am determined to find Ferncliff and put the fear of the devil into the Allbrights." But he still didn't say anything about his suspicions of Serena.

"Excellent," said Nicholas. "Ferncliff isn't at Simmon's place."

Francis took a seat. "How did you find that out?"

"Sent Steve over. You should have remembered that the tyrant always had a soft spot for Steve. Soon mellowed enough to say that Ferncliff was out the day you invade his rooms and was warned not to return. By the way, both Simmons and Ferncliff seem to really feel that you intend the man harm."

"Perhaps I do. What else can he expect when he goes around pestering my womenfolk?"

Stephen Ball spoke up. "Simmons, at least, believes Ferncliff an innocent victim. Ferncliff was up at Balliol with him, by the way. Simmons had no clear idea of the problem, but thought it was a personal matter between you and Ferncliff and entirely your fault. He is now confirmed in his opinion that the Rogues are villains. I was lectured on the text, *'Every man is like the company he keeps.'* " Wryly, he added, "In Greek."

"Personal matter? I've never even met the man!"

Nicholas said, "If Ferncliff really is into blackmail, he would hardly tell his old friend about it. Anyway, we're back to searching the urban haystack for a needle."

Francis knew he should tell them that Ferncliff seemed to be in the habit of hanging around his own garden, but he didn't. The Rogues had taken Serena to their hearts; he wouldn't reveal her duplicity unless he had to.

"Now," said Nicholas to Francis, "what do you have planned for the Allbrights?"

"In my dreams, the torments of hell. But there is a limit, I suppose, to what I can do to my wife's brothers. Probably sheer weight of status should have them on the run. I intend to put the fear of the devil into them, and immediately."

"Crude but effective. Why don't you and Lucien handle it? You comprise the most weighty status we have to hand. You were definitely not the right team to send against Simmons, but should be perfect for the

Allbrights. They're staying at the Scepter Inn, by the way. Since they are using their own names, that was easy enough to discover."

The Dowager Lady Middlethorpe had agreed to dine with her sister and the Countess of Cawle. She knew it was time to untangle the web of deceit she had woven and hoped they could help. She shuddered at the thought of revealing her foolishness to her sister and her friend, but the time of cowardice was past.

Cordelia hoped for advice, and perhaps some support, but she mostly hoped that her confession here would serve as a rehearsal for the horrible task of revealing her foolishness—her wickedness, in fact—to her son and her lover.

She did not approach her dinner with a hearty appetite.

Alone in her bedroom in Hertford Street, Serena put the solitary daffodil in a vase, and it promptly became the focus of some maudlin thoughts. She had hated to see a flower destroyed, and yet there had been something rather exciting about her husband's steady hand and cool eyes as he had prepared the shot. The excitement was still with her, tingling her nerve endings, speeding her heartbeat, and making her hearing sensitive to any sound that might announce his return.

She wished she knew what Francis really felt toward her. When she had agreed to this marriage, she had hoped for nothing other than respect and kindness. Now, she longed for more.

The trouble with a good and well-bred man, however, was that it was hard to decide what was courtesy and what was emotion. He was always courteous, but when he retreated behind that icy manner, Serena wondered if Francis even liked her, never mind loved her.

If only they hadn't been plunged straight into this hectic life. It was necessary in order to avoid scandal, but it meant that their time alone together had been very limited. Not bed-time—though they had not often been together in a bed—but time to talk during the day. No wonder the idea of a honeymoon was so popular these days. Some privacy in order to become acquainted sounded delightful.

Tonight, at least, they were to dine alone. Perhaps that would be an opportunity to grow closer.

She was wondering what to wear to dinner—whether fine or informal would be more effective for the mood she wanted to create—when a package was brought to her.

Serena recognized her brother's messy writing immediately and was tempted to throw the small package into the fire unopened. Her nerve wasn't strong enough, however. It felt like a box, for heaven's sake. What now?

She broke the seal. A letter formed a cover for a chased silver snuff box. She recognized it as one belonging to her first husband, but Serena couldn't imagine why Tom had sent it to her. It must be worth a few guineas at least.

She suspected an unpleasant surprise and so eased up the lid cautiously. The box was empty, even of snuff. Serena stared into the space, wondering what to make of it all, and then her eye was caught by the underside of the lid.

Dear Lord above!

Fitted into the inside of the lid was a meticulous miniature of one of the more disgusting pictures. Her mouth slackened with shock to think that when Matthew had sat in their drawing room, smiling at her as he took a pinch of snuff, he had also been ogling this picture of her in a compromising situation.

Oh, but if there was any justice, he was roasting slowly in the lowest pits of hell.

She remembered the original pose for this picture. Beehan had directed her to lie on a chaise on her stomach, head resting on her hands on the raised arm. She had seen the drawing when it was finished and it had been rather charming, as if she were a young girl having a pleasant daydream.

In the final product, however, she was naked except for some jewels—some of her own jewels. The chaise was shortened so that her knees were on the ground and a man was using her from behind. He held a whip in his hand and marks indicated that he had recently used it on her. She—no, the woman in the picture, for it was not her at all—was smiling out of the picture with the utmost contentment.

Serena used her nails to gouge the paper out of the box and hurled it into the fire. It caught and flared, then flew up the chimney, but her fear stayed leaden in her heart. What would happen if the world saw pictures like *that?*

Quickly, she scanned the letter.

Serry, have you forgotten what's at stake here? Here's something to jog your memory. Destroy it if you want, there's more as you know. Seems a shame, though. Your husband might like this little box as a gift. I had to wear out two whores after I'd finished looking through all these pretty pictures.

Now, why not be sensible? We'll start with the jewels. Bring them to me at the Scepter Inn, Crown Square, and I'll give you half the pictures then and there. Cheap at the price.

If you don't pay before half past six this evening, though, the first ones will go to a printer I know. He's very keen to start engraving them.

Serena hurled the letter, too, into the flames, but that did not destroy the threat. Pity of heaven, it was nearly five already!

She needed Francis. Where *was* he?

Why on earth hadn't he said where he was going?

Why on earth hadn't he told her *anything* about his plans to handle her brothers? He clearly had just ignored them, and this was the result!

She rang for a footman and scribbled a note asking Francis to return home immediately. She directed it to Belcraven House, as his most likely location.

Serena paced the room, praying that he be there.

In fifteen minutes the footman returned to say that he had failed to find the viscount. He offered to do the rounds of the clubs, but Serena dismissed him. That could take forever and she had little over an hour left.

While the footman had been gone, Serena had realized why the Scepter Inn sounded so familiar. It was where Charles Ferncliff was staying as Mr. Lowden. That gave her the germ of a plan, and now there was nothing for it but to act.

She was going to try to steal the pictures, but she'd take the jewels with her in case she had to stave off disaster by paying.

She ran to her room, grabbed the pouch from her drawer, and flung on her cloak. How on earth, though, was she to get to the Scepter Inn? It was already dark outside.

She returned downstairs and ordered Dibbert to find her a hackney. "Certainly, milady. You will require a footman to attend you, milady?" Though phrased as a question, it was more of a command.

"Yes, please," said Serena. A footman seemed like a very good idea. Francis had two, and she was pleased to see the bigger, stronger one appointed for the task. She wished she could tell him to bring a weapon if he had such a thing, but that would raise altogether too much alarm.

Darkness had already fallen, and as she rattled along in the musty vehicle, Serena was glad of the gaslights that illuminated much of this part of town. Surely nothing too terrible could happen in such well-lit streets. The Scepter, she was pleased to find, was not far away and in a respectable location. The worst of her tension began to ebb. She entered the bustling inn, escorted by her footman, and asked for Mr. Lowden.

A maid directed her to number eight on the first floor. Serena told the footman to await her in the hall and headed for the stairs. She halted, however, at the sound of a familiar voice.

Will.

In the taproom?

Serena slipped back to peep into the low-ceilinged room. The ale-soaked air swirled with smoke, but she could make out Will at the bar downing a tankard and chatting. Was Tom here, too? That could suit her plans very nicely. . . . But he was nowhere to be seen.

More likely he was in his room awaiting her.

Since it didn't seem to be the custom here to take guests up to the rooms, she stopped a passing potboy and asked what room Sir Thomas Allbright and his brother had.

"Numbers eleven and twelve, ma'am."

Armed with this information, Serena climbed the stairs, wondering whether Will being in the tap helped or hindered her cause. Though Will was small beer compared to Tom, having him out of the way should be helpful.

She knocked on the door of number eight.

Mr. Ferncliff opened the door cautiously; at the sight of her, his eyes widened with shock. Serena slipped in quickly, not wanting to risk being seen.

"Lady Middlethorpe, what on earth are you doing here?"

Serena took in the room with alarm. In her limited experience, people staying at an inn took both a bedchamber and a private parlor, which also served as a dining room. Ferncliff, perhaps for reasons of economy, had not.

She was in his bedchamber.

She put it to the back of her mind. "I've come to ask your help, Mr. Ferncliff. If you assist me, I will do all in my power to sort out the problems about your marriage to Francis's mother."

"That is a strong inducement," he said, but with a great deal of suspicion. "What is it you want me to do?"

Serena paced, keyed up by nerves, by outright fear, but also by the excitement of finally doing something. "My brothers are staying in this inn. They have some pictures of me, pictures I want destroyed. I have to find a way to steal them before half past six."

He looked startled, as well he might. He pulled out a watch. "It is already gone half past five, Lady Middlethorpe! Besides, surely this is a matter best handled by your husband."

Serena had not expected to find him so stuffy. "Very likely, Mr. Ferncliff, but he is out and I could not reach him. Will you assist me?"

Ferncliff held up his hands. "My dear lady, I am willing to help, but I am not an adventurer. How are we to commit this daring burglary?"

She had hoped he would have some ideas, but it clearly was not to be. It was up to her to find a plan. "My brothers have taken rooms number eleven and twelve. Do you have any idea whether that will be two bedchambers, or a bedchamber and a parlor?"

"Almost certainly the latter. Why would they need two bedchambers? It would be unusual."

At least the man had some knowledge to contribute. "Very well. At the moment, my brother Will is below stairs in the tap. I assume Tom is in his parlor awaiting me. We will have to draw him out by some means so that I can slip in and take the pictures."

"Good heavens. We are both likely to land in the watchhouse!"

"Let us pray not," said Serena tartly. "I hope to prevent scandal, not cause it."

Ferncliff shook his head. "Do you have any plan in mind to draw your brother out of his room?"

"No," Serena admitted.

"And what is likely to happen if half past six comes without success?"

"I will have to pay them and buy another day's grace. I have with me the price they demanded, but I would much rather not give them a penny. Perhaps we could cry fire. . . ."

"No," Ferncliff said firmly. "The chances of someone being injured in the panic are too great."

Serena paced the room fretfully. "I have to try *something!*"

"What would draw your brother away from his appointment, do you think?"

Serena pondered it. "Tom is pretty fond of Will after his own fashion and in the habit of looking out for him. What if Will were to get into trouble?"

"A fight? My dear young lady, I am not engaging in fisticuffs even for you."

Serena eyed him. "Not even for Cordelia?"

He groaned. "No, not even for her. I am not a man of violence, Lady Middlethorpe, or I would have faced your husband weeks ago and drawn his cork!"

"You most certainly would not," Serena declared, "for he would not have permitted it!"

He opened his mouth, then said, "Let us not fall to childish squabbling."

Serena glared at her reluctant accomplice. "I don't think you *deserve* Cordelia. You're a pudding-heart."

"A man is not a coward for wanting to avoid violence."

Serena sighed and looked for a way to achieve her ends without drawing blood. "We do not actually need for there to be a fight. If Tom were told Will was drunk and in a dangerous fight, he would have to act, wouldn't he?"

"And I am to do the telling, I assume. On what pretext?"

"An innocent well-wisher?"

"I know neither man."

"Oh, do stop being so difficult! Tom cannot possibly know that. The question is, what will he do with the portfolio when he goes downstairs?"

"Take it with him in all likelihood, so your plan would come to naught."

"No, he could not do that. It is about two feet by two feet. He'll either just leave it or hide it. The trouble is that I will only have moments to search . . ."

"I really doubt this plan will work," said Ferncliff, not without relief.

"Yes it *will*," said Serena fiercely. "I will make it work. What if I were already in the bedroom when you come to bring Tom the news. I will be able to peep through the door to see where he hides it."

"Good Lord, what a flimsy plan. What if the door is shut?"

"I will open it!"

"What if it creaks?"

"What if the sky falls? Mr. Ferncliff, I am desperate! This is the price I demand for promoting your connection with Cordelia. Stop being so difficult."

Ferncliff looked at her with dislike. "You may want to consider what you will do if he decides to hide this portfolio in the bedroom."

"I'll duck behind the curtains!" Serena declared with exasperation. "I don't know what I'll do, but this is the best chance we have." She saw that arguing was not at all helpful. "My dear sir," she said as piteously as she could, "the results of failure could be disastrous, I assure you."

He sighed. "Very well, Lady Middlethorpe. But I have the feeling I am going to regret this. How do we proceed?"

She opened the door and peeked out. The narrow corridor with doors on both sides was deserted, though there was plenty of noise—snatches of conversations from behind some doors, louder talk and laughter floating up from the tap, and bangings from the kitchens.

The doors were numbered in order, so numbers eleven and twelve were just down the corridor toward the end. The question was, which was the bedchamber, which the parlor?

She ducked back into the room. "Do you think it possible that the even numbers are bedchambers and the odd parlors?"

"Possible, I suppose. There are travelers requiring parlors who do not intend to spend the night, and those wanting a bed without need of a parlor."

"Very well," said Serena. "You will stand knocking at number eleven. You're pretty well big enough to conceal me from a casual glance. As soon as he opens the door, I'll slip into the bedchamber."

"And if the door he opens is the one by which you are hovering?"

Serena shrugged. "He'll be expecting me. I'll give him the price he has asked, and we'll have at least postponed disaster. You can come back here and forget all about it."

He smiled ruefully. "You make me feel a very feeble fellow. Very well, I hope the plan works."

Serena smiled back at him. "Thank you. Then you tell him of poor Will's plight. After that, we can only hope that it will work as expected."

He shook his head. "You are a rather frightening young woman."

"Frightening?"

"Resourceful, brave, decisive, and far too beautiful. Your husband showed remarkable courage in choosing you."

Serena sighed. "Perhaps it was just fate. Ready?"

"Just one more thing. I am not making difficulties, but when you have these pictures, what do you intend to do with them? I fear it will not take your brother long to realize he has been tricked and to come in search of me."

Serena was keyed up for action and in no mood to hesitate further. She heard a clock strike quarter to six. "I will burn them," she declared, "and then Tom can do his worst."

"Not here," Ferncliff said, indicating the small hearth. "That would surely set the chimney on fire. The best thing is for you to leave immediately with your loot. But not, I think, by the main entrance."

"What other way out is there?"

"A side stairs at the far end of the corridor, which leads down to the coach yard."

"Good. I have a footman, though, down in the entrance. . . ."

"Once the deed is done, I will go down and speak to him . . . tell him to meet you in the coachyard." He suddenly smiled. "That will have the added advantage, you see, that if your irate brother comes after me, he will find me in a very public place."

Serena smiled and reached up to kiss him on the cheek. "Wonderful. And I will do all in my power to assure your happiness with Cordelia. Ready?"

"Yes."

Just as they emerged into the corridor, a potboy came up the stairs with a tray and headed down the other arm of the corridor to knock at a door. "Do we wait?" asked Ferncliff quietly.

"No." Serena could not bear any more delay.

They went to number eleven. Then, screened by Ferncliff, Serena hovered by the door of number twelve. Ferncliff knocked, and Serena listened. She heard someone going to answer the door to number eleven and gathered the courage to turn the knob of the door in front of her. It opened without noise, and she slipped into the room.

It was empty.

She let out a sigh that was nearly a gasp. Despite Ferncliff's words, she was not feeling particularly brave, just frantically determined. The only light in the room was from the fire, and so she was very careful as she crept over to the adjoining door and pressed her ear to it.

Tom's voice: "Yes?"

Ferncliff's voice, rather loud: "I believe you are Sir Thomas Allbright."

"What of it?"

"I am afraid your brother is in difficulties below, sir." In the middle of this, Serena turned the knob and opened the door the slightest crack. The catch clicked, but the door did not squeak. By now her heart was pounding like a team of galloping horses, so she felt as if Tom should hear it. The small crack did not allow her to see the men, but their voices were now louder.

"Difficulties? What d'you mean, sir?"

"To be blunt, sir, drunk and belligerent. He is picking a fight with a brawny boatman. I thought you might want to know." Serena held her breath and eased the door open another inch. She had to be able to see more of the room. When she saw the red portfolio on a chair, she almost let a sound escape.

"Devil take the young fool," Tom muttered, but then said, "Thank you, sir. I'll see to it."

Serena heard the door shut, presumably with Ferncliff on the other side of it. She kept her eyes on the pictures.

Tom came into view and picked up the portfolio. He scanned the room, still muttering curses. Serena froze as his eyes passed over the door, but nothing about it seemed to bother him. With an irritated grunt, he shoved the pictures on the windowsill behind the curtains. Then he slammed out.

Serena was into the room in a flash. She grabbed the portfolio, then froze, wondering if Tom had other pictures in items such as the snuff box. It was unlikely, and a miniature picture was much less identifiable anyway. She needed to be away to destroy what she had. She whipped out into the corridor, checking swiftly.

Empty.

Ferncliff poked his head out of his door. "Got them?"

"Yes!"

He grinned quite boyishly and came toward her, intending to go down to alert her footman. Serena clutched the portfolio under her cloak out of sight and headed past the stairs toward the other end of the building. A bellow froze her just short of the stairhead.

Tom!

He had realized too soon.

She turned, and she and Ferncliff fled back to his room and closed the door.

The man groaned. "I knew I was going to regret this! He'll be here in a moment!"

"Do you not have a pistol?"

"No, of course I do not."

"Well, you *should* have."

Serena pressed her ear to the door. Ferncliff crowded behind her and they both listened to Tom's footsteps pound past, then to the crash of his door as he charged back into his room.

"Now!" Serena said, and flung open the door.

They came face to face with Francis.

He, it seemed, had been in hot pursuit of Tom, but now he focused entirely on her.

The moment seemed cast in a sculpture of ice. Francis took his hand out of his pocket, bringing a pistol with it, which he pointed with deadly intent at Ferncliff's head.

Chapter 20

Ferncliff and Serena backed up, and in moments they were inside his room again. It was only when the door clicked shut that Serena realized someone else was present.

Lucien.

The silence was so complete that she had no trouble hearing Tom's bellow of rage at finding the pictures gone. She wanted to say something, but her throat appeared to be frozen by some force.

She realized it was terror.

It was Ferncliff who spoke, and with resigned dignity. "Lord Middlethorpe, if you intend to shoot me, get it over with, for I am heartily sick of this cat and mouse game."

Francis actually cocked the pistol with an audible click, but then let the lock return to safety. "You're not worth hanging for, Ferncliff."

The choking grasp on Serena's throat eased, "Francis, we—"

"Not another word." He didn't even look at her, and yet the command was absolute. She looked for help to

405

Lucien, but his expression was nearly as cold as Francis's. Why did they hate Ferncliff so much that merely an association with him could put her beyond the pale?

"My lord," said Ferncliff with careful moderation, "I have been wanting an opportunity to speak with you for some time now. As you have apparently thought better of your intention of shooting me, perhaps we can have a rational discussion about myself and Lady Middlethorpe."

"I doubt it," said Francis with deadly calm.

Even moderate Ferncliff began to color with anger. "You will continue to unreasonably block our happiness?"

"*Unreasonably?* You have a damned funny notion of reason!"

"And you, sir, have no notion of it at all!"

"Francis," said Serena, "you must listen to him!"

He turned on her and the fury blazing in his eyes almost made her faint. "I would like to listen to him scream in agony. If you do not want to see him dead, be silent."

Her legs gave way, and she sat on a chair with a thump. Again she looked at Lucien, but he stood against the wall, arms folded, as if this were the most common of occurrences.

Bloodthirsty reprobates.

It was the simple truth.

Francis looked back at Ferncliff. "If I thought I could believe a word you'd say, I'd ask for an explanation. I have one question: Just what did I do to deserve this?"

Ferncliff folded his arms. "You talk like a spoiled child."

"Spoiled child! Am I supposed to turn a blind eye to

this? Accept a cuckoo in the nest without cavil? And if you wanted ten thousand pounds, why mess the whole thing up with a marriage?"

Before anyone could respond, the door burst open and Tom appeared, eyes red with anger. The anger flared to rage when he saw Serena, who was still clutching the portfolio. "I knew it! I'll have 'em back. *Now.*"

Lucien pushed off the wall and produced a pistol, cocking it in one smooth motion. The dangerous click alerted Tom to the fact that there were others present, and he looked around in growing uneasiness.

Francis turned and impaled him with a look. Tom blanched and Serena was not surprised. The deadly rage emanating from Francis would terrify anyone.

"You," said Francis in a voice of burning ice, "are a blight. Your whole family is a blight, but I suppose I will have to deal with your sister. You I do not have to deal with at all. Come near me or mine in the future, and I will ruin you so absolutely that you will never dare set foot in decent company again."

Tom tried to bluster, but nothing of sense came out.

"Get out of my sight."

Since Tom seemed stuck, Lucien gripped his arm, propelled him into the corridor, and shut the door on him.

Serena would have cheered if it hadn't been for the words *I suppose I will have to deal with your sister.*

Was that the main problem? That she was her brothers' sister and she carried their blood?

And now she had been caught associating with a man Francis considered a deadly enemy, though for the life of her she could not see why. He clearly considered it a betrayal.

Francis was in such a rage just now that there seemed no chance of bringing him to reason, and she was not sure she wanted to. If this was his idea of correct and reasonable behavior, she doubted she could live with him at all.

Ferncliff was frowning. "What's this about ten thousand pounds, my lord? Is that Lady Middlethorpe's portion?"

Francis was now superficially calm. "If she chooses to go with you, she goes with what she wears and nothing more."

"Really, sir! You cannot do that. Not only is it heartless, it is illegal!"

Francis shrugged. "You may be right. You can have the three thousand and the jewels."

At that familiar amount, Serena frowned. Surely Cordelia's widow's jointure was more than three thousand pounds, whereas Francis had given her exactly that amount. She pulled the pouch of jewelry out. "These jewels?"

"Already have them with you, do you?" Francis asked with a superficial cordiality that was even more wounding than his rage. "I suppose if you failed to get your hands on the whole amount, you were intending to flee into the night with what you had. Or do you just like playing with them?"

Serena stood, clutching the portfolio and the pouch. "I don't have the slightest idea what you are talking about, except that you are being totally unfair to poor Mr. Ferncliff. He is an honorable man!"

"Are you going to claim to be an honorable woman?"

She raised her chin. "Yes." At his scathing look, she

asked, "What in heaven's name are you accusing me of, Francis? Is being here——"

"Adultery."

The word stopped her cold. *"What?* With whom?"

"Oh come, Serena. And to think I believed you were not capable of acting a part!"

"We are all capable of acting a part, it would appear. You have been acting the civil gentleman for weeks, whereas now I see that Mr. Ferncliff is right. You and all the Rogues are headstrong, foolish, wicked reprobates!"

He snarled at her. "If I were a headstrong, foolish, wicked reprobate, you worthless tart, I'd be beating you. If I hadn't throttled you first!"

Serena hit him.

He hit her back.

Serena gasped with outrage and slammed him on the head with the portfolio. It had wooden end boards and made a most satisfying noise against his thick skull. He staggered.

She looked around at the gaping men, positively growled with rage, and ran out of the room. Down at the entrance to the inn she found her footman patiently waiting. He leapt to his feet. "Is something wrong, milady?"

Heaven knows what she looked like. "No. I wish to return to Hertford Street. Now."

Adultery! How dare he? How *dare* he?

"Yes, milady. Immediately, milady."

Francis collapsed into a chair and held his reverberating head. "Christ Almighty," he muttered. The blow had somehow knocked away his rage, leaving him empty, miserable, and bereft.

He hadn't actually lost much, he tried to tell himself. Just a lying, unfaithful wife. The pain and dizziness faded, and he looked up. Lucien appeared thoughtful, and Ferncliff—damn him—was sitting in a chair looking stern.

It was Ferncliff who spoke. "Could you possibly be suffering from the misapprehension that your wife has been committing adultery with me, my lord?"

"Yes," snapped Francis. "I think I could have that strange notion in my head, when I find her creeping out of your bedchamber, sir. I know she has been meeting you in my garden, and on one occasion at least returned from the tryst disheveled and muddy. Not to mention the fact that you just admitted it."

"How could I admit such a falsehood?"

"For pity's sake!"

"My beloved is your mother."

Francis stared at the man. "Do you take me for a complete fool?"

"Yes."

Francis just stopped himself from lunging for Ferncliff's throat. "Let us by all means be clear about this. You are claiming to be in love with my mother, Cordelia Lady Middlethorpe. And she with you, no doubt?"

"Precisely. See," said Ferncliff with awful sarcasm, "even a dull mind can comprehend an issue if given time."

"Oh, certainly I can," said Francis with equal sarcasm. "It is completely credible that you have been conducting a passionate affair with my mother in the

410

cold and muddy gardens of my house in Hertford Street."

"You believe such a thing of your wife, my lord."

"But she . . ." Francis could not bring himself to say the words that came to his lips.

Ferncliff provided them. "Is a worthless tart, I suppose."

Francis instinctively leapt to his feet.

"Your words," said Ferncliff, "not mine."

Good God, had he really said that to her?

"As for your mother and I, my lord, I would that we had been conducting an affair, even in a muddy February garden, but she and I are at outs at this moment."

Francis collected his wits. "Doubtless because you are trying to extort ten thousand pounds from her so you can run away with my wife."

"Plague take you!" shouted Ferncliff. "When I spoke of Lady Middlethorpe earlier, you numbskull, I wasn't talking of that child, I was talking about your mother!"

"Numbskull, am I? At least I'm not a lying thief."

Ferncliff rose, fists clenched. "I am no thief, sir!"

"Not again," muttered Lucien, and stepped forward to stave off a fight.

The door opened. "Why are you shouting in here?" asked Cordelia severely. "The whole inn can probably hear you." She froze, and her eyes widened at the sight of her son, but after a moment she resolutely continued into the room.

Arabella came in behind her. "I detect all the signs of men making complete fools of themselves."

"Cordelia!" exclaimed Ferncliff.

"Mother!" exclaimed Francis.

Cordelia went to Charles Ferncliff and said, "Hold me, please, Charles. I'm very frightened."

His arm went around her without hesitation. "Don't worry, my dove. No one will hurt you."

The mists of anger in Francis's head cleared, and the whole picture—or the essential parts—were revealed to him. "Serena . . ." he murmured.

He headed for the door, but Lucien gripped his arm. "I know. But you had best discover what is going on here first. You don't want to make yet more mistakes. She'll probably be better with a little time to cool down, anyway. I'll go and make sure she's safe."

Francis could hardly begin to grasp the disaster that he might have made of his marriage. He wanted desperately to dash out and start mending things, but he knew Lucien was right.

As Lucien left, Francis turned back to the couple in the center of the room. He was revolted to see Ferncliff stroking his mother's head and comforting her between kisses.

"Damnation! Stop that!" When his mother turned, looking amazingly young and frightened, the picture began to clear even further, though it was as bizarre as a painting by Fuseli.

Francis took a deep breath. "Why don't you start by explaining the ten thousand pounds, Mother?"

"Don't bully her," said Ferncliff, and led Cordelia gently to a settle, where he sat beside her, patting her hand. "Now, Cordelia, if you really have been foolish, you had best make a clean tale of it. Honesty is the best policy."

Seeing his mother treated like a young, slightly naughty girl both amazed and upset Francis. His world

412

was swinging upside down, and somewhere Serena was crying. . . .

"Ten thousand pounds," he prompted sharply, and saw guilty color flare in his mother's face.

"I shall have to start at the beginning, dearest, so do not heckle me. It started when you agreed to court Lady Anne, you see. That was when I realized that my life would change upon your marriage. Oh, I knew that I would be welcome to live in any of your homes, but it would not be the same. That knowledge changed something in me, so that when I met Charles, I was open to him as I had not been since I was a girl."

Open to him! What the devil did that mean? Francis wondered, but kept the words back.

"At first we just talked of his work—so very interesting—and my concerns. He helped me think about my future, and I helped him with his researches. We have some useful records at the Priory, you know. . . ." She glanced at Francis nervously and broke off. "But I must not be distracted." Her voice sank to a whisper. "The intimate side of it . . . that caught me unawares. . . ."

Despite all the evidence, Francis couldn't quite believe it. "Do you mean you . . . ?"

She nodded, positively red-faced. "On the chaise in my boudoir!" She looked desperately at her lover and he patted her knee, though he, too, looked acutely uncomfortable.

Francis glanced at Arabella and she made a droll expression. "I've heard it all in the past hour, dear boy. Brace yourself for evidence that foolishness does not end with youth."

Francis turned back to the couple. "If that was the way of it, then why the devil didn't you marry?"

413

His mother sighed. "I lost my nerve. It seemed such a terrible thing to have done. I have always felt that to remarry would be a betrayal of your father, but to be carried away . . . to . . . to do what we did . . . where we did . . . It *was* a betrayal, because what I experienced with Charles was unlike anything I had ever experienced with your father, dear though he was to me." She turned adoring eyes on her lover. "I had not known."

Francis was acutely embarrassed, but he said, "All the more reason to marry, I would think."

"Oh, no. I wanted to deny it, to pretend that it had never happened. And in addition, you know, I was sure that the world would laugh at me for marrying a younger, poorer commoner. In fact, they very likely will, but for some reason now it doesn't seem quite so terrible."

Francis was receiving revelations about some matters, but most of the events that had turned his life upside down were still as clear as a mud-splattered window. "But if this was the state of affairs, Mother, why did Ferncliff try to extort ten thousand pounds from you?"

"What?" asked Ferncliff.

His mother's eyes shifted between the two men. "He didn't."

"It was all lies? Good God, Mother. Why?"

"Yes indeed, Cordelia," Ferncliff said sternly. "Why?"

She held on to Ferncliff's hand but addressed Francis. "I am truly very sorry. You see, dearest, in my first panic over my weakness I just wanted Charles gone, so I would have no reminder of my frailty and no more

414

temptations. I advised the Shipleys to dismiss him. But he wrote to me, again and again. He would not give up. It was driving me to distraction! When he finally wrote to you, I had to think of a reason. That was all I could dream up at the time."

"Why on earth could you not tell me the truth?"

"I thought you would despise me for my wickedness."

"Mother . . ."

She eyed him with a much more familiar look. "Well? What would you have thought?"

He sighed. "I would have been shocked," he admitted.

"When you turned up demanding explanations, I could not think. I came up with that ridiculous story, and matters grew worse immediately. When you said you would confront Charles, I was in a panic. I could not let you meet."

Ferncliff spoke up. "So you wrote to warn me, Cordelia. Your actions deserve censure, but so do mine. I wrote that letter deliberately to push you into honesty. I hoped you would confess all to your son. It was my opinion that the problem would have been solved." He looked at Francis. "Would it, my lord?"

"Of course. I would have checked your background, but if you are the poor but trusty fellow you make out to be, I would have had no strong objection."

"Oh, don't!" cried Cordelia. "You make me feel so much more the wicked fool. From that moment, things just became worse and worse. You were pursuing Charles, and poor Charles was bombarding me with angry letters, and then I realized that all this was interrupting your courtship of Anne. . . ."

She gave a deep sigh. "Then you turned up with another bride, and one I could not easily approve of. When I came to understand that in some way my foolishness had brought this about, I felt ready to *die*. Everything was being destroyed and it was all my fault. But still I lacked the courage. I lacked the courage to tell Charles of the wicked lies I had told about him. I shivered at the thought of telling you, Francis, about my improper behavior and all the other lies I had told you afterward. Each day made it worse!"

" '*Oh what a tangled web we weave,*' " quoted Arabella, " '*when first we practice to deceive.*' "

Cordelia glared at her sister. "Oh, do be quiet!" She looked up at Francis. "I have finally come to my senses. I hope it is not too late to mend some of the damage I have caused."

"So do I," said Francis, and rose to his feet. "I have to confess that your behavior over this has left much to be desired, Mother, but it's not my place to berate you. I'll leave that to your future husband." He shook his head. "Judging from his besotted expression, you'll get off scot-free. I doubt I will be so lucky with my spouse."

"Oh, dear. Have my affairs tangled yours very badly, dearest?"

Francis smiled ruefully. "Oh, most of it we've done to ourselves, but Mr. Ferncliff has created a few more knots, particularly with a tendency to call both you and Serena Lady Middlethorpe."

"You cannot have thought . . . !"

"Can I not?"

"Oh, dear. I am sorry. . . ."

"You are forgiven. After all, I have to remember

that if none of this had happened, I would not have met Serena. And that would have been a shame."

He raised a brow at Arabella. "Why exactly are you here, dear aunt? Come to see justice done or to gloat over human failure?"

"Don't sneer at me. I'm the only innocent party here! I came to make sure she didn't turn chicken at the last moment. What a tale of foolishness! If you're at outs with Serena, though, you had best go and make it up with her. She deserves better than you, but she'll doubtless make do, as most women have to."

"That is my intent."

"And I warn you, I intend to make it clear to Serena that she can always have a home with me, so don't think you can bully her by threatening poverty. And if you think to deprive her of her child . . ."

Francis threw up a hand. "Peace! I would never dream of such a thing. All I want to do is love her and cherish her."

Arabella harrumphed. "So I should hope. By the way," she said when he was already at the door, "Maud had an interesting tidbit to impart over dinner tonight. Apparently, she knew Serena's mother when they were girls. They lived close by in Sussex. Said Hester had those slanty eyes and a fair bit of Serena's beauty. But no money, which was how she ended up married to Allbright."

"So? I am in some urgency."

"Thing is that Hester had been in love with someone else. A doctor's son, I think. The point is that when Maud set eyes on Serena, she recognized that man's hair color and something else about the features. She's as sure as one can be that Serena ain't an Allbright at all. Given her brothers, I thought it might be good news."

Francis laughed. "Given her brothers, it certainly isn't anything to be ashamed of." He glanced back at his mother and Ferncliff, who were holding hands and murmuring to one another. He shook his head. "My family carries strange enough blood without mixing that lot with it. Are you going to stay and play chaperon?"

Arabella rose. "God forbid! Sickening sight. And I don't suppose you want me, either. Maud sent us here in her two damn sedan chairs, but at least it means I've independent transport to take me back."

Francis saw his aunt into the lacquered, gilded box and watched as she was carried off by the two chairman. A dying profession, that. He looked at the other men, standing by the other vehicle. "It could be a while." He tossed them a crown. "Have something to keep you warm, and if Lady Middlethorpe doesn't appear within the hour, you have my permission to go home."

Then he set off to walk to Hertford Street, wondering just what he would have to do to mend his marriage.

Chapter 21

Serena had arrived home and run up to her room to weep. Once there, though, she found she couldn't. She flung off her cloak, tore off her bonnet, and paced. When her maid came to attend her, she snarled at the woman to go away.

It slowly dawned on her that she couldn't weep because she wasn't so much miserable as she was in a royal rage.

How dare he!

What cause had she ever given Francis Haile to doubt her fidelity? A night in the Posts' farm came to niggle at her conscience, but she chased it away. She hadn't been married to anyone then.

Since her marriage, she hadn't so much as looked at another man. It was his Roguish friends who insisted on flirting with any woman who crossed their path.

A simpering china shepherdess caught her eye. She picked it up and smashed it. That's what she'd like to do to Francis Haile's thick head!

No, all she'd done since their wedding day was to be sweet, kind, and forgiving, and to work and work to make something of their marriage. When did he think she'd had *time,* damn him, to commit adultery?

The shepherd lad with his pipes went to join his shepherdess.

The portfolio caught her eye. She ripped open the ribbons and spilled the pictures on the floor. Horrible, horrible things. Her own stupid girlish face simpered out from them, and though they didn't show reality, they showed truth. She *had* submitted. She'd done every damn thing she'd been told to.

Why the devil hadn't she murdered Matthew Riverton? There must be ways.

Why hadn't she run off to Harriet Wilson and become an honest whore?

But no, she had wept and wailed, but she'd sucked in the lies about duty and obedience to a husband, and had been properly submissive. . . .

She picked up one picture of her smiling as two men groped at her and began to tear it into tiny pieces.

Adultery! She didn't even *like* what men did to women.

A scratch on the door brought Dibbert. He looked around and his eyes bulged. "Go away!" Serena shrieked, and hurled the handful of scraps. They traveled a few feet and then fluttered gaily through the air.

Dibbert tottered down the stairs wondering where on earth Lord Middlethorpe or the dowager was. Where was someone able to take command of the situation? Had the poor mistress lost her wits entirely?

There was a rap on the door and he hurried to open it. He immediately recognized the Marquess of Arden, one of the master's friends. "I am afraid they are not at home, my lord."

"Lady Middlethorpe isn't here?" the marquess asked with quick concern. Something on Dibbert's face must have given the truth away, for the marquess relaxed and walked forward.

Blocking the way of a marquess who was also a friend of the family was not possible, and so Dibbert closed the door on the night air and hoped Lord Arden could offer help.

"She don't want to see anyone, I assume," said the marquess. "But Lord Middlethorpe asked me to come and look after her."

"I am afraid she is a little upset, milord."

"Having the vapors?"

"Not quite."

"Just weeping?"

Dibbert cleared his throat. "There have been a number of crashes, milord. When I went up to investigate, her ladyship appeared to be tearing up some papers. She . . . she screamed at me."

The marquess laughed. "Like that, is it?"

Dibbert could not see anything amusing in the situation. "I do hope she will soon recover, milord."

"Oh, I would think so. Let's hope Lord Middlethorpe soon returns home."

"Oh, yes, indeed." There was a distant but distinct tinkle of broken glass. Dibbert wrung his hands. "Do you know if he will be long, milord?"

"Not long at all if I'm any judge." Still looking amused, Lord Arden announced, "I don't think there's any point in me staying here. My advice is to leave Lady Middlethorpe alone unless she rings."

Dibbert saw the marquess leave with dismay. It was all very well for Lord Arden to dismiss the matter, but what if her ladyship was even now doing herself harm?

Lucien walked home and found his wife dining off a tray in her boudoir. He came upon Beth eating with one hand and holding a book in the other. He grinned at the endearing image of his wonderful bluestocking.

She looked up and smiled. "Hello. Now tell me, what adventure have you been up to?"

"How did you guess?" He came over and picked up an untouched chop from her plate and began to nibble at it.

Beth put down her book and fork. "One," she said, "you went to Nicholas's. Two, you sent a note saying that you had some business to attend to, and in Town that rarely means estate matters. Three, you have a certain glitter to you."

"Do I? I'm thinking of anger."

"Why is that so pleasant?"

He considered her. "Beth, we've had words, but you've never really raged at me or fate, though you've had reason enough. Have you never wanted to?"

"I don't know. I don't think so. It seems so unproductive."

"But the hot intimacy we're going to indulge in at any moment will be unproductive, too, since you are pregnant. Will that make it less enjoyable?"

A warm flush rose in Beth's cheeks. "No, but that's different."

"How so?"

"It's pleasant, productive or not. Temper isn't."

422

"Isn't it?" He pulled her up.

"Lucien, are you angry?"

"Not in the least." He slid one of her sleeves slightly off her shoulder and nipped at her skin there.

Beth squeaked. "Then why are you biting me?"

"Perhaps I'm hungry. You taste better than cold pork. In fact, I am excited by anger. I hope Francis and Serena are, too."

Beth grabbed his ears in an attempt to control him. "What's been going on? Who's angry and why?"

He released her and took over her chair by the tray. He picked up her fork and started in on her sponge cake. "Take your clothes off and I'll tell you, one fact for each item."

Beth stared at him. "Lucien! You are in a most peculiar mood."

He raised his brows and grinned.

Beth giggled, then took off one slipper and dangled it.

"The Allbright brothers had some scurrilous pictures of Serena and were trying to sell them to her for ten thousand pounds."

"*What?* What did you do?"

He just smiled. She took off the other slipper and threw it at him.

"Francis and I went to the Scepter Inn to confront them. . . ."

Francis entered his house trying to taste the atmosphere. What did he have to face here?

Dibbert appeared so quickly that he must have been

hovering. "Welcome home, milord." It sounded intensely honest.

Francis shed his outer clothing into the man's hands. "Is Lady Middlethorpe at home?"

"Yes, milord. She is in her chamber."

"Excellent." Francis headed toward the stairs.

"My lord!"

He turned impatiently. "Yes?"

"Dinner has been ready for some time. . . ."

"Do what the hell you like with it." Francis took the stairs two at a time.

At Serena's door, he braced himself. No sound could be heard. Was that good news or bad? Perhaps she had cried herself to sleep. . . .

He opened the door and went in.

Serena was kneeling on the floor over a piece of paper, scribbling. Her jewels were scattered around the room amidst more sheets of paper and a great many torn scraps. There seemed to be a lot of broken china as well.

He closed the door carefully.

She looked up and her eyes flashed. "Hah!" She grabbed the nearest solid item and hurled it. "Go away!"

A silver manacle missed his head by an inch, leaving a scar on the mahogany doorjamb. He looked back just in time to dodge the other. She was scrambling to her feet, doubtless to try to improve her aim.

He launched himself at her and trapped her on the floor, but her writhing, maddened body could hardly be controlled. "Stop it, Serena! What the devil's the matter with you?"

She froze, glaring at him. "What's the matter with

me? You called me a worthless tart and an adulteress!"

"I'm sorry. . . ."

"Sorry! I'll make you sorry!" Now she was back to struggling with an intensity that made him afraid he might hurt her. He released her and backed away.

"Serena, let's talk about this sensibly."

She leapt to her feet, hair wild and loose, eyes burning with a passion he had never seen in her before. *"Sensible?* That's what I've been all my life. I've been *sensibly* quiet, *sensibly* docile, *sensibly* obedient. Well, I won't be anymore."

"Good."

She jerked with surprise, but then her eyes narrowed. "Oh, no, you won't cozen me that way. I am very angry with you!" She grabbed a candlestick and hurled it. He ducked it, but it hit a picture on the wall, shattering the glass.

"Goddamnit, Serena, stop this! I made a mistake, but what else was I to think when I saw you in Ferncliff's bedroom?"

"And I suppose you've killed him for it, haven't you? Why aren't you after me with a gun, too, you bloodthirsty monster? That was the point of that shooting exercise, wasn't it? Not to reassure me, but to show that you could kill!" She picked up the vase containing the daffodil and threw it. It missed, but the water didn't.

"Ferncliff is in excellent health," snarled Francis, brushing water off his face, "which is more than will be true of you if you don't cease this disgraceful behavior!"

"Are you going to whip me?" She whirled around and grabbed the jeweled silk-thronged whip. "Here." That, too, flew through the air at him.

425

He caught it by the handle. "I am very tempted."

Serena planted her fists on her hips. "Oh, why not? It's what I'd expect from a man. I warn you, though, it only stings and reddens the flesh for quite a while. You have to have patience if you want it to really hurt."

Francis threw the whip aside. "Serena, stop this. I misjudged you. But all the evidence was against you."

"What *evidence?*"

"I saw you coming out of a man's bedchamber for a start!"

"And could conceive of no explanation except that I was having an affair with him? For your information, Charles Ferncliff is a prosy bore!"

"Even boring men become lovers now and then. I have proof of that. I might not have leapt to conclusions if I hadn't found his card in your pocket and heard that you were meeting him in the garden."

"Meeting him! Bumping into him, more likely. You need to do something about that garden of yours. No one is safe there!"

"The gate is now locked."

"And why," demanded Serena with scarcely a pause for breath, "were you going through my pockets? And who did you have spying on me? I had my fill of that from Matthew. I will not stand for it again."

"I didn't set anyone to spy on you!"

"So, a card, two accidental meetings, and finding me in Ferncliff's room . . ."

Serena paused, considering that list. Despite her longing to cling to her delicious anger, her sense of fairness was reasserting itself. She tried, though. "You wouldn't have given a thought to those things if you didn't think me a loose woman."

"Of course I don't think that."

Now Serena was distracted by the very look of him. His hair was damp and disordered, and his clothes had a somewhat disheveled look, but it was the energy crackling around him that stole her breath. She wanted to devour him.

"What *do* you think, then?" She grabbed a picture and thrust it at him. It was one of the more innocent ones. She had been drawn sitting on a stone balustrade, one arm around an urn. The urn was now a monstrous phallus. "What do you think of *that,* then?"

He looked at it for a moment, then burst out laughing. She flailed at him, but he caught her arm and trapped her close. "I'm sorry, love, but it is so silly. Is that what has you so upset? These pictures?"

She wouldn't surrender and held herself rigidly. "No. *Men* have me upset. My brothers, my husband, his friends, your friends, and *you.* I am very angry."

He looked beyond her and let her go. He picked up the picture she had been scribbling on when he came in. She could feel the color in her cheeks at having been caught in such a childish impulse. He picked up one, then another. She had been changing them so the naked victims were men and the clothed oppressors were women.

"I have a right to be angry," she said. "I like being angry. I am enjoying my rage!" It was a rear-guard action, though, for the genuine tender concern in his eyes was leaching away her fury.

Without a word, he began to remove his clothes.

"What are you doing? I'm not doing bed-work with you now."

He stopped, in only his pantaloons. "Bed-work? Is that how you think of it?"

He was hurt. "No. Matthew called it that."

He continued to strip. "You just called it that."

Serena didn't know what to say. When he stood naked before her, he was aroused. "I suppose these pictures excite you," she accused. "Tom said he wore out two whores after looking through them."

"Your brother is beneath contempt and no indication of men in general."

"No? I have experienced little else."

"Really?"

She looked away arms tightly folded. "I suppose that's another reason you're ready to believe the worst of me. My brothers. You probably think I'm cut from the same cloth."

"No, never. Actually, Lady Cawle is of the opinion that you and your brothers have different fathers."

Serena swiveled back. "What? Oh, this is beyond anything! Now I'm not just an adulteress, I'm a *bastard!*"

He gripped one of the bedposts, and she saw his knuckles gleam white. "Serena, I am losing patience. For the last time, I do not think you are an adulteress. I hope you are a bastard, though, because the less connection between you and your brothers the better, but I don't much care either way. If I'm to be crudely honest, I am suffering a violent excess of lust."

Serena could see it was true. "Suffer, then."

"I will until you feel the same way."

She stared at him. "But I can't . . ."

"Can you not? Perhaps if you funneled all your rage into abusing my naked body . . ."

"Francis!" But something was uncoiling like a serpent in her belly—rage, lust . . . Both?

He walked across the room, all lean muscular grace, and picked up the manacles. He inspected them for a moment, then clipped them on his wrists, even though they must be cruelly tight.

"Stop it," she whispered. But by the stars, the silver and jewels on his wrists made him look like a magnificent creature of dreams.

"Do you want to tie me to the bedposts?" he asked. "Do you want to whip me?"

"No! Stop it." Without conscious thought she walked to him and laid her hands on his rib cage. "I feel very strange."

A flame lit in his eyes. "I hoped you might." He grabbed her by the hair and kissed her, and the metal on his wrists was cold against her neck. He twisted her so they tumbled onto the bed in a tangle of limbs and hair.

But Serena fought free. "No. I want to undress!"

After a reluctant moment, he let her leave the bed. He watched her, though, his eyes dark with the passion that showed in his erection, in his color, and in his unsteady breaths—the passion he held under ruthless control. The balance of beauty, lust, and powerful control weakened Serena so her fumbling fingers could hardly manage her fastenings. She hummed with a need that was new to her, that frightened her even as it drew her, for it could become a master and she its slave. . . .

When she was finally naked, she faced him and asked, "Am I your slave now?"

He held out his hands. "I'm the one in shackles."

Serena picked up the barbaric slave collar and considered it a moment. Then she fastened it around her neck with a sharp click. The heavy golden chain hung cold between her breasts and brushed against her thighs as she approached the bed.

She thought perhaps he trembled, but there was nothing hesitant in his action when he caught the loose end of the chain, wound it once around his shackled wrist, and slowly pulled her down to him.

She was both afraid and desirous, unsure of this strange world. "Now we are both prisoner of the other," she whispered and gave her lips permission to explore his torso, to move lower and lower down his body toward an anticipated target . . .

That thought chilled her, and she stopped her gentle foray. She had never wanted that before, never dreamed of it as anything except a loathsome duty. If she had come to like these things, what did it make her? She looked up at him. "Francis, this isn't right. What if I desire many men? What if I have the soul of a whore? Look at my mother."

He pulled her up to face him. "Serena, there's no right and wrong between us. Anyway," he added with a gentle kiss, "if Lady Cawle is to be believed, your mother only ever wanted one man, and it wasn't your legal father."

Serena thought of her quiet, unhappy mother. "Oh, I do hope that's true, though it makes me very sad for her."

"But she had her moment of delight. Do we not deserve ours?"

Serena was still not sure, but she would give him anything she could. "You certainly do."

He shook his head, but asked, "Do you like being kissed yet?"

She slid her hands into his hair. "I think I might."

They experimented and proved that she did indeed like being kissed.

His hand brushed lightly over her breast. "And this?"

"Yes, that is sweet . . ."

His lips and teeth replaced his fingers and Serena gave a cry of desperate astonishment. "Francis, Francis!" How was it that everything was changed, that touches that had left her cold now inflamed her . . . ?

She heard him murmur, "Perhaps the books were right after all," but thought was drowned by the fevered pounding of her blood.

His hand and mouth worked magic on her and he whispered, "Let it happen, Serena! Let it."

She wanted it to, for him as much as herself, but it was as if a part of her was locked, chained by fear, unable to trust . . .

In the end, Serena could only moan, thrashing her head, tormented by the impossible. She cried out her desperation and begged him to stop.

When he did she rolled away, aching with shame and frustration. Why could he not just take? Why did he have this terrible need to *give?*

He turned her back to face him and she prepared to face anger, but there was nothing but love on his face.

"I'm sorry," she whispered, tears blurring her vision.

He kissed them away and said hoarsely, "By all that's holy, Serena, this isn't a test, but you can break free." He rolled half off the bed and grabbed the picture she'd been altering. He held it in front of her. "Look at it, damnit, and hate it. Don't let something like this rule you. Don't let Riverton rule you from the hell he's surely in!" He grabbed a handful of her hair and made her face him. "I'm not that man. I'm not Riverton. I'm Francis. You can trust me."

He kissed her deeply, demandingly, arching her back. "Gather your anger, my siren, and break free. Come to me."

His words, dragged rough from his heart, started the magic, and when he touched her again, Serena arched like a bow as flame ran through her.

"Trust me, Serena. Be free. You are safe . . ."

Yes, this was Francis. She would *not* let Riverton rule her from hell!

She took her rage and turned it into fire, finding at last the trust to surrender completely to the flames. She heard herself scream as the furnace consumed her, and she did not care.

She both fought him and loved him, and when he thrust into her, she didn't give a damn about her hard-won skills or whether she pleased him. She just shattered the chains that had bound her and burned free at last.

The aftermath found her immensely peaceful and incapable of movement, of thought, certainly of anger. "Am I dead?" she asked.

He groaned. "You've killed me, I think." Heavily,

he shifted them both into a more comfortable position and removed her collar. He kissed her neck. "It's marked you. We'll have to get rid of these things."

She raised his wrists and smiled. "I rather like them now."

"On me, not you, I assume."

She nipped his arm. "I don't know. When I think of *you* tying me to the bed it seems as if it might be fun." She knew the message was that she trusted him, and saw it pleased him.

His gentle eyes smiled into hers as he said, "Repeat that when I'm not feeling scoured and dismembered, wench."

She let her fingers wander over his beautiful, sweat-dampened body. "Have you ever done that? Tied someone up?"

"No."

She picked up her collar and trailed the chain up his thighs, across his belly, admiring the gold against his skin and noting the shiver of reaction that ran through him. How strange that this horrible thing was now an amusing toy. "I just wondered how common it was."

"Not very, I don't think." He captured her hand and met her eyes. "But you'd have to ask someone else."

"Why?"

He smiled rather ruefully. "Confession time. I am singularly lacking in experience, love. You are the first and only woman I have ever shared my body with."

She stared at him, seeking another meaning to his words. "Do you mean that at the Posts' . . . ?"

He nodded. "Disappointed?"

"Horrified!" She could feel tears threatening. "To do that was bad enough, but . . ."

He wrapped her in a warm embrace. "Hush, don't cry. It was a remarkable initiation. In retrospect, I feel blessed."

She frowned up at him. "I'm not sure I believe you. You're such a *good* lover."

He grinned with delight. "That's a salve to my pride, but how would you know, my virtuous one?"

She was struck by that. "That's true! After all, compared to Matthew, who cared nothing for my pleasure, any kind man would appear—" She broke off with a shriek as he tickled her.

And then, of course, she had to tickle him back.

They collapsed in a heap again, hands idly caressing. "But how is it that you are so skilled?" Serena asked.

"I'm very well read. But I'd rather learn from you." He ran a finger lightly up the underside of her thigh. "Is this as pleasant as it is supposed to be?"

"Hmmm. But it might be better with a feather duster."

"What?" He laughed.

She glanced at him mischievously. "I've read books, too. In the past they were part of a very unwelcome education, but now I think I might appreciate the learning."

Francis groaned. "I always suspected that it was a bad idea to educate women."

"You mean it might overheat our poor delicate brains?"

"I mean it might overheat something, though it wasn't your brain that came to mind. I'm feeling rather hot myself. But," he added seriously, "there's more to all this than knowledge and mechanics." He ran his hand over her belly. "I delight in simply touching you, my precious one, my wife."

Serena sucked in a breath. "Why do the books never mention the beauty of words? Your words are like a caress on my soul. Your words have set me free." She shifted to look straight into his eyes. "Have I told you that I love you, my husband? My only husband in the sight of God."

His hand paused. "I'm not sure I deserve that yet. But I will."

"Of course you deserve it. No man would have been as kind and gentle as you."

"Perhaps I'm just fortunate that you only have Riverton to compare me with."

She laid a finger over his lips to stifle such nonsense. "Every woman has more. It is something we have in our hearts. That's why even with my brothers and my father as models, I knew from the first that Riverton was a monster. But I didn't know it fully until I met you."

She kissed him gently. "Riverton created a well-trained wife . . ."

"Hush—"

She silenced him with another kiss. "But in that marriage, there was much that was forbidden me—love, tenderness, respect, decency. As a result, I was a woman who would use her body to snare a stranger."

"Hush," he said again. "I understand why you did that."

"That's what makes you so wonderful. That's why you have been able to teach me the other things—love, tenderness, respect and decency."

"You did not need teaching, Serena."

She kissed away his frown. "Reminding, then. You reminded me, revived me, released me. Even if I didn't love you I would be devoted to you for that."

She saw he was uncomfortable with this and changed to a lighter tone. "Now I am free, though, on your head be it, my lord!" A sliding glance indicated one head she had in mind. It moved and she grinned at him.

"Tongue, teeth, ice, feathers. . . ." she murmured speculatively. She picked up the whip and tickled him with it. "In love, my love, nothing need be forbidden."

After a startled moment he burst out laughing and she joined him, to roll naked among forgotten, irrelevant, chains.

Author's Note

I hope you enjoyed FORBIDDEN, the fourth book in the Company of Rogues series.

I must have been inspired when I came up with the name the Rogues, for the books have been rogues of a sort in the area of Regency romance. According to the dictionary, one definition of rogue is, an individual exhibiting a chance, and usually inferior, variation. Now I wouldn't agree with inferior, of course, but chance and variation both fit.

Traditionally, Regency romance has focused on a narrow segment of that society. My Rogues are, I think, creations of their time in all its variety. This is because when I created most of them back in 1977, I didn't know there was a fixed idea of what "regency" meant. I was a great fan of Heyer, and reread her books constantly, but when I sat down to write my own Regency, I made no attempt to follow her path. That will be clear from my working title—A REGENCY RAPE!

Though I finished the book in 1977, I remained

unpublished until 1988, and this first Rogues book wasn't published until 1990. What happened in the meantime?

I grew discouraged for a start, since I had no idea how to go about getting a book published, and there were few organizations available to help. I came up against a couple of blank walls and gave up. That's one reason I am now very willing to help aspiring writers.

I also got pregnant, and most of the intervening years were taken up with raising our two children.

The need to write did not go away, however. (I had, after all, been writing historical romance since my teens, and still have some efforts to prove it.) There's a wise saying: If you can give up writing, do. I couldn't. But when I returned to writing fiction, I knew more and settled to writing a traditional Regency in the approved mode.

That was LORD WRAYBOURNE'S BE-TROTHED, published in hardcover in 1988 and then in paperback by Zebra in 1990.

It received critical acclaim, and I settled to writing more books in the same style. I enjoyed writing these books, and still do, but I wanted to do more. I wanted to write more complex stories, and to include more sensuality, which for me meant marriage stories. I also decided my heroes were all too polite and civilized, and I wanted to write an arrogant, damn-your-eyes Regency blood.

The slang order of men of fashion in the Regency was greenhorn, jemmy, jessamy, honest fellow, joyous spirit, buck, and blood. Lucien de Vaux, Marquess of

Arden, heir to the Duke of Belcraven, was decidedly a blood. As I should have realized, he was a challenge to write, and even managed to shock me, but it was great fun.

I was preparing to send this book out to publishers when I took a strange urge to tidy my filing system (believe, me, any urge to tidy is strange for me!) and discovered the part-handwritten, part-typewritten manuscript of A REGENCY RAPE. Simply out of curiosity, I sat to read it, to see what I had been up to all those years ago before I learned the craft.

Hours later, I was still enthralled. Yes, there were technical flaws, and a sub-plot that was irrelevant, but it was a gripping, moving story, perhaps the stronger for not recognizing any rules.

I typed it into the computer, re-wrote and polished, and sent it off along with Lucien's book.

At this point the Company of Rogues did not yet exist. Nicholas, the hero in the first book, had a group of friends, but it was only later, in a flash of insight, that I realized I could make Lucien one of those friends and have a series. I love series because I hate to let any of my characters go away completely.

It was fun for other reasons. Nicholas is a commoner (not a member of the peerage) but is unquestionably King Rogue. Lucien is heir to a dukedom, which means that only royalty are higher, but he has to accept Nicholas's leadership. Reluctantly at times. It makes for interesting dynamics within the group.

It wasn't easy to sell these books. Editors of traditional Regency were dismayed by the untraditional elements; editors of historicals found them too Regency. Back then, just a few years ago, the idea of the Regency historical was only beginning to take shape.

But Zebra saw the light and bought the two books, publishing AN ARRANGED MARRIAGE in 1990 and AN UNWILLING BRIDE in 1992. Both Zebra and I have been rewarded by a string of awards, including the highest one in Romance, the RITA of the Romance Writers of America.

People often ask for a rundown of the Rogues. Here it is.

There were twelve Rogues at Harrow, all born in 1789 or 1790.

Nicholas Delaney, younger twin brother of the Earl of Stainsbridge. (AN ARRANGED MARRIAGE)

Lucien de Vaux, Marquess of Arden, heir to the Duchy of Belcraven. (AN UNWILLING BRIDE)

Leander Knollis, Lord Haybridge, heir to the Earl of Charrington. (CHRISTMAS ANGEL)

Francis Haile, Lord Middlethorpe. (FORBIDDEN)

Connaught (Con) Somerford, who becomes Viscount Amleigh.

Lord Darius Debenham, younger son of the Duke of Yeovil.

Miles Cavanagh, nephew and heir to the Marquess of Kilgoran.

Stephen Ball, now Sir Stephen Ball, member of Parliament.

Hal Beaumont, who becomes a professional soldier.

Simon St. Bride, who went into the army and then into administration in Canada.

Two Rogues died before the opening of the first book. (Remember, this was a time of war, and anything else would be unlikely.) Captain Lord Roger Merryhew died in the Peninsula, and Commander Allan Ingram died at sea.

But there are enough Rogues left to provide a few more stories. Hal and Blanche will doubtless resolve their situation one day, and Miles will have to do something with Felicity. Will he persuade one of the Rogues to take her on, or will he decide to guard her himself? And what of Térese Bellaire, who was cheated out of her loot by Lord Deveril? Will she decide to seek revenge?

Now, what about my other books?

I don't just write in the Regency.

I have always loved the Georgian period—1714–1811 in theory, but really the eighteenth century. I love the elaborate costumes, though I'd hate to have to wear them. I love the aristocratic men who wore high-heeled shoes, satin, lace, and powder, and were possibly the most dangerous males ever. Did you see the movie DANGEROUS LIAISONS? Then you know just what I mean.

I have created a family of Georgian men, the Mallorens. The head of the family is the Marquess of Rothgar—cool, cynical, with a controlling finger on every button. Then we have Lord Bryght, mathematical genius who loves a high-stakes game; Lord Brand, high-spirited but interested in the land; and Lord Cyn, who rebelled against Rothgar's control and joined the army.

There are sisters, too. Hilda is married, contentedly it would seem. Lady Elf is still waiting for a man different enough to stir her interest, and brave enough to face her brothers.

Where did they get such strange names? You see, their father had an absorbing interest in his blood-lines, and was convinced he could trace the male line back to Anglo-Saxon nobility, which would be quite rare. So he called his children after Anglo-Saxon notables. Elf is Elfled, Lady of the Mercians. Hilda was a famous abbess and saint. Cyn (Cynric), (Bryght) Arcenbryght, and Brand were all minor kings or heroes. And Rothgar? Rothgar, of course, was named Beowulf, but you'll have to wait for the next Malloren book to find out what his brothers call him informally.

The first Malloren book, MY LADY NOTORIOUS, was published in March 1993. The next will be published by Zebra in late 1994, and is Bryght's story.

My other abiding interest is the middle ages, and I have settled on the early middle ages as my period, from 1066 to the early twelfth century. It was so much more gritty than the later times. Life was lived closer to the edge, and men and women of all classes needed to work together to survive. Since that is my philosophy—that men and women need to find ways to work together to survive—it appeals to me.

LORD OF MY HEART was published in 1992, and DARK CHAMPION in October 1993.

So, there you have it.
Traditional Regencies
The Rogues.
The Mallorens.
The medievals.

442

Somewhat to my surprise, the flavor is different for each of them, but that is because I try to stay true to the period.

The traditional Regencies are rather orderly, because those characters inhabit the more orderly parts of that period. They have emotions and passions, but it is all kept decently within bounds.

The Rogues, however, are less constrained by their society, or perhaps just reflect the wider aspects of it. Evil does invade and must be combatted, and because these are marriage books, we can explore the characters' relationships in a deeper way.

The Mallorens are full-blooded products of their cynical, amoral age. It is part of their code to gamble and not flinch when the stakes get high; to fight for their honor, to the death if necessary. It is part of their time to regard sex as both amusement and weapon. Remember DANGEROUS LIAISONS, a book written at exactly the time I have chosen for my books.

The medievals are generally less complex. The issues are clearer here—usually matters of survival. Marriage and mating is not a game, but often a matter of gritty practicality for the man as well as the woman. But there's space for romance, too.

There's the warrior male for a start. He is so appealing, isn't he, particularly if all that strength and power is completely under his control? And in those early times, women still had a great deal of power and responsibility. That sort of woman appeals to me. Not the "feisty" heroine, rebelling and throwing out silly challenges, but the woman of her times, taking up her responsibilities and powers and using them wisely to be a true partner to a worthy man.

Here is a complete list of my books to date:

Traditional Regencies

LORD WRAYBOURNE'S BETROTHED
THE STANFORTH SECRETS
THE STOLEN BRIDE
EMILY AND THE DARK ANGEL (RITA
Winner, Regency)
THE FORTUNE HUNTER
DEIRDRE AND DON JUAN

Rogues

AN ARRANGED MARRIAGE (Reader's
Choice Award, Regency.)
AN UNWILLING BRIDE (RITA Winner, Regency. Golden Leaf winner, Historical.)
CHRISTMAS ANGEL (Reader's Choice
Award, Regency.)
FORBIDDEN

Mallorens

MY LADY NOTORIOUS (Golden Leaf winner, Historical.)

Medievals

LORD OF MY HEART
DARK CHAMPION

If you can't find all these books on the shelves, they can be ordered through your favorite bookseller, or directly from the publisher.

I hope this guide to my works is useful. I love to hear from readers, both about what you have liked, and what you have not. I also have buttons to give away as long as the supply lasts: either EVERYONE LOVES A ROGUE or for Malloren fans, WAITING FOR ROTHGAR.

Please write c/o The Alice Orr Agency, 305 Madison Avenue, Suite 1166, New York, NY 10165. I do appreciate a SASE to help with the costs.

LET ARCHER AND CLEARY
AWAKEN AND CAPTURE YOUR HEART!

CAPTIVE DESIRE (2612, $3.75)
by Jane Archer

Victoria Malone fancied herself a great adventuress and student of life, but being kidnapped by handsome Cord Cordova was too much excitement for even her! Convincing her kidnapper that she had been an innocent bystander when the stagecoach was robbed was futile when he was kissing her until she was senseless!

REBEL SEDUCTION (3249, $4.25)
by Jane Archer

"Stop that train!" came Lacey Whitmore's terrified warning as she rushed toward the locomotive that carried wounded Confederates and her own beloved father. But no one paid heed, least of all the Union spy Clint McCullough, who pinned her to the ground as the train suddenly exploded into flames.

DREAM'S DESIRE (3093, $4.50)
by Gwen Cleary

Desperate to escape an arranged marriage, Antonia Winston y Ortega fled her father's hacienda to the arms of the arrogant Captain Domino. She would spend the night with him and would be free for no gentleman wants a ruined bride. And ruined she would be, for Tonia would never forget his searing kisses!

VICTORIA'S ECSTASY (2906, $4.25)
by Gwen Cleary

Proud Victoria Torrington was short of cash to run her shipping empire, so she traveled to America to meet her partner for the first time. Expecting a withered, ancient cowhand, Victoria didn't know what to do when she met virile, muscular Judge Colston and her body budded with desire.

Available wherever paperbacks are sold, or order direct from the Publisher. Send cover price plus 50¢ per copy for mailing and handling to Penguin USA, P.O. Box 999, c/o Dept. 17109, Bergenfield, NJ 07621. Residents of New York and Tennessee must include sales tax. DO NOT SEND CASH.

FEEL THE FIRE IN CAROL FINCH'S ROMANCES!

BELOVED BETRAYAL   (2346, $3.95)
   Sabrina Spencer donned a gray wig and veiled hat before blackmailing rugged Ridge Tanner into guiding her to Fort Canby. But the costume soon became her prison — the beauty had fallen head over heels in love!

LOVE'S HIDDEN TREASURE   (2980, $4.50)
   Shandra d'Evereux felt her heart throb beneath the stolen map she'd hidden in her bodice when Nolan Elliot swept her out onto the veranda. It was hard to concentrate on her mission with that wily rogue around!

MONTANA MOONFIRE   (3263, $4.95)
   Just as debutante Victoria Flemming-Cassidy was about to marry an oh-so-suitable mate, the towering preacher, Dru Sullivan flung her over his shoulder and headed West! Suddenly, Tori realized she had been given the best present for a bride: a night of passion with a real man!

THUNDER'S TENDER TOUCH   (2809, $4.50)
   Refined Piper Malone needed bounty-hunter, Vince Logan to recover her swindled inheritance. She thought she could coolly dismiss him after he did the job, but she never counted on the hot flood of desire she felt whenever he was near!